MINDSTALKER

Also by Patricia Weenolsen

The Art of Dying

Transcendence of Loss over the Life Span

REMEMBRANCE OF THINGS
THAT NEVER HAPPENED SERIES:

BOOK ONE
The Cave of Storms

BOOK TWO
Daughter of the Morning Star

BOOK THREE
The Persistence of Memory (forthcoming)

BOOK FOUR
At the Back of the Stars (forthcoming)

WITH ADDITIONAL WORKS TO FOLLOW

PART I
1985

PROLOGUE

WHEN THEY BROUGHT HIM here with his hands tied behind him, it was still light outside. Some other little boy's home with sailboats on the shelves and balloons hanging from the ceiling.

"It's your birthday, my little cinnamon bun," said Toyman, the sweet one with the pale hair.

No, Robbie shook his head. Not my birthday. "My birthday's March."

"You're our new best boy. It's the start of your new life," Toyman said, releasing his hands and rubbing his sore wrists.

"Where's my ice cream?"

"It's coming. It's coming. What kind would you like?"

"I told you. Spistachio."

But Toyman brought vanilla. Robbie took a taste. It made him feel barfy.

Now he sits alone on the lower bunk in this strange darkening room. A slash of light from the open door that he's not allowed to shut. Their voices down the hall — the sweet one and the big dark growly Monsterman who scares him. But only occasional words, and he can't make sense of those.

Over and over, he whispers to himself:

"My name is Robbie Merrow. I'm five years old, and I live in Santa Cruz. With Mom and Dad and my big sister, Becca, she's ten. 212 Beechnut Street. That's my address. My phone number is 324-8122.

"My name is Robbie —"

At that moment, the room darkens, like a storm passing over the sun. Slowly, the door swings wide, and the shadow of Monsterman stands on the threshold, blotting out the light. Robbie strains to see the eyes, but there aren't any.

It looms closer, and then it speaks.

"Who are you talking to, Damon?"

1

IN THE POLICE STATION, the walls are smudged white, the filing cabinets gray, the desks and chairs brown. Horrible crimes and wrenching sorrows have bleached all color from the world.

Becca perches on the edge of a wooden chair as if, at any second, she might take flight. Police officers encircle her, standing, sitting, lounging on desks, answering phones or ignoring them, their eyes curious or skeptical or boldly intrusive with no fear of being called to account. They focus on every part of her body, judging her. Her long brown hair feels tangled and unkempt at her neck, greasy even, although she shampooed it this morning. Sweat does that to hair. She sees their attention snag on it, as if it might hint at the reliability of what she says. Does a girl with dirty hair tell the truth?

Officer T.'s name is too long to pronounce. She's said it a different way each time until he told her impatiently, "Just call me Officer T." Not an invitation, an order, rather. Now, he's questioning her too quickly, his words rapid-fire like a machine gun on a TV show.

"Was the van white or off-white?"

"White, although not as white as snow, I don't think." She must be as accurate as possible. Robbie's life may depend on it.

"Not as white as snow. I see." Officer T. scans the room as if calling on everyone to witness what he must contend with. "Well, let me ask you this. The man you saw. Was the van as white as his hair?"

"No, his hair was sort of a silver white, like platinum, whiter than Robbie's which is more yellow —"

"We know the color of your brother's hair."

They've been through this all afternoon, so they've heard it before, and they cut her off. "Don't waste our time," they seem to say. She doesn't have a chance to finish her answers the way she did at first. But maybe that's because she wanders off the topic. She tends to do that. One idea leads to another, and before you know it, you're on to something else completely. Her fifth-grade teacher, Ms. King, calls her "creative." When you write poetry about the ocean on the beach or play the sunrise on the piano, it helps to let your mind wander.

"I was too far away to see the driver," she tells them again.

President Reagan looks down on her benignly from the wall, as if he understands.

She's on automatic now. She doesn't even hear all their questions, but somehow she gives appropriate answers, her mind elsewhere.

Her mother has gone home to wait for Robbie. Wait for him to come through the door with his big grin, saying, "Scared ya', didn't I?" Wait by the phone for some word — of ransom, perhaps. Her dad's flown out of town to see Grandma Emily, who's sick again. That was this morning after he and Mom fought and before Robbie was taken. He doesn't even know yet. Becca wishes her mother had stayed here at the station with her. Maybe then she wouldn't feel so alone and afraid. But her mom was right to leave. She even waived a lawyer for Becca. Robbie is more important now. It was Becca's fault. She shirked her responsibility. The least she can do is stay here in this miserably stuffy room and answer their sweaty questions over and over. She tells herself she's doing it for Robbie. If it will bring him back . . .

"No, I didn't notice anyone closer to the van who could describe it. They were all on the playground or sitting on the benches. But maybe there was one . . ."

"Who? Why didn't you mention this before? Describe them." Officer T.'s face reddens, and his cheeks quiver with fervor as he whips out his pad and pencil from his top pocket.

"There might have been a woman with a baby carriage on the sidewalk. No," she corrects herself. "I'm just imagining it."

"You have a hard time telling real from imaginary, do you?"

"Come on, Pete," says Officer Samantha "call me Sam" Von Trier. "No need for that." She wears a thick blonde braid pinned to the back of her head and the skin on her raw-boned frame is milky.

"Did you imagine the van?"

Becca stares at him. Could she possibly have imagined the van?

Now Officer T. and Officer Sam are arguing, oblivious to Becca, like her mom and dad who can argue about anything — the cost of apples, whether it will be foggy tomorrow, and Mom staying home instead of going with Dad to his mother's, so that he has to be alone with her while she's dying. Except Mom said Grandma Emily wasn't, "and don't talk about it in front of the children," meaning Robbie, of course. Becca knows all about death.

What was the question?

"I told you, I ran after the van. And then I ran home to call Mom."

"Why didn't you call from the playground?"

"I don't know. I didn't think I had a quarter. And if I did, it would take too long to find it."

"You don't need a quarter to dial emergency."

"I didn't know that."

"You can dial 911 from a pay phone without any money."

"Oh. I'll remember that next time" my brother's kidnapped.

"Next time?"

"I need to."

"Didn't your friend, Annalyn, have a quarter?"

"I didn't ask — I was too — home's only a few minutes away, and I just felt it would be quicker. I had to get back there."

"Quicker than dialing from right there on the playground," and then under his breath, "for Chrissake?"

"I don't know." The ultimate refuge. She doesn't know anything anymore, her eyes wandering back to the pictures of missing children and crooks all over the walls so that you're not sure which is which. Some of the crooks are young and the children old, and the pictures fuzzy, as if taken long ago. They're all WANTED, either to lock up in jail or give back to parents who'll hug them to death.

Will Robbie's picture be up there soon? Will it be on a milk carton? Robbie always talks about the milk carton children, the ones who are missing because somebody snatched them away and did horrible things to them, and they're probably dead anyway. But Dad says they just ran away because their parents weren't nice to them. "That won't happen to you," he says.

"I could play ball with him," Robbie said over his Crunchy Bunchies this morning, pointing to the little boy about his age with a grin as wide as a jack-o'-lantern's.

"How do you know he plays ball?"

"I know. Just look at him. Besides, everybody plays ball."

"I don't," Becca said, turning up her nose.

"You're a girl. Aw-w, it's okay Bec-Bec, you can't help it."

"Being a girl's better than being a silly old boy any day."

"Becca!" her mother warned. She thinks being a boy is better.

"Are you going to put Robbie's picture on the wall?" she asks Officer T.?

"Would you like that?"

Becca feels the tears choking up her throat again.

"No," she manages to get out, breathing hard, trying to get enough air, only it doesn't come.

"Why not?"

"That would mean — " She snuffles back the tears. "That would mean he's missing."

Officer Sam hands her a tissue, and she blows loudly. Officer Sam's the nice one. She and that cute Officer Slewski, except his name is twistier than that. They've brought her a cheeseburger and a Coke and said she'll be going home soon, but that wasn't true, was it? She's still here.

"He is missing," says Officer T.

"I — what?"

"Becca! Becca!" Officer T. reaches over and shakes her arm.

"She's exhausted," says Officer Sam.

"So's her brother, most likely," Officer T. snaps. "In the best case scenario," he adds. Probably, he thinks Becca doesn't know what he means.

"What do you think they've done with him?" Becca asks again.

They never answer straight on. They say, "We're doing everything we can to find him." "Not much evidence to go on." "Searchers, dogs, no eyewitnesses except you and your little friend." "Combing the area. The creek, the river, the beach."

"You think he's drowned?"

The whole afternoon, they've been hinting that Robbie's had horrible things done to him and is now at the bottom of the San Lorenzo River or in the cold cold ground. Every time the phone rings, some officer picks it up gravely and snaps his name. Becca watches and listens intently, until Officer T. drags her back to the same questions over and over. She wants to search, too, but she's stuck here while everyone else is being useful, including Mom. Becca can almost see her sitting at home by the phone in her white nurse's uniform, still stained with the blood of the last baby she helped deliver.

Sue Merrow had gotten the call to take an extra shift at the hospital this morning. Sunday morning. Great! Dad had just left for another flight to Chicago to be with his dying mother, Grandma Emily, and they'd had a fight about it, because Dad wanted his family with him, and Mom didn't like to come. She'd never gotten along with Grandma Emily. She'd gone a few times for her husband's sake, but Emily ignored her.

"You'll have to watch Robbie," her mom said to Becca.

"But, Mom, I'm supposed to meet Annalyn at the park."

"Emergencies happen," said her mother, smoothing her uniform. "Too many babies being born. Sometimes they're inconvenient. They don't plan around your social life."

"We'll have to take him with us, I guess." Becca heaved a dramatic sigh. "If we stay here, he won't give us a minute's peace. Hear that, Robbie? We're going to the park. I'll make your favorite bologna and cheese sandwiches if you promise not to bug us. You can play on the slide."

It was at that point that Mom hesitated.

"No, I don't want you going to the playground today. Stay home."

"But I promised Annalyn."

"She can come over here."

"But Robbie'll just hang around us with nothing to do."

"No, and that's final. I've got enough to worry about with an extra shift and your dad away and your grandma sick, what that's going to do to him. I don't need any more."

That was Mom for you. Solved problems by eliminating them!

Or could it have been a premonition?

"Becca? Becca?" Officer T. is shaking her again. "Stay awake here."

"I am awake," she says, shrugging his hand from her shoulder.

"Well, were you?"

"Was I what?"

"Mad at your brother?"

"What do you mean?"

"Did you ever fight?" Past tense. As if they'll never fight again.

"I — no — well, not much, just little things."

"Like?"

"He takes my stuff."

"What stuff?"

"Just stuff. Pennies from my collection. My Hanon Studies — that's my piano exercise book. My diary. He can't read it. He just does it to bug me. And he calls me Rebecca. Just to tease me. He does it all the time."

"Didn't that make you mad?"

"Sometimes."

"Is that why you left him alone on the playground?"

"I told you," she bursts out. "I didn't. Only for a minute. I had to go to the bathroom with Annalyn."

"Seems pretty convenient for the kidnappers."

As if she'd planned it!

She hadn't really needed to go. Annalyn had seen her boyfriend, Nick, walking down the street with a group of his friends. At least, she liked to call him her "boyfriend", but only to Becca. It was their secret. She had the hugest crush on him and enlisted Becca to ask him stupid questions.

"Did he see me?"

"Not yet, I don't think."

"How do I look? I've got to get to a mirror."

They had dashed for the bathroom, Becca telling her she looked fine while Annalyn fussed with her hair and smeared on lipstick so pale it hardly showed, but that's all her mother allows her to wear.

Becca remembers the vague sense of unease she had then. Now she thinks it's because she felt it was wrong to leave her brother alone on the slide even for a minute.

"If you don't step on it, Nick will be gone," she told Annalyn impatiently.

"Guess what. Mom's gonna have a baby," said Annalyn, smoothing her eyebrows with spit, because it worked better than water.

"Oh, no, Annalyn, you poor thing. You don't know what you're in for."

"Are you kidding? I can't wait."

"You'll have to do all this work and baby-sit and get him his food and clean up his mess."

"Maybe it'll be a girl."

"Same difference!"

She recalls this warning with guilt now. She hadn't felt guilty then. Just resentful.

They emerged from the bathroom, still talking about Annalyn's baby sister, because that was what they had decided it was. At that instant, Becca spotted Robbie half a block away getting into the white van with a man. It's like a picture in her mind now. The only picture, nothing else. It will never be erased, never dim. Robbie will always be just inside the van door in his red sweatshirt with the bears on it, waving jubilantly at her and shouting something she can't hear. The man with the white hair will always look back sharply at Becca, then twist around to Robbie and push him farther inside, leaping in after him and sliding the door shut. The van will always carom down the road with a roar. Becca will always run after it, screaming, "Robbie! Robbie!"

"Blue," she tells Officer T. "His pants were blue. Jeans, I think."

"Whose pants?"

"The kidnapper's." Who else's? Hasn't he been paying attention? Becca starts to giggle. Maybe she should shake his shoulder!

Officer T. reddens all the way down his neck. "What's so funny?"

"Nothing," Becca says. Even Officer Sam looks taken aback.

"Your brother's been kidnapped and you're laughing? I don't think it's funny at all." His jowls quiver with anger. How long does it take him to get his sideburns just right in the morning? Does he comb them or brush them? Does he mousse them? She giggles again. He must think they make him handsome, but Becca doesn't.

"Blue jeans," Officer Sam interrupts. "That's good. Isn't that good, Pete?"

Officer T. gives her a long look. Some of the other officers drift away, and others drift in to stare at Becca's hair. Officer T. turns back to her.

"Have you any idea what they do to little boys? If you'd seen what I've seen, you wouldn't laugh."

"Pete, she's just a child."

"People always talk about what gets done to little girls — and I'm not saying little girls don't deserve the sympathy. But little boys get raped, too."

"Raped?"

"Pete, we need to talk," says Officer Sam, grabbing his arm and pushing him down the aisle, while the other officers shift uncomfortably. Becca is trying to get her mind around what Officer T. just said. How could a boy be raped? She's pretty sure they don't want her to ask.

"You're sure you can't remember part of the license number?" cute Officer Slewski asks before she can think too much about it. His nose is tipped upwards, but when he smiles, she sees he has bad teeth. Probably afraid to go to the dentist. She is, too, and Robbie yells.

"I told you. It was way too far to see."

"Any letter or number would help."

"There might have been a 'B'. Or an '8'. It could have been an 8." Now Becca isn't sure how much she's remembering and how much she's making up.

"Was there anything on the side of the van? A sign or a picture, maybe?" She's already told Officer T. there was nothing. But perhaps there was lettering after all.

"A picture maybe. No, I think I'm remembering the diaper van with the stork on the side."

"Was it the diaper van?"

"No."

"You're sure?"

"Yes."

In disappointment, he subsides. "We'll check the diaper van just in case." He makes a note. "Maybe there were stickers on the front window?"

"I didn't see the front, only the side and the back."

"Bumper stickers. Do you remember those?"

"There might have been."

"What color?"

"I told you, it was too far. Maybe green."

"Green, that's good," says Officer Sam, returning with Officer T. who looks, if possible, even grimmer. Becca notices his arm muscles rippling under his blue shirt. Does he want to hit her? No one hits her, even boys. They know that Becca can beat them up. The secret is to twist out of their reach and make your fists fly.

"Or blue, maybe?" asks Officer Slewski.

"Might be blue-green. I want to go home now." Why hadn't she demanded to go before? She had a right, hadn't she? Well, she'd stayed to help, and now she was just wasting time.

"We need you here," Officer T. interrupts, and Officer Slewski gets up to make way for him. "You want to find your brother, don't you?" Prove it!

"I want to help with the search."

"You're more help here," says Officer Sam.

"I don't feel I'm helping. You've got everything I know."

"We'll decide that," says Officer T. "Poor little fella," he adds to the officer standing beside him. Officer Sam gives him a stony look.

"You really are a great help, Rebecca," she says.

"Becca," she corrects. We've been here all afternoon. Don't you know my name yet?

"Tell you what let's do. We'll put you with a sketch artist so you can describe the kidnapper, and she can draw him. Then maybe you can go."

"If we don't need you further."

They've said this several times, but it's not happening. It seems to Becca that it would be more important to help a sketch artist than answer the same stupid questions over and over. Maybe not. She was way too far away to see the kidnapper's face, and she's already told them his hair was short and white-blond. Twenties, long, thin and graceful, the sleeves of his blue shirt rolled up —

"His sleeves were rolled up."

"Rolled? How far?"

"To the elbows."

"Why didn't you tell us this before?" another officer asks, leaning over to peer into her face. She winces, not because he's too close, really, but he feels too close. "You been holding out on us?" he seems to ask.

"I forgot," she says.

"She remembers now," says Officer Sam, popping a Coke can and handing it to Becca. Becca takes a sip, all eyes on her. She'd better not drink too much. She can't tell why that would be wrong, but it would be.

"So, you say your mom told you to stay home, and then you left for the playground," Officer T. continues.

"I told you, I called Annalyn first. I said I couldn't go like we planned. But Annalyn said, 'Who'd know?' And 'We have to eat lunch sometime, somewhere. Why not at the playground?'"

Actually, it was Becca who'd said that. She felt a little guilty, but she was the one being blamed, not Annalyn. At least, Annalyn got to go home. Probably. And if they hadn't gone to the bathroom because of Annalyn's stupid boyfriend, none of this would have happened.

Hungry now. Maybe it was thinking about the bologna sandwiches she'd made them, the chocolate milk in Robbie's dinosaur thermos, Crunchy Bunchies in baggies, fruit rolls for something healthy. Later at the picnic table on the playground, Robbie smacking his lips, his chubby little chipmunk cheeks chewing away. Her eyes fill with tears.

"You've remembered something else?" Officer T. presses.

She shakes her head. She can't tell him about Robbie's chipmunk cheeks. The cheeseburger sits on the table in front of her, cold, its fat congealed. She can't see it, but she knows it's there, like the bottom of a frying pan the morning after. If only she could have a few crackers, just to hold her. She looks to Officer Sam, who seems to divine what she wants, nods, and goes to get something from the machine. Peanut butter cheese crackers. Officer T. watches her bite into one as if he resents anything that goes into her mouth. But Robbie may not be eating anything. Anything at all. She chokes again, and puts the cracker down.

"You have to eat something," says Officer Sam, giving her permission, but Becca senses that Officer T. will only approve of her if she never eats again. After what she's done to her brother. She lays her head down on the table and gives in, sobbing, her heart breaking into chunks that rattle around in her chest like pinballs.

Officer T.'s voice cuts the air. "This isn't helping us find Robbie."

Now, everybody's arguing in tones so low that she can't quite hear what they say.

Officer Sam's hand is on her shoulder.

"Come along, Becca. Let's go see the sketch artist, and then you can go home."

"I love my brother!" she bursts out, jumping to her feet, suddenly furious. She returns their stares with a shake of her dirty hair. "I love my brother," she says again, trying to impress it on them. They'd looked a bit bored until now. Now, they just look startled. "I didn't do it on purpose, you know. It's not my fault!"

"It's the kidnapper's fault," says Officer Sam.

"Why aren't you out looking for him instead of asking all these stupid questions over and over." She ignores Officer Sam's hand on her arm. "Because it's easier to just sit on your fat rears and look like you're getting something done?" She shakes off the hand meant to gentle her. "They're getting away!"

Shocked stares and silence. Not a move. She's done it now, but she doesn't care.

Officer T. finally breaks the tension.

"But you weren't supposed to go to the park, were you?"

No, she wasn't supposed to go to the park. She's sitting across from Robbie at the breakfast table that morning. He's building a house for the milk carton child. The cereal box with the empty "sugar" bowl on top, turned on its side, its blue sugar substitute packets spilled out, and a tilted slice of bread on top of that. Building, always building.

"He could be my friend," Robbie says.

"Relax," says the sketch artist, whose name is Eileen and who smells of lilies. "Go ahead, eat your crackers. Just don't get crumbs on my table."

She has a warm Irish accent, and Becca feels less condemned here, without all those eyes prying into her head. So she nibbles at her crackers while Eileen talks steadily.

"Let's begin with a full figure, shall we? They tell me you didn't get a very good look at the face."

She sketches quickly, Becca correcting her.

"His chest isn't so broad, I don't think. He wears the sleeves of his shirt rolled up. His waist's narrow, longer, I think. His head's narrow, too. His hair's short, yes, like that. Maybe he wears an earring. I think I remember a flash at his ear, just as he turned."

Bit by bit the man emerges on the paper, in his twenties, small and slight, graceful even, no facial hair, sleeves neatly rolled, a belt at his waist. And it's amazing that Eileen can do this. Even Becca hadn't realized how much she can remember. It's almost as if she's seen him somewhere else before today. Or is she imagining it — imagining the man who would have taken Robbie?

They're eating lunch at the picnic table under the trees, Robbie munching his bologna and cheese sandwich.

"Is Toyman coming today?"

"Toyman?" Annalyn asks. "Who's Toyman?" She's ignored Becca's picnic because it's too fattening, preferring the apple she's brought with her. She plans to be Miss America, although she admits it might be boring.

"One of his imaginary friends, remember? I told you about him," Becca answers. "It's very common at the age of five," she adds expertly.

"Why do you call him 'Toyman?'" Annalyn asks. "Do you have to wind him up?"

She and Becca both laugh, but Robbie suspects she's teasing him and frowns.

"He brings me toys," he says defiantly.

"You mean like Santa? Down the chimney?"

"Uh-uh," Robbie shakes his head. "He gives them to me at the mall. I'm finished now."

"You haven't eaten your fruit," Becca says, pushing a grape fruit roll at him. "Come on, just a bite."

"Fruit rolls aren't real fruit," says Annalyn sternly. "They're just sugar. Not like an apple."

"It was all we had."

"At least, take a bite of mine. There. So, what kind of toys does this Toyman bring you?" she asks, winking at Becca.

"Boats, mostly. I gonna play on the swings, now," he adds, sliding off the bench.

"But you don't even like boats," says Becca. "You like trucks and blocks. And wipe your mouth." She always gives him trucks and blocks for his birthday and Christmas. He has a collection.

"Toyman likes boats." says Robbie. "He says I'm his toy."

"Toys are *things*, stupid. You're alive."

"He says I'm gonna be on a milk carton."

Had he really said that last? Or was she imagining it now, because of what had happened?

He runs off to play on the slide, giving Becca and Annalyn a chance to talk. He never stays in one place for long. Now he's on the jungle gym, and now the swing where Becca pushes him without his begging, because she's feeling just the tiniest bit guilty for bringing him to the park. Maybe if he has fun it'll be okay. Now he jumps off the swing to chase a little friend, and they play "Monster," which means they dash around after each other screaming "Monster's coming."

"Stupid game," says Annalyn. "No one's tagged. No one's 'It.'"

"Finished?" asks Officer Sam.

"She did very well," says Eileen.

"Come on, let me take you home."

On their way out, they pass a glass office where Annalyn's parents, Mr. and Mrs. Woodward, are giving information to a detective. Mrs. Woodward looks up at Becca and scowls furiously. Mad enough to ground Annalyn for a week, Becca thinks.

Outside, the October air is crisp with the hint of winter already, the branches flinging their leaves about like a child having a tantrum.

In the front seat of the car, Officer Sam explains some of the dials and knobs.

"I don't understand," Becca says. "Why would anyone want to take Robbie?"

"Sometimes, people can't have children of their own."

"But what was that Officer T. was saying about — " she breaks off, embarrassed. "I mean, I don't understand how they can do things to a boy that they do to a girl."

"Oh, it's way to early to worry about anything like that."

"But I don't understand it."

"When you're a little older."

Becca hears a tick on the window pane, and then another. She looks up quickly.

"Rain," she says, the full implication dawning only gradually. "Do you think Robbie's out there?"

"He's a smart little boy. I'm sure he's found a place to stay dry."

"Probably the man who took him, too, don't you think?"

"No one likes to be out in the rain."

"Will they keep searching?" Becca asks, anxiety burrowing into her chest.

"It depends on a lot of things. If they think they're making progress, how heavy the rain is, how muddy it gets, lots of factors," says Officer Sam, meaning to reassure.

Alarmed, Becca asks suddenly, "Can the search dogs smell in the rain?"

"Sometimes. Some dogs can smell anything anywhere. We have real talented dogs."

"But you wouldn't want them to get soaked."

"That's true," says Officer Sam.

They're driving up Mission Street now, and Becca is suddenly exhausted. She leans back. In her mind's eye, Robbie chews his cereal like a chipmunk as he stares at the milk carton boy.

"He could be my friend," he says. "We could play ball."

2

ROBBIE WASN'T SURE WHAT woke him. He thought it was a scary dream that he couldn't remember. Or maybe the sun streaming through the windows and casting barred shadows across his face. Or the sound of voices arguing, or the smell of food. The colored balloons drifted limply just below the ceiling. For an instant, Robbie wanted to be home so badly that he thought he was.

He sat up and rubbed his eyes. The yellow, red, and blue boats still sailed across the bookshelves beside his bed. The curtains and bedspread as well. Some other little boy's room. He tugged at his pants. He had to go pee-pee real bad, but he was scared to, and that made him need to go even worse.

He got up and padded toward the open door. He must have lost his shoes in the struggle, maybe in the van. Although he wasn't struggling at first. Toyman had said they were going for a ride to get spistachio ice cream, and he was excited. But Monsterman drove a long time, way past the Mission Ice Cream store with the Halloween pumpkins outside the door, and even 31 Flavors and Ben and Jerry's. Robbie began to get tired. "I want to go home now," he'd said finally. That was when he tried to slide the door open, and Toyman grabbed him and held him down, laughing as if they were just playing, and Monsterman said, "Kenny, tie him up." So Toyman tied his wrists but kept asking, "Is that all right? Does it hurt? Is it too tight?" and Robbie said, "Yes! Yes! Yes!" But Robbie could see that Monsterman, whom Kenny called "Carl," was watching him through his dark glasses in the rearview mirror, and Robbie settled down, staring at the dark gray curly hair at his neck and the dark glasses that made him look like a movie star.

He didn't get ice cream until they reached the apartment. When Toyman Kenny brought him a dish of vanilla, where he sat on the bed as he was told, he took one lick, and suddenly he wasn't hungry.

"I knew this was a mistake," said Carl. He was as big as this room, practically, and when he took his glasses off, his eyes were stormy.

"He's just excited," said Kenny.

He remembered now. Carl had taken his shoes. What did he want with Robbie's shoes? His own feet were as big as a clown's.

Now Robbie peered down the hall and saw what he thought was the bathroom door where Kenny had taken him before.

"There's my good boy, all bright and awake," sang Kenny coming toward him. He danced on tippy toes when he walked. "Does my Damon need to take a whiz? What a good boy! Right in here, Damon. Do you need me to help?"

Robbie shook his head and shut the door behind him. The weird pictures of kids on the walls and the smells of toothpaste and after-shave and stranger things almost dried him up. But not quite.

When he came out, Kenny asked, "Did you wash your hands? You didn't, did you? Come along, we'll do it together. You don't want to let the germs grow into great big boogers that eat you up, do you?"

At the sink, Robbie struggled to wash them himself, but Kenny insisted, rubbing soap into his hands, talking all the while, using a brush to scrub under his nails, rinsing, and rubbing them dry with a towel.

"There's my good Damon, nice and clean. We'll have breakfast first. Later we'll give you a bath from head to toe."

As he said this, he traced a line from Robbie's hair all the way down his back.

In the dining room, Carl was shoveling scrambled eggs, bacon, fried potatoes, and toast into his mouth that opened wide like a tunnel. He needed a lot of food because he was so big. As his dark eyes fixed on Robbie, Robbie felt there was something wrong with him.

"Come on," said Kenny. "Upsy-daisy into the chair."

Robbie started to climb onto it, but Kenny lifted him up and set him down.

"You're spoiling him," said Carl.

"He's my baby, not yours. You gave him to me, and I can spoil him if I want."

Robbie slipped off the chair and followed Kenny into the kitchen. On the refrigerator was a calendar with a photo of a little boy, naked except for a tie, holding a pumpkin.

"How come he don't got no clothes on?" Robbie asked.

"How come he don't got *any* clothes on," Kenny corrected as he bustled around the kitchen.

"Isn't he cold?"

"I don't know. Does he look cold?"

"His sister might see him," Robbie giggled.

"Silly! Go back to your chair and keep Uncle Carl company."

Minutes later, Kenny bustled in carrying a plate of eggs that smelled like barf, with bits of bacon and toast around them like a flower. Robbie pushed the plate away. He wanted his Crunchy Bunchies.

"Would you rather have cereal?"

"He'll eat what he gets, if he's hungry enough."

"It's his first morning in his new home. Everything's strange to him. Let him eat what he wants."

Kenny got down a box.

"I'm afraid all I have is Raisin Bran."

That was what Dad ate every morning. Robbie didn't like it, but it felt safe, almost like having Dad here in the room with him. He nodded, yes, he wanted Raisin Bran just like Dad. Kenny poured milk on it, and picked up the spoon, brought it to the table, sat down, and started to feed Robbie. Robbie took the spoon from Kenny's hand and shoved it into the bowl.

"See?" said Carl. "You're babying him too much." He had an earring that glittered in the light just like Kenny's. When the phone rang, he answered it. Robbie stared into his face to see if it was for him, maybe Mom saying he had to clean up his room, maybe Bec-Bec promising to make his favorite cheese and bologna sandwiches if he'd hurry home. But Carl talked into the phone in a deep Billy-Goat Gruff voice from way down at the bottom of his stomach like Dad.

Kenny didn't leave the cereal box in front of Robbie for him to read the pictures, but before he put the milk back in the refrigerator, Robbie saw that the carton had a kid on it.

"Damon needs new clothes," Kenny was saying. "His are dirty, and he didn't have a chance to pack, did you, Damon? We should take him shopping."

"Are you crazy?" asked Carl, off the phone again. "Kid's picture's plastered all over the papers by now."

"The Santa Cruz papers, maybe. Not San Francisco."

"You could dye his hair."

"Then he wouldn't be the spitting image of me, would you, Damon?" Kenny reached over and stroked the hand that held the spoon. "Don't you think we look like brothers?" And to Carl, "There are millions of little blonde five-year-old boys who look just like him. You worry too much."

"I knew this was a bad idea," said Carl, interrupted by the phone again.

"Come on, Carl, you promised."

Robbie stared up at Kenny and Carl, trying to understand. Around the dining room hung the weirdest pictures from floor to ceiling, except where the windows were, pictures of soup cans, umbrellas, and rows and rows of noses. At home, Mom loved mountain posters, with suns whirling through the sky, and Dad liked photos of people doing things.

"Oh, he's looking at my paintings. Isn't that sweet? You know who painted these, Damon? Big brother Kenny painted them."

"You're not my brother," Robbie said through a mouthful of milk and cereal.

"Oh, yes, I am, Damon, I'm your new brother," Kenny said quickly, and he glanced at Carl like he was scared of him.

"I told you before, my name's Robbie, not Damon."

"Maybe you need to be tied to your bed," said Carl, who was eating fried potatoes off Kenny's plate, "until you remember your name."

Robbie frowned at Carl. Could he do that? Could he really tie Robbie to the bed? Nobody'd ever done that to him before.

"I'll just get myself more potatoes," said Kenny. "Want another helping, Carl? Oh, that's right, the doctor said you're on a diet." Kenny returned with a heaping plateful, which Carl proceeded to gobble. "Damon's just not used to us yet, Carl. Give him a chance. He'll be fine, really he will." Then, to Robbie, "I'm an artist, you see? And I'm going to have a gallery showing in a few months. If you're real good, maybe you'll get to come."

"You're crazy," said Carl between mouthfuls.

"It's a big honor, you know."

Robbie finished his cereal.

"I'm ready to go home now," he said, sliding to the floor.

Carl scraped back his chair and started toward Robbie, saying, "I'm real sick of this kid contradicting us," when the phone rang again. Maybe, that was a good thing. Maybe Carl had been about to tie him up.

"Oh, you can't go anywhere before we've opened your birthday present," Kenny said, grabbing Robbie's hand.

"It's not my birthday."

"Come and look at the big box in the middle of the living room that big brother Kenny got for you."

There was a giant TV in the living room, and the walls were covered with more photographs of boys without any clothes on.

"Your Uncle Carl took those. Aren't they brilliant? And what do you suppose that is?" Kenny was pointing to the box.

It had the picture of a train on it.

"A train?" Robbie guessed.

"Reading already? Such a smart boy! And guess what we're going to do. We're going to put it together and make it run. It'll go round and round the track, and we'll be the engineers. I'm so excited. I had one of these when I was a boy. My little brother, Timmy, and I played with it for hours. Before I had to run away."

"Bad news," Carl called out from the dining room. "That was Madison. Cops are onto their O'Farrell studio again. He wants to use ours. I told him after seven."

"Your Uncle Carl's an important movie producer. Oh, I'm sure you'll sort it all out," he called back.

"It's a cinch *you* won't. I gotta get down there," Carl answered. "Back in a couple of hours. And you'd better have this kid in line."

"Damon's already in line, aren't you, Damon? Good, good! Then we can take Damon shopping."

"Yeah, yeah, yeah!" The door slammed.

Robbie watched Kenny take the train tracks out of the box and lay them on the floor, where they buckled a little because the carpeting was bumpy.

"Come on, Damon. You help."

"I'm not Damon. I'm Robbie!" He wasn't scared of Kenny, like he was of Carl.

"Oooh, you better not let Carl hear you say that again. Here's a piece of track. Where do you think it goes? You see, Damon, you used to be Robbie. But you're not any more. Of all the little boys we could have chosen, we picked you. We drove around all the playgrounds and schools and malls for months, looking for you. Carl spotted you first. You're our little boy Damon, now."

"Am not! I'm Robbie Merrow. I want my mom and dad, and I want my sister, Bec-Bec."

"They gave you to us, Damon."

"Did not!" Robbie started to cry.

"Did so! You don't live with them anymore. You live with Carl and me. Tell you what. Let's put the train together later. Let's make out a shopping list."

Kenny got up and returned with a pad and pencil. "What do you like to eat, huh?" He sat down beside Robbie in his blue jeans and blue shirt, the sleeves rolled up to his elbows. He smelled like soap.

"Do you like turkey?"

In his mind's eye, Robbie saw a turkey on the big dining room table at home, with Dad, Mom, and Bec-Bec, saying a prayer around it. Aunt Cordelia, too. Maybe Grandma Emily. Each of them took turns. Now it was Robbie's.

"God's neat! Let's eat!" Robbie would always say, grinning when they pretended to be shocked. Then he'd stuff himself with stuffing and cram himself with cramberry sauce.

"Turkey?" Kenny repeated.

He shook his head gravely, saying, "No." He didn't feel like turkey the way he used to.

"Apples?"

Robbie squirmed. Annalyn had given him a bite of hers for lunch, and it was pretty good. Except that it was "healthy."

"Pizza? Oh, come on, everyone likes pizza, with sausage and cheese on top? Extra cheese?"

No.

"No pizza?"

Robbie shrugged his shoulders. He used to like pizza. Now his tummy hurt.

"Tell you what. You come to the store with us and point out what you like."

Crunchy Bunchies.

"I'm sick."

Kenny leaped to his feet.

"Are you gonna barf?" he asked, pushing Robbie out of the dining room toward the bathroom. "You better not. I won't love you any more."

"I got bugs in my stomach."

"You mean, like a flu bug?"

"Crickets."

"Crickets!" Kenny looked mystified.

"And spiders."

"Spiders!" Now he looked horrified.

"And pillbugs and ants." Robbie tried to smother his giggles.

"Not ants!"

"And beetles and snails, and mice. All kinds of bugs."

Now Kenny was laughing.

"Where?" he asked, poking at Robbie's stomach. "Here?"

"Uh-huh."

"Or here?"

"Yeah."

"Here, here, here? Here, here?" He asked, poking all around until Robbie squealed.

"Yes! Yes! Yes!" he shouted.

"Boy, my Damon's full of bugs."

"Not Damon. Robbie."

"You used to be Robbie. Not now. You're our little boy, and you're Damon. Damon's a much nicer name, don't you think?"

"I wanna go home now."

"This is your home, Damon? Think of all the new toys you have. Look at these cool boats like the ones Timmy and I used to play with in the tub. I bought them just for you. What do you say? Do you say thank you?"

"I want my Bec-Bec." Robbie started to cry. Kenny led him over to the bed with the sailboats, sat him down, and put his arm around Robbie's shoulders. Then he took a tissue, put it to Robbie's nose, and told him to blow, as he said very gently,

"Bec-Bec gave you to us. You're our little boy now. Mine and Uncle Carl's."

"No! No! No!" Robbie cried, and he pounded his fists against Kenny's chest.

Kenny laughed. "Ow, you're hurting me," he said, but Robbie could tell it was in fun. So he hit Kenny harder.

Suddenly, Carl was standing in the doorway with a phone to his ear. They hadn't heard him come in.

"I can hit you a helluva lot harder than that, Damon, so pipe down."

"Shhh, Damon," Kenny said. "Uncle Carl's doing business. He's a big-time movie producer. He can't have his customers hear you fussing over the phone."

Robbie tried to shush as hard as he could, but his chest kept heaving up and down all by itself, until he had the hiccups. Kenny rubbed his shoulders and his back. Then he kissed him on the forehead.

"Don't worry, Damon. I'll protect you," he promised.

3

BEECHNUT STREET WAS SO jammed with news trucks and nosy neighbors that you couldn't even see the Pacific ocean in the distance, but the rain had stopped. In Becca's driveway, a police car stood ominously vacant while two officers examined the ground beneath the bushes in the front yard.

"Did something happen?" Becca asked.

"They're just covering all possibilities," Officer Sam reassured her, and she really did sound as though this was true.

"But he disappeared from the playground six blocks up that way."

"We know. Don't worry, honey."

They swung into the driveway and were instantly mobbed by reporters jockeying for position like football players and yelling so many questions that Becca couldn't hear any.

"I'd better get you inside."

Becca felt indignant. Bad enough to have to come home and face her mother without a mob of sensation-seekers.

"Are they allowed on our property like this?"

"Technically, no. Try telling them, though."

"They're wrecking Mom's begonias."

"That's right." Officer Sam's mouth was a grim line.

She got out and came around to the passenger door, shielding Becca with her muscular Scandinavian body, yelling, "Back, back, all of you, stand back, coming through."

"They should pay for them." Becca struggled to be heard.

"Becca, honey —" called one reporter.

"I'm not your honey," Becca lashed out.

"Steady, there," said Officer Sam.

She put her arm around Becca's shoulders and hustled her across the lawn. Lights popped, and Becca ducked to shield her eyes. Reporters poked microphones into her face, everyone pushing until they lost control, jamming her teeth into her lips.

"Do you miss your brother, Becca?"

"Do you think they'll find little Robbie?" from someone who'd never laid eyes on him.

"Rebecca, is he still alive, do you think?"

If they thought that question was going to get her to cry into the cameras, they had another think coming!

When Officer Sam reached the front porch, she wheeled on them.

"Not one step farther or I'm arresting the lot of you. Back, back, Jean, Howie, Finn, I know you all."

"Just a word, Becca."

"A comment, Becca."

"You'll be on TV," — as if it were a lollipop!

Sam was shoving her inside the front door when Becca twisted around and faced them.

"Ms. Merrow to you," she said. "Only my friends call me 'Becca'. You're not my friends. I don't even know you."

"You're not to blame, Becca."

"Ms. Merrow," someone corrected.

To blame?

Then they were through the door.

To Becca's surprise, the living room with its factory-carved Spanish furniture was empty, although it showed signs of previous occupation — official-looking papers strewn about the coffee table with saucers of cigarette butts — "Mind if I smoke?" Must have sent her mother round the bend. As an obstetrical nurse, she regarded the habit as filthy and dangerous. Becca had tried a few puffs with friends. They made her sick. Her father and his easy chair were banished into the garage, where he smoked his pipe and read his papers in peace. Comfortable when it wasn't cold.

The phone rang, and a woman Becca vaguely remembered from the neighborhood slunk in, answered it, and said, "No, not now." Ignoring them, she slunk out again.

They headed toward the voices in the kitchen, past Becca's beloved upright piano, with her John Thompson music book open to a tarantella and *Hanon Studies* on the rack beside it. Had it been just yesterday when she'd played?

Six women sat at the table laden with rotting food, the room oven-warm, the heat a security blanket against the crisis that enveloped them. Someone had just made a fresh pot of coffee.

The minute her mom saw Becca, her eyes snapped. Becca couldn't tell if it was welcome or anger. For herself, Becca was shocked at her mother's appearance. Gray hair unwashed, eyes rimmed with purple bruises as if someone had hit her, she wore her old bulky tan cardigan over the same dirty uniform with the smear of blood on her chest.

Her mom's attention swiveled to Officer Sam, waiting for an answer to a question she hadn't asked.

"I'm sorry, Mrs. Merrow. No news yet," she said, implying that there would be news eventually, good news, even, a certainty, not ambiguous at all. They had only to wait.

The rest of them just stared at Becca, as if she were the last person they expected to see in her own home. Aunt Cordelia's bright nails covered her mouth to keep from saying something she shouldn't. She must have rushed over from the beauty salon she owned. Mrs. Bergmann from next door had probably left the children with her husband. Would she ever leave them with Becca again? Mrs. Leonetti, who girdled her capacious opinions less tightly than her stomach, didn't even like her mother, but perhaps crisis resolved old enmities or at least merited a truce.

Their comfort gifts sat cold and limp on the kitchen table — the remains of a fried chicken, coleslaw, gelatin mold, a pot of soup, plates of cookies and brownies, melted ice cream, macaroni and cheese, something green and drippy. Almost irrelevantly, Becca wondered why no one had put it away.

Then Aunt Cordelia picked up a plate and asked, "What will you have, Becca?"

Even the condemned sister was entitled to a last meal. The air was thick, as if everyone were holding their breath. She shook her head and turned toward the stairs.

"Wait," her mother called. "I want to ask you something."

Here, in front of all these neighbors? Who'd blab to cameras for a chance to be on TV?

"I can't, Mom. Not now."

"She's been answering questions all afternoon," Officer Sam proffered the excuse. To Becca, she seemed to be the only one in the world who didn't see Robbie's kidnapping as Becca's fault. "I'm sure she's told us everything she knows. Many times over, in fact. She's exhausted." And a good mother would let her daughter rest. Except that Becca had deprived her of mothering her most cherished child, so Becca didn't count.

Becca gave Officer Sam a grateful look and mounted the stairs while the officer slipped out the front door. The conversation restarted, as if the radio had been switched off at her entrance and was switched back on, everyone talking at once, the words "she" and "Becca" and "sister" rising above the din. She felt betrayed.

Becca's breath caught in the doorway to her room. Someone had been in here and left dirty fingerprints all over her white and gold-trimmed French Provincial furniture and fat fanny prints on the ruffled bedspread with the intertwining roses across it. Someone had pulled the miniature furniture pieces from her dollhouse, then heaped tiny chairs, couches, beds, china plates, and dried flower bouquets on the bottom shelf. Someone had pawed through her tubes and jars of make-up on her vanity and messed up her books and papers on her desk. And where was her homework? Frantically, she scrabbled through everything, finding odd papers in her night table. Nothing was where it had been. And what was her diary doing in her top desk drawer? She picked it up and noticed immediately that the clasp was broken. Whoever had been in here had forced it. Even Robbie had never done that! Her chest drawers were only half closed, her panties and starter bras ever so slightly disarranged. Did they get their kicks out of rifling through a young girl's underthings, these men? Because she was pretty sure men had done this, not women. Police officers. Or could it have been her mother?

She walked around her room, reading other signs. Her Sweet Amanthus cloth doll in its white chenille dress embroidered with pink, blue, and yellow yarn flowers flopped lazily on the floor by the door. Becca would never have left her there. Picking her up, Becca cradled her, looking for a clear clean place to set her down. Finding none, she perched her on the windowsill to look out at the trees turning gold and magenta.

"You'll be happy there," she said.

The window was open a third of the way. Why? Perhaps because the place stank of something like smoke and metal. In her closet, too, boxes put back crooked on the wrong shelves, a blouse hanging with her skirts, everything pulled to one side to search behind, shoes in a pile. How could her mother have allowed them?

Becca was neat and orderly, but even when she forgot to put her things away, the disorder was predictable. This room was no longer her own.

Her home had changed. Someone else's idea of what a home should be. She was quite sure that it would never be the same. She'd lost it. But with that loss, a scrap of independence glimmered faintly like a tinsel ring in the grass. She was on her own.

Slowly, Becca approached Robbie's room, dreading what she might find. If only Robbie were there, running his squeaky trucks across the floor, or bouncing his ball. "Not supposed to play with it in the house," he'd sing when he saw her. But his room was noiseless. Maybe he'd be lying on his bed with something of Becca's that he wasn't supposed to have, her power bar, or her secret picture of a naked man that she'd gotten out of one of Mom's magazines. Oh, God, they'd seen that, too, hanging inside her closet door. She ran back and flung the door open again. It wasn't there. How embarrassing! Maybe her mother had taken it before the police searched. Not likely. She hadn't even known about it. Or had she? Even if she'd known, she hadn't saved Becca from anything else.

Back to Robbie's room, still fantasizing, still praying, hope against hope, that he was lying on his bed with something of hers that he wasn't supposed to have. The minute he saw her, he'd — quick! — cover whatever it was with his body and try to act as though it was nothing at all, with no idea of how obviously he gave himself away. Whatever it was, she'd gladly let him keep it if only . . .

Or he might be "reading" his Peter Pan and Wendy book. Becca and Annalyn were putting on a play for the neighborhood in Annalyn's garage, and Robbie was going to be a "lost boy."

Lost boy?

As Becca entered his room, a shock like a cold wind blew across her forehead. In the fading light she saw that his bed was torn apart and empty. The place was a mess, but what was heartbreaking was that it wasn't Robbie's mess. Fire trucks, dumpsters, racers, ambulances and police cars scattered, not ranged along the road to Timbuktu. "Timbuktu." How he loved to say it! His block towers, bridges, and houses tumbled and his toy spacemen strewn, some already broken underfoot. Why couldn't they have been more careful?

Absently, she picked up a little sailboat from the windowsill, remembering how Robbie had brought it to her and Annalyn in the mall a few months ago, August, it was. Mom had dropped them off to shop for school clothes. When she picked them up, she'd approve and pay. All of a sudden Robbie was gone. Their search became frantic, dashes in and out of stores, announcements played over intercoms, a security guard jotting her brother's name on a report — when Robbie reappeared.

"Robbie, where have you been?"

"We were looking all over," said Annalyn, a second sister to him.

"I was with Toyman," he'd explained to them.

"Not Toyman, again! His imaginary playmate," Becca had explained to Annalyn. "They all have them at this age. Especially the more creative ones." As if it were a sign of superiority. "And what's that you've got? A sailboat? Where did you get this?" Becca had demanded.

"Toyman gave it to me."

"Robbie, how many times do I have to tell you, you're not sup-posed to take things from stores. It's called 'stealing.'"

"I didn't!" he'd yelled indignantly.

"Come on, show us where you got it. We have to give it back."

And they'd hunted through the mall in widening circles, but they couldn't even find a toy store, and no wonder! They'd chosen the section that had the best school clothing shops around. They weren't dummies, after all.

But Robbie's imaginary friend hadn't been just a phase, as Becca had predicted to Annalyn. Instead, Robbie'd talked about him more and more often, including this morning.

Another memory jiggled the edge of Becca's mind. It was some-thing she'd paid no attention to at the time. Someone standing by the water fountain in the mall, someone Becca thought she remembered Robbie had said "Hi!" to. But then Robbie was a friendly boy. He said "Hi!" to just about everyone, and Becca and Annalyn were at pains to explain to him that he mustn't talk to strangers.

The thing of it was, though, Becca thought she remembered that the man had white-blond hair, that he wore a shirt with the sleeves rolled to the elbows, and that something flashed at his ear.

Now *she* was imagining things.

She walked around Robbie's bed to the other side. There on the floor was his *Peter Pan* book. It's spine was broken.

Exhausted, Becca returned to her room and collapsed on her bed. It stank of police uniforms that had been in back alleys and God knows where else. She was very hungry, her last food the cheese and peanut butter crackers that Officer Sam had gotten her, but she couldn't bear to go downstairs and face those women again. Usually, she kept a cache of power bars in the top drawer of her night table. Probably, they wouldn't be there. She opened the drawer. Pencils and pens from her desk, pink lip glosses from her vanity. No address book with the white lace on the cover. What could they have done with that? How was she supposed to call her friends? If she still had any. Probably, she'd find it eventually — maybe in the linen closet, or the 'fridge, or the woodpile!

Nothing to eat. Who knew where her stash might be? Inside some officer's growly stomach, most likely. Two fat fannies sitting side by side on her bed, munching power bars and discussing her dirty hair. Doesn't take a detective to figure *that* out.

She lay across her bed remembering breakfast this morning.

Was it just this morning?

Sun shadows of hibiscus on the patio outside the back door trail down the yellow kitchen walls. Robbie's chipmunk cheeks nibble Crunchy Bunchies as he "reads" the picture of the little boy on the milk carton.

"He could be my friend," he says, grinning up at Becca with milk oozing from his mouth.

"That's right," Becca sings.

"Why is his face crooked?"

"An artist sketched him, and sketches are often crooked." Becca doesn't really know why. She doesn't even think the boy looked particularly crooked, but she wants to eat her toast in peace.

"Did he run away because he didn't get any toys for Christmas?"

"Silly! That's no reason to run away. Lots of poor kids don't get toys. If they don't get them this year, they get them the next."

"Did he run away because he was bad?"

"No, most runaways are good little children."

"Then why did they run away?"

"Some of them couldn't help it. Somebody took them."

"Becca," warns her mother.

"Will somebody take me away?"

"Not a chance," Becca says. "You're too ugly." Mom frowns without looking up from the list she's making, so Becca adds, "We wouldn't let them." The whole aim of rearing children successfully these days is to raise their self-esteem, not lower it.

"Toyman says he's going to take me on a trip."

"That's only your imagination."

Robbie thinks about this for a few minutes, leaving Becca to spread strawberry jam on her second slice in peace.

"Did their sister leave them behind because they were a pain in the rectum?"

His ability to quote her exactly is exasperating. "Of course, not. Sisters don't do that."

"You always say you will."

"Do not," says Becca, with a quick glance toward her mother who's washing a pan. Apparently, she isn't listening. "Well, only to make you behave. I wouldn't really do that."

She hopes she said that. Probably she did. "Some bad man took them," she says.

Upstairs, Dad bangs around the bedroom, getting packed to go see Grandma Emily, who's in the hospital dying again, except they're not supposed to call it that. They're supposed to call it being "very very sick." Sunday is one of his best days to sell houses, and he hates the fact that he has to go to see his mother in Illinois instead. He's also scared of flying — a secret that he never tells anyone but they all know. The doctor has warned, however, that he might miss a last sight of Grandma alive if he waits any longer. Mom and Becca and Robbie aren't going with him, and he's upset about it.

Downstairs, he says for the sixth time by Mom's count, "Wish you'd come, Sue." He's carrying his garment bag to the front door while Becca listens from the kitchen.

"We've been through that," Mom says. "It's always the same. She's about to die and then she gets better. Besides, I can't take any more sick leave."

"If she dies this time, I don't think I can handle it."

"Silly, Tom! We always manage to handle the things we think we can't."

He's opened the door to wait for the taxi.

"She'd love to see her grandchildren one last time."

"She already has. Three last times. It's not good for them. Becca obsesses so on death — all that death poetry."

"Maybe he ran away because he had to eat spinach," Robbie says, interrupting Becca's eavesdropping.

"Shhh," Becca tells him. She wants to listen.

"And Robbie's always in his own world. Too imaginative for his own good. Look at him. He's on about the milk carton children again."

Robbie's feeding bits of toast to someone in the empty dinette chair beside him.

"Jeez, maybe we should get him a shrink."

"Lots of five-year-olds have imaginary friends."

"Hey, don't take such big mouthfuls," Robbie says. "Leave some for me. Selfish!" He slaps his friend's hand on the table. "Owwww, he slapped me back." Robbie turns tear-filled eyes to his sister.

"I'll kiss it and make it better," Becca says, grabbing the pudgy little hand by its fingers. It really does look a bit red. She's noticed this about him before, that there's something different about his body for no reason. She bends over it. It smells of Crunchy Bunchies.

"Mmm, you smell delicious. I could eat you up."

"No, don't eat me up," he giggles.

"Okay." She kisses his hand and says, "There," as the front door closes.

"Ewww!" Robbie says. "Beccaspit."

Some time in the middle of the night, Becca awakened. It was dark now, and the phone was quiet. But she felt as though someone were in her room. She lay motionless, not even breathing, waiting for whoever it was to step forward from behind the curtain, or out of the closet, or to get up where he crouched at the desk. But whoever had been here was gone. Even *she* didn't belong.

She tiptoed into Robbie's room. Nothing had been disturbed since she had been in here earlier. He hadn't returned. The bed was still a mess, and she had to walk cautiously so as not to trample his fire trucks. The moon cast an eerie glow over everything as if it belonged in another world. She lay down on Robbie's bed. His pillow smelled of him, sweet and milky with a dash of garden dirt.

As she began to drift, the sailboat gleamed larger as if it were the only thing in the room. She should tell the cops about Toyman. But she couldn't face another session like the one this afternoon. Maybe tomorrow.

Nestled beside Robbie, she fell asleep.

4

"LISTEN TO ME, DAMON."

They were in the sailboat room, where Kenny knelt in front of Robbie the way his family did in church on Christmas. Easter too. Not birthdays. One other time, Robbie thought, Mom in her feather hat; Dad in his real estate suit with the red and blue striped tie so he could dash off to sell his houses at the sound of the last "Amen;" Bec-Bec in her "stupid beret" with the pom-pom on top that Mom made her wear; and Robbie in his blazer.

Kenny was shaking Robbie's shoulders. "Damon? Are you with me here?"

Where else am I? Robbie wondered. Panic tugged at his chest. Aren't I here? Am I there?

"We're going to take you shopping. These clothes are real dirty, and they don't suit you anyhow. Whoever bought them for you has no taste. No sense of style," Kenny said, dismissing Bec-Bec's choices with a wave of his hand. He smelled of the same soap he washed Robbie with, and also vanilla candles. "So we'll take you shopping, but you've got to be good. No mouthing off. No wandering away. Understand?"

Robbie didn't move. Where would he wander to? He was lost anyway.

"Understand, Damon?" Another shake.

Robbie leaned over and whispered in Kenny's ear.

"I'm not Damon. I'm Robbie."

Kenny bit his lip.

"That'll be our secret, okay?" He brushed Robbie's hair from his eyes. "Just pretend for now you're Damon. Pretend you're acting a part."

"Like in the movies?"

That upset Kenny, although Robbie didn't know why.

"No, television," he said. "Or better yet, on stage. Have you ever seen a play? No? TV, then."

"Sesame Street?"

"That's good. I'll bet you'd be terrific on Sesame Street. Just don't get Carl mad. He's not nice when he's mad. Believe me, I know."

Kenny had tiny red bumps on his nose like chicken pops. Robbie had had chicken pops last year, and Bec-Bec had made him chicken noodle soup, so the chicken pops wouldn't be hungry, and they'd go away.

"If you're real good, we'll get you an earring just like mine. Would you like that?"

Robbie's eyes alit on the diamond. It was pretty like Mom's diamond ring, and it flashed in the sun as Kenny turned his head this way and that, so Robbie could admire it.

"See the rainbow colors?"

Robbie nodded. Yes, he saw the rainbow colors, and yes, he'd like a diamond like Mom's. He'd like that very much.

"You have to promise me you'll be good, though. Promise?"

Robbie stared into Kenny's eyes, kind eyes, sort of a watery blue with bits of black floating in them like the dead leaves in the San Lorenzo River. Kenny liked Robbie and wanted him to like him back.

"How about it, Damon? Do we go shopping for clothes," and then, in a sudden inspiration, "and afterwards we can have cheeseburgers and fries, and a shake, how about that? Will you stay close and mind?"

Robbie nodded.

"Yes?"

"Yes."

"Good boy! Carl," he shouted, "Damon promises to mind."

"Then can I go home?" Robbie asked.

"Shhh!" Kenny looked around, but Carl wasn't standing in the doorway with a storm in his face. "This is your home, Damon. Get that into your noggin," and he tapped Robbie's forehead as if somebody were in there. "Look at all the great toys I got you. You haven't even played with them yet."

"At home I got blocks."

"Tell you what. We'll go to a toy store in a few days, and you can pick some out. Would you like that?"

Robbie thought about this. He'd like to go to a toy store, but more than that, he wanted his old room back, just as it was, with his red, blue, orange, and green blocks, and his fire trucks, and his *Peter Pan and Wendy* book.

"I want to go home."

"Okay, tell you what. We'll take you back for a visit to your old home. So you can see it."

"Later?"

"Not today."

"Tomorrow?"

"I'm not sure when. Sometime."

Robbie felt the sniffles filling up his nose again. "That's not soon."

"As soon as we can," Kenny promised, kissing him on the forehead where he'd rapped. Robbie liked that. His Mom did it, too. And Bec-Bec kissed wherever it hurt. Even Dad kissed him on the cheek while he was on his lap, if he had time.

"Kiss back?"

Robbie had to stand on tiptoe to reach Kenny's cheek. It smelled of aftershave.

"Oh, that was a wonderful kiss," Kenny said, rubbing circles into Robbie's back.

They took Robbie for a ride in the van. Carl drove in his lumpy black sweater, brown pants, and dark glasses.

"Carl likes to wear his dark glasses. They make him look like a big-time Hollywood producer. Which he is, practically."

Kenny sat in the Mommy seat. He reached over to the black hair curling at Carl's neck, and then the gray above his ears.

"Time for another job," he said.

Every time Robbie looked up, he caught Carl's black eyes watching him in the mirror, glistening like the sequins on Mom's best dress. As if he were waiting for Robbie to do something bad. But Robbie couldn't think of anything bad to do, and he'd be too scared anyway.

This time it was just a short drive. When they parked and got out, they were on a busy street full of people jabbering in what must be French because Robbie couldn't understand a word and French was the only other language he'd heard about besides Spanish. Dressed in colorful skirts and big blouses — even the men — they bumped into each other and laughed and talked to everyone. The trouble was, the town was called "Hate-something", and Robbie didn't think a place should be named "Hate." Carl and Kenny each took a hand and squeezed it very firmly, and they walked a little too fast, so Robbie had a hard time keeping up.

"Relax, Carl," Kenny was saying. "See the papers? Not a word."

"Not on the front page, anyway."

"No one knows up here."

"Doesn't hurt to be vigilant," Carl said, scanning the street and not looking at Kenny or Robbie at all. "The sooner we get him out of those clothes, the better."

"They really are a disgrace," Kenny agreed pleasantly.

"That's not what I meant," Carl growled.

"I know what you meant."

"Of course you do."

Robbie stared into their faces, wondering if they were going to have a fight. What would happen to him if they did?

In and out of stores they traipsed. On a mission to buy. Blue jeans and tees, sweaters, and shirts in colors Robbie had never heard of, like "puce" and "chartreuse" and "aubergine" and "coral" and gold, too, because Kenny was much too great an artist to be satisfied with plain old yellow or green. "Too common," he said.

Kenny picked out several scarves to go with them, tying one with a lot of bright nonsense figures around Robbie's neck. Each time they tried on a shirt or a pair of pants or a jacket, Kenny turned Robbie to the mirror so he could see it on himself.

"The mirror never lies," he said. "Always check to see if it approves of what you're wearing. The mirror knows who you are. Brilliant," he exclaimed. "Now you look just like your Kenny."

"Your little brother?" asked the beaming salesman.

"Of course! My youngest."

"He looks just like you."

"Uncanny!" Carl proclaimed, tossing Robbie's bright red sweatshirt with the bears into the wastebasket.

"Hey, I wanted that."

"It's dirty."

"Bec-Bec can wash it."

Kenny and Carl exchanged glances, as if Robbie had said something bad. Was he in trouble?

"She does sometimes," Robbie added. Didn't they believe him?

Kenny bent over him.

"You have nice new clothes, now," he said to Robbie. "You look much handsomer in them than you did in the old ones. Doesn't he, Carl?"

Carl nodded as if he didn't really think so.

"You have to develop a sense of style," Kenny said. "Aren't you going to thank your uncle Carl for your brilliant new clothes?"

"Thank you."

"Thank you, Uncle Carl," Kenny corrected.

"Thank you, Uncle Carl."

And they were off, leaving the sweatshirt behind, one sleeve poking out over the rim, crying, "Help! Help! Save me!"

Next was the underwear department, where Kenny made Robbie try on new undershorts to be sure they fit. He snapped the waistband and tested all around Robbie's legs and pee-pee, or "penis" as Kenny called it, then bought a whole bunch of them with matching under-shirts.

"Look how much whiter they are than your old ones. Practically rags."

Robbie hadn't thought they were rags at all.

"You're such a good mommy," Carl said to Kenny, and both of them laughed, although Carl didn't think it was as funny as Kenny did.

"Let me see," said Kenny, "What have we forgotten? Oh yes, socks and shoes."

In the shoe department, they bought several new pairs of tennis shoes as well as a pair of dark blue shoes for best.

"A *dozen* pair of socks?" Carl asked. "Does he really need a dozen?"

"You've got a dozen," Kenny said.

"I'm the man of the house. I have to go to work."

"I work too. Art is hard work."

"Of course it is. But you don't need socks for it."

"I do for my gallery showings."

"Your one showing?"

Kenny thrust out his lower lip.

"There'll be others."

"A dozen pair of socks for one showing," Carl said, as if he hadn't heard Kenny. "What are you going to do, change socks every fifteen minutes? Or maybe you'll wear them all at once. The new artist fad. Anything to attract attention. It'll be the Kenny Warhol style. At least, it'll give the critics something to write about."

Kenny had turned pink all over his face, even his neck and ears. "You're just jealous."

"Who knows, you might even sell something. Your dirty socks, maybe," Carl laughed.

"All you can sell is dirty movies," Kenny blurted out.

"Shut up!" said Carl through gritted teeth. "Not in the middle of the street." People passing by were peering curiously into their faces. "And they're films, not movies."

What was going on, Robbie wondered. What were they fighting about? Would Carl hit Kenny?

Robbie stole his hand deeper into Kenny's. They walked along in silence, past an incense shop, a gallery, a fruit stand, a cheese shop and into a barber shop where Robbie had his hair cut short just like Kenny's.

Finally, Kenny paused in front of a restaurant, saying, "I promised Damon a hamburger if he was good, and he's been a little angel."

"He doesn't fool me."

"Oh, how can you say that?" Kenny took Robbie's arm affectionately, as if to protect him, and led him inside.

They stood in line and ordered cheeseburgers, fries, and shakes.

"Spistachio," Robbie said.

"They don't have pistachio."

"Chocolate."

"Strawberry," Kenny said. "It's better for you. It's fruit. Fruit and milk, that's good."

"Only a apple's fruit. Annalyn says."

"I say strawberries are fruit, too," said Kenny, his eyes sliding back and forth between Robbie and Carl. "You've got to learn not to contradict."

As they settled into the yellow chairs at the orange table with the plastic ivy dripping over the divider beside them, Kenny continued, "We've got to get you healthier food, Damon. You'll rot your teeth. Do you like oranges?"

Robbie nodded. He'd learned it was the safest thing to do. He was watching Carl, who sat glowering at him across the table. Kenny sat beside Robbie, and Robbie didn't think Carl liked that, although he had no idea why not. Kenny sat here because he wanted to keep Robbie boxed in like a spaceman in a toy chest. Or maybe Kenny sat here because he liked Robbie best.

"How about salads?" Kenny was asking. "I'll make you a fresh salad when we get home."

Carl gobbled his cheeseburger in a few bites, his mouth wide enough to fit the whole thing if he wanted. It reminded Robbie of a train tunnel. Then Carl downed his big bag of fries in bunches as if they were a snack.

"I told Damon we'd buy him an earring like mine."

"Not today," Carl said. "Are you going to eat those fries?"

Kenny pushed them toward Carl, who grabbed a fistful while eyeing Damon.

"I guess you're right," said Kenny. "We've done enough shopping for one day. Little fellow's plum tuckered out."

When they got home, Kenny had to try the new clothes on Robbie all over again.

"Let's look at you in the mirror. Are your buttons straight? Are the shoulders just where they should be? Is everything neat and clean? Well, of course, it's clean. We just brought everything home. Is that my new boy?"

Robbie nodded. He did look like a new boy in the mirror, not like an old boy at all.

"Nothing's too good for my Damon, is it? Does he look like a proper little man, now, or what?" he asked Carl, who was lounging around the room, hands thrust deep in his pockets, as if he didn't quite know what to do with himself.

"He looks like a proper little Kenny, that's what he looks like."

"Doesn't he, though! Oh, Carl, thanks so much for letting me have him." And he threw his arms around Carl's neck and hugged him, while Carl's face turned as soft as butter. Robbie blinked. Was he seeing things again? He'd never seen a face do that before. It looked melted!

"Carl's right, you know," Kenny said to Robbie as he tied another scarf around Robbie's neck. "You look just like me. You're the spitting image of my brother Timmy, when he was your age. The minute I saw you, I knew you were my little boy. And Carl knew I wanted you, so he made me a present of you. Wasn't that nice of him?"

"Like Toyman," Robbie said.

"Exactly."

"You're his new boy-toy," said Carl.

"Carl, don't say that."

"Why not? He doesn't know what it means."

But Kenny didn't like it. Not one bit. Robbie wondered what was wrong with a boy-toy.

That night, Robbie lay in bed planning what he would do. Get up in the middle of the night and tiptoe into the dining room where Carl always left the phone. Pick it up very quietly. Don't make a sound. Punch in the numbers for home like he did on his own telephone with the duck head. When Mom or Dad answered, whisper he was with Kenny and Carl, and Kenny was nice but Carl wasn't. Come and pick him up, please. Say "please" because that was the magic word. Bec-Bec said. That was how you got what you wanted. Then sit in the living room and wait. When they banged on the door, let them in. And he'd be home before you knew it.

Robbie fell asleep going over his plan.

When he awakened, it was still dark outside. It must be early because there were hardly any sounds from the street. Sounds didn't happen until people started going to work at a quarter to fifteen. Time to do it.

His heart thudded against his chest as he got up. If Carl caught him, he'd beat him until his blood ran out of his ears. Or stick a knife in his stomach and twist 'round and 'round until all his innards were mashed like potatoes. Or the tomato soup like Mom made in the blender. Innard soup, that's what he'd be. Robbie clutched at his innards. He could really feel the knife, and it hurt. Even Kenny couldn't save him.

He didn't put on his shoes because they might make a noise. Slowly, he tiptoed down the hall. The floor creaked once, then a second time. The door to Kenny and Carl's room was closed, and he didn't hear anything, even snores.

It was hard to see his way in the dining room. He pretended he was a cat, but it didn't help much. There was just enough streetlight to show him the telephone. Sure enough, there it was, right on the table in front of Carl's chair. He was so excited he almost forgot to be quiet.

But not quite.

Holding his breath, Robbie picked up the receiver and pressed the numbers 324-8122.

5

THE HOUSE EXPLODED, SHAKING Becca awake. Earthquake, she screamed to herself. Quick, dive under the bed! Stand in the doorway! She couldn't remember the school drill and lay rigid, watching the ceiling for cracks to spider across before it caved in.

But there were none. No rattling of the windows, no books and framed pictures falling to the floor. Why was that?

The slam of the front door still echoed. A minute later, her dad's voice cut through the air. She sprang to her feet, still wearing the shirt that smelled of sweaty metal from the police station the day before, and she hustled out of Robbie's room to the top of the stairs to listen.

"Just about got there when I had to turn around and come back," Dad grumbled angrily, his suitcase thudding to the floor. "Any news of Robbie in the last hour?"

"No."

"I called the police from the airport. They said they still have no clues. What the hell happened here anyway?" *Can't I go visit my dying mother without the roof falling in? Can't you take care of the children, instead of running off to a job we don't need? That costs us more in taxes and expenses than simply being a one-earner family?*

Becca not only heard her parents' words; she heard all the arguments down the years that these words echoed. Like a code that she'd become proficient at cracking.

"Becca left him alone at the playground."

It wasn't that way at all!

"Why would she do that?"

Thankfully, Dad didn't believe it.

The door of the refrigerator banged shut, and dishes clattered to the table. Her father had to eat every few hours. It was a stomach thing. Mom said it was a "big" stomach thing. Becca herself was so hungry she felt as though animals were gnawing through her insides, but she couldn't bear to go down and face them yet. First thing today, she'd stock up on fruit and energy bars and hide them around her room. Robbie's, too. They wouldn't think to look there.

"She had better things to do," her mother was saying.

"Where is she?"

"Upstairs. Hasn't affected her sleep any." Mom managed to make it sound like an accusation. "How's Emily?"

"How should I know? Didn't get to stay long enough to find out, did I? The doctor says she's stable, the nurse says she's going downhill, and as for Mom herself, she just groans."

"I told Becca not to —"

The phone was ringing again. Becca's Mom cut off her explanation and picked up quickly. It might be news of Robbie, found wandering in the Santa Cruz Mountains, cold and hungry but otherwise okay, they were taking him to the hospital for observation as they did all little lost boys who had spent the night outside, just a precaution, visiting hours at ten —

"Hello," her mother said. "No, Cordelia, no news. I have to go." She put down the phone and resumed, "I told her not to take Robbie to the park but she deliberately disobeyed me. She left him with Annalyn to go to the bathroom."

Becca began to creep down the stairs.

That's not how it happened, she wanted to shout. But she didn't want to face her father. Or her mother. Anyone.

She had to.

She didn't sneak down the rest of the stairs, because it was no use.

Instead, she thumped, giving them plenty of warning that she was coming. Both of them watched her take the box of Crunchy Bunchies out of the cabinet, as well as a cup, because there were no clean bowls.

"You'd better save that for your brother," her mother said sharply. You have no right to take the food from his mouth.

Without a word, Becca replaced the box and snicked a piece of bread from the open loaf on the counter. It was stale. She quickly spread peanut butter on it with a knife, also on the counter.

"Knife's dirty," her mother said.

Becca nodded in acknowledgment. I don't care if it's been soaking in pig slop. She tore into her breakfast like the lion over the zebra corpse that she'd seen on TV.

"Tell us what happened from beginning to end," her father demanded, stuffing bread and bologna down his throat without benefit of mustard, mayo, lettuce, or any of the other usual amenities. He ate straight from packages, drank from the orange juice carton, opened cans and spooned out whatever was in there. "Cutting out the middleman", he called it.

"Annalyn was the one who went to the bathroom," Becca said.

Recognizing that her own account was being challenged, her mother frowned. "Doesn't make any difference. He's gone."

"So who was watching Robbie?"

"I was — except just for a minute —" She tried to swallow, but the tears had her throat in a vise. Robbie was his favorite, hands down. As soon as he could walk, she'd watched them play ball together from her perch up the tree. She couldn't join them because she was too old. The one thing that her Dad had always praised Becca for was how well she cared for her little brother, made his lunch, found his other shoe, and bandaged his knee. She glowed in his praise. This was Becca's own little island of attention and even love from her father. Now she'd lost Robbie, she'd lost that. His desertion of her was that much bitterer.

The phone rang again, and Becca raced to it to get herself off the hook. Phones had always been so full of possibilities — friends, gossip, news. Now, the only thing she wanted from the phone was relief.

"Give me that," said her mother, snatching it from her. "You don't need to talk with your friends just now."

"Probably some stupid reporter. I didn't think it was a friend."

"Don't argue."

"You tell me from beginning to end exactly what happened," said her father. "And don't miss a detail." *Your brother's life may depend on it.*

So she told them, with frequent breaks by her mother to answer the ever-ringing phone, or slam the door on reporters, or welcome neighbors dropping by with moral support and deviled eggs in exchange for news fit for gossip. Becca hadn't thought it was a long story, but their questions drew it out unendingly. What was Becca doing in the bathroom? How long were they in there? Didn't it occur to her that Robbie might be in trouble? No sooner had Becca begun one answer than her father thought of another question. Her mother — who wasn't there, as Becca recalled — corrected her account as if she had been. At some point, Becca recognized that her father wouldn't be through with her until he'd stuffed himself, and judging from past performance, he had a long way to go. Another question about his son legitimized another spoonful of refried beans.

"Didn't your mother expressly forbid you to go to the park?" He was opening a jar of olives.

"Didn't I?" her mother chimed in.

At least, I finally got you two to agree on something.

"Yes." Short answers might get the agony over with sooner.

Becca's eyes escaped to the ceramic canister set, a little Dutch boy like Robbie in blue pantaloons and clogs on the flour jar, his sister on the sugar, green-leaved yellow tulips over all. When had she thought they were a family like that?

"Then why did you disobey?" *You're not too old to spank, you know.*

Puh-lease!

"She thought she could get away with it," her mother fake-explained.

"Why do you think we tell you not to do things?"

Because you're too lazy to think it through, Becca hazarded the guess, although not aloud, of course.

"Did I tell you not to go so you'd go?"

"Is that why we tell you things?" He tore open a bag of corn chips for emphasis.

"Or perhaps you know better than we do? Is that it?" her mother pressed. "You think you know better?"

"No."

"Of course she does. She's a ten-year-old, for Chrissake!"

"Almost eleven."

"Why did you leave her to baby-sit Robbie in the first place?" Dad suddenly wheeled on Mom and tore into her as efficiently as he had the bag of chips.

"I told you, I got a call from the hospital. They were short-handed."

"Again?"

"Babies don't wait to be born just because it's inconvenient." Besides, I CAN'T STAND staying home!

"Saying 'No' is another option, you know. You can't be expected to come up with a babysitter at the last minute. Children are a valid excuse to get out of working," if you care more about your children than you do about your job like any normal mother which, of course, you don't.

"Taking care of *our* children isn't just *my* responsibility."

"I was off seeing my dying mother, for Chrissake." Now Robbie was gone, he could use the offending word with impunity. Becca didn't need protection.

"Quit your own job if you're so all-fired set on guarding your kids every minute of the day."

"Oh, sure, we'd get along great on *half my salary*!"

"It's not my fault women get paid less."

Becca stared at them, not quite believing her eyes. Had Dad always had those hairs growing out of his ears? Had Mom always been so lumpy and dumpy? When had they changed, or was it just that she'd never noticed how her Mom's extra chin shook when she argued?

The phone was ringing again, and neither of them was answering it.

"You're the one who wanted kids. You should take care of them. You know damn well Becca isn't old enough to be left with such a responsibility."

"I know it now."

"You've said so yourself."

"She's old enough. Just not mature enough."

"Well," her dad wheeled on Becca. "Make yourself useful. Get the phone."

"Are you two through with the inquisition?"

"Don't get snotty with me."

Becca answered the phone. It was just a reporter. Becca told her to leave the phone clear for important stuff. She could hear the silence from the kitchen as they listened in, so she added sweetly,

"Mom and Dad are much too busy fighting to come to the phone just now. Any message?"

Her father's footsteps thudded into the hall.

"Just one comment from you, Rebecca dear," the honeyed voice persisted.

"I'm not your dear and drop dead. There's your comment."

"You wouldn't want me to print that!"

"I don't give a damn what you print!"

The sharp intake of breath on the other end of the line sucked the air out of it as she slammed the receiver. Such language from a ten-year-old! A girl, at that!

"I told you not to let her answer it," said her mother.

They both glared at Becca as she returned to the kitchen. She must get something more inside her while she had the chance. She hooked a couple of apples from the top of the refrigerator, the rest of the stale bread loaf, the peanut butter, and a fork to spread it with. Then she headed for the stairs.

"You, come here, you," her father called out angrily. "We're not through with you yet." I'm not through eating yet. "Not by a long shot. Aren't you even the least bit sorry?"

Becca could scarcely believe her ears. Not sorry that her brother was gone? Not sorry that it was because of her own inattentiveness that he was missing?

"The kidnappers took him, not me," she snapped.

"You gave them the opportunity," her mother said. "All you think about is your social life."

"Right. And you knew it. And you made me baby-sit him anyway," she said — her father's argument. "If you cared anything about Robbie, you'd be out searching for him. Which is where I'm going just as soon as I've finished eating."

"You're grounded," her father exploded.

"We have to stay by the phone," said her mother.

"You don't both have to."

"You don't think of anyone but yourself."

Maybe she could hide out in the yard for a few days. She and Robbie had hung a sleeping bag in the garage rafters last year. Probably it was all buggy. Annalyn's playhouse?

"Who Becca thinks of isn't the issue," said her dad, wheeling back on her mom. "She's a normal ten-year-old. She's not supposed to think about anyone else. The issue is that she disobeyed. She left her post. She was on duty, and she left her post."

"Oh, Lordy, Lordy," as Aunt Cordelia would say, now with the military metaphors. If they were particularly unlucky, they'd be treated to interminable tales of army life and how they all suffered and saved each other and bunches of Viets into the bargain. During his whole month of active duty.

Becca started out the back door.

"Where do you think you're going?"

"Just out to eat." But a media type was lurking behind the fence.

"I told you, you're grounded!"

"From the yard?" Becca asked incredulously.

At that moment, they both became aware of the reporter's camera whirring and picking up this tidbit of family life for posterity. Her dad scowled at the face across the fence and slammed the door so the house shook. He was doing a lot of that lately.

"Upstairs this instant. We want you available for questions."

Predictable! Becca supposed they had to take it out on someone. At least, she had enough food to last her awhile. In case they decided never to feed her again. That that would be her punishment.

Today's copy of the *Santa Cruz Sentinel* was lying on the hall table. Dad must have brought it in. A picture of herself on the front page stared up at her. She was leaving the police station, her long stringy hair askew, her pink shirt rumpled, Officer Sam's arm around her shoulders to shield her, as if she were a criminal or something. The kids at school would be commenting about the whole thing right now between classes. "Did you hear about Becca? Her missing brother? Didn't she look awful? I wouldn't let anybody take *my* picture looking like that." Like she'd had a choice. They'd be passing notes, shaking heads, giggling to each other, and giving the boys the news as an excuse to talk to them without appearing to flirt, which, of course, was exactly what they were doing. Annalyn was probably telling Nick right now.

Her parents seemed not to have noticed that Becca was missing school. But she didn't see how she could face her friends, not today, not tomorrow, even if Robbie came home. Maybe Annalyn was sticking up for her.

Maybe not.

Beside her photo was an inset of that old picture of Robbie on his way to church, looking holy. Might as well have a halo. Had Mom given that to them? Why hadn't she given them a decent picture of Becca? The story quoted Becca as saying that she was "filled with guilt and regret." Becca supposed that was better than assuming she didn't care, as her parents had.

After squirreling away her food stash, Becca paused on the threshold of Robbie's room. Already it didn't look the same as it had the afternoon before. Maybe it was the difference between sunset, with all its reds and golds, and daylight that somehow bleached the color out, shadowing the red of his bedspread, graying the walls, sapping the life from his trucks and blocks and spacemen until they were only bits of plastic now. The bedclothes seemed more rumpled and not as fluffy, the pillows flattened. Well, she'd slept on them. Flatter, too, the red cushions on his little desk chair and on the window seat that looked out over the trees now yellowing, where he curled his legs and read his picture books aloud to himself. Red was Robbie's favorite color, fire engine red.

"How about a navy cushion?" Becca had suggested to him once. "And yellow curtains would be nice to go with your fire engine. And what about little gold stars on the ceiling that glow in the dark? I bet I could do that."

"Who ever heard of a yellow fire engine!" Robbie had ridiculed.

"Go with, not match."

Their mother hadn't come in here since yesterday, Becca was quite sure. Probably she couldn't bear to. Their father would be up, but he wouldn't stay long. He was too pragmatic to be sentimental. Lingering in his missing son's room wouldn't help find him.

Perhaps I should tidy up the place a bit, Becca thought. Then it will be all ready, neat and clean for Robbie when he returns. So he can just come home all exhausted from his journey and climb into clean, sweet-smelling PJs and a well-made bed and have a nice long sleep. I'll bet he'd love that.

But if Becca straightened, less of Robbie would remain. Even his dirt was precious somehow. He had left those sticky strawberry jam fingerprints on his bookcase; his grubby little hands had arranged his wooden blocks and run all his trucks into the far corners of the room, although the feet of police officers had knocked them askew. Even his precious skin cells were on the dirty sheets and pillows and pajamas. So Becca hesitated, picked up the sailboat, and returned to her own room.

She lay down on her bed and contemplated the disagreeable task of telling the police about Toyman. She couldn't bring herself to endure all the questioning that Officer T. would subject her to under the condemnatory stares of the rest of the force, to explain over and over how she hadn't even believed in Toyman at first, had thought he was a figment of Robbie's imagination, didn't start putting the sailboat together with the flash of an earring and a platinum young man in blue until yesterday.

Oh, God, she couldn't bear it. Maybe Mom would come with her? Not bloody likely. Dad? He honestly wouldn't understand the need. His supportiveness was limited to offers to take her to the mall because he figured shopping was what she did best, and he knew he spent a lot of time with Robbie that Becca resented. But, of course, she wouldn't be caught dead in the mall with her father. Aunt Cordelia! Aunt Cordelia was something called "a feminist," which meant that she wouldn't stand for any nonsense from a "passel" of men! She'd come.

Becca made the call to the salon surreptitiously, but Aunt Cordelia wasn't available.

Back up in her room, Becca watched the police, volunteers, and dogs going door to door. The neighborhood looked ever so slightly different, as if there were a new vibration shimmering up from the ground. She'd heard that Santa Cruz was a center of magnetic forces and energy fields. Perhaps it was these she saw. The poor lived in the woods, grew their own food, wore homespun, and sported ponytails — men as well as women — part of a back-to-nature movement. A few months ago, a biker had zoomed up Center Street, yelling, "I love this place!" That was how she felt, too. She loved this place, the bougainvillea crawling up the patio, the hibiscus lounging in the sun, the Penny University's philosophical discussions, and always the ocean with its gold satin pathway of promise or illusion. But also "frail Santa Cruz," a place of earthquakes, fires, floods, and new waterfalls in the haunted meadows where the ground periodically gave way.

An hour later, her father climbed the stairs, hauling more than the weight of his body with him, the heaviness of his loss finally settling inside him, Becca surmised. She saw him pause on the threshold of Robbie's room, just as she had. Finding nothing there of value, because he did not perceive the precious traces of her brother as she did, he shifted around and peered in at Becca. Evidently, he saw nothing of value here, either, and headed for his own room.

By noon, Becca decided to get Robbie's room ready for his return. That would be more comforting than leaving it as it had been when he disappeared. The police had contaminated the scene anyway.

She stripped his bed and obtained fresh sheets and pillow cases from the linen cupboard in the hall. There, now his bed was all ready for him to crawl under the covers, where he'd play house until he fell asleep. The weather was getting colder, so he might want an extra blanket. The red one, of course, folded in half and laid across the foot.

She piled his dirty laundry in the hall, his pajamas, his pants and shirts, in fact, almost everything needed washing, although she had done his laundry just last Thursday. She did two loads, tiptoeing past the room where her mom lay resting in the dark. She didn't know where her dad had gone. Probably searching. She must find a way to sneak out of the house to look for her brother, too. She might see signs of him that strangers would not recognize as his.

Back in Robbie's room, she returned everything to where it belonged, his blocks to the net bag inside the toy chest, his Legos and Lincoln Logs to canisters just inside his closet, and his spacemen to his shelves with his books. He doesn't like to keep his clean clothes in his bureau, because it's hard for him to tug his drawers open; he just likes them in a pile on his beanbag chair, but he really needs to learn to open his drawers. Maybe I can wax them so they don't stick. With a candle, maybe.

And a fresh pair of pajamas waiting for him on his bed.

And *Peter Pan and Wendy*, did those bad policemen break your spine? Come here, I'll mend you with tape. Good as new, practically.

Open the window to let the stale air out with its weight of strangers and grief, and let the fresh in, with its promises from far away.

That night the room still waited expectantly for Robbie's return. Becca lit votive candles in each of the windows, careful to keep them well away from the curtains.

But with the candles lit, she couldn't see out into the dark where Robbie might be. She saw only this room like the duplicate in *Alice through the Looking Glass*, as if it were someone else's. What if he were signaling her? Perhaps he needed help and was waving at her to come down? She pressed her forehead against the glass. She could barely see outside. No sign of Robbie, not in the street or on the sidewalk, not by the bushes where he and Alex played, not on the neighbor's porch, not under the pine tree.

Why was it that she could only see outside when it was dark inside? Why, did light prevent her from seeing into the dark? Why did the candles merely reflect themselves in the windows, distorting reality?

"I wonder what God's doing now," she thought to herself, the God she felt so close to up in her backyard tree, the God of her poetry, the God of the sunset over the Pacific. Was he grieving over Robbie or protecting him? "Protect him, please, God."

Then her Mom was standing behind her, chenille robe open, sash hanging down one side to the floor, breasts sagging to her waist — what would Becca want with breasts? Already she had breast buds. Breasts seemed unavoidable.

"What are you doing?" her mother demanded.

"I was just cleaning up for Robbie."

"You have no right to be in here."

"See the candles? If Robbie's lost, the light will show him the way home."

"I said, get out. You have no right."

6

A SIREN WAILED IN Robbie's ear. How come there was a siren at his house? Could it be the fire department? Oh, no, was there a fire at his house? Was everything burning up? He could smell the smoke. The siren stopped.

"Thank goodness!" he said to himself.

Now there was a busy signal. Maybe he'd made a mistake. He punched in his home number, but got the busy signal again. Uh oh, he'd forgotten to hang up first so he could start over. He pushed in the plastic hang-up thingy, got the dial tone, and pressed the numbers for his home more carefully, 324-8122. The line was still busy. Must be Bec-Bec with Annalyn. He wished he had his duck telephone. It was never busy. He could speak to anyone he wanted any time.

Huffing in frustration, he hit the numbers wildly now. "Oh, you booger, you!" he said into the phone.

Laughter behind him. Side by side in the doorway stood Kenny and Carl in their matching striped pajamas.

"Are you trying to call your parents, Damon?" Kenny stepped forward and switched on the lamp. Then, to Carl, "Isn't he cute?"

"You forgot the area code," Carl said coldly.

"Do you know what an area code is?"

"You're in a different one now."

Robbie let go of the phone, and it clattered to the table. He'd done it wrong, and now Carl and Kenny knew. Were they mad at him? Kenny wasn't, but Carl, he just couldn't tell. Sometimes he hid his anger like it was a secret.

As if in answer, Carl lunged at him and grabbed his wrist.

"Any more of this nonsense and we'll tie you up," he said, propelling him toward the boat room.

"He didn't mean anything, Carl," Kenny said, tugging at Carl's other arm. "He's just a little boy." But Robbie saw that Carl was much stronger than Kenny.

"He meant to call home," Carl said, his grip tightening, "to get us into trouble."

"No, he just wanted to talk, didn't you, Damon?"

Robbie nodded without speaking, trying to free his wrist. But the harder he struggled, the harder Carl squeezed.

"You're breaking my wrist," Robbie said.

"Or were you calling the police?"

Robbie shook his head "no." Maybe he should, though. He probably wouldn't have trouble reaching them. What was their number, he wondered.

"Answer him, Damon. Tell him who you called."

"Just Mom," he said.

"You want us to tie you up, huh?" Carl whipped him around by his arm, so he landed on the bed.

"Ow!"

"Of course he doesn't, Carl," Kenny said, throwing himself down beside Robbie and rubbing his sore shoulder gently. "He was just playing a game, weren't you, Damon? See, Carl? No biggie. It was just a game."

"You don't fool me," Carl said to Robbie, but Kenny was in the way of further damage, so he stalked off.

Then Kenny lay Robbie back down in his bed, covered him gently with his sheet and blanket, and patted him.

"Be a good little Damon," Kenny told him. "I wasn't going to tell you this, because I didn't want to get you too excited. But we're having a big party for you to celebrate your new birthday. On Christmas Day. With cake and ice cream and trucks. And all your new friends are coming, the boys in Carl's films. There's Dickybird, Mickey, Adam, Hank, Flip, and I forget who else. They're bringing lots of presents and they'll be nice because Carl said. Would you like that?"

Robbie nodded.

"But it's not my birthday," he said. "My birthday's after Christmas. It's March a hundred."

"You have a new birthday, Damon. Your new birthday is October twentieth now. That's the day you came to live with us. The day before yesterday when you were born into our family. We're going to be a little late celebrating it, that's all. Are you excited?"

Robbie yawned. "Yes."

"Good. Now it's almost daylight." And indeed the light was sneaking in under the blind. "You nap for a little while. I have to go to work in my studio today, and if you promise to be good, I'll take you with me. Then you can paint and be an artist, too, just like your big brother Kenny."

Kenny dressed him in his new blue shirt and sweater over his jeans, and a little navy blue pea jacket because it was chilly out, although the sun rimmed the buildings and windows. Around Robbie's neck, he'd tied one of those scarves that had pictures on them of nothing at all, just a lot of weird shapes that Kenny called "geometric," but kind of pretty, though. Red and green, although Kenny called them "cerise" and "chartreuse." Kenny showed him again how to check himself in the mirror.

"Does the mirror approve?"

Robbie nodded gravely at the little boy who didn't look like him anymore, but the little boy in the mirror nodded back that he approved. The twisty gold frame made him look like a portrait in Grandma Emily's home.

"Oops, there's a thread on your shoulder." Kenny plucked it off. "There. New clothes often have little extra threads on them. You have to be sharp-eyed." Kenny smiled at him in the mirror. "My handsome angel," he said. He did look like a big brother, didn't he?

They marched toward Kenny's studio at a brisk pace, although every time Kenny remembered that Robbie's legs were shorter, he slowed down, and once he picked him up and carried him, nuzzling his cheek. Robbie liked that.

Kenny pointed out a gilt Chinese Buddha in the window. "He has a Buddha belly like yours."

"A booty belly?"

"Buddha belly. All nice and fat. Don't you have a Buddha belly?"

"No!"

"Oh yes, I think you do." Kenny put him down and poked him in his stomach, which made him laugh. "There it is, right there."

"*You* have a Buddha belly," Robbie teased.

"I do not. My belly's flat as a board."

"Yes, you do. Right there," and Robbie, reaching up to poke him.

"Do not."

"Do so."

"Do not."

"Do so."

"I have a separate studio, because I'm a real artist, you see," Kenny was saying as they hurried along, passing a costume store where a naked wax man stood in the window with a boa around his waist. "Carl doesn't appreciate that. He's a photographer, but he hasn't had much success at it. Ansel Adams got there first. And Carl's not much good with wedding portraits. He hates weddings, especially brides. They're so full of themselves. That's why he has to make those films. So he's kind of jealous of me. I have the talent in the family. He owns the building, but he lets me work in the studio to humor me. I go there every day, just like a regular business."

"Like Dad?"

"Probably. You have to do that if you're going to be a serious artist. No painting an eyelash one day and nothing the next. That's not the way. This is how I earn my living. Well, I haven't sold anything yet, and Carl's helping me out. Sort of like an arts patron. But it's how I'm *going* to earn my living. In January, I'll have my gallery show. My friend Carmine owns it. Right after Christmas. It's the dead season.

Probably we won't get many customers. But it's something. Remember that, Damon." Kenny bent down to re-tie Robbie's scarf which had come loose in the wind and might blow away. "If you're going to do anything serious in life, you have to be disciplined. Maybe you'll be an artist, too, what do you think? Do you think you'll inherit your Kenny's talent?"

The studio turned out to be kind of fun. First, they went inside this great big room with ladders, paint cans, and brushes. White sheets that Kenny called "tarps," spattered with paint, caught their feet in deep wrinkles so you had to be careful not to fall. Paintings that smelled of gasoline were everywhere. The ceiling plaster was crackled like the one in nursery school.

"Adam lives upstairs. He's a little boy like you, and he forgot to turn off his bath. Thank goodness my paintings weren't ruined. I'd have died!"

Startled, Robbie looked up at Kenny, but Kenny paid no attention, giving him the tour, pointing out various works of art that he had done. One wall had nothing but pictures of green ladders.

"That was when I was in my verdigris period," he explained. "Can you guess what I call this one?"

Robbie couldn't, because it looked just like all the others.

"'Phase,' that's the name of it. Because when you're on a ladder, you're kind of between one stage and another. I thought of calling it 'Stage,' but that's been done. That ladder's 'Voting Booth,' because it changes our lives. It's important that your paintings make a political statement. That's what art's for."

On one wall, there was just a piece of canvas with a big orange square on it.

"You see, Damon, what's so marvelous about this painting — everybody says so — is that you can turn it upside down, and it's the same painting. You can even turn it on its side," and Kenny demonstrated by lifting it off the wall and turning it one way and then another, and yes, it was exactly the same, an orange square, no more, no less. "People say the conceptualization of this alone shows huge talent. I call it 'Political Perspective' because no one way is the right way."

He rehung it. "I'd thought of calling it 'Democratic Perspective,' but the Republicans are the ones with money to buy it. Tell me, Damon, which one do you like best?"

Robbie looked around the room, bewildered, so many paintings towering over him, one on the wall itself, "a mural," Kenny called it. "When I was in my coffee period. I call it 'Diversity' because it's all one shade of brown. You see, people think they're all colored differently from each other, but they're really the same. My fellow artists say it's brilliant. Which one is best? Which one? Which one? Don't be shy. There's no wrong answer," Kenny giggled.

At last, Robbie pointed to the ceiling patches. He liked the design they made, like Grandma Emily's patchwork quilt.

"The leak?" Kenny laughed. "I guess you can see things in it if you look hard enough. That's okay. No biggie. You'll learn. Well, come on, we've got to get to work. Here's a table for you and a big shirt so you won't get paint on your nice new clothes, and some watercolors."

At that moment, another artist shambled in, wearing a painted shirt that Robbie thought looked like fun and a stupid beret like Bec-Bec's. In his hand, he carried a long paint brush between two fingers like Aunt Cordelia's cigarette holder, which she held unlit because she no longer smoked.

"Trent, this is my sister's boy who's visiting us. Name's Damon."

Trent looked quickly from Robbie to Kenny and back again.

"Damon," he stuck out his hand to shake. And then to Kenny, "Damon Two?"

"Shhh. Just Damon. He's here to paint with me today."

"Another artist? Splendid. The world needs more of us."

"Not nearly enough," Kenny agreed. "Trent's paintings are brilliant," Kenny explained to Damon. "Everyone says so."

"Except the critics." Trent's laughter boomed.

"Critics! What do they know? No, really, I ask you, what do they know? If they knew anything, they'd be painting themselves."

"Stuck on Rauschenberg," Trent muttered in disgust.

"Where's Adam?"

"Upstairs sleeping. That boy spends more time sleeping than a cat. Wildest dreams, too."

Then they chatted in low tones that Robbie could barely hear and couldn't understand. But that was okay, because he was very happily painting the big pine tree in their yard that Becca liked to climb to watch baseball games between him and his dad.

When Trent finally left, Kenny asked, "What's that you're painting, Damon?"

"It's my yard," Robbie said loudly, as if any fool could see that this was exactly what it was.

"I see. Come on, I just realized I have to go to the art store for burnt sienna."

"But I gotta finish."

Kenny whipped off Robbie's shirt, saying, "We'll leave it right here so you can paint some more later." As they were going down the stairs, Kenny was saying, "Burnt sienna's a gorgeous color, very profound, echoing the whole history of art as it reverberates from one space to another." but Robbie didn't get any of this.

"Echoes," Kenny began to translate when he saw the look of puzzlement on Robbie's face.

"I know what a echo is." They'd yelled off the top of a mountain in Yosemite and gotten echoes. But he didn't see how a color could do this.

In the store, Kenny introduced him to his good friend, Harmon, the sales clerk, who also happened to be an artist in his spare time. He painted real bridges, but dreamed of opening his own sign-painting business some day. They didn't have burnt sienna in stock, so Kenny bought cadmium orange.

Back at the studio, Kenny threw the new tube in his paint box and set them both up again. Robbie began to paint Becca at the top of the tree. Kenny, after a long gaze at his big empty canvas, took up his brush and made a sudden swish across it.

"Know what that is, Damon? That's an aubergine sneeze. I got the idea when the mayor had the flu and couldn't keep his appointment with our arts group. We were protesting."

It looked like a purple blob to Damon. Maybe it was a germ. Or a booger.

"All that walking around made me hungry," Kenny said. "Are you hungry?"

Not really. Bec-Bec peeked down from the top of her tree, but he hadn't finished Dad, and he himself wasn't in the picture at all.

But he answered, "Sort of." Better to agree with everything than say how he really felt.

"Great! Let's go to lunch."

So they went out for a cheeseburger, fries and a shake, and Kenny promised him again he'd make a salad for dinner that very night. At the next table, a group of kids the color of Kenny's coffee mural were having a great time snapping fries at each other, while their mother kept telling them not to do it. It had sort of a rhythm to it.

Snap. "Stop!" Snap. "Stop!"

"That's why I took Andy Warhol's name for mine," Kenny was telling him as he slurped the last of his shake. "He's a great painter, and I didn't really have a last name. Or else I'd forgotten it or something. It wasn't my real name, anyway. See, I had to leave home when I was fifteen. Left my brother Timmy behind. God, I miss him. I felt terrible, but Mom didn't beat him nearly as much. Still doesn't. I was her favorite." Kenny made a face.

"I'm Mom and Dad's favorite," Robbie said. "At least, most of the time. Bec-Bec even says."

"I didn't mean it that way exactly. Anyhow, I met Carl at the bus stop, and he took me in, and I've always been grateful for that. He does that for boys, if they're lost, or running away from home because their moms beat them or whatever, and they don't have a place to sleep. He puts them up in his loft over the movie studio and gives them plenty to eat. Even jobs to pay their way. They're really pretty safe there. He's very kind. Just a little rough sometimes, but nothing to be afraid of. Exciting, actually. You're too young to understand. So, I had to have a last name, and I took Andy's."

"Was he your friend?"

"Sort of, in a way. I felt as though he's my brother."

"If you took his name, whose name did he take?"

"No, you see, I just copied. He's still named Warhol, too. God, you're cute."

"I don't understand. Did you steal it?"

"No. I borrowed it," Kenny said with a big sigh.

"Did you give it back?"

"No, no, we both have the same name. He's Andy Warhol, and I'm Kenny Warhol."

"People shouldn't take things that's not theirs."

"Oh, like you never did!"

"My last name's Merrow."

"No, Damon, you're Damon Warhol now."

"I don't like that name. It reminds me of poo-poo," Robbie giggled. His eyes connected with the little boy's at the next table.

The boy said, "Poo-poo. Hey, poo-poo head."

"I'm not a poo-poo head. You're a poo-poo head," both of them twisting around with laughter.

Snap.

"Stop."

"Silly," Kenny said. "It's a very famous name."

Robbie and the little boy mouthed "poo-poo head" back and forth until Kenny said, "I'm terminally disgusted." He wrapped up the rest of Robbie's fries, and they left.

Back in the studio, Robbie had just started painting himself and was feeling confused. Should he paint a red sweatshirt with a bear on it or blue pants and shirt with a print scarf? Kenny was contemplating his swish from several different angles.

"Maybe I should leave it as it is. It's so perfect."

The phone rang. It was Carl, and Kenny told him about their day.

"Damon? Oh he's painting a landscape," he said in answer apparently to a question. "I know, but he's young yet. You want to say 'Hi' to him? Damon, say 'Hi' to Uncle Carl."

"Hi," Robbie said.

There was no one on the other end, so Robbie returned the phone to Kenny.

"Nobody there."

"Huh!" Kenny grunted. "Must not have heard me. Come on, Damon. We'd better clean up. Uncle Carl's coming by to take us home. We've had a busy day, haven't we?"

As the three of them walked along the street, Robbie spotted a gray suit with a red and blue striped tie coming toward them. The suit covered an ample paunch, the walk was sort of a swing from side to side to balance the weight, the hair was dark, and while he couldn't quite make out the face, he was instantly sure.

"Dad!" he cried out. He broke from Kenny and Carl and ran toward the man, who'd stopped to look at something in the window.

"Damon! Get back here," Carl yelled.

As Robbie got closer to the man, he was no longer quite as sure, but he'd already begun to throw his arms around him, burying his head in the man's stomach. He wanted him to be his dad so badly.

Startled, the man jerked back.

"Hey! I don't know you, little boy," he said.

Kenny caught up with them and grabbed Robbie's hand.

"Yes, you do," Robbie cried. "I'm Robbie, remember?"

"So sorry," Kenny was saying. "He's my sister's child. They're going through a messy divorce, and he's visiting me for a while. I think it's been too hard on the little tyke."

Robbie's eyes were filled with tears. The man was almost his dad, but not quite. But he could have been. Why wasn't he?

Carl and Kenny each snatched a hand and held it very firmly.

"You'll pay a nasty piece for that little trick," Carl hissed.

"It was a natural mistake, Carl. An accident. I'll punish him," Kenny promised.

"Suppose the guy reads in a newspaper that a boy named 'Robbie' is missing? What do you think he'll do then, huh? Tell the police that the boy they're hunting for is right up here in San Francisco?"

"You naughty boy," Kenny said. "You know you're not supposed to talk to strangers. I'm going to punish you just as soon as we get home."

"He needs a lesson. And I know just how to teach him."

"Leave it to me," Kenny said. "He's my little boy, and I'm responsible."

They fell silent until they got home. Carl got a rope out of his bedroom, threw Robbie on the bed, and tied his feet to the foot of the bed and his arms to the top. It hurt a lot, because the ropes were too tight, but Robbie didn't dare complain. Evidently, Kenny didn't dare either. He stood to one side, wringing his hands.

"There," Carl said to him, "now I can do anything I want to you. And there's nothing you can do about it. Just wait until Kenny leaves. Kenny," he said in a friendly tone, "run over to the market and get us some food, will you? The list's in the kitchen."

"I just shopped last night," Kenny said.

A little while later:

"Oh, Kenny, the laundry needs doing."

"I'll do it tomorrow. Damon can help."

Later that evening, when Robbie's arms and legs were numb, Kenny came in with a tray of soup and a cheese sandwich. Of course, he had to untie Robbie so he could eat.

7

DAD WENT BACK TO work, where he got a helluva lot more sympathy than he did in his own home. His real estate firm was offering a sizable reward for Robbie's return, alive or whatever, and he said he felt he owed it to them to show up, but he wasn't fooling anyone. When he wasn't at work, he was at the police station, demanding more searchers and better snacks.

Mom dropped in at the hospital for a few hours, more as a break from grieving than out of any real dedication to new mothers and their babies.

"I can't bear to be around them," she said one night to Dad, who was reading the paper and grunted in reply.

Probably the nursing supervisor sensed this, because she put Mom on desk duty.

Becca could only practice the piano when Mom was gone, because Mom couldn't "stand the noise." Just as well. Becca's fingers stumbled over her *Hanon Studies* as if they'd lost their way. She didn't really feel like practicing anyway. Or writing poetry.

During one of Mom's hospital drop-ins, Becca called Aunt Cordelia, explained about Toyman and Officer T., and asked if she'd accompany Becca to the police station.

"I'll say I will!" Softly feminine Aunt Cordelia was on the warpath. No one was going to mess with *her* niece if she had anything to say about it.

At the station, they dumped the whole story on Officer Sam, who insisted they report it to Officer T. So there was Becca again, in an interview room this time, away from the prying eyes of the rest of the force, although her hair was clean. Aunt Cordelia shone in full battle regalia — piled blonde hair lacking only her Miss Artichoke tiara, brows arched over emerald eyes, "tasteful" studs, imperially immaculate in a peach pantsuit. Officer T. alternated between scowls at Becca and gentlemanly explanations to Aunt Cordelia that seemed to imply she wouldn't understand without his help.

"Why didn't you come forward with this sooner?" he demanded, as if Becca had spirited her brother away herself.

"I didn't realize at first. I'd forgotten."

"She's doing it now," Aunt Cordelia reminded him.

"You see," Officer T. explained patiently to Aunt Cordelia, "this puts the case in a different light. The kidnapping was planned, not random. The perps are more intelligent than average and organized. This explains why there's been no ransom demand, so we can't call in the FBI."

"What about a profiler?" suggested Aunt Cordelia. She didn't watch TV at night without absorbing its lessons.

"I'm profiling now," he replied.

"I meant a professional."

Officer T. snorted, as if the suggestion were offered out of pure ignorance. "This Toyman thing narrows the field from someone who had it in for Mr. Merrow to a couple of men who've had their eye on Robbie for some time."

"Why would they?" Becca asked.

In answer, Officer T. shrugged his shoulders at Aunt Cordelia.

"Did you bring the sailboat? No? We'll pick it up. Probably handled so much there are no useful prints, but we can try. Maybe we can trace it. Have there been others?"

"Other boats? Come to think of it, several. We always wondered where he got them. We never get him boats. He likes trucks."

"I want all the boats you have."

Mom was mystified when Officer Sam showed up to spirit away a toy, but thankfully the officer kept mum about Becca's and Aunt Cordelia's visit to the police station.

On the fifth night, like the twelve days of Christmas except that they were counting off to Halloween, Dad told Becca, "You have to go back to school. You'll get behind."

Her mother didn't say anything.

Already the phone wasn't as frantic, and they no longer expected news from the police every time they answered, although of course they hoped. Annalyn hadn't called. Probably she'd tried and couldn't get through. Becca sneaked a few calls to her when Mom and Dad weren't home, but Mrs. Woodward told Becca coldly that Annalyn couldn't come to the phone. What was that about? Thankfully, the reporters had deserted them for a broken water main in the valley and then a two-headed calf somewhere else. Or vice versa. The number of neighbors with their food drops was trickling, although there was plenty left over from the first days. No one ate it. Dad liked his food straight out of the bag or the box or the can, neat as it were, on the rocks, unadulterated with sauces and mystery ingredients. Mom didn't eat, and Becca told Aunt Cordelia the food was so germ-laden from being unrefrigerated that she wouldn't put it in the trash lest the street people get hold of it.

On Friday morning, Becca appeared at the breakfast table in her plaid skirt and black turtleneck. It was the only way they were going to let her out of the house. With a great show of heaviness, she slung her bookbag to the floor, bit into a power bar, and swiped lunch money from the creamer with the little Dutch brother and sister dancing over the tulips. Or perhaps they were just classmates, unrelated to each other. And she left on time. To all appearances, she was headed for school.

"Come straight home," her mother called after her.

Or what? Or I'll worry that something's happened to you as it did to your brother? Because I love you every bit as much and couldn't bear to lose you? Not bloody likely! Mom just wanted to check Becca off her mental "to do" list. Didn't want to have to even *think* of something else, for instance, where Becca might be if she were late. Like Sunday, when she told them they couldn't go to the park.

Becca stowed her backpack under Alex's bushes and quickly skirted the school bus stop without the others spotting her. At the downtown transit station, the street kids were milling about with the desperate laughter Becca had come to expect and bumming cigarettes. Here, she caught a bus for the woods.

According to the news, the search by neighbors and police had progressed from door to door, on to the banks of the San Lorenzo River and the Santa Cruz Boardwalk amusement park along the Pacific Ocean, to the University of California Campus, more secluded beaches, and the Cowell Redwoods. Becca couldn't have said at what point she realized that they weren't looking for a living little boy any longer, but a dead one whose body had been dumped somewhere. To her, Robbie was still alive.

The road wound through the town past Spanish-style whitewashed and brick buildings with red-tiled roofs, bookstores, cafes, small apparel shops, and gift emporiums, all hung with baskets of flowers. Tourists without a care ambled along the streets carrying their trophies in bright plastic bags. Past a scattering of warehouses and a tanning factory, the bus emerged onto a narrow two-lane road that led into the sun-dappled redwood forest. Robbie's kidnapping hadn't changed it.

Not very far in, they began to pass an area cordoned off with yellow tape, and then police and volunteer searchers with their dogs, walking along the road. Becca hopped out and joined them.

They were involved in something called a "grid search," which just meant that they divided the area up on a map with criss-crossing lines, and each team was to cover one area, walking back and forth, eyes on the ground so that they wouldn't miss a body.

"I don't think you're supposed to be with us," said the leader, a middle-aged woman in a windbreaker and hiking boots. "Are you with Search and Rescue?"

"They told me to come here," Becca replied, as the German shepherd loped over to get a good sniff. Becca kneeled down and put her arm around his neck, ruffling his fur.

"He's a trained dog. You're not supposed to do that."

"I know," she said, straightening up.

"You're not even dressed for this," said the leader, eyeing her mini-skirt and black tights. "Without long pants, you're exposed to poison ivy, oak, sumac," and she listed a bunch more that Becca had never heard of — a walking encyclopedia of botanical disasters. Probably just their scientific names, Becca sniffed.

"I'll be careful," she replied. She caught a quick picture of herself at home, lying in bed with a horrible, life-threatening, disfiguring rash, Mom nursing her tenderly, even cutting the crusts off her bread, always the sign to Robbie and Becca that they were seriously ill.

To avoid any further confrontation, she fell in behind the team as they turned into the woods. The dank air smelled of dead things — dead leaves, dead animals, mushrooms, dirt, molder and decay. She had written poems about it, but she had no urge to do so now. Trees had always comforted her, welcoming her into their branches and holding her in their safe embrace, but now they threatened, as if they knew something she didn't, that Robbie had come over to their side and joined their own cycle from life to death (and back?). The forest floor was spongy with piles of fallen red, gold, and brown leaves damp from a rain, so that unwittingly you could step on a branch or into a hole or even over a body without seeing it.

Her eyes scanned charred tree hollows where a little boy might be hiding — or his body hidden — and beneath the brush, the rocks, the fallen logs sprouting new growth. She thought she spotted a red sneaker and was immediately on her knees, scrabbling through leaves, but it was a piece of red paper. When she got up, her knees smarted with scratches. Farther on, she imagined that she and Robbie were playing hide and seek, darting in and out among these trees. She'd glimpse him out of the corner of her eye, but when she turned, he'd hidden himself from her again. Pretending she hadn't seen him, she'd let him win. He'd be so pleased he'd chortle as he did when she tickled him.

As they plodded on, however, Becca grew increasingly frustrated. Robbie wasn't here. He never had been. She was sure of it.

At lunch, she sat on a log with the others to eat her peanut butter and lettuce sandwich, Dad having scarfed down all the bologna. It was at that point that the eyes of a police officer flickered across her in recognition. Affecting casualness so as not to attract attention, he sauntered over. Becca caught the name on his breast pocket, Creagan.

"Aren't you the sister?"

Becca had been noticing that she'd somehow lost her name during the last few days, in the newspaper and in casual neighborhood talk. Perhaps it was just as well, except that the corollary was "the notorious sister who left her brother alone on the playground." The only one who ever had. Her sole identity. No longer ten-year-old Becca Merrow, secretary of her fifth grade class, tomboy tree climber, an A-minus student who helped out at home a lot, played the piano, and wanted to grow up to be a poet. Just "the sister." To name her would be to acknowledge that she was human.

Officer Creagan crouched beside her, his manner gentle. He had a thin reddish blond moustache that she imagined he was very proud of. In her mind's eye, she saw him manicure it every morning as carefully as Aunt Cordelia tweezed her eyebrows. When she acknowledged that she was indeed "the sister," he went on, "I don't think you're supposed to be here."

"Why not? Who better than me?"

"Of course, you'd feel that way, but . . ."

"I could recognize his stuff that you couldn't. I could recognize signs he'd been here. But I don't think he was," she added.

"Why not?"

"Just a feeling. I think we'd have seen something by now."

"Well, I appreciate intuition. I really do. We've solved a lot of cases by going on gut feeling. Then we pretend we had some logical reason for what we did." His smile crinkled his eyes and extended beyond her to the team leader with the dog, who was sitting on her other side and hanging on every word.

"Oh, we're great at pretending we have good solid reasons for what we do," she joined in with a hearty laugh.

"Marjorie's right. Fact is," said Officer Creagan, "we're just covering all bases. You want us to do that, don't you?"

"Yes, but the way you're looking for him, it's as if you think he's dead already."

"Not at all. He could have been dropped off here and not know how to find his way back. He could be cold and hungry. Then we'd get something hot inside him."

"Soup, probably," said Marjorie.

"Did you bring soup with you?"

"We could get it fast."

But they hadn't brought any. Becca turned to Officer Creagan. "Is that what you think happened to him? That they dropped him off here?"

"Can't say," he replied, clamping his mouth into a line. Which meant he had a theory, but it was supposed to be a secret. Police officers didn't divulge their trade secrets. Nor did real estate agents, for that matter. What would they talk about if they didn't have their little cabals? The possession of secrets made them belong.

"Do you think those men in the van drove him far away?" This was the latest theory in the papers.

"It's possible."

"But why would they do that? What would they want with him?"

A sadness passed over Officer Creagan's face, like a curtain drawn discretely across a memory.

"There are so many possibilities."

"That's what everyone says, but no one tells me what they are."

"Not to worry your little head," injected Marjorie.

"I think you need to finish your sandwich and go back to school. Isn't that where you're supposed to be?"

Her clothes had fooled more than her family.

"Not until tomorrow," she fumbled.

"Tomorrow's Saturday," Marjorie reminded her.

"I mean Monday. But how can I go back to school with my brother missing?" She gritted her teeth to keep the tears from her eyes.

"Skipping school won't bring him back," said Marjorie.

"I want to help."

"You'll just hold us up and make mistakes, perhaps. We've got everything in hand. I promise," said the Officer.

"That's right."

"You've already helped — a lot! You've given us all that information. And we may need to call on you again."

By now, Becca's identity was spreading "like crab grass," as her realtor Dad would say, and the others leaning against trees and sitting at the occasional picnic table began to catch on to who she was, murmuring to each other, casting her sympathetic glances that made it only that much harder to keep from crying. Marjorie steered her dog closer to Becca, saying, "Come on, Star, give us a kiss."

"Can I feed him part of my sandwich?"

"Here's a biscuit. Better for his digestion. He loves them."

Becca held it out to him, and he took it with his lips as delicately as if she were a baby, his tongue with its furzy taste buds licking her fingertips.

"We'll drive you back to the bus stop," said Officer Creagan. "It's kind of a ways. You've walked quite a distance this morning."

Becca rewrapped the rest of her sandwich and put it back in her purse. No way that she could eat with the tears in her throat again. Do tears have calories, she wondered? Probably not. Just water and salt. She could drink her tears without worry about packing on the pounds.

Other searchers dropped by to say "Hello" and shake her hand, and assure her that they were doing their very best. Oddly enough, they didn't seem to blame her. Perhaps, they hadn't read the papers.

When it came time, Becca dropped down beside Star and put her arm around his neck, burying her face in the bristly fur, while he stood patiently allowing it.

"Please find Robbie for me," she whispered in his ear and kissed him.

And Star promised that if Robbie was around, he'd find him.

On the bus back, Becca kept seeing places that Robbie might be, places she was sure others had not searched. What about behind the leather tanning factory? Under the hotel where they stored beach furniture? In the bookstore behind the stacks? If the kidnappers had let him go, figuring he was way too much of a nuisance — and that she'd witness! He'd have no idea how to get home. Like the birds, he'd eat bits and pieces of food as he found them. At night, he'd be afraid without his Pooh nightlight, and he'd squirrel himself away somewhere. Perhaps he'd ask someone for help, but very likely this would be a tourist who didn't want to sacrifice a minute of his or her precious vacation shopping time to help a lost boy. At the library, he might be reading picture books all day like the other kids and go virtually unnoticed. When the library closed, he might hide under a desk and go to sleep. Did they keep the heat on all night?

Or what about that old Victorian haunted house on Beach Hill? Or the innumerable nooks and crannies of the rides at the Boardwalk like the wooden Giant Dipper roller coaster. Or even the Coconut Grove Casino? The Boardwalk would be a terrific place to play hide-and-seek as long as you didn't fall into the machinery.

What was needed was a thorough search of the whole Santa Cruz area! Becca's hopes brightened. She could scour the town this weekend, go back to school next week for a few hours each day, and then search until nightfall. At school, she'd say she had to help Mom or answer more questions down at the police station. At home, she'd say she had to make up schoolwork — that one was good for endless days — or research a paper at the library. After the first few days of inquisition, Mom and Dad had ignored her.

Becca arrived at the transit station, ate the rest of her sandwich and bought herself a Pepsi, hopeful determination giving her an appetite. As she ate, she planned her own grid search of Santa Cruz, one sector at a time, much more thorough than the police.

The number of homeless kids had grown. They gravitated to the West Coast in the fall because it was more temperate than the places they'd come from — Boise, Denver, Ottumwa, Chicago, New York. Here, they milled about with spiked violet hair, yellow skin, clothes smelling of sleep, talking about others they'd run into someplace else under the pathetic illusion that they were family and would care for each other as their families had not. Well, Becca could understand

it. Crouched against the stucco wall, they smoked cigarette butts retrieved from deep inside their pockets, petted mutt dogs, and gnawed
on leftover bits of Danish.

Mom always told Becca to "just ignore them." They were filthy
and diseased — their own fault — they could have called child welfare services if they were abused, and they should get jobs. Don't give
them quarters; that just encourages them.

Yet, if she was lucky, her own brother was milling around a transit
station somewhere, just not this one. Someone was being kind to him,
just as she could be kind to these. Except that she was a little afraid of
them.

Becca's heart jerked around in her chest when she spotted the wall
of the transit center covered with pictures of missing kids. Technically, she had seen it before but had been blind to it. Hurrying over,
she scanned quickly for a picture of her brother but did not find one,
so she went back to the beginning and went through them methodi-
cally.

Becca had always assumed that the children whose pictures were
posted here had run away from home. Many had. But some had been
kidnapped. Others were simply labeled as "MISSING" in bold capital
letters.

Officer Sam had told her that every year over 200,000 children
were kidnapped, usually by a parent, but thousands were "stranger
abductions." On TV, a reporter had interviewed an agent with the
FBI who said that in the case of stranger abduction, most kids were
killed within twelve hours. What happened to the rest?

As she stared at the photos, they took on a life of their own. Before,
they had all been just a blur, but now they were individuals with parents as heartbroken as her own. Age, birth date, height, weight (did
they get to lie about it?), where last seen, what last wearing — the
statistics were impersonal, but the faces were not. Each wore her best
smile as if she had never imagined a day when it would be posted in
publication of her tragic disappearance or possible death. "She could
be my friend," Robbie would say.

Some pictures were awfully old. Imagine waiting ten years for
your child to come back! One day, and then another, and then a week

has passed. Months, years, and you need a computer-enhanced photo that somehow isn't as appealing as the original. Last seen in Florida, now possibly in Iran, a father had taken the two children to a place where a mother could only follow at risk of her life. Messages at the bottom of some. "Please come home." "Forgive us." "We're waiting for you." Parents pleading for their children to return, no matter what had happened to chase them out. Now dead themselves, perhaps.

Many of the flyers were obviously home jobs, crude replicas of photos, shakily lettered. Robbie's picture wasn't there.

How did they get up on the walls, anyway? Was her dad supposed to see that it got done? The police? They couldn't just make up a picture and post it, could they? Could she?

8

KENNY PLANNED TO TAKE Damon to get his ear pierced on Tuesday.

"I promised to get you a beautiful diamond stud just like mine, and I always keep my promises, don't I, Damon?"

Robbie nodded agreeably, but what promises had Kenny kept? Not the spistachio ice cream. Not the visit home. Not the new blocks.

Carl said no way were they leaving the house again without him, not after that stunt Damon pulled a few days ago.

"He didn't mean anything by it," Kenny reasoned sweetly. "He's just a little boy. He got confused, that's all. You won't do that again, will you, Damon?"

Robbie shook his head No, eyes fixed on Carl. What was he going to do to him next? His ankles and wrists still hurt from being tied up for so long in the dark with just a slash of light from the hall.

Now Carl was saying, "I'm coming with you to get Damon's ear pierced. I want to see his face when the needle goes in."

Needle?

"Why didn't you say so?" Kenny said lightly. "By all means, come with us. Isn't that nice, Damon? Uncle Carl wants to come. He'll even take time off work to help get your ear stud."

The place was just a few blocks away. Going into it was like stepping into a comic book, with floor to ceiling colored pictures of flowers, bats, snakes, butterflies, skulls and skeletons, hearts, naked women, motorcycles, fists, and masked muscle heroes. It smelled of incense and machine smoke, like when Dad worked on his car.

"Wow!" Robbie said. "Why don't you paint pictures like these, Kenny?"

Kenny laughed.

"Look at those wide eyes of his. He's just a child," he said to the dragon-covered giant who waited on them. When he moved, they rippled and blew fire across his chest.

"First, we have to choose a plain gold stud," Kenny explained. "Then, when your ear's healed, we go to the jewelry store, and you get a beautiful diamond chip just like mine."

They stood in front of the jewelry case with the studs inside that all looked the same.

"Which one do you like best, Damon? What do you think, Carl? I like this one, the color is just a little bit antiquey. Damon? Damon?"

But Robbie's eyes were fixed on the lettering of one tattoo on the wall.

"M-O-M," he read aloud. Carl's eyes narrowed, as Damon worked it out. "That spells 'mom'."

"That's right," said Kenny. "You can read. What a clever little boy!"

"I want my mom," Robbie said, looking up at Kenny.

"Of course you do," said Kenny, getting red and flustered.

"I want my mom!" Robbie shouted.

"Shh, in a little while," Kenny said, trying to calm him as the comic book man took the stud they'd selected, sat down on his stool, and prepared to get to work.

"That's enough," said Carl, grabbing Robbie's ear and yanking it over to the comic book man as if it were a separate part of Robbie's body, which followed after. "Here, get it done."

Robbie was crying. His ear hurt like crazy, and he wanted Bec-Bec to kiss it and make it better. Carl had his arms inside Robbie's, pulling them back and holding him tightly, his legs wrapped around Robbie's so he couldn't move, and Robbie's head in his hands like a vise, while Kenny was trying to calm them both. The comic book man, paying no attention to any of this, swabbed stinky alcohol on Robbie's ear, picked up a steel machine, and gave his ear a shot. Robbie yelled, "Ow!" as much in surprise as pain. Carl jerked his head hard, and yanked his arm across Robbie's face to muffle his cries. Robbie couldn't breathe. In panic, he twisted his body trying to get away, screamed, and managed to bite Carl's arm.

"He bit me! You little brat, I'll show you."

"No, Carl, let go, let go," Kenny cried, trying to twist Carl's fingers backward to loosen his grip. "You're hurting him! He's suffocating!"

"Little bugger!"

"Carl, you let go this minute or we'll both leave you, I swear it!"

Carl released him, and Robbie buried his face in Kenny's chest with great big heaving sobs.

"I still gotta get the stud in," said the comic book man.

"Listen to me, Damon. The hurt's all over now. Now he just has to put this pretty gold stud in your ear, that's all. Doesn't hurt, but you have to hold still. Will you do that for your Kenny?"

Robbie sniffled and finally mumbled "Yes," and the comic book man futzed around with his ear for a minute, and it was done.

"Now, that didn't hurt a bit, did it?"

"Did so," Robbie said, wiping his nose on his sleeve.

"Let Kenny blow your nose. Come on, that's it."

As Kenny wiped, Robbie caught a glimpse of Carl standing in the shadows. He could see that Carl was furious, and he wasn't quite sure why, but it was the kind of fury that boiled inside, red and dark, like one of those volcanoes on TV.

As they left the shop, Kenny said to Carl, "I meant it, Carl. I meant every word. We had a deal, but if you hurt Damon again, it's off."

To Robbie's surprise, Carl didn't say anything.

When they got home that night, Kenny said, "Go on into your room, Damon, and play with your new toys. I want to speak to Uncle Carl about something."

Then Kenny and Carl fought for a long time, their voices rising until Robbie was afraid that Carl was going to hurt Kenny, then falling. Loud and low, loud and low. Sometimes, Carl would get louder, and Kenny would interrupt him, and Carl would immediately quiet down.

Robbie didn't want to play with his Kenny toys. He wanted his own toys back, his Robbie toys — trucks that he could drive to Timbuktu and his wooden blocks. He wanted to take a red block and then another the same size and put it on top. Just like that. He imagined the red block on the bottom and another red one on top of it. And then a green and a yellow. Block by block, his imaginary tower got higher and higher. Only this was better, because the tower didn't fall over after five or six blocks. It was getting to be the highest tower he'd ever built. He had to kneel to put another block on top, and then he had to stand.

"High as this room," he said to himself gleefully.

Pretty soon he'd have to stand on his bed.

"Higher than this whole house! Higher than the sky!"

He didn't even notice that the fighting in the dining room had stopped and that the whole place was silent. He was too busy building his wonderful tree tower to the sky.

"Then I gonna climb to the sky and walk across like Jack. I gonna climb down the beanstalk and go home.

He heard a slight noise behind him. He turned to find Carl and Kenny staring at him curiously. They had funny expressions on their faces. Robbie wasn't sure if they were angry or what.

"He's putting nothing on top of nothing," Carl said finally.

"Just a game," Kenny said. "A kid's game, that's all."

"He's talking to himself, for Chrissake!"

"Kids do that. They make up stories to themselves."

"Something's wrong with this kid. Maybe we should put him back."

"Take me back," Robbie said, jumping down and sending his tree sprawling. "Uh oh, I knocked it over. You made me."

"Knocked what over, Damon?" asked Carl calmly.

"My tree tower to the sky." Robbie stamped his foot.

"There's nothing there. Nothing at all."

"It's indibisible."

"I say we take him back."

"Yes, I want to go back. You said I could see my mom."

"Get rid of him."

Kenny knelt down, straightened his scarf, and brushed back the hair.

"Your turn."

Obediently, Robbie straightened out Kenny's scarf and brushed his hair, although it was shorter and prickly.

"Damon, you can't go back."

"You said we could."

"I made a mistake. Your parents don't want you anymore, Damon," Kenny said.

"Yes, they do. They're coming to get me."

At this, Carl laughed. "They're not coming. Not your mama or your dada or your sis."

"Sister. She's not my sis. She's my sister!"

"Proper little egghead, are we? Well, you'll get over it."

Robbie scrunched up his face to keep the tears back. "They are so coming."

"Then why aren't they here?"

"They'll be here in a minute."

"What's taking them so long?"

"Dad has to get gas."

"Now, listen, Damon, for the last time," Kenny said. "They gave you to us because you fussed too much. If you don't behave, we'll give you away, too."

"I'm not Damon. I'm Robbie. And I wanna go home."

In an instant, Carl had taken three long steps into the room and slapped him to the floor, and when Kenny cried, "Oh, no, Carl," Carl replied, "He has to learn who he is or we're all going down."

He threw Robbie to the bed and tied him up again, arms to the headboard, feet to the footboard, so tightly that he was stretched out and couldn't move. "Now stay there until you know who you are."

Robbie could hear them talking again. Had Mom and Dad really given him up? Mom wouldn't. She always said she loved him better than chocolate. Whenever he asked her, she said that. Dad, maybe. He didn't have that much time to play baseball and acted as though it was kind of a nuisance when Robbie asked. Becca got angry with him sometimes, but he didn't really think she'd give him away. Although she had left him alone so Carl and Kenny could take him. And when they drove away and she ran after the van, she didn't run as hard as she could. He'd seen her run harder.

His arms ached, and his legs. He ached all over. Then his wrists began to turn numb. He dozed.

Hours later, Carl walked into the room.

"What's your name?"

"Robbie," he said so softly even he couldn't quite hear himself.

"What is it?"

Kenny appeared behind Carl, so Robbie said it a little louder.

"You don't get to sit up and eat dinner until you know your name," Carl said.

"I have to go pee-pee."

"Not until you know your name."

"But I have to."

A while later, he couldn't help himself, and he felt it trickling out of him like a river, the San Lorenzo maybe, because it had no place else to go. On and on, it ran. Now his pants were sopping and getting cold, and his bed was wet, too. He tried not to cry because he couldn't wipe his nose, and when it got stuffed up, he couldn't breathe right.

He dozed again, imagining he was back in his own bed, with the red bedspread, and his trucks running around the edges of the room. Only they ran all by themselves with nobody pushing them, and the drivers waved and nodded to him. They ran past houses and under bridges that he had built with his wooden blocks and his canister of Lincoln Logs, while he read his *Peter Pan and Wendy* book. He was a Lost Boy, Lost Boy, Lost Boy.

"What's your name?" Carl's voice jolted him awake.

"Robbie, no, I don't know," he said miserably.

"Your name's Damon. Say it."

"Damon," he cried.

"My name's Damon. Say it."

"My name's Damon. Say it." Now he had the hiccups and barely could.

"You being smart with me?"

Robbie didn't know how to answer. He just lay there frozen in the cold wetness of his bed.

"Ah, you wet your bed. That's disgusting, you know? Really disgusting."

"Carl," said Kenny softly.

"Stinks, too. What's your name, boy?"

"Damon?" he guessed.

"My name is Damon."

"My name is Damon."

He still thought his name was Robbie. Maybe they were right. Maybe he was Damon after all. Maybe people changed their names as they got older. Or whenever they moved. Or depending on who they lived with. Or because other people wanted them to.

"And what happened to Robbie?"

Damon didn't answer, so then Carl answered for him.

"Robbie's dead. Say it."

"Robbie's dead," he repeated. But somewhere inside him, a little boy named Robbie was crying.

Kenny untied him, and he hobbled toward the bathroom while Kenny rubbed his wrists and arms.

"You'll feel better soon."

Kenny drew a bath for him and helped him get out of his wet clothes, saying, "That's okay, Damon. Accidents happen. We all have them. I had them once in a while when I was a little boy. I'll tell you a secret if you promise not to tell."

"What?"

"Promise?"

"Uh-huh. I promise."

"Uncle Carl had accidents, too, when he was little, I'll bet."

Kenny floated the yellow boat "out to sea. That's what Timmy and I used to play." And he talked on as he washed Robbie all over.

Robbie didn't like it when Kenny washed him all over. He washed his pee-pee for a long time with lavender soap, saying it was "sanitary," and Robbie didn't like it one bit. It made him feel funny. He pushed Kenny's hand away, but it did no good.

Kenny put Robbie in a pair of clean pajamas.

"I can do it myself," Robbie said, but Kenny insisted on helping him.

"Into the dining room with you now. Don't worry about Uncle Carl. He isn't mad at you, now that you know your name."

Uncle Carl was in the living room, drinking out of a bottle and watching a wrestling match. Damon tiptoed past, but Uncle Carl didn't pay any attention to them.

"See? I told you."

Damon sat at the table, and Kenny brought him an apple cut into quarters and a bowl of peas.

"Don't make such a face. You have to eat some vegetables so you'll stay nice and healthy," Kenny said. "Finish your peas like a good little Damon, and I'll give you ice cream and chocolate sauce."

As Damon was eating, Kenny left him alone, saying, "I'll clean up your bed." A few minutes later, he was back. "We'll air out the mattress tomorrow. Right now, I made up the top bunk all nice and clean.

Damon ate his ice cream quietly, with Kenny taking the tiniest spoonfuls that he could. "Just a dot. You don't mind, do you? Just a drip." He was laughing, which made Damon laugh, too.

"Just a mouse nibble," said Kenny.

"Just a ant dribble."

"Just a dog kibble."

"No, a gum bubble."

"Oh, you silly Damon, bubble doesn't rhyme with kibble. What am I going to do with a word that doesn't rhyme, huh?"

Once Damon was in bed, Kenny stood on the bottom bunk railing for their goodnight talk and said, "You've got to stop with the crazy stuff. All that building a tower in the air, what were you doing?"

"That was my tree tower that I builded with my blocks. At home I have blocks, and I build them."

"We'll go to the store and buy you blocks tomorrow, okay?"

"I like doing it in my head. It gets higher."

"And talking to yourself. It's got to stop. Here's your good night kiss. I love you."

"Kenny?"

"Yes, my darling little boy."

"Do you love me better than chocolate?"

"Well, that's a pretty big decision. I'm crazy about chocolate. But, yes, I love you better than chocolate. How about you? Do you love your Kenny better than chocolate?"

"No."

"No! You hurt your Kenny's feelings."

Damon giggled, "I *like* you."

"Better than chocolate?"

"No. But almost as much."

"Not better?"

"I'll love you better than chocolate tomorrow. Kenny?"

"What is it, my little chocolate drop?"

"If you leave Carl, will you take me with you?"

"Don't worry, we're not going to leave Carl. If we did, we'd have no place to go. Besides, Carl would be so lonely he couldn't bear it. You wouldn't want Carl to be lonely, would you?"

Damon considered this in silence.

Kenny added, "I promised him I'd stay if he helped me bring you to live with us. And he did. It'll all work out, you'll see. But you've got to stop with the crazy stuff, the invisible towers and the talking to yourself. Or Carl will put you in the movies."

What would be so bad about that?

9

MOM WAS SITTING IN the kitchen over tea with Aunt Cordelia. Oh, no, had her aunt betrayed their visit to the police station? The two sisters, always a study in contrasts, today were even more so — Mom in her plain yellow sweatshirt with the logo of the charity she volunteered for occasionally, clipped salt and pepper hair, new lines in her face and circles around her eyes — soul bruised. She'd never recover, Becca realized with a pang. Aunt Cordelia, her cosmetics impeccably applied, her blonde hair piled and French-twisted behind her head; she'd never let them forget that she'd been Miss Artichoke.

"Becca, dear, how are you bearing up?" she asked, as if she hadn't seen her a few days ago.

"Lots of homework," Becca said, a word about school being a necessary prerequisite to peace. Parents could say they were dutifully keeping abreast of their children's education, and children could say they were communicating. Didn't matter if the actual questions got asked; in fact, answering them in advance relieved them of the chore — a plus on the child's balance sheet.

"Your hair needs trimming," Aunt Cordelia said. "Why don't you come in on Monday?"

Mom didn't say anything, just sat there sucking an invisible lemon.

"I'll try," Becca replied. "I'm behind in my school work."

Upstairs, Becca changed from her school clothes into pants and a tee shirt. Then, as she did every day now, she wandered into Robbie's bedroom to check if anything had been disturbed. Nothing had. His clean pajamas awaited his return on his bed, the extra red blanket still neatly folded at the foot, his fire engines and dump trucks, ambulances and squad cars marshaled along the edges of his room with his spacemen and aliens sitting atop them. *Peter Pan and Wendy* lay on his nightstand now with one of Becca's bookmarks holding Robbie's place, at least, the place where it had fallen open when the police barged through. He could read the pictures when he got back. His laundered clothes hung neatly in his closet, the canisters of Lincoln Logs and Legos below them. In his toy chest, his net bag of wooden blocks lay ready for his chubby little hands.

Perhaps his pajamas were getting dusty on the bed. They'd been there for some time. Becca couldn't see the dust, but she knew it was there, one of the many invisible menaces like germs and atoms that people took on faith. She shook them out and folded them in a neat square. Then she tucked them into his second drawer down, leaving it ajar just a sliver so he could get it open.

The votive candles had melted down on the several nights that she had left them burning until someone, Dad she assumed, had blown them out after she was asleep. She got replacements out of the linen closet and stuck them in their holders, making sure there were plenty of matches left to light them tonight. She'd heard of people disappearing from their homes and waking up in a strange city, not remembering their names or where they lived because they'd been hit on the head. Was it possible that Robbie had escaped? She imagined him, traumatized by his kidnapping, wandering toward home confused, seeing the light burning in his window, drawn to it even though he remembered nothing.

In the garage Becca cleared off a space on Dad's workbench, moving his old sax aside, the last remnant of his college dream. The space cleared but dirty, Becca removed a bunch of old clothes from a department store box, and flattened it to use as a work surface. On this she laid a sheet of typing paper.

Now, she needed a picture of Robbie. Back in the house, she found the newspapers announcing his kidnapping piled up in the den. Everyone had brought a copy by, as if the family would want plenty of mementos the way athletes save pictures of their trophies. She took one out to the garage with a pair of scissors, clipped Robbie's photo, and pasted it onto the sheet of paper. Then she threw the newspaper in the neighbor's trash down the alley so that her parents wouldn't figure out what she was up to. No reason for them to object, just that they objected to everything on principle.

The space above Robbie's picture glared at her like an empty eye socket. It needed something. "MISSING" she began to print, and then stopped. The word "MISSING" was so banal. People even used it for lost wallets at school. In her best hand, she added in large black letters the word "KIDNAPPED!" That would get their attention! Beside Robbie's snapshot, she lettered, "Height." Becca paused, unsure as to how tall her brother was. Back to the den threshold, where Dad had kept up his ritual of marking their heights and weights every birthday.

"Height 3 feet 8 inches. Weight 44 pounds. Hair light blond. Eyes blue." Beneath this, she printed: "Last seen on Santa Cruz Playground October 20th. Kidnappers: Two men in white van." She thought of writing "Family Heartbroken," but that made Robbie sound like a pet. Instead, she printed "REWARD" in big capital letters on the bottom. She was about to write the "$50,000" from Dad's real estate company, but she'd saved $150 herself, and Dad must have at least $5,000. So she changed it to $55,150. If they were a little short, they could work it off. At the bottom, beside an asterisk, she wrote, "Robbie, if you see this, call home, 324-8122." Then she remembered the area code and inserted a small (408).

Annalyn was forbidden to see Becca ever again; they held Becca responsible for that whole "sordid episode" of police questioning. She joined Becca in adding the flyer to the wall of missing children at the transit center. To do so, they had to move a few aside to make room in the middle. They did this very gently, as if to deny the desecration of appropriating another child's space. They did not say that the child was dead anyway, and Robbie deserved a chance. Maybe the child they were replacing had returned home, and her parents had forgotten to take down the picture.

They stood back, admiring their handiwork.

"Pretty cool," said Annalyn.

"Thanks. I'm thinking of making a career creating flyers for kidnapped children when I grow up."

For Becca, there were no other pictures now except Robbie's. It seemed to stand out and apart, as if there were a spotlight on it, and none of the other tragedies counted.

They'd made copies, and they posted them all over town, on food market bulletin boards, in cafes and restaurants, stores and movie houses. They brought one to the police station, where Officer Sam said, "Nice flyer. Did you make it yourself? Give me a few extras to pass along to other officers."

They trudged all over the University of California campus in the middle of the redwoods through the crisp cleansing air, over bridges, across deep ravines, below which the deer tiptoed softly with the dusk. Each time they left a building, they were soon in the woods with only trees in sight, but they followed paths on faith that they led somewhere, and sure enough another concrete or redwood building gradually emerged ahead. Department bulletin boards, eateries, the bookstore — nothing escaped their notices.

On their way home, they passed a tree on which they had taped a flyer, but it was gone.

"Maybe they took it because they had a lead," Annalyn said.

"Or maybe to throw it away," Becca replied, swallowing tears.

10

BECCA WAS SHAKING HIM awake to get him dressed for school, but he was still asleep because his scary dreams woke him up all night, and he was tired.

"Do you know what day it is tomorrow, Damon?" Only it wasn't Becca's voice. It was Kenny's. "It's Halloween, and we don't have a costume for you. Oh, Carl," he called in his upset voice, hurrying out of the room and down the hall. "Tomorrow's Halloween and Damon doesn't have a thing to wear." Back in the room, he said, "Carl's on the phone. We have to get you a costume."

"Don't wanna costume."

"Of course, you want a costume. You want to go trick or treating, don't you?"

"No."

"Of course, you do. You can't go trick or treating without a costume."

"Don't wanna go tricker treating."

"Now, Damon, no more nonsense. You get up this instant."

Damon flung himself back under the bedclothes and curled up, but Kenny tore them off him. "Up, up! What do you want to be?"

"Wanna sleep," said Damon, pulling at the sheet. Now he and

Kenny were in a tug of war, Kenny laughing and Damon trying to stay serious. "It's cold," he whined.

At that instant, Carl marched in with a storm in his face, talking on his phone but glaring at Damon, who immediately sat up and rubbed his eyes. Kenny pulled off his pajama top and pushed his arms into his tee shirt, first one arm, then the other.

"Timmy was a pirate once," Kenny was saying, pulling off his bottoms, "with a black patch over his eye and a black beard. Would you like that?"

"No. Don't wanna be a pirate. The crocodile will eat me."

"What? Silly! Crocodiles don't eat pirates."

"Yes, they do," Damon said loudly. "And they have clocks ticking in their bellies."

"Of all the nonsense!" Kenny tugged on Damon's jeans. "Stand up, that's right. What do you want to be, then?"

"Lost Boy."

Damon didn't know what he'd said wrong, but Kenny shushed him with a quick look at Carl, who was mad at somebody on the phone and had turned away to concentrate on bawling them out.

"You're not lost. You're found."

"Peter Pan, then."

"Okay, we'll see if we can find a Peter Pan costume."

"Are you crazy?" Carl demanded, as Kenny and Damon swallowed a few mouthfuls of cereal before heading out. "We're trying to hide him, not show him off to every crackpot in the neighborhood."

"Only our friends. We'll get him a mask to hide his face. It's a great way to introduce him around without anybody actually seeing him. Get them used to the idea. Oh, I'm so busy today. There isn't time." He swept up the dishes in an armful and dumped them into the sink. "I'll stack later."

"I'm coming with you then," Carl announced. He got his brown leather jacket and cap from the hall closet, put them on, and checked his appearance in the mirror as he always did, first full front face, then each side. Damon wondered why, because he always looked the same, the gray hair curling at his neck, the dark glasses, even if it was foggy outside, because he thought they made him look handsomer and more like a movie producer, although Damon had never heard him say this in so many words. "So Hollywood!" Kenny had said.

They couldn't find a Peter Pan costume. In fact, there weren't many costumes left in the Haight because it was so late and because so many people loved to dress up here anyway, not only for parties but for parading down the street in their feathered snakes and sequins. A few animals, witches, ballerinas, and TV characters left. No Peter Pans, alligators, or even pirates.

"Guess you'll hafta sew it," Damon said to Kenny, shrugging his shoulders, and adding, "No biggie."

"Are you kidding? Me sew? I'd rather go naked."

"Mom can do it."

"Your mom's dead," Carl snapped.

Damon stared up at him, the meaning of his words slowly sinking in, but Damon couldn't see Carl's eyes through his dark glasses, and that made them scarier still.

Kenny said mildly, "Don't tell him that."

"No sense in spoiling him."

"Your mom isn't dead, she's just gone, that's all."

"Gone where?"

"On vacation," Kenny said.

Carl gave that explosive laugh of his and shook his head.

Had something happened to Mom?

They stood in front of a rack of costumes, Kenny saying, "Come on, choose, choose."

Damon picked an astronaut, but then a ghost caught his eye. It had a horrible twisted mouth, like in his nightmares. Either it was screaming, or it was making other people scream. Damon couldn't take his eyes off it.

"That one."

"Oh, that's not a good one. That's a horrible one. The astronaut's much better."

"The ghost," Damon said, a tiny smile beginning to curl his mouth upwards.

"Oh, you're teasing me," Kenny laughed. "What do you want to be a ghost for? You'll scare everybody."

But Damon had already taken it off the rack and was dragging it along the floor to the line at the register, Kenny hurrying after to pick up the bottom.

"I got a stomachache," Damon said after they returned from trick or treating.

"Told you it was a bad idea," Carl said.

"He didn't eat much candy." True. Kenny had eaten more. Kenny loved candy, especially at night, when he and Carl were smoking those sweet cigarettes that Kenny rolled and watching Carl's videos.

"Looks like he ate enough," Carl said.

"Are you gonna hurl?" asked Kenny.

Damon looked at him blankly.

"Upchuck, vomit, puke your guts out," Carl translated sharply.

Damon shook his head "No", because obviously Carl didn't want him to. So upchucking was not a good idea, although that was exactly what he felt like doing.

"You get a lot of stomachaches, don't you, Damon?" Kenny said, taking the plastic jack-o'-lantern from his hand with its load of treats. "Let's put this away for now."

He put it on the dining room sideboard with the bowl of phony fruit. Becca didn't like phony stuff, not fruit, flowers, or even sugar-free soda. "Too much phony stuff, and you become phony yourself," she'd warn.

"It's *my* candy. I want it."

Carl snorted and reached his big hand crawling with black hairs like spiders over to the pumpkin. Eyes fixed on Damon, he plucked out a chocolate bar, Damon's favorite. Eyes still on Damon, he peeled off the wrapper and popped it into his big mouth.

"Mmmm, delicious," he said, chocolate oozing out the corners as Kenny sighed loudly.

Damon sniffled, afraid to say anything but furious at the unfairness of it.

"My dad says big people shouldn't take little people's candy," he said in spite of himself.

"*Who* says?"

"My dad. He says big people who take little people's candy are pigs!"

Kenny gasped. "He didn't mean that."

"Did you just call me a pig?"

"No," Damon said, backing away. Then, to Kenny, "I gonna up-chuck now."

"Oh, jeez," Carl said in disgust, as Kenny hurried Damon into the bathroom.

Damon stood over the toilet, trying to throw up, but it wouldn't come. He'd learned a valuable lesson, however. Now, whenever Carl got mad, Damon could get sick to his stomach.

Damon felt someone clambering step by step up the ladder to the top bunk. The whole bed was shaking.

"Alex?" he called to his friend softly. If it was a monster, maybe it wouldn't hear.

No answer. But the top bunk creaked and shook like something very big getting comfortable.

Maybe it was Kenny. But Kenny would just crawl under the covers with him. Carl? He was too big. The only reason Carl would be up there would be to shake the whole bed down on top of Damon. Or on top of Robbie. That was it. It was Robbie who was in danger, not Damon.

Whoever was up there made snuffling sounds like a pig. But Damon heard a lot of odd sounds lately. Usually he paid no attention.

Leaving Robbie huddled under the covers, Damon slipped out, crawled to the very edge of his bunk, got to his hands and knees, and pulled himself up to a standing position, holding onto the top bunk frame, careful not to clutch the mattress itself before he could see whatever lay there that might snatch up his hands and gnaw on them like a giant rat.

Slowly, slowly, he stretched up and peered over. What he saw made him scream and scream until Kenny was beside him, shaking him awake. Damon threw his arms around him, tears streaming, trying to tell him, but the words wouldn't come.

"Did you have a bad dream, my little Damon? A nightmare?"

He sniffled his tears back up to where they made giant achy puddles in his forehead.

"I have those sometimes. When I was little and had to leave home and get on the bus to come here, I had them a lot. Want to tell Big Brother Kenny about it? Come on, you can tell me. Then you won't be so scared anymore. What was it about?"

"Don't remember."

"Was there a monster?"

"Yes," Damon nodded. Not that he remembered it. It just *felt* like a monster. Now he had the hiccups.

"Was the monster chasing you?"

"Yes." Damon clung to Kenny for safety. "Can I come into your bed?"

"I don't think that's a good idea," Kenny said.

"I get into Mom and Dad's bed when I have scary dreams."

"Carl's in there now, fast asleep. We wouldn't want to wake him up, would we?"

Damon shook his head. The monster was fast asleep. Don't wake him.

"Tell you what, though. Move over, and I'll come into bed with you."

Damon made room, and Kenny lay down on his side, taking him in his arms, stroking his hair, nuzzling his cheek. Kenny was nice and warm.

When Damon awakened the next morning, Kenny was gone, and the bed was cold again.

"That's a Becca tree," Damon said, pointing it out to Kenny on their way to the studio. They'd taken a little detour through the park and paused in front of a giant pine.

"What does Becca do with her Becca tree?"

"I don't know."

"Does she-e-e — water it?"

"No."

"Does she-e-e — take pictures of it?"

"No."

"Then why is it a Becca tree?"

"She puts her arms around it like this."

"She hugs it," Kenny giggled. "So Becca's a tree hugger."

"She climbs it, too."

"So Becca's a tree climber."

"Becca loves trees."

Damon liked it when he and Kenny were alone. Carl had to go to his movie studio and make his films, and Damon was freer to talk about things. In fact, Kenny even asked him about his family when Carl wasn't around. Damon quickly caught on that, when Carl was gone, he could talk about Mom, Dad, Becca, Aunt Cordelia, and Alex all he wanted.

"Why don't I still go to nursery school?" he asked Kenny.

"You don't need to. You're a big boy now."

"Am I going to kindergarten?"

"You bet, but first we have to have special papers for you in order to register you — birth certificate, that sort of thing. And they're not finished yet. Then we have to take you to the doctor for your check-up and shots."

"I don't like shots."

"It's not for a long time yet."

"I gonna cry," Damon warned.

"What do you want to go to school for, anyway? Don't you have fun at the studio with your Kenny? We meet our friends in the street and chat with Trent and Harmon and paint and go out to lunch. Isn't that fun?"

"Uh-huh."

"You'll start kindergarten next year. Meanwhile, we'll go to the library and get some books so you can learn your numbers. Yes, that's what we'll do. Good idea, Damon!"

If they had time after they'd finished at the studio, they stopped in at a toy store to buy Damon another Robbie toy, except that he didn't call it that because it upset Kenny and made Carl mad. One day, they brought home a bag of blocks, just like the ones he had at his old home. They were big and different shapes and colors — red, orange, yellow, blue and green. They were exactly the same as his Robbie blocks, only they weren't. They were newer, shining clean, and smelled of paint. Damon liked his real Robbie blocks better, but he didn't tell Kenny because that would hurt his feelings. Kenny got his feelings hurt a lot. Damon imagined them as a bunch of fingers all mashed and mangled in the car door, bloody and bruised.

When Carl and Kenny weren't looking, Damon still played with his old Robbie blocks, building towers in the air, castles, and even skyscrapers with those bridges that connect between. Now he could build whole cities with cars that raced through the air and people that flew with power packs on their backs and sisters who never let their brothers out of their sight.

He was careful not to let Carl and Kenny see him do this. He knew it made Carl want to get rid of him, and then where would he go? He was pretty sure they wouldn't take him back home as they'd talked about once. It was a long way away, and he didn't think Carl would bother. He'd just take Damon some place and dump him. Kenny had said as much. Damon didn't think he could find his old family again. Kenny said it would be dangerous to try. They'd walked all around here, and he never saw anything that looked like his old neighborhood. Besides, his mom was dead, maybe.

When they got home, Kenny would get down on the floor with Damon and help him build a wood block train to Timbuktu. Only, he called it "Timbukthree." Damon was supposed to say "Timbuk-four," and Kenny would get silly and say "Tim'sbuttfive." When Carl came home, Kenny told him that Damon could count to ten.

"I have so many errands to run I'm all a-dither — the cleaners, the laundry, the market, the cheese shop, the bakery. I just don't have time to take you with me today, Damon. Can you stay here by yourself for a little while without me tying you up? I'll be home as soon as I can." Then he turned back. "I'll bring you a treat. But don't tell Carl I left you. He doesn't trust you yet. I trust you. I can trust you, can't I, Damon?"

Damon nodded. Kenny could trust him, although Damon wasn't

quite sure what it meant. Kenny could trust Damon not to tell Carl, that was for sure, if trust was like a promise.

The minute Kenny was out the door, Damon took a deep breath. It was the first time he'd breathed since he came to live here. He felt his heart blow up and lift like a balloon. Suddenly, he was no longer afraid. He was free.

He wandered around the living room, listening to the clock. It ticked and then it tocked and then it ticked again, as if making up its mind between times. The sun glowed on Kenny's sweet potato vine as it ran up the window like a beanstalk. Outside, through the curtain, people laughed back and forth along the street, talking strange languages that Kenny said weren't even French.

Damon turned back to the living room. He hadn't had a real chance to look at all the pictures of the boys on the walls. There were no mommies or daddies or even sisters, just big brothers. There was one whole wall full of boys. Some of them were alone. Others were skinny dipping, although he didn't see the pools. Carl had taken all these pictures, and Kenny told Damon that they were "brilliant masterpieces" and "award-winning" and that Carl was a genius. Carl had taken pictures of Damon, too, and of Kenny and Damon together, on the couch, in the bathtub, in bed after one of Damon's nightmares. None of them were hanging on the wall, though.

As he stared at them, Damon heard a creak. Startled, he looked around, trying to figure out where it came from. He heard lots of odd sounds lately. Smelled things, too.

Damon wandered into the kitchen just like he did at home. Except there was no salad from Aunt Cordelia or home-baked cookies from Mrs. Wickman, and there was no ceramic jar with the Dutch brother and sister like him and Becca to store them in. Or was that for coffee? Or rice like Kenny's gold cookie tin? Damon was forgetting things, and it upset him. He wanted the tin to hold cookies, so it did. He just had to lift the lid, but he didn't. Why take chances? Instead, he got down a bag of potato chips, and suddenly he smelled home-baked chocolate chip cookies fresh from the oven. He even peeked inside the oven, but there were none there. Where did that smell come from?

The phone rang, but he didn't dare answer it. Suppose it was Carl wanting to speak to Kenny? Damon wasn't allowed to answer the phone anyway, not after that time he tried to call home. Besides, he was supposed to be tied up. So he just stood over it, listening to the message from someone named Jeff.

Damon wasn't supposed to go into Carl and Kenny's room either, so he just stood on the threshold. From there he studied the room as he'd never had a chance to before. It smelled of Carl's aftershave and Kenny's vanilla candles. Also something pukey, like dirty laundry.

The bed was big with a blue satin cover and several stuffed dogs, a golden retriever like Alex's and the dog that pulls sleds. Maybe it was one of them that had squeaked a minute ago. On the dresser were pictures of an old woman and a younger one in fancy gold frames. They looked full of themselves. Carl's hairbrush was there, and his jewelry chest where he kept his fancy cufflinks. In the corner was a stuffed black dog with a brown mouth like the kind that always barked at Robbie when he passed the house on the corner in his old neighborhood. Damon wondered, if Carl and Kenny liked dogs so much, why didn't they have any real ones? Damon heard a whisper, and a minute later, a sigh. Just once. He wasn't even sure he'd heard it. That was the trouble with odd noises. You heard them once, and you held your breath to see if they came again, and they never did, so you couldn't be sure what they were and where they came from. Once he'd heard Mom's tea kettle whistling, but that couldn't be right. They didn't have a tea kettle here.

After they got home from the studio every day, Damon had to have his bath. He didn't like it, even with the sponge duck and the Timmy boat that he didn't have time to sail. Kenny washed him all over, saying, "Got to get my Damon clean so there are no germs left to make him sick. You don't want to be sick for Thanksgiving, do you?"

"I don't want to be sick at all."

"Of course not. Remember what we do on Thanksgiving?"

Did they do something on Thanksgiving? Damon remembered the turkey that Mom cooked, but he didn't remember anything about Carl and Kenny.

"No," he said.

"We go visiting all the friends we're going to have over for Christmas. Absolutely everybody feeds us. Doesn't that sound like fun?"

"Do we get turkey?"

"Turkey, pumpkin pie, everything. Then at Christmas, your Kenny cooks a great big thirty-pound turkey with apricot and sausage stuffing." Kenny was rubbing him all over with the washcloth, even hurting him, although he didn't mean to. "And we have cranberry orange relish and roast potatoes. Remember?"

Damon thought he did.

"And creamed spinach — "

"Ew-w-w-"

"Don't ew-w-w your Kenny's spinach. I make delicious spinach with cheese in it. You'll like it."

"Ew-w-w-" Damon laughed up at him.

"Silly."

"Is that gonna be my birthday?"

"Silly. Your birthday's over. That was October 20 when we got you."

"But you said — "

"What did I say?"

"I don't 'member. Do we get presents?"

"Of course, you get presents. It's Christmas. That's when we have three kinds of pie — apple, mince, and pecan with vanilla ice cream. Know why we have so much dessert? Because all the boys come for dinner."

"The lost boys?"

"What is it with you and lost boys?"

"I'm a lost boy."

"You're not lost, you're found," Kenny said irritably, scrubbing behind his ears much too hard. "How many times do I have to tell you? We found you. We picked you out from all the little boys we could have chosen. You were the one we wanted. Okay, that's enough. Get up and I'll dry you off."

"I can dry me off."

"I'll do it. You'll just stay wet, and wet your PJs, and Uncle Carl will point at you and say, 'Ew-w-w, Damon wet his PJs.' Turn around.

The boys who are coming for Christmas are from Carl's movies. We're their only family, and they're very grateful. Well, a few of them have daddies, but the rest live in the orphanage above the studio. They wouldn't even have Christmas dinner if it weren't for us. They're all very talented actors, and they're going to be your new friends. Do you want some friends?"

"Uh-huh. Alex is my friend."

"These are your new friends. Uncle Carl told them to be friends with you, and they do what Uncle Carl tells them. 'Cause he's the producer, you see. And the director, too. He's the boss of them."

One day, Kenny dried Damon off and got him into his pajamas. Then, instead of showering, he ran himself a bath, too, with the boat and the sponge duck.

"Help me undress, Damon. Help me take off my shirt."

"You're not a little boy. You can take off your own shirt."

"This time I want you to help me."

At last, Kenny was naked and got into his bath. Then he said, "Damon, come here."

He was lying in the bubbles with his candle lit on the sink, smelling of vanilla.

"Your turn," he sang gaily.

"My turn for what?" Damon asked.

"Your turn to wash me. I wash you every day, now it's your turn to wash me. Come on, kneel down here by the tub and take the washcloth. Here, I'll soap it for you."

Damon had to wash Kenny's chest, his shoulders and back, his arms and stomach, and his legs.

"Isn't this fun?"

"Uh-huh," Damon said. But really, it wasn't fun at all. He had to pay special attention to Kenny's pee-pee, that Kenny called his "cock and balls." Kenny had big ones that floated in the water like the yellow duck, and when he washed the cock, it stretched longer and longer like a rubber band, and Kenny said to him,

"Oh, Damon, you make me feel so good. Mmm. What a good boy my Damon is."

Damon knew he made Kenny feel good, but for some reason he didn't like to. He felt icky and tried to get out of doing it. But, when he said he didn't feel like it, Kenny said, "Damon, you ungrateful child. After all I've done for you."

So he did it. He tried to do it only for a minute, but Kenny insisted on longer.

"Damon, it's no biggie, you know. It's just a little thing you can do for your Kenny. You see, we have a special relationship, you and I. The bond between a man and a boy is very special, and not all little boys have it, and the ones that do feel very lucky. They wouldn't trade it for anything. But it's our secret. Lots of people just don't understand. They're jealous, and they try to stop it. So you mustn't tell anyone. Okay?"

Damon nodded gravely. He wouldn't tell anyone whatever Kenny had just said. He liked to keep secrets with Kenny.

"Besides, you don't want your Kenny angry at you, do you?"

Could Kenny get mad at him? No, Damon didn't want Kenny mad, because then, who would save him from Carl?

11

DAMON SCRAMBLED UP THE ladder to the top bunk where his tree tower stretched through the ceiling now into the sky — his very own beanstalk. The roots dangled like ropes and the branches sprang from the wooden blocks, so that he could climb to heaven. Nobody else could, not even Carl because he couldn't see it. Besides, it was Damon's tree that he'd built himself. Up in the sky, he'd be safe forever. He was making friends with the birds up there. Sometimes when he was brushing his teeth or eating soup, he'd hear one sing a note — just one. They'd take him anywhere he wanted to go, home to Mom and Dad and Becca and Alex and then other places, too. He'd wanted to go on Thanksgiving, but Carl and Kenny had kept him busy visiting their friends.

"Damon, are you in bed?" Kenny called from the hall.

Damon scooted under the covers, pulled them up to his chin, and peered down at Kenny mischievously. Kenny didn't know about the tree tower. Should he tell him?

"Oh, come on, Damon, that's not your bed," said Kenny clicking into the room. "That's the top bunk. The lower one's your bed, you little minx."

"What's a minx?" asked Damon, his voice muffled by the covers.

Kenny took a couple of steps up the ladder, swooped Damon into his arms right through the tree tower that he couldn't see and plunked him into the lower bunk.

"A minx is a mischievous little boy."

"Does a minx stinks?"

"Not if he's had his bath."

"Is a minx a jinx?"

"Not if he's my Damon boy. But a minx finks."

"Does not."

"Oh yes, he does."

"Who does he fink on?"

"Anybody who climbs into the top bunk, that's who."

"Does he got his finking cap on?"

"Why Damon, my clever little boy! If he's my smart Damon, he does."

"Who's the top bunk for?" Damon asked, as Kenny tucked him in.

"To tie you up when you wet the bottom one," replied Carl, who slouched in the doorway, gnawing on a salami stick.

"Oh, Carl, don't tell him that. The top bunk is for your friends when they visit."

"Alex?" Damon asked, momentarily forgetting that the subject of the past was forbidden.

"Who?" asked Carl.

"Adam," Kenny said quickly. "He meant Adam, didn't you, Damon?"

Damon shook his head "yes."

"Trent's little boy, the one you met on Thanksgiving. Just a few years older than you. He's always at school when we're at the studio."

"School for crazies," said Carl.

"Shame on you, Carl."

"More likely sleeping."

Kenny tried to ignore it. "He'll be at our big Christmas dinner. Isn't that nice?"

Damon nodded again. He really wanted Alex. He hadn't seen him in about a year, he thought. But he knew better than to mention his name again.

"Bring Damon down to the studio, why don't you?" Carl suggested pleasantly. "He can meet the boys."

Damon could see that Carl was teasing Kenny.

"Carl, will you stop with that? I've told you, he's too young," Kenny said. "He needs boys his own age."

"You weren't much older," Carl said.

"Oh, yes, I was. Fifteen's a lot older than five."

"Emotionally, I mean."

"Damon doesn't have to work. He has a home."

Carl was staring hard at Damon with his "I'm on to you" look. And Damon knew that some day he'd have to go down to "the studio," whatever that was, because Carl wanted him to, even though Kenny didn't.

On Christmas Day, the house smelled of turkey and hot apple cider with cloves and cinnamon bubbling on the stove. In the living room, it smelled like Becca's pine tree that she climbed to the top of on the old Perkins lot where the parents had been murdered, their heads split open with axes like watermelons, and the house burned to the ground.

Kenny's tree with the angel on top was almost as high as the ceiling, although Damon didn't think it could grow through it. It wasn't magical enough. You could hardly see it because it was so smothered with decorations.

"You shouldn't put too many decorations on a tree," Becca said. "That makes it phony."

"You shouldn't put so many decorations on a tree," Damon said.

But Kenny just ignored him and explained where the most important ones had come from, proudly swirling his cerulean blue silk moiré cape over his dusty rose velvet suit and tossing his head so that the jewels in his hair glittered. Carl, who wore chocolate satin pajamas with a gold crown on his breast pocket, said Kenny looked elegant. But Kenny whispered to Damon that Carl looked anal, whatever that was.

"That ecru clay bell my little brother Tim made at school. He gave it to me because it didn't turn out good enough for Mom. She'd have fussed and fussed. I miss my little brother more than anything."

"If you missed him that much," said Carl, "you'd visit more often. You haven't been home in two years."

"Well, I might just," Kenny's voice rose, as Damon grew very quiet, wondering if they were going to fight again. "This frosted bell I got on sale at Filson's. I had to hide it in the ear of a stuffed elephant until I could come back with some cash because I'd maxed out my credit card."

"Can I come with you?" Damon asked Kenny.

"Where? Home? With me? Of course, you can, you little dear. Isn't that sweet?"

That relieved Damon's mind, but then he got to wondering how he could take his tree tower with him. He didn't see how he could pack it in a suitcase. If Kenny left Damon alone with Carl, Damon might have to climb to the top of his tree and never come down again.

Underneath Kenny's tree, the presents were piled high on phony snow, but Damon wasn't supposed to open any until the boys from the studio got here. Then they'd each get one, and Damon would open the rest after the boys left so they wouldn't be jealous.

"Don't you think that's a good idea?" Kenny asked absently, as he bustled about. He moved a decoration on the tree a fraction of an inch lower, a glass on the table a smidge to the right.

"I think that looks better, don't you?" Kenny asked no one in particular.

"Oh, stop fussing."

"I want it all to be perfect for them. This is the only home they have."

"This isn't their home, and don't pretend it is."

"Carl, what's wrong with you? Are you in a mood? Whatever for? Come on, Damon, we need to get you dressed in your Sunday best."

"It's not Sunday. It's Christmas."

Kenny opened his closet door and immediately spotted Robbie's old red sweatshirt with the bear.

"What's this? Where did that come from? We threw it out months ago."

Damon shook his head, mystified.

"I dunno."

The last he'd seen it was when it was in the wastebasket with its arms hanging over the side, trying to climb out and yelling, "Help! Help!"

Robbie must have done it. He probably sneaked it from the trash and stuffed it under his jacket and hid it behind his shoes when he got home. But how did it get hung up in the closet? Did Carl do it to get him in trouble? Or a ghost, maybe?

Kenny had paper plates set out for the boys with Santa Clauses on them. The adults had china. Kenny didn't want to do more than two loads in the dishwasher.

Kneeling in front of Damon, smelling of vanilla perfume, Kenny said, "I want you to be my good little Damon all day. Make me proud."

"Is that a biggie?" Damon reached out and touched a green jewel.

"That's a biggie. There are lots of presents for my good little Damon," said Kenny. "None for naughty Damon. None at all."

"Naughty Damon went away."

"He did! Where did he go?"

Damon stretched his arm up as high as he could but didn't say anything because Carl was watching.

"One stunt from you — just one — and I'll tie you up forever and never let you loose," Carl said.

"Oh, Carl, you're always expecting the worst."

"I know him."

"Meaning I don't?"

The doorbell rang over and over, and Kenny sang his greetings to everyone who entered, Trent and Barry with little Adam, who looked straight through Damon to a spot on the corner of the couch; Jeff, Madison, Torq, and their twelve-year-old boy Eric; and then old Uncle Paulie with a bunch of the studio boys, most of whom looked about nine or ten. Dressed in their suits and flowing ties, they filed awkwardly into the living room, trying to decide where they should stand and ending up in a line.

One, about fourteen in navy corded pants and a ruffled blouse open to his waist, shambled in and looked around very carefully, noting everything as if he needed to memorize it. Then he stood in front of Damon, eyeing him up and down. Damon was in his good powder blue suit with the pink and purple scarf and his new diamond stud, and he figured this boy was approving him like the mirror did.

"You're Kenny's new kid, aren't you? Damon?"

"Kenny's and Uncle Carl's." Close up, Damon could see that his face was full of little holes and white freckles and scars, and he wondered what had happened to him. His sandy hair was piled on top of his head in an unruly cascade of curls, and he stood sort of tilted as if he were bragging about something.

"I'm Mickey," he said. "You probably heard."

"No," said Damon truthfully.

"Carl said to be nice to you, so I am."

Damon's eyes were on his bare chest and the largest jeweled cross Damon had ever seen, like the one the minister wore only bigger.

"I'm Celtic," said Mickey. "That's a religion. Come on, pretty boy, suppose you show me your room."

"I'm not pretty boy. I'm Damon."

Once inside and out of hearing of the rest, Mickey said, "You really are a spoiled little bugger, aren't you? I live in the dorm at the orphanage."

"What's that?"

"Upstairs of the studio. The studio's in the basement to keep prying eyes from looking through the windows while we're shooting our movies. If you show too much of what you got, no one will buy. Remember that."

Damon thought it sounded wise, so he said, "I will."

"Good bugger! On the first floor's the bookstore that Jeff owns, full of weirdos looking for something to get their rocks off 'cause they can't do it on their own. Can you?" He was touring Damon's room as he spoke, opening the closet, riffling through his clothes, taking down the boxes on the top shelf and peering into them, examining shoes, and flipping the lid off the Lincoln Logs can. "Well, can you?"

"Yes," said Damon, because that was usually the answer that was expected. Of course, he had no idea what Mickey was talking about, but Mickey seemed to.

"Good boy! Then, upstairs of the bookstore is our dorm," Mickey continued, yanking open the drawers of Damon's bureau. "It has six beds. Nathan's the seventh, so he hasta' sleep on the floor until one of us leaves, probably me. He's glad to have a roof over his head, though. You will, too, if Kenny gets sick of you or leaves Carl or something." Mickey was pulling everything out of Damon's toy chest, stuffed animals, spacemen, cars, Kenny's boats and yo-yos. "Jeez, you got a lot of trucks, y'know?"

Damon knelt beside him and ran the ambulance from the toy chest to Mickey's foot, at which he laughed.

"Don't you wanna know why I'm leaving?" he asked, taking the puzzles and books from the shelves and examining them one by one. "Can I have this?" he asked, waving *The Wizard of Oz* at him.

"Sure, okay," Damon said, wanting to be polite.

"Super! Probably I can sell it after I've read it. I read pretty good, you know. Got lots of practice on magazines waiting around for my scenes. Bor-ing! I'll give you something next time I come. Is Damon your real name or your stage name?"

"I don't know."

"Well, what was your name before you got here?"

Damon got to his knees, walked over to Mickey on them, put his hands to Mickey's ear, and whispered "Robbie."

"Oh, so that's how it is, eh? It's a secret. Don't worry, I won't tell. You can trust me. I'm your friend. Kenny's my friend, too."

"Kenny's my friend," Damon said.

"You bet. So Damon's the name they gave you, huh? Did you know the other Damon? Probably not. That was a few years ago. He — "Mickey paused, staring intently into Damon's face until he rubbed it, thinking it was dirty. "He went away," Mickey finished. "So Damon's your stage name. Mickey's my real name. Stage name's Clint, but I only use it when I'm acting. When I go to Hollywood again, I'll be Reginald. That's classier. Been there once, 'cause I told them I was going home, so they sent me there. Stayed with Vince. Even had an audition. I'm my own man," he said proudly.

"What are you two doing in here?" Kenny demanded, bustling into the room, his cerulean duster floating behind him.

"Nothing!" said Mickey, as if hurt that Kenny might think they were doing something wrong.

"Damon, you need to greet your other guests. Come along, Clint, you too."

"Mickey," he said.

"Whatever."

Back in the living room, Kenny introduced Damon to Little Dickybird.

"Hi!" said the boy in a grown up, manly fashion. "I'm really eleven, and I'm little because I smoke."

"At the rate he's growing," said Carl to Trent, "he's got a career ahead of him until he's twenty-five."

"Why you think I smoke for?"

"Aw, you smoke 'cause you're a dirty little bugger," said Flip. "I'm named after Flip Wilson."

"Can we open our presents now?" asked Mickey.

"After dinner," Kenny said. "Oh, my goodness, I forgot the rolls."

Mickey tried to sit next to Damon, but Kenny said Damon should sit at the foot of the table between himself and Adam, Trent's boy, Trent's and Barry's. Mickey was down at the other end by Carl, but he made twisty silly faces at Damon, who grinned back at him.

"First, we say Grace," said Kenny.

"Grace," Mickey replied.

"Enough, Mick," Carl said sternly, reaching over and patting his knee. Damon wondered if Mickey was too big to tie up. The orphanage had bunk beds, Mickey had said.

"Damon, would you like to say Grace for us?" asked Kenny.

Grace? They'd never asked him to say Grace here. He began to panic. Maybe he could remember Becca's.

"God is great, God is good, let us thank him for our food."

"Oh, that's so nice," said Kenny, but the boy named Hank with the ruffled handkerchief in his breast pocket, stuck his finger down his throat in a puke sign.

"Hank, do you want to be excused?" Carl asked.

"No."

"'Cause you look like you're going to be sick. We don't want anyone sick at the table."

Hank twisted and wriggled around in reply.

Mickey, Flip, Little Dickybird, and the rest exploded in laughter.

"You shouldn't eat if you're sick," Carl pressed.

"I think you should apologize to Damon," said Kenny.

"Sorry."

"What do you say, Damon?"

Damon knew what to say because Becca was always telling him. "S'okay."

"I've been teaching him manners," Kenny announced proudly, beaming at Damon. "But he's just naturally a very polite boy."

"Can we eat now?" Mickey asked impatiently. "I mean, we said Grace a hunnert times."

"Do you want to say it, Mickey?" Carl asked.

"God's neat, let's eat, for crying out loud."

"Pass this plate of turkey to Adam, Damon. Adam's dad can help him with the yams and the rest."

Obediently, Damon passed the plate to Adam, who said, "Turkey lurkey."

He didn't say it as if it were a joke. In fact, he looked very serious. Damon was puzzled.

"That's enough, Adam," said Trent.

"Jerky," added Adam as if he hadn't heard. Or was he being sassy? He was a pointy little kid — pointy nose and mouth, and even his hair came to a point at the back of his head.

Kenny leaned over to cut Damon's meat, but Damon said, "Don't. I'm not a baby," he added in a low voice.

"How old are you, Damon?" Trent asked.

Carl gave him a warning look, but Damon didn't understand it.

"I'm almost six," he said. "I'll be six in a little while."

Adam's dad plopped a spoonful of spinach on his plate, but Adam smooshed it away.

"Mean green," he said.

"That's Kenny's best spinach," Damon said, but Adam paid no attention. Down at the other end of the table, Mickey was grinning at him as he tipped his glass of water so it just reached the edge but didn't quite spill over, making Damon laugh and start to try it himself, but Carl put his hand on Mickey's and guided the glass back to its proper place.

"No more for you," he said. "What are you on, anyway?"

"Nothing!" Mickey said indignantly.

So far as Damon could see, Mickey was on the chair.

Little Dickybird gobbled up so much food, Damon wondered where he fit it.

"You don't have to eat it all at once, Bird," said Kenny. "I'll send home a foil package with you."

"You will anyway," he replied. "Paulie'll eat it all."

"Yeah," said Mickey. "All he cooks is corn. Corn, corn, corn."

"And peanut butter sandwiches," Hank added.

"I give him money for a lot more than that," Carl said with a scowl.

"Maybe eats it," said Little Dickybird with a straight face. He reached into his pocket and took out a cigarette stub, but Carl said sternly,

"No smoking at the table, Bird."

"But it's Christmas," the boy wailed.

"We don't want smoke with our dinner," Kenny said. "I went to a lot of trouble to make this delicious food. And the rest of us haven't finished eating."

"Eating," said Adam.

"Enough, Adam," said Barry and Trent together.

"Is the therapist helping, do you think?" Kenny asked pleasantly.

"Think stink," said Adam, and Damon giggled.

"Not so's you'd notice," said Barry at the same time as Trent said "A little."

"How long has it been?'

"About a year."

"Since you got him, then?"

"It began a few months afterwards. Pass the cranberry sauce, will you, Dickybird?"

"Pass the gravy."

"At last, the rolls are ready."

"This spinach is delicious, Kenny."

"Turkey's smirky," said Mickey.

"Enough, Mick!" said Carl.

"What'd I do!"

"More yams, please," said Flip, followed by a chorus of "Me, too's."

After dinner, everyone cleared their plates. Then came the gift giving. Kenny scuttled around under the tree, finding a gift for each boy, including Damon. They all received scarves in Kenny's inimitable style. There were small boxes with bits of jewelry in them for the dads and from them as well, while Carl lounged in the recliner and lit his pipe.

"Time for movies," he said.

"Don't see why I can't smoke if you're smoking," grouched Dickybird, but at Carl's snarling frown, he added, "Okay, okay."

"Ooh, my movie, my movie," said Flip.

"Everyone gets a turn."

"I get to sit up front," said Mickey. "I don't see so good," he explained to Damon.

"Why don't you wear glasses?"

"Movie stars don't wear glasses. I'm saving for contact lenses."

Kenny caught Damon's hand and sat him down at his side on the couch. Carl flicked on a movie, but it was like the ones they showed at night when Damon was supposed to be asleep that he'd only caught glimpses of. First, there was Mickey and Dickybird getting naked and rolling around in the snow.

"Yeah!" the boys cheered. And they said things that Damon didn't understand.

"Are they wrestling?" Damon asked, because he was confused.

"They're just playing," Kenny said, hugging Damon's head to his shoulder, so it was harder for him to watch. Kenny put Damon's hand on his thigh. He was getting affectionate again. Damon always dreaded it, because Kenny made him do things he didn't want to do.

Suddenly, something in the corner of the ceiling caught Damon's eye. It was a shadow, but it kept moving, changing shape, and Damon couldn't think what it might be. At first, he thought it was a cat on the ceiling, but how was that possible? Then it was a glob of cookie dough that Becca was rolling out, except how could she be doing it up there? Maybe it was a branch from his tree tower that had stretched all the way across his ceiling and closet into the living room.

Kenny turned Damon's head to him, and he saw Flip and Hank in a pool doing the same kind of thing, and then three other boys playing in the tub like Kenny and Damon did while they made weird noises.

"Are they hurting each other?"

Now the boys had stopped watching and were around the living room for real, smacking each other with cushions, grabbing each other's pee-pees and yelling with laughter until Carl called, "Enough!" Kenny jumped, then stopped what he was doing, and Damon saw that the shadow had stopped moving, too.

Uncle Paulie showed up, and Kenny presented him with a huge a gift package of turkey with all the trimmings.

"For *all* the boys, Paulie, not just you."

"Why don't you invite me over to spend the night some time?" Mickey suggested to Damon at the door.

"Sure!"

"Damon wants me to spend the night," he told Kenny immediately.

"Some other time," Kenny said.

"How 'bout I sleep over at your place?" Damon suggested.

"We can have more fun here," said Mickey. "You gots more stuff. Besides, you come down there, you hafta work."

"Don't you like work?"

"It's okay. You hafta if you're gonna be a star."

"Did you make new friends today?" Kenny asked, bending over Damon in his bed.

"Why does Mickey got all those holes in his face?"

"They're from chicken pox and acne, stuff like that. He looks kind of scrofulous, don't you think?"

"Yes."

"'Scrofulous' means kind of diseased like you have the plague or something."

"Am I gonna look like that?"

"Not if you keep yourself really clean. Some people like scrofulous-looking kids. They get off on them. There's a call for scrof in some films."

"Will I ever be in a movie?"

"Told you so," Carl guffawed from the doorway.

"I don't think he should even be seeing them."

"You protect him so much he's gonna end up a ninny."

Kenny ignored him.

"Have you said your prayers? No? Come on, kneel down, we'll say our prayers."

Damon scrambled out of bed and knelt beside Kenny, putting his hands together in a church steeple as Becca had taught him.

"Thank you, God, for a wonderful day," Kenny said. "And God bless Uncle Carl and all the boys, and everyone else."

When Damon held his hands up together, he could see his tree growing strong through the ceiling.

"Is God in our hands?"

"No, silly. He's up in the sky."

"Up there?"

"Up there."

"My tree's up there. I'm praying to my tree."

"You're what?"

Damon heard Carl shift in the doorway behind him, but he went on as if they were alone.

"My tree. See, up there, it's growing through the ceiling. It's up to the first star already," Damon said gleefully.

"Enough of that. Into bed with you."

"Why can't I have Mickey over?"

"He's too old for you, and he's not very nice. Adam's nicer."

"Madam Adam?"

"Now, Damon, that's cruel. If you had a limp, would you want people to make fun of it?"

"I don't have a limp."

"Yes, I know, but if you did."

Kenny gave up, tucked Damon in, and walked out saying to Carl, "Adam really doesn't seem any better."

"Worse. Kid's sick. They should have taken him back. That's what happens when you don't do your research. Sounds like Damon's headed in the same direction, if you ask me. Him and his tree."

"Oh, he's imaginative, that's all."

They left the door ajar. Damon wasn't allowed to close it all the way. He climbed back into the top bunk and followed his tree with his eyes all the way up through the ceiling into the night sky until it reached toward the second star, the one called Scrofulous. He thought he could see Becca at the very top of the tree, a tiny figure no bigger than his thumbnail because she was so far away. She was waving to him.

12

ENDLESS PHONE CONVERSATIONS BETWEEN Kenny and his younger brother, Tim. Much hand-wringing as Kenny paced the room, talking to Carl, to Damon, to himself.

"I mean, I don't *have* to go. There's really no reason why I should, except that Tim's half out of his mind. He doesn't know how to handle things, never did." Kenny was now addressing Carl, who sat on his dining room chair, the only one with arms, his cell phone on the table in front of him, his jaw set. "He doesn't know how to handle the doctors, fill out the forms — I mean, you just fill them out with any old thing to make it look as though you did their fucking paperwork for them — it's not as if they read them. But he thinks you have to answer every single question with some fact he doesn't know."

"Can't he get a social worker at the hospital to help him?"

"Of course he can. I told him that. He's afraid of dealing with those people because they might find out something about him that could land him in trouble."

What trouble? Damon guessed Carl knew because he didn't ask. Trouble was trouble, no matter the reason.

"You're in some kind of time warp. Your baby brother's nineteen, for Chrissake. Four years older than you were when you struck out on your own."

"He's young for nineteen. He doesn't know — "

"You remember him as a baby. He can take care of himself."

Damon watched this scene with increasing anxiety. Kenny might go away, and what would happen? Would Kenny leave Damon with Carl? Would Damon have to run just as Kenny did?

"I mean," Kenny said, distractedly pulling out a drawer from the mahogany sideboard to look for something and then pushing it shut again, "it's not as if I'd be going to see her or comfort her or anything. My mother was very mean to me, Damon. You never saw such a mean, mean mother."

"What'd she do?" Damon asked, his voice unexpectedly hoarse. He couldn't imagine what a mean mother would do. He didn't know any. The microwave was dinging, but Kenny didn't seem to notice.

"What'd she do to me? Well, she beat me, for one thing. She beat me with everything she could get hold of, with a rubber spatula, with a wooden pudding spoon, with the belt from my dead Dad's trousers. She said she'd saved it special to use it on my sassy behind."

"Sissy," Carl corrected.

"Whatever."

"The rolling pin," Carl reminded, and then answered his phone.

"Oh, yes, she swung that rolling pin as if it were a baseball bat. Trouble was, she didn't have very good aim, so it landed all sorts of places — on my legs, my arms, and my back. Once she hit me upside my head and laid me out cold. I had to stay in the hospital with a concussion."

"Why?" Damon asked. He couldn't conceive of somebody hitting somebody else with a rolling pin. Mom and Becca used it to roll out cookie dough.

"She's just a very violent woman. She did the same to Tim before her stroke, only not so much."

"Why doesn't Tim run away, like you did?"

"Tim's too scared. He lives with her because he lost his job. It's cheaper to live at home. When he gets another job, then he'll leave. So you see, I don't owe her anything."

"Did she beat you with a candlestick?" Damon asked, his eye on the silver ones atop the sideboard with the Christmas red drip spills running down.

"Isn't that cute?" he asked Carl, who was off the phone again. "He's trying to think of something I didn't get beaten with. Yes, she beat me with anything you can think of."

"Did she hit you with the TV clicker?"

"Now you're being silly, you little darling. But what am I going to do with you if I go?"

"Take me with you," Damon said quickly.

"I'd love to, darling, but that just wouldn't be practical. You see, they don't know about you, and when I go home, I'm sort of in disguise."

"Like a spy?"

"More like an actor."

"Do you wear a costume?"

"Yes, I guess you could call it that. I certainly don't wear my real clothes."

"I want to go with you," Damon said. "I can be in disguise, too. I can wear my Halloween costume."

"Did you hear that, Carl? Oh, what a funny boy. Oh, I forgot my tea." Kenny was back in a moment with a steaming cup, the bag steeping. "How would you like to spend a few days with a friend? Adam, say?"

"Madam Adam? He's not my friend. He's crazy."

"Damon, shame on you, that's not nice. Not nice at all. Adam just thinks differently. It's a game with him. Suppose I give Trent and Barry a ring? But you have to promise to be nice to Adam."

"Damon could spend a few days down at the orphanage," Carl suggested mildly.

"Yes, with Mickey," Damon said.

"Don't start with me, Carl. Damon's much too young for them," Kenny said, and then to Damon, "Those boys are too old for you, Damon. That could be bad for you."

"Why? I could be in the movies."

"Out of the question," Kenny said. "Let me give Trent a call."

Damon listened tensely to Kenny talking to Trent. They lived upstairs from the art studio, so Damon would be able to come down and paint any time he wanted to. Problem was, Adam was spooky. Damon didn't want to be with him at all. There was no telling what he'd do. Still, it was better than being with Carl. Anything was better than that.

"That's odd," Kenny said as he hung up.

"They can't take him?"

"Well, they didn't really want to. Trent said they were sort of in crisis there, that things were unsettled, something to do with Adam, I think. But he finally said 'yes.'"

There followed more long conversations between Kenny and Tim, until Kenny decided to fly up to Portland for three days, and Damon would spend the time with Trent, Barry, and Adam.

The next morning, Damon hardly recognized Kenny in his navy business suit, white shirt and striped tie like the kind Dad wore.

"What do you think of your Kenny in these duds?" he asked.

To tell the truth, Damon didn't like how Kenny looked at all. It was him and not him. But he didn't want to hurt his feelings.

"Does the mirror approve?" he asked finally.

"I don't think I'll ask the mirror today. The mirror might barf."

"What happened to your earring?"

"I'll put it in again just as soon as I get back."

As Trent's door, Kenny put down Damon's suitcase so that he could knock, a bottle of merlot in his other hand. But Trent was still in his yellow pajamas with the crossed tennis rackets over the pocket, and he acted as though they didn't have any arrangement at all.

"Oh, Kenny, yes, of course, well, things are kind of a mess."

"I'm sorry to hear it, Trent, but you did say you'd take Damon, and my plane leaves in an hour."

"I suppose he could have Adam's room."

"Where's Adam?"

"He's not here. Barry finally had to take him back to Pismo Beach. We decided to drop him off there. That's where we got him, you know. We think we're probably safe. He's too far gone to remember us or this place or be of any help to the police. Still, we may have to leave."

"You didn't, I mean he's not — "

"No, it's nothing like Damon One, thank god."

"Damon. That's *my* name."

"This was another Damon, sweet."

"I couldn't have done that," Trent said.

"Could Barry?"

"Not without my say-so, and I wouldn't give it. No, we just had to take him back, that's all. He'll probably be okay. They'll give him the care he needs in Pismo Beach. But I miss him so," and now Trent was bawling, and Kenny didn't know what to do.

"Look, I'm sorry, Trent, are you really up to this?"

"He can stay in Adam's room."

"Because I could cancel. I mean, I owe my mother *nothing*, I mean *nothing*."

"I know how she treated you. That's why I was surprised."

"It's Timmy. He's so scared of everything. It's just for a few days."

"And Carl's out of the question?"

"Well, Carl's so busy and all, and Damon's a little, well, you know, I thought it would be better for him to be with someone his own age, although now he isn't — "Kenny floundered.

"Okay, if it's just a day or two."

"Goodbye, my sweet Damon," said Kenny, covering him with hugs and kisses. "I'll be home real soon, I promise, and we'll have so much fun. We'll go to the zoo. How about that? Why, you're trembling."

"I got to ask you something."

"What is it, my dear boy?"

"Do you love me better than chocolate?"

"I do. I love you better than chocolate. Better than chocolate bars, syrup, drops, sauce, hot cocoa, better than every kind of chocolate there is."

"Then come back."

"Of course I'll come back. Three days. That's all. You count them. Uncle Trent will help."

After Kenny left, Trent asked Damon if he needed to eat, and when Damon shook his head, Trent led him to Adam's room. It was

a mess, the bed rumpled and smelly, clothes thrown around everywhere, and no tree, of course. The phone rang, and Trent left him
standing there.

Damon set to work building a tower out of Adam's blocks.

The problem with Adam's blocks was that there were no bumps
in them. Damon didn't understand why this should be so. They
were made of wood, same as his own. They should have bumps for
branches to grow out of, but there was nothing. He built a tower as
high as he could and then started to finish it with his imagination. He
couldn't even get it up to the ceiling.

The apartment was quiet at first except for the phone ringing
every few minutes. But then Trent was running around, jabbering
excitedly, "Oh, no, no, this is awful." Damon tiptoed out of his room
to find out what was going on. Trent was flinging off his pajamas and
pulling on his underwear without even stopping to shower.

"Oh, Damon, don't worry. I called Carl. He'll be here for you in
a few minutes."

Damon backed away.

"No," he said, shaking his head, but Trent wasn't paying attention.

"I have to go. It's Adam. Barry needs me."

Carl was coming to take him? Where could he hide? The studio?
The orphanage? Damon was in a panic. He had to think of something. He had to find a place to hide for three days until Kenny came
back.

Now, Carl was at the door, his big, burly frame concealed in a tan
trench coat, his hat, and his ever-present sunglasses.

"I'm so sorry I couldn't follow through with this," Trent said
quickly, the words stumbling over each other in a race to get out
of his mouth and be done with it. "Barry can't get Adam to move.
Barry's parked with him at the playground. When he tries to get him
out of the car, Adam just screams. Barry doesn't want to cause a fuss,
of course. He thought he'd just open the car door, and Adam would
go running off. I told him that wasn't realistic. I told him that. I've
got to rent a car and drive down there."

"What about giving Adam a little something to make him drowsy. I have some if you need it."

"We may have to. Barry, the dodo, didn't think to bring anything with him. I have to do everything in this family."

"I always have some on hand," said Carl, taking a brown vial from his pocket. Instantly, Damon recognized it. "This'll work, believe me. A few drops. Takes all the fight out of them. Don't park right at the playground. Park a block or so away, so parents can't identify your car later. You can just sit him down at a picnic table with a bag of burgers and shakes. Sit down with him for a minute. Take a bite. Get him distracted with that. Once he's chewing — vamoose!"

"Thanks loads, Carl. Tell Kenny I'm sorry."

"Come along, Damon. Where's your suitcase?"

Carl's footsteps thudded to Adam's room, always menacing.

"Where are we going?" Damon asked, dreading the answer.

"Why, we're going to the studio, Damon, just like you wanted. I'm in the middle of a film, and I can't stop now, and I certainly can't leave you at home alone, can I?"

"Yes, you can. Kenny does."

"What!"

"I forgot. No, he doesn't. I'm not supposed to tell."

Carl grabbed his hand and yanked.

Damon's feelings were very mixed up. He was scared of Carl, but the studio sounded okay. Kenny didn't want him to go, and Kenny wanted what was best for him, but Kenny and Carl fought a lot, and it wasn't all about him. Mickey would be at the studio. Maybe Damon could stay with him at the orphanage. Damon didn't think he'd mind sleeping on the floor. It was probably a little like camping out with Becca in Robbie's backyard. The ground was hard, but the fun was worth it, all the woodsy night smells, and little animals scurrying around, and Becca giving him bites of her energy bars while they told each other ghost stories. The orphanage might be like that.

In one hand, Carl held Damon's overnight bag which was really Carl's, and he clutched Damon's wrist in the other, squeezing the bones together so they rubbed against each other. Damon didn't dare complain. Outside, Carl walked so fast that Damon had to run to keep up with him. Sometimes Carl jerked his arm to move him along, and his feet left the ground or scraped his shoe tops.

Carl muttered something about "Holding up production because of you." Damon wasn't quite sure what that meant, but he knew it was bad. Something Damon shouldn't have done.

"Do I get to stay in the orphanage?" Damon asked, out of breath but hopeful. He got no answer from Carl, who was yanking him through crowds and traffic as quickly as he could.

They came to a gray wooden building several stories tall, with yellow paint around the windows. Through a window, Damon saw Jeff's bookstore on the bottom, but they went in at the side and down into the basement. There was a flight of stairs leading up, too, and Damon figured that was where the orphanage must be.

Downstairs, they entered a large room with a big bed in the middle, surrounded by lights brighter than Damon had ever seen, except maybe at the dentist's. The walls were lined with mirrors, so it made it seem as though there was at least two of everything. Several of the boys were there, but the minute they spotted Damon, they got up and crowded around him to say "Hi!" and punch him in greeting.

Mickey said, "Damon, great! Welcome to our humble home. Are you going to be in the movie? Stay here for a while?" He looked like they'd added more holes and bumps in his face, so he was even more "scrof" like Kenny had said.

"All right, all right, time to get back to work," Carl said, swinging off his coat and hat and hanging them on a hook near the door. "Damon, you sit in this chair right here on the side and watch. You might learn something. Places everybody."

The boys jumped on the bed and started doing silly things to each other and making noises like they were in pain. This between coughing and sneezing in each other's faces because they had the flu and thought that spreading germs was great fun. A couple of men were behind cameras that made whirring sounds. Every minute or so, Carl yelled "Cut!" and then told some boy to do something different. Damon thought Carl was very bossy, but he was bossy at home, too.

"That's what directors do, dear," Kenny had explained. "They boss people around."

"Roll camera," Carl yelled, "Action." He liked to yell. The boys seemed to be trying their best to do what he wanted.

Actually, it got pretty boring. Damon began to swing his legs and dream of other things. His eyes wandered around the set, the racks of costumes that each looked like two racks in the mirrors, the tarp a picture of the ocean with an island in the middle, and an assortment of handcuffs and other shiny objects, most of which he couldn't identify.

Then he noticed the man leaning in the corner of the studio with his hands thrust deep into his pockets, watching him. Damon had no idea how long he'd been there. He wore a black business suit and a black turtleneck, and his shoes were polished to a high shine. He didn't wear studs in his ears, but his lapel glittered with one stone. He looked like Dad, just before he went to work, only finer. Kenny would have said he was too "conservative." Exactly how Kenny looked when he left this morning. "Conservative" was a bad thing to be. Like "retro." Damon looked at the man, then felt his eyes skitter away, feeling slightly guilty for thinking bad things about him. When his eyes flickered back as if they had a mind of their own, the man was still staring. Damon began to feel uncomfortable. Didn't this man know that it wasn't polite to stare?

A few minutes later, Damon saw the man jerk his head in Carl's direction. It was the kind of nod that meant, "Come here."

"Take five, everybody," Carl said and went over to him, and they had a discussion. It wasn't an argument, but they didn't seem to be agreeing either. Finally, Carl shrugged and called, "Time for lunch break. Mickey, show Damon where it is."

"Are you all finished?" Damon asked Mickey as they climbed the steep narrow staircase up to the orphanage.

"Hell, no! We could go to midnight," Mickey said, wiping his nose on his sleeve. "Just depends on Carl's sense of high art, how long he's willing to roll. And I think they'll have a part for you when we get back."

"Because of Mr. Martingale," said Little Dickybird.

"Yeah, Mr. Martingale," said Flip.

"He's our biggest customer," Mickey explained to Damon.

They passed through a room stuffed with bunk beds and a couple of sleeping bags on the floor. Through that was the bathroom and then a kitchen with a table and an assortment of stools and crates to sit on. Paulie greeted them, patted Damon's head, and dished out bowls of macaroni and cheese, bread and orange quarters, and glasses of milk that was too thin because Paulie had added too much water to the milk powder.

"Mmm, Paulie's macaroni is the best. He makes it real cheesy," said Hank between deep rumbling coughs that seemed to come up from his stomach, while Flip scooped the bread from Damon's plate, saying, "You don't want this, do you, pretty boy?" and Mickey snatched it back, calling him a "baby-robber."

"I'm not a baby," Damon objected.

"Looks like Martingale wants Damon in the movie," said Hank. "If he does, pretty Damon won't be a baby anymore." And he and Flip snickered to each other.

"Don't worry about it, Damon," said Mickey. "I'll show you what to do."

"Yeah, baby Damon, we'll show you," said Hank. Flip farted, and they exploded in laughter.

Damon worried. "Kenny doesn't want me in the movies," he said.

"Probably just a little part," Mickey assured him. "Where is Kenny, anyway? And how come you're here?"

Damon told him everything about Kenny, Timmy, and Madam Adam, and everyone listened in, including Uncle Paulie.

When they got back to the studio, Carl came over to Damon and took his hand, not too tightly this time. Seated on a high stool, Mr. Martingale was watching.

"This'll be easy, Damon," Carl said. "Just stand by the bed and watch. That's all. Don't have to say anything. Don't even have to move. We'll take pictures of you doing that. Just watch with that innocent angel face of yours that will turn every kid-lover into a seething mass of hormones. Understand?"

Damon nodded. He supposed it was all right. The boys started doing their weird stuff again, and Damon watched as he was instructed, although it was very boring. He got tired after awhile, and started shifting from one leg to the other.

"Damon!" Carl warned.

Damon straightened up fast, then caught the Martingale man laughing at him. He tried to keep his eyes on the boys, but something about it made him uncomfortable. He didn't like looking at them. They were all naked now, doing things to each other like Kenny did to him. He really hated it, although he didn't know why.

Then he began to notice the boys in the mirrors on the wall and the ceiling as well. What puzzled him was that there seemed to be more boys in the mirrors than there were in the room. How could that be? He started counting but got mixed up. Mickey, Flip, Hank, Dickybird, Nathan, no wait a minute, there was a boy Mickey's age in a purple shirt and a long black coat and hat. No one else in the room was wearing that outfit. In fact, most weren't wearing much of anything. Damon's eyes began to swim.

"Damon!" Carl shouted angrily. "Focus!"

That night, Carl didn't leave Damon at the orphanage as he had hoped, and as Mickey tried to persuade him to do. Instead, Carl took him home with him.

"Get undressed and take your bath," Carl told him. "You're spending the night with me."

Those words filled Damon with terror.

"No," he said.

"Kenny isn't here to spend the night with me, so you're going to do it."

"No," Damon said. Then seeing the storm gathering in Carl's face, he sprinted for his room as fast as he could.

He could hear Carl's heavy footsteps thumping down the hall like a giant. He sprang for the upper bunk where his tree grew thick and strong now through the ceiling. He grasped a branch of the tree close to the ceiling, then swung onto it, climbing as fast as he could, although his head kept bumping the sky.

Carl came into the room and stopped short, a look of surprised puzzlement on his face.

"What are you doing up there?" he asked.

"I'm climbing my tree into the sky, and you can't catch me," said Damon.

Carl shook his head.

"What tree? There's no tree in here."

"This tree, my tree, I builded it all myself."

"My God, you're as loony as Madam Adam. There's no tree."

"Oh yes, there is. See, I'm climbing it to the sky, and you can't come up it because it's not your tree."

Carl stood below him, his face darkening by the minute, as he seemed to consider this. Then he took a step forward.

"I can do better than climb up your tree. I can chop it down."

"No, you can't, it's my tree."

"Yes, I can. See this axe?" And he held out his hand as if he were gripping the handle, except there was nothing there. Damon was mystified.

"You don't have a axe."

"Oh yes, I do. I have an imaginary axe, and I'm going to chop down your imaginary tree, and then I'll have you."

With that, he took a swing at the tree. His hand passed right through it, but the tree trembled, and Damon called, "Stop! It's my tree, and you can't cut it down." But Carl took another swing and then another, and to Damon's horror, the tree began to ooze bloody sap all the way down its side to the bottom.

"No, no, you're hurting it," Damon cried out.

But Carl chopped away. Suddenly, Damon felt himself plunging with his tree, all the way down to the top bunk, all the way down to the floor.

13

EVERY MORNING, BECCA FELT as though she had been crying all night. Yet her eyes were dry, and there were no discarded tissues on the floor beside her bed.

Ms. Zinnia Jefferson, the school counselor, closed the door, commented on the rain, and nodded her head invitingly toward the jar of jelly beans. A smart young black woman in a purple angora sweater, knee-high black boots, and African beads, her manner was sympathetic.

"How is the search for your brother coming?"

What could Becca reply to that? It wasn't coming at all, was it?

"How about your family? How are they taking it?"

Well, they weren't, were they? Dad had run away from home.

There was just one goldfish in Ms. Jefferson's bowl. Becca had never heard of only one. They were always in pairs. Had the second died? Was it flushed? Did it get to be replaced, so no one would know the difference?

"I know you came to see me about something," the counselor prodded gently.

In the end, Ms. Jefferson gave Becca a test and suggested she see a psychologist in town. Maybe she'd flunked, although Ms. Jefferson said it wasn't a pass-fail thing. Adults say things like that so you won't worry.

"Let's make an appointment for you with Dr. Connie."

The psychologist's secretary barely glanced at Becca as she checked the appointment book. Becca wondered if this was to make her feel more comfortable. Instead of staring at her — "so this is what a crazy kid looks like!" — she gave Becca a brief smile and then was busy with her books and her computer. The name on her badge was Linda, comfortably blah — blah dusty hair, blah colorless complexion, blah cream sweater and beige skirt. Becca would have a hard time remembering what she looked like and hoped that Linda felt the same way about her.

"Down to the end of the hall. Go on in. Dr. Connie will be with you in a few minutes."

Troll dolls peeked around at her from behind the books in the floor-to-ceiling mahogany bookcases. They sat on the shelves, swinging their legs or peering over the edges. Why had the Santa Cruz street people living under bridges been named for such charming creatures as if it were derogatory?

Becca took a book down, and then another, all psychology, of course, with titles like *The Basic Writings of Sigmund Freud, Listening with the Third Ear, Psychological Assessment, The Fifty-Minute Hour* and *The Minds of Billy Milligan*. A strange science with its own foreign language. Becca felt as though she had suddenly popped her head above the clouds into a new universe.

She was browsing through *I'm Ugly, You're Ugly, But That's Okay* when Dr. Constance entered — a diminutive woman in a powder blue suit, her face a map of wrinkles amid lush white hair.

Becca replaced the book, slid the naked troll with the orange hair in front where it had been, and asked, "Do I have to lie on the couch?"

"Not unless you want to. Some people find it comfortable."

Becca sat in the black leather recliner. She didn't deserve comfort. Dr. Connie seated herself beside her desk, not behind it.

"So tell me, I understand you lost your brother a few months ago."

That was all it took. Becca burst into tears and couldn't stop, although she kept trying. She'd pluck a tissue from the box beneath the white nurse troll doll, blow her nose, and start to speak when the grief overwhelmed her again. "I'm so sorry, I can't seem to . . ." And then she cried some more. "Really I'm fine . . . This is so embarrassing," she gasped.

"Have you cried much since it happened?"

"I've been too busy looking for him."

14

ALL NIGHT LONG, DAMON'S body ached where the fallen tree towers branches and twigs poked into his back and bottom. Could he build it again and make it so strong that Carl couldn't chop it down? So that the trunk was so hard every time Carl swung his axe it bounced back and hit him in his leg? No, his pee-pee? Damon heard himself groan in his sleep. Where was Becca? She'd been up at the top of the tree, waving encouragement to him. But when it crashed, she was gone. Maybe she was still safe in the sky, waiting for him.

When Damon sat up in bed, naked and shivering in the early morning light and surrounded by the ruins of his precious tree, he discovered to his horror that his sheets were all bloody. Had his tree branches poked him that hard?

"Kenny," he cried out. But his voice was weak, and the next instant he recalled that Kenny was gone.

He began to shake with fear. What had happened to him? Carl had dragged him off into his and Kenny's room. That was all he remembered.

He got up to go to the bathroom. Why did his bum hurt so much? The blood dripped down between his legs.

"Oh-h-h," he cried. "I got blood on the floor. Carl'll be mad at me."

But he couldn't wait to clean up first, because he had to go number one and number two real bad.

Feeling weak, he sank onto the toilet. His pee-pee hurt, but when he tried to make a BM, it hurt so much he cried out and tried to hold it in. It came out anyway and filled the toilet with blood. He screamed in pain and fear.

Then Carl was standing in the doorway in Kenny's red dragon kimono. He had a strange look on his face. Not mad, not disgusted, not evil exactly. Maybe a tiny bit afraid?

"Take a bath."

"But I'm bleeding."

"We'll have the doctor check you out. Clean yourself up and get dressed."

"What's wrong with me?"

"Stop sniveling. You're not a virgin anymore, that's all. Snap to it."

Damon wiped himself and filled the tub. Maybe the water would stop the bleeding. He wasn't supposed to bathe alone. Guess Carl forgot. The hot water turned pink, and he felt so dizzy that everything started to go black. When he got out, he didn't think he was bleeding as much, but the towel was bloody. He held it to his rear end, so he wouldn't bleed again in the hall. On his way to his room, he heard Carl's low voice on the phone.

"Just a little blood."

Damon wadded up a whole bunch of tissue and stuffed it in his crack before he pulled on his underpants. Still woozy, he was slower than usual getting dressed. His pants pressed the hurt so much that he tugged them down around his hips. He fumbled with his scarf, trying to make his fingers go and looking into the mirror as Kenny had taught him.

"Does the mirror approve?" he asked weakly. This reminder of Kenny provided faint comfort. If he could picture Kenny, Kenny might return.

To Damon's astonishment, his wasn't the only reflection. Another face stared back at him, the boy he'd seen at the studio, maybe Mickey's age, dressed in a long black coat and hat, purple shirt, brocade vest, and a silver tie, all too big for him as if he hadn't grown into them yet. Damon wheeled around, but there was no one behind him. He turned back to the mirror. The older boy smiled at him and put a hand on his shoulder. Damon could feel the pressure, but no one stood beside him. He rubbed his eyes and shook his head.

"Don't you remember us, Damon?" asked the older boy in a slightly clipped accent like Trent's that Kenny had called "British." His eyes were hazel — nice eyes, Damon thought.

"How do you do that?" Damon asked.

"Do what?"

"You're in the mirror, but you're not out here."

"Easy when you know how. Don't you remember how we helped you last night?" The glass rippled slightly like the surface of a pool when you skim a flat rock across it, and Damon thought he could just make out the vague outlines of other people. Then the glass was still again, and there were just the two of them.

Damon shook his head. He didn't remember anything about last night.

"I'm Gregory. When Carl hurt you, we took you out of his bed into the closet and up through the hole in the ceiling to the attic. Remember now?"

Damon squinched up his face in concentration. Yes, he did think he was beginning to remember.

"I don't 'member the attic."

"We played Candyland with Robbie."

"Damon, are you ready?" Carl asked, coming into the room. "Who are you talking to?"

"I'm just asking the mirror if it approves," Damon said quickly.

"One of Kenny's silly sayings. Never mind the scarf. We're only going to the doctor."

"What's he going to do to me?"

"More horrible things than you can possibly imagine."

"How many times do I have to say it?" Doctor Phillip demanded. A granddaddy with thin white hair over a red apple head, he smelled of nasty medicines. He lay Damon on the examining table and began to pull his pants down, but Damon clung to them, whimpering. "I won't hurt you," he smiled, then scowled up at Carl.

"So I tore him a new one, so what?"

"He needs stitches. He should go to the hospital." Dr. Phillip smiled at Damon as he said it, as if he were making Damon a present.

"Those buggers ask too many questions," said Carl. "When I brought Damon One in, I ended up into my lawyer for thousands to get me off. Fortunately, we got Judge Flaherty."

"Club member," Dr. Phillip nodded.

"Sew him up here. You've done it before. That's what you get overpaid for."

"There's nothing overpaid for what I do. I'm taking a big risk. I'm supposed to report it," he snapped at Carl, then turned and smiled at Damon.

"Just do it. I'm late for work."

"You're going to sleep, Damon. And when you wake up, it'll still hurt a bit, but soon you'll be good as new." Dr. Phillips assistant wheeled in a metal canister that he said was gas. "I'm going to put this mask over your face. You've worn masks before, haven't you?"

"Halloween," Damon said hoarsely.

"Halloween, that's right. Bright boy! Breathe just as you usually do. The gas will help you sleep. You won't feel a thing. What do you want to dream about?"

"Mom and Dad and Becca."

"Shut the fuck up!"

Now the mask was in place, but Damon didn't like the smell of it and tried to struggle away. Carl got a lock on his head.

"Stop squirming, you miserable kid."

"Easy, Carl, easy. They all try to get out from under. It's natural."

"Kenny," Damon called. "I want my Kenny."

"Kenny's gone to visit his stupid brother, remember?"

"By the way, I should check Nate's lesion again. And Mickey needs his contact lenses, and their shots are all way past due."

But Dr. Phillips voice was fading. Even panic fading.

When he awakened, Dr. Phillip said cheerfully, "All done. Here's a prescription for pain medication." He tore off a slip of paper and handed it to Carl. "Don't exceed the dosage. He should be feeling a lot better in about a week. And for Gods sake, don't mess around with him until then. Or I won't be responsible for the consequences."

"Don't worry. He can mess with me instead."

Carl didn't fill the prescription because he was late. He took Damon to the studio instead, where he unceremoniously planted him on the stool.

"Ow, ow, that hurts," Damon cried out.

"Stay," Carl barked.

A few minutes later, Damon was so woozy he started to slide off the stool.

"What's wrong with Damon?" Mickey asked.

"Nothing that concerns you." Carl picked Damon up and dumped him on the bed. "We'll do the beach scene today."

As the gas wore off, the pain began again, only much worse.

"Oh, no," Damon cried. "Oh, oh, oh."

"What's the matter with the angel kid?" Mr. Martingale asked.

"Nothing that a whipping wouldn't cure."

"He doesn't look well enough for that."

"Shut the fuck up," Carl gritted at Damon. "We can't have your groans in the middle of this scene."

Flip and Hank were on the beach throwing a ball. They were fully dressed, but every time one of them dropped the ball, he had to take off a piece of clothing. It wasn't an honest game, though. When Flip had dropped the ball twice in a row and was down to his undershorts, Carl said, "Okay, Hank, your turn." Hank dropped the ball and had to take off his shirt. Stupid game, Damon thought through the haze of pain.

Mickey crawled onto the bed beside Damon and whispered, "What happened to you? As if I didn't know."

Tearfully, Damon told him, "Carl hurt me in my rear end, I think." He couldn't really remember.

"Cheer up, kid. Happens to all of us. You stay here. I'll get you something."

A few minutes later he was back with a little blue pill.

"Open your mouth. You'll have to swallow it dry. Know how to do that? Just put it way back on your tongue, that's right. Now swallow. Good job! You'll stop hurting in no time."

Damon began to drift. The pain was gone, and he was feeling good. Mickey was his good friend. He watched them make the movie for a while. Behind them, the mirrors reflected the scene. Like yesterday, there were more people in the mirrors than in the room. But this time he recognized Gregory.

Damon didn't remember much of what happened the rest of the week, except that the ruins of his tree tower were gradually fading away. When he made a fuss about the pain, Carl left him handcuffed to his bed and went out and got him the medicine.

"Maybe this will shut you the fuck up," Carl said, stuffing pills into Damon's mouth without water, although Damon was pretty sure he was only supposed to have just one. Hadn't Dr. Phillip said he shouldn't take too many? No matter. Pills made him feel better, like Mickey's medicine, so he didn't care as much about the hurting. When the bottle ran out, Carl got a big refill.

Even when the pain subsided, Damon still said, "Ow, ow, ow," because he liked the way the pills made him feel. He wasn't so upset. They calmed him down and made him forget about the rest of it.

Carl took him to bed every night and made him do "the nasty." That's what the boys called it when they were playing. The first night, Damon thought he was going to choke to death. Then he thought he was going to throw up. Suddenly, he remembered from Halloween what a great defense this was. Carl didn't like hurling, and he didn't like anybody else doing it either. It made his own stomach tighten up and turn over. Carl would curse and stop whatever he was doing to Damon if he said he was sick. Trouble was, then Carl would beat him. His fists were harder than anything Kenny had said he got beaten with. A pudding spoon would be a feather compared to Carl's fist. At least, Damon thought so. So he couldn't use the "hurl defense" every time.

One night in Carl's bed, what Carl was doing to him was particularly disgusting. Damon couldn't stand it, and he thought he was going to throw up for real, except he'd used that excuse last night, and Carl had beaten him something awful. Keep doing it or get beaten up? Damon was in an agony of indecision.

Suddenly, he found himself standing in the corner right beside the dresser, with Carl's fancy gold hairbrush and jewelry case and the picture of the old woman and the younger one so full of themselves. How had he gotten here? It made no sense. Carl was still doing those disgusting things, but nobody was there. Damon started to giggle. Carl was doing it to himself. Then, as Carl raised himself up in his bed, Damon saw himself underneath him. How could that be? How could a person be in two places at once? Maybe that was his body with Carl, and where he stood in the corner was what Becca called his "mind" or his "soul," an invisible something like a ghost that everybody's got inside them. Or, if that was the real Damon in bed with Carl, who was he? Could he possibly be someone else? Robbie, maybe? Even then, he'd have a body, and how could he possibly have gotten out of it?

And if he could get out of his body, why was he staying here? Why wasn't he skedaddling home? He could ask somebody directions. "Excuse me, sir. Could you tell me the way to Santa Cruz?" He'd sleep in secret places and maybe fast food restaurants would give him French fries. If Mom was dead like Carl said she was, Bec-Bec would take care of him. He'd promise not to steal her stuff ever again. Before, he'd have been way too scared to run away, but now it was worth anything to get home again.

The next night, when Carl took him into his room, Damon went quietly, wondering if he could get out of his body again. How had he done that? There was no way that he knew of. As Carl began, Damon tried to get out. He tried lifting his shoulders. That didn't work. He took a deep breath and held it. He made himself as light as he could, "light as air, light as air," he told himself over and over. He stared up at the ceiling light. He prayed. "God, get me out of here, please."

Damon was about to throw up for real, when he was floating along the ceiling, watching Carl again. His sickness began to fade. Carl went on for a long time, but Damon didn't feel a thing. This would be his secret. His only worry was that he still didn't know how he did it, and someday he might be trying with all his might to get out again, and he might not be able to. What was the last thing he'd done before he got here? He'd prayed. That was it. God was lifting him out of his body when things got too bad. "Thank you, God," he breathed. "I owe you."

After Carl finished, he rolled over onto his back. To Damon's amazement, there was that other little boy lying underneath him. He was about eight, Madam Adam's age, and he was crying but doing as Carl told him.

Then he heard Gregory's voice whispering, "That's Leroy. It's his job to take the pain, and he's good at it."

Damon looked around, but Gregory was nowhere in sight, not even in the mirror. On the floor were Leroy's clothes, apparently — paint-stained pants and shirt, no undershorts. Damon guessed that Leroy was an artist like Kenny and Trent. But Damon still didn't understand why he did it. Why would doing the nasty with Carl be anybody's *job*?

Now, this was silly. Carl would have noticed if he suddenly had a different little boy in his bed. Wouldn't he have asked him, "Who are you, and where did you come from?" Wouldn't he have said, "Get the fuck out of my bed. Where's Damon?" Didn't he see that Leroy's nose was pushed up, and his eyes were brown, and his voice (when he grunted) sounded like a foghorn? Leroy didn't look anything like Damon. Then again, maybe Carl didn't care. Maybe he even knew Leroy. Maybe Leroy was from the orphanage. Maybe Carl didn't care *who* did "the nasty" for him as long as it got done.

Damon was mightily puzzled, but not too upset by this strange experience. The fact was, he got to escape, and that was what was important. He'd find out later how and why. Maybe he'd ask Kenny. Kenny would know.

The next day, Carl left him alone for a few minutes to run to the market next door and buy some bread and stuff. He didn't even tie him up because he was in a hurry.

"You're damaged goods, anyhow," he said to Damon. "Nobody'd pick you up."

Damon grabbed the chance to look for the stairs to the attic that Gregory had told him about. He opened Carl's and Kenny's closet door, and there were a lot of clothes in there. In fact, it was stuffed. There was a square in the ceiling that they kept shut tight so mice couldn't get in. But there was no way to get up there without a ladder. Probably no attic either. Gregory had fibbed.

Damon dreamed he heard Kenny calling to him.

"Damon, my sweet dear boy. Did you miss me? I missed you so. I thought of you every single day."

Damon opened his eyes, and in the light from the carousel bedside lamp, he saw his Kenny.

"Kenny, oh Kenny, you're back." He flung his arms around Kenny's neck and pulled him down. "Oooh, Kenny, you stink."

"What do you expect after a four-hour wait for a bus and a three-hour ride crammed up against the great unwashed? We stopped in every town in the Bay Area — Concord, Milpitas, Walnut Creek, Hayward, Tuscaloosa, Ponderosa."

"And Stinky Town?"

"And Stinky Town."

"And Bathroom Place?"

"And Bathroom Place. I thought we'd never get here. I'm going right in to take a shower so my Damon loves me again."

"You're still in disguise."

"Is he irresistible or what?" he turned to ask Carl who, of course, was lounging in the doorway, sucking on a pepperoni stick. Carl didn't answer, and Kenny seemed to take that as agreement.

"Are you really really back forever?"

"Yes, of course, I'm back, sweetheart. I didn't expect to be gone so long, but it was just one problem after another. I'm sorry it didn't work out with Trent and Adam. Did Carl take good care of my sweet little boy?"

Carl didn't tell Damon to shut the fuck up. He didn't have to. Damon wasn't about to say anything against him. Anything at all. He wasn't sure what would happen if he did. Kenny was here now, but if Kenny left again, Carl would hurt him worse than anything. Maybe murder him.

"And you'll never leave again?" he asked Kenny.

"Of course not, my little chocolate drop. I told you. Now, I've got to go change out of these wretched clothes."

"Put on your Kenny clothes," Damon told him.

"You want me to put on my Kenny clothes? I'll do just that, then."

"And your sparkly stud like mine."

"Then I'll look like myself again, won't I?"

"Don't forget to ask if the mirror approves."

"Sickening," mumbled Carl, disappearing down the hallway.

"Have you been doing that while I was gone? Oh, you good boy! Remember, you have to keep yourself looking beautiful so everyone will love you."

Damon whispered to Kenny, "Then you'll meet Gregory."

"Gregory?"

"Uh-huh. He's nice."

"A new little friend?"

"In the mirror."

Kenny frowned, but then seemed to figure he'd misunderstood.

"You tell me about him later. Now I want you to sleep, and tomorrow we'll go to the studio and paint important pictures and have hamburgers and fries just like always. Would you like that?"

"M-m-m-m."

"Hurry up and go to sleep. It'll be tomorrow before you know it."

"Like Christmas?"

"Just like Christmas."

"And Kenny, oh Kenny, come here, I got to tell you something."

"What's that?"

"It's my birthday."

Kenny checked the door to be sure Carl wasn't there. "No kidding, really?"

"It's March."

"What day?"

"Today and tomorrow."

"What about yesterday?"

"Yesterday, too."

"And I have to buy you a present for every day, huh?"

"Uh-huh," Damon brightened.

"What a scam you've got going, my little Damon."

Damon could hear the shower running, and he pictured Kenny getting out of his stinky clothes and tossing them into the white wicker laundry hamper, and rubbing his vanilla soap all over his body with the curly little white hairs on his chest and between his thighs all lathered up, and then letting the water run over him, the foam trickling down his legs. The water stopped, and Damon knew Kenny was toweling himself off and singing under his breath.

A few minutes later, Damon heard the bathroom door open, and Kenny padded down the hall to the bedroom where he and Carl talked about his trip as Kenny unpacked.

Damon was so excited to have Kenny back that he couldn't sleep. He got up and padded over to the doorway where he could hear Kenny and Carl more clearly. In the hall, he slid down to the floor. He noticed the blood spots were gone. Had Carl cleaned them? Never mind. He wanted to hear Kenny say again that he was back forever and would never leave.

"I swear, Timmy doesn't have the sense he was born with. He's scared to death of Mom, even though she's in the hospital and can't do anything to him. Oh, don't drop those crumbs, here, use your plate," Kenny mimicked Timmy in a high scared voice. "Mom'll have a cow. Even if you sweep them up, she knows you dropped them. There's always one you missed, for God's sake! I mean, yeah, in the old days, she could whip us with a broomstick or a belt or anything else that came in handy. But now she's flat on her back with a hose up every hole, she's not about to take after us."

"She's still alive, then?"

"Well, to hear her tell it, she's on her deathbed. To hear the doctors and the nurses tell it, she's on her deathbed. She's got them all snookered — neighbors, social workers, postman, the lot of them. She doesn't fool me. She can't die. If she does, she'll be one of those freaks who suddenly sits up on her gurney in the morgue and starts ordering the morticians around. Neither God nor the Devil would have her, that's for sure. They're used to giving the orders, not taking them."

Carl was laughing, and Damon could imagine his chest shaking up and down, his chest where his heart was, which was why they called it a hearty laugh. No wonder Kenny loved him. Why couldn't Carl be that way with him?

"So did you visit her?"

"Timmy made me. He was too scared to go alone," Kenny said in his disgusted voice.

"I'll bet she was glad to see you?" Carl teased.

"Are you kidding? 'Who the Hell are you?' she asks, like she doesn't recognize me. 'And what the Hell are you doing in my room? Timmy, get that stranger out of here.' 'But Mom, you remember Kenny. Your son. He came back to visit you.' 'Get the fuckin' Hell out of here. Nurse! Nurse!' she's screaming and stabbing that button like the rooms on fire. 'Just came to wish you more of the same,' I says."

"Ha! Good one!"

"Timmy didn't think so. He wouldn't speak to me for the rest of the day. Until I said I might as well go home, then he gave in. So anyway, that was my reunion with my long lost mother. God, Carl, how can I ever thank you? You saved me from all that. If you hadn't, I'd be like Timmy, afraid of my own shadow."

It had never occurred to Damon that his shadow was scary.

"You can give me another hug," Carl said.

Then there was hugging and kissing, and Damon knew what they were doing. Thank goodness, Kenny was back to do the nasty with Carl so Damon and Leroy wouldn't have to.

Damon's head sagged to his chest, and he was almost asleep when Kenny started banging around the room again.

"Yes, that was the last of my dear departing mother." Damon could hear the rattling of hangers. Kenny must be hanging his clothes up in the closet.

"Good riddance, I say. So where's Timmy in all this?"

"Likely to inherit something so he can keep the apartment. Not much, just a big closet, really. She's got the kitchen with the bed. Biggest room in the place. Real old time with those white five-sided porcelain tiles on the bathroom floor. I forget what you call them."

"Pentagons? God, that is old."

"They made kitchens big in those days. Timmy sleeps in the foyer they call the living room."

"Will you get anything?"

"Not bloody likely. Timmy will give me whatever junk he doesn't want and remind me about it every time he hits me up. But what do I need anything for? I have my dear Daddy Carl, who gives me everything my heart desires, even my little boy."

"But what's Timmy going to do? He's still got to earn money for food and the like, without his Mum's social security coming in."

"I told him. He says he can't get another job. He's already been fired from a hundred of them. Moving man, garbage collector, bricklayer, factory parts assembler, roofer — you name it, he's done it. He says there isn't room on job application forms to list all the jobs he's been hired and fired from."

"What? You mean he's listing them *all*?"

"With dates of employment. January 16 to January 23, February 6 to March 1."

"You've got to be kidding!"

"He says the forms say he has to. I told you, he doesn't have the brains he was born with. And what he has are pretty pickled with cheap wine, let me tell you. I said to him, 'Timmy, you don't list all the times you've been fired' 'It says to.' 'You just list one job you've got a good reference from that you've been at the longest. Then you say you had to take care of your dying mother for a year or whatever!' He's got the perfect excuse, for crying out loud."

"Other deadbeats would kill for that excuse."

"Oh, Timmy's not a deadbeat. He's just immature. So I helped him fill out applications, and wasn't that fun! Among them, an application to the local community college. Guess what he wants to study?"

"I haven't a clue."

"Art."

"He's going to earn a living painting pictures?"

"I don't think earning a living is much on his mind."

At that moment, Kenny came out of the room in his red dragon kimono, carrying a load of dirty clothes for the washing machine.

"Damon, what are you doing there?"

Carl appeared behind Kenny, arms around his waist, and Kenny leaning back into him.

"I couldn't sleep," Damon said quickly. "I need my pills is all."

"What pills?"

"In the medicine cabinet. On the top shelf."

Kenny dropped his load of laundry to the floor and was back with the pills in a flash, as Carl scowled at Damon.

"What do you need pills for?" Kenny asked.

"For the hurt."

"Why would you hurt?" Kenny was reading the label. "Dr. Phillip! Carl! Why did you have to take Damon to Dr. Phillip? What did you do to him?"

"Nothing. Nothing. Kid fell, that's all."

"Is that all that happened, Damon? Did you fall?"

Damon started to cry.

"I don't 'member," he said. "Are you going to leave again?"

"Not without you, I'm not."

Damon got to his feet and limped as quickly as he could back to his bed, where Kenny knelt down beside him. He was so upset he was shaking all over.

"Now, here's a pill."

"I need sixteen."

"You only need one. That's what it says. Oh, I forgot the water."

"I don't need water. I swallow it dry, like Mickey said."

"Proper little junkie, aren't we? Where does it hurt? Show me."

Slowly, very slowly, Damon pulled down his pajama bottoms.

15

KENNY WAS SITTING AT the dining table in his red dragon kimono, nibbling English muffins with raspberry jam and reading the paper. The bedroom door opened on an empty room, a sign that Carl had left for work already. Damon inhaled the sweet free air. Sun streamed in from the window, and through the curtain Damon could see the people parading back and forth, "but they can't see us," Gregory whispered. Damon jumped and looked around for him, but Gregory wasn't even in the dining room mirror. "Like being invisible," Gregory added. Invisible to the passing people? To Kenny? Safe?

"My, we slept late this morning, didn't we? Come over here, dear boy, so I can get a good look at you in the light. You don't look well, not well at all. Want a muffin?" He held out his own.

Damon hadn't slept for listening to the horrible fight between Kenny and Carl. Would Kenny leave Damon again and go back to his brother? Relieved that Kenny was still here this morning, Damon crawled into the chair beside him and took the muffin drippy with butter and jam.

"Your food always tastes better," he said.

"And we're going to see that you get plenty of it," Kenny said. "Know what we're going to do after breakfast?"

"Uh-huh. We're going to go to the studio and eat French fries."

Kenny threw back his head and laughed, the diamond in his ear glittering in the light from the chandelier. Damon knew his own glittered, too, but he couldn't see it.

"You make it sound as though that's what we do at the studio. We eat fries. Well, we'll do all that, but first we're going on an adventure."

"What kind of 'venture?"

"We're going to pack up all our clothes and move out."

"You mean we're not going to live here anymore?" The pictures of the boys who had befriended him in his loneliness looked down sadly, even the April boy licking an ice cream cone on the kitchen calendar. They seemed to know already and to be saying goodbye.

"We're going to camp out in the studio until we find a place of our own. Trent's got sleeping bags we can borrow. Won't that be fun?"

"Will we have a tent?"

"We don't need one, silly. We don't need one here, do we? The walls and ceiling shelter us from the rain."

"Can we take my toys?"

"I only have one luggage cart for our suitcases of clothes this trip. We'll come back for them."

"Is Carl moving, too?"

"No, Carl's staying here. The studio's his, but he won't bother us there. I've told him if he so much as — well, never mind, we'll be okay. We'll visit Carmine at his gallery. That's where I'm supposed to have my show in a few weeks. Remember it got put off again? I'll get an advance for my paintings. Then we'll have enough to live on."

At Trent's, an armful of yellow and purple flowers splashed across the hall table, and a new golden puppy dog darted out at them, barking happily. He made straight for Damon, who laughed with glee and bent down to pet him. The dog licked his fingers and wagged so hard he looked as though he'd send his little body spinning off into space.

"That's Noodles," said Trent. "At least, temporarily. You won't tell Carl?"

"Why would I tell Carl?"

"We're not supposed to have pets. I've got the sleeping bags here and a couple of pillows." He scooted them over to Kenny. He was still in his pajamas. "I'd ask you to stay here but — "

"Oh, no, we'll be fine in the studio."

"You know what a temper Carl has."

"It's only temporary."

"It's just that, if he comes here looking for you, we don't want to be in the line of fire."

"He won't. I've got too much on him. He'll leave us alone."

"We're friends with both of you," Trent said.

"I know, I know. We'll be out of your hair in no time. We're getting a place of our own as soon as I get some money, although I'm not sure how much I need. Carl's always handled the finances."

"You're definitely split, then?"

"Forever."

"Sad. We always said that if anyone was going to stay together, it would be you two. What happened?"

"Nothing. We broke up that's all."

"Carl hurt me," Damon ventured.

"Oh!" Trent's eyes fluttered from Kenny to Damon to Kenny again, and Damon had the feeling that Trent knew just how Carl had hurt him.

"Have you heard anything about Adam?"

"It's good news," Trent said with tears in his eyes. "Our friends say his parents had moved, but they came down to pick him up. He's in a hospital now. A very, very sick boy."

"What's wrong with him?" Damon asked. "Did he got to have stitches?"

"Damon!"

"Did a bad man hurt him?"

"Oh, no, nothing like that. We're just glad he's being taken care of."

"Maybe you'll get him back someday," said Kenny.

"I don't think so."

Through the door, Damon could see that Madam Adam's room was empty.

"We could stay in Adam's room," suggested Gregory suddenly. Damon didn't think Kenny had heard, so he nudged him.

"Gregory says we could stay in Adam's room," he repeated.

"Who's Gregory?" asked Trent.

"Some friend Damon met while I was gone. You heard Uncle Trent. It's not convenient."

"It's not convenient," Damon told Gregory.

Trent and Kenny stared.

"Where should we have our bedroom?" Kenny asked as they walked around the studio. "Where do you think, Damon?"

Damon was mystified. It was all one room. How could they make a bedroom unless they built a wall?

"Should we have it in the bathroom? We could lay out our sleeping bags in there."

Damon shook his head.

"Yuck! Suppose one of us wants to sleep and the other one wants to go smelly?" He wasn't sure if he or Gregory had said this.

"How about by the front door?"

"Then we'd be in the way. We couldn't get out."

"We'd stumble all over ourselves. Where do you think? Under 'Phase,' maybe?" He nodded toward one of his green ladders. "That would be appropriate, wouldn't it? We're going through a transition, you and I, from one phase to another."

"It's bad luck to be under a ladder."

"Oh, you darling boy, you're absolutely right. There's plenty of room under my 'Diversity Mural,'" he nodded toward the coffee-colored wall. "Room for everyone, actually. I don't think we should have 'Political Perspective' in our room — it's so — so orange."

"How about on top of a ladder?"

"On top of 'Phase?'"

"No, one of the shorter ones."

"How would we get up there?"

"We'd climb." Damon picked up a bag, hauled it over to a green ladder and made climbing motions. "There. We're nice and safe up here. Carl can't get us unless he chops it down."

Kenny laughed at him.

"Oh, Carl can't chop it down. That ladder's made of a special steel that can't be chopped."

In the corner by the ladders, they lay their sleeping bags side by side, fluffed the pillows, and then hung up clothes on the rungs of the only real ladder in the room.

After a lunch of burgers, fries, and shakes, they returned to the studio to paint.

Then, the weirdest thing happened. Damon was standing at the little easel that Kenny had bought him. Suddenly, he wasn't. He was sitting on a rung of a ladder right up there on the wall, and in his place was the boy Gregory called "Leroy," the one who had saved him by doing "the nasty" with Carl. Leroy was about eight and wore paint-stained pants, a denim shirt, and a baseball cap with a tree on the front. He must have done a lot of painting to get his clothes in that state. Damon watched him, but he couldn't see what he was doing from the ladder. He felt himself getting sleepy and lay down on a rung, which was surprisingly wide enough for him, like a little shelf.

The next thing he knew, Kenny had walked over from the nail he was painting, looked at Leroy's painting, and exclaimed, "Damon!"

Damon assumed he was calling him. He slid down the ladder and ran over. Then it was him standing in front of the painting, a portrait of Becca in her white blouse with the embroidered collar and pink sweater. Her eyes had little trees in them that were reflections, and her dark hair framed her face with every strand perfectly in place. That was something Leroy was able to do for her that she couldn't do for herself. She stood against the sky in the backyard, only the fence wasn't there. Neither was the Bergmann house. Damon thought that was much better.

"That's my sister, Bec-Bec."

"Not bad!" Kenny exclaimed. "Kind of retro."

"Is retro good?"

"Well, it isn't modern, but it's good for a kid. I mean, I can even tell what it is. It's not like anything else you've painted. If you can paint people this well, why are you painting silly landscapes?"

"I didn't really paint it," Damon confessed.

"Shhhh," hissed Gregory in his ear. "It's our secret."

Kenny's forehead wrinkled.

"Well, you've been standing right here all afternoon. Who else painted it?"

Confused, Damon whispered, "I don't know."

"Oh, you know what that is?" Kenny asked, taking him by the shoulders. He bent closer, face to face, his sweet breath blowing Damon's hair in that brotherly way he had when he wanted to share something special. "Sometimes when we're doing a real important project, we're so into it we forget we're doing it. That's all. You just forgot."

"Not a word," warned Gregory.

Every day, Carl came by to fight with Kenny. Then Kenny sent Damon out of the studio to sit in the hall on the stairs to Trent and Barry's place so he wouldn't hear; but, of course, he heard every word.

"How could you do that to him?" Kenny would say.

And "I trusted you."

"You didn't trust me. You trusted Trent and Barry. It backfired, that's all."

"I never thought you'd hurt him."

"You did so, or you'd have left him with me in the first place."

"I thought you might get a little rough with him. Nothing like that."

And again, "You've ruined him. That poor innocent boy."

"You just wanted him for yourself."

"I'd never hurt him."

"What a crock!"

"You'd better stay away from him if you know what's good for you."

Damon had no idea what Kenny was warning Carl he'd do. Certainly, not beat him up. Kenny was no good with his fists. "Marshmallows," whispered Gregory. "Sponges," blasted Leroy in his foghorn voice. Whatever it was, it scared Carl off.

Carl always slammed out of the studio, making a fist at Damon, while Kenny rushed to him.

"Don't you touch him! I warn you."

After Carl left, Kenny would sink down onto the floor and cry, great big shoulder-shaking sobs, saying, "I love him so much. And I miss him. It's like a pain right here," and he'd point to his chest.

Damon knelt beside him and tried to console him.

"Don't worry, Kenny. I'll never leave you."

After a while, Kenny dried his eyes with his handkerchief that was only supposed to be for show.

"Now, I'll have to wash it," he'd laugh, his eyes red-rimmed. "How can I paint when I'm so upset? Come on. We'll get an early dinner. How about Mexican? Taco salad, that'll be healthy."

"Really?" Damon said dubiously. He remembered Bec-Bec talking about how unhealthy fast food was.

"It's salad, isn't it?"

"We have to move where Carl won't always come barging in on us. We need money. We'll go to Carmine's today. They've put off my show twice." Damon was pretty sure it was more than that. "Three's the charm. I'll get an advance on my sales. We'd better bring a little something to tempt him. Now let me see. Which painting shall I bring? Which one? They're all so good." And Kenny moved from painting to painting, contemplating it as if he'd never seen it before.

At last, Kenny selected his most recent, "Nuts and Bolts," each nut and each bolt exactly like the other in a line, gray on gray with yellow and red highlights. Damon had learned to praise Kenny's work as super, but Gregory whispered that Leroy said Kenny'd got the shadows wrong.

Into a big black portfolio it went, with straps to hold it in place and a zipper across.

"Can I take mine, too?" Damon asked.

"Of course, dear boy, why not? Let's wrap it in bubbles."

The Bel'Occhio Gallery was in what Kenny called "the Mission warehouse district," a huge brick edifice with neon signs all over it, announcing the name in orange, and "Fine Art" in red, and "Open" in green, and "Layaway Available" in blinking yellow.

"Bel'Occhio means 'good eye' in Italian. There, now you know a foreign language. Better than 'evil eye.' I'm not sure if it means people who buy here have a good eye for art, or they'll have good luck. A fine name for a gallery, don't you think?"

The front was all glass, of course, with art works on easels in the windows, and hanging on the walls behind. As they went through the glass door, it seemed to Damon that Kenny's footsteps got softer, like the footsteps of his parents entering church when he was Robbie, and they all attended together.

They stood just inside, Kenny seeming unsure as to how exactly to proceed. An African mask leered at them with colorful red and blue feathers hanging from its head; a red, black, and white button blanket covered the wall behind it; a syrupy blue glass urn stood on a pedestal to one side; an enormous yellow hammock with white feathers swooped down from the ceiling next to a pink Indian print blanket. The whole was encircled by a bunch of neon tubing that went on and off while a car battery beeped. Damon felt bewildered as Kenny identified all these for him.

A saleswoman approached them, her neck stretching toward the ceiling like the bronze bird in the corner, standing on one leg at the pond's edge. Kenny started to ask for Carmine but found his voice had disappeared and he had to clear his throat several times.

"Tell him it's Kenny Warhol."

"Who?"

"Kenny Warhol. As in Andy. I'm having an exhibit here in a few weeks."

"Oh. Do you have a card?"

Kenny put down his portfolio and made a show of fumbling through his pockets, saying, "I think I left them at home." But Damon was pretty sure he didn't have any. Damon had never seen them, and he'd seen everything else of Kenny's. At that instant, a man strode out of the back room, and Kenny's face lit up. "Carmine, Carmine, how are you?" he said warmly, grabbing his case and half-running towards him.

Carmine was an older man with wisps of hair above his ears and the perfect nose and full lips of a Greek God, as Kenny had described him to Damon periodically. A silk business suit encased his not inconsiderable bulk, and what Kenny told Damon later was a "foulard" encircled his throat. Silver rings covered his fingers to the first knuckle. They must be heavy. Apparently on some other errand, he swiveled his head and stared at Kenny blankly. Then his blankness turned to irritation. Kenny held out his free hand, as if expecting Carmine to kiss it, saying,

"It's been too long. Always phone calls, never in person."

"You could visit, you know. Just to keep up with the scene."

"I'm so busy painting," Kenny fumbled.

Now Carmine's eyes fell on Damon, his face softening. "And who is this lovely boy? A new addition?" His eyes fluttered from Damon to Kenny to Damon again. "Come here, dear heart, let's get a look. Yes, lovely." He took him by the shoulders and spun him around slowly as Kenny introduced him. "So, Kenny, what can I do for you?"

"I came to ask you for a little advance on my exhibit. Just a small one."

"It's a small exhibit. What did you bring?"

Kenny unzipped his portfolio and removed his new canvas, holding it to the light.

"It's brand new," Kenny said proudly. "So. What do you think?"

"A bit familiar, Kenny."

"Familiar! Well, of course, they're familiar. They're nuts and bolts." Kenny didn't add "for God's sake," but Damon could feel it coming.

"A tad retro."

Kenny went pale.

"What do you mean, 'retro'?"

"You know what 'retro' means, Kenny." Damon noticed that the woman called "Gina" was rearranging her desk, pushing the tape dispenser from the left to the right by the wire basket filled with papers. Then she pushed it back to its original spot. "Nuts and bolts went out a year ago, at least," Carmine shrugged, as if he was not to be held accountable for the vagaries of the market. "Paint by numbers was a seventies thing."

"But these are original," Kenny reasoned.

Carmine shook his head. "It's cups and saucers this year." He pointed to the wall behind them. "Rows of cups, rows of saucers, cups alone with every other cup turned upside down, saucers the same, a cup and matching saucer together, and here, this is brilliant, cups and saucers that *don't* match. Everyone's so busy matching. See how the light strikes the imperfections? Positively highlights them. I'm calling the entire exhibit 'Failure.' Now, *that's* art. I've got boomers bidding on them. It's an actual auction. But even they're fading," Carmine's voice dropped to a confidential tone as if he didn't want anyone else to know. "The hottest new thing is computer disks. They all look the same, but everything on them is different, so they are, too. It's metaphorical, you see. It's the meaning of life. Over here is my prize, written up in *Art Weekly* and *Genius World*." It was a bud vase or test tube filled with yellow fluid and stoppered; inside it was a photo of a bunch of men that Kenny later told Damon was the Congress. "It's called *Piss Government,* and the genius of it is that it keeps evaporating, so you have to keep pissing." Carmine gave a little laugh, adding, "The things I do for art. I told Robert he should add my name to his." Turning to Damon, he said, "Gina, find an Easter egg for our boy."

From a tall distance, Gina held out a cool hand while Carmine took Kenny inside. Gina's wasn't an office at all, just this desk outside Carmine's, where she could see customers come in the door. She handed Damon an egg with a smile and then popped up to greet a man and woman who looked as if they'd never been in a gallery before.

Damon bit into his chocolate egg, which melted in his mouth until only the crunchy nuts were left, as he listened to Kenny plead for an advance. Carmine explained that he was going to have a tough time selling Kenny's bolts and ladders as it was. Customers wanted the latest thing that might become another Warhol. A real one. Probably not, but they could hope, and that was the business Carmine was in, giving the customers hope — like a psychologist — and taking a hefty fee in return. In fact, Carmine stood to lose money on the exhibit and was only doing it as a favor to Carl.

Finished eating his egg and bored with waiting, Damon wandered toward the many rooms of the gallery. Mosaic fish swam across the floor. Neat!

One exhibit featured a bunch of computers piled in a heap on bales of straw. Damon didn't think it was even pretty, but maybe it meant something. In another room, a bunch of clay animals were busy doing human things. A cow in a pink apron stood on her hind legs cooking at a play stove like the one that Becca had when she was little. A horse drove a toy car like Alex's. A goat on a bicycle waved a scarf. An elephant typed. Damon lifted the typing elephant. It was surprisingly light. He carried it over to the stack of computers and put it on top of a bunch of disks. In still another room, a huge plain wooden cross hung on the wall, surrounded by smaller crosses made out of foil or wrapping paper with all kinds of dolls in the middle of them, Trolls with huge pee-pees, Barbies with nipples down to their waists, other crosses of vegetables — zucchini, celery, and green onions with tomato blood. The celery was shriveling.

To his delight, Leroy discovered a bunch of paintings in a back room next to a pile of broken furniture — dim portraits of people wearing old-fashioned hats and gowns in ornate gold frames. Damon felt Leroy's breath stop. Then Carmine and Kenny were there, Carmine saying,

"This is the latest batch from one of our moving companies. They're splendid at finding old art. Keep us well supplied."

"Don't you think it's kind of retro?" Kenny asked, still stung by Carmine's verdict.

"Seventeenth and eighteenth century painting isn't retro, dear boy. It's antique. We have retro clients who are simply mad for this stuff. That bridge with the wagon and horses is a genuine Charles Henshaw."

"Never heard of him."

"I wouldn't brag about it if I were you. These windmills are by Charlotte Buell. Worth a few thousand at least."

"Stolen from one of their customers, undoubtedly."

Damon studied Kenny, his lips pursed, his face and neck pink. Damon had never seen him so angry, not even when he found out what Carl had done to him.

"Who probably didn't even know the value of what they had," Carmine replied. "We'll clean it up and sell it for fifty times what we paid the movers to someone who really appreciates it. Everybody's happy. The movers. Our customers. Us."

"Except the original owners."

"Bad luck happens. What do you have there, dear boy?" Carmine asked Damon, who handed over his package

Carmine unwrapped it on Gina's desk.

"Very good!"

"Kind of retro," Kenny said savagely.

"Kenny, don't be so upset. You have to learn to take criticism. It's part of being a professional painter. If you visited here more often, you'd find out what's in and what isn't. All my painters absolutely haunt this place. Real artists paint what the customers will buy." Carmine was holding Damon's painting up to the light and turning it every which way. "I like it. Want to sell it? I'll give you five dollars for it," Carmine said.

"Is that enough for an apartment?" Damon asked.

Carmine's head shot up.

"Why? Aren't you still with Carl?"

"Of course we are," Kenny said quickly, and Damon could tell he'd said the wrong thing, although he wasn't sure why. "Damon sometimes gets mad at him."

"I can imagine," said Carmine. "That's quite an operator you have there. Tell you what. I'll give you $50."

"Oh, we can't accept that," Kenny said.

"I think maybe I can get it," Carmine said. "When they hear the boy's age. I'll throw in my commission."

"You mean this painting's worth more than mine?" Kenny said it very quietly but his face and neck deepened from pink to a fiery red.

"Kenny, Kenny, if you were only six and had painted this, I'd pay the same. Gina, take it out of petty cash. Damon here's a comer, aren't you, Damon? Will you come visit your Uncle Carmine sometime, eh?" He put his arm around Damon's shoulders and gave him a squeeze.

Damon nodded, although he wasn't sure what a "comer" was. If Carmine said it and Carmine was giving them enough to rent their own place, then Carmine was right.

"Besides," Carmine added, clapping Kenny on the back and at the same time moving him toward the front door. "*You're* having a show."

On their way home, they stopped for a milk shake, and Kenny said that Carmine's so-called "art" was mostly junk, and the stuff that wasn't, was stolen. It was a side business with moving companies who often picked up estates left by a deceased parent to their grieving children and drove off with the most valuable furniture and paintings. If the owners filed a claim, the movers made them try to prove the value of shipment, but most of them hadn't had their art appraised in years and could only prove it had been worth much less than it was now. Or better yet, the appraisals were on the stolen truck. The movers ended up paying the customers a fraction of their inheritance, if they paid at all. It was one thing for the heirs to sue and win a judgment, and it was altogether another to collect. Then, the driver was free to steal again, and the movers made a pretty penny on sales to people like Carmine, who, of course, had no idea what was going on.

"Sweet racket!" Kenny said in disgust. But Gregory, who understood much more than Damon did, wasn't sure if Kenny's disgust was at the moving companies or at Kenny's own work being labeled with that horrid word.

"What about our apartment?"

"Guess we'll have to stay in the studio a little longer, that's all." Back in the studio, however, Kenny's foul mood didn't last. "I could show these nuts and bolts in different settings. In joists, for instance, in a nut dish, even in a loony bin." He got all excited. "Now *that's* brilliant!"

"What's a loony bin?"

"Where Adam ended up and you will, too, if you don't stop talking to people who aren't there."

Kenny spent the next days painting in a fury to get ready for his show.

"Don't forget to put the shadows in the right places," Damon reminded him.

"What do *you* know about shadows?"

"I don't. Leroy told Gregory that all the light's supposed to come from one place, like the sun or a light bulb."

"You know, I'm getting real sick of Gregory and his friend Leroy."

16

"YOU MUST HAVE A high tissue bill," Becca tried to joke through her tears, "if everyone who comes here cries as much as I do."

It was her sixth visit to Dr. Connie, and Becca hadn't done much else. She plucked another tissue from beneath Nurse Troll, who perched on the lamp base in her white uniform and cap, her arms extended toward Becca in sympathy. "Take all you need," she seemed to say, stroking Becca with her gentle doggie eyes.

"Don't you cry at home?" Dr. Connie asked. Becca thought she resembled a bird, small delicate bones, her suit today a soft dusty rose, white hair a crest. Even the room seemed to smell faintly of roses. Yet, here was Becca, crying in the garden.

"I don't cry. For one thing, I don't have time."

"For another?" When Becca didn't answer, Dr. Connie added the obvious, "You cry here."

"It seems safe."

"Isn't it safe to cry at home?"

"Someone might walk in. Not that much privacy."

"Who would see, besides your family?"

"No one."

"Don't they cry?"

"I never see Mom crying, but her eyes are always red. So I guess she must."

"It's been, what, four months?"

"Going on five."

"Do you think she's feeling better?"

"I suppose she must. She still looks awful, but no worse than after Robbie was taken. But then, she couldn't look any worse. I mean, I can't tell the difference. She's gone back to nursing full time. Dad's quit work and gone to live with his girlfriend and play his saxophone. Mom's pregnant, but Dad says they're not his. Twins, Aunt Cordelia says. 'Mystery meat,' Annalyn calls them. Probably some doctor at the hospital."

"What does your mom say about Robbie being gone?"

"We don't talk."

"Why is that, do you suppose?"

"*I* talk. She doesn't answer."

"Does she listen?"

"She listens, but she doesn't hear."

"Oh, a fine line, but an important one. How long has this been going on?"

"Since Robbie was taken."

"Maybe if she saw you cry, she'd understand a little better how hard it is on you. That you're grieving, too."

"No. She'd say I don't have the right to cry. I'm the one who caused it, aren't I?"

"Is that what you think?"

"I took Robbie to the playground when I wasn't supposed to. Mom distinctly told me to stay home." The next minute, Becca realized that she had slipped into her mother's inflections. Years later, she would trace the start of her separation from her mother to that realization, but now her mother's opinion of her and her own were one and the same.

"But you took him anyway."

"I wanted to meet with Annalyn. It was selfish of me."

"Really? Do you think it's selfish of a little girl to want to play with her friends?"

"Well, no, I guess not, exactly." Becca felt a bit relieved, then guilty about that. So she hastened to add, "But I disobeyed."

"Yes, you disobeyed. Was there some alternative? Could you have had Annalyn come over to your place?"

"You don't understand. When friends come over, Robbie bugs us out of our minds."

"How, exactly?"

Dr. Connie seemed a little like a lawyer in her relentless questioning. Becca had heard that other psychologists sat back and listened, and you could say anything you wanted. Dr. Connie had done just that the first few sessions, but now she questioned everything. Becca wasn't sure which was better, but she was getting to speak of things she couldn't anywhere else without feeling judged. Even Annalyn had limits as to how much she could tolerate.

"He hangs around and listens to our conversation."

"What's wrong with that?"

"Some of it's personal, like interesting guys and things the kids did at school. He doesn't understand much, but he asks questions. And he pesters us to play games."

"Don't you like games?"

"Not Candyland! It's a stupid baby game."

"You're too old for baby games."

"I am," Becca insisted. "Sometimes, when we're alone, I'll play a game with him and let him win. But that's not what I want to do with Annalyn."

"All you and Annalyn want is a few minutes of peace to tell each other what you need to."

"Exactly."

"And when you take him to the park?" Dr. Connie asked.

"He runs off and plays. Then we can talk."

"So it hasn't always been easy having Robbie around."

"No, but I never wanted him dead or anything!" She gasped. She'd actually said the word. Dr. Connie seemed not to have noticed, but Becca amended, "I mean, kidnapped."

"Of course you didn't," Dr. Connie went on. "Still, you caused your little brother to be kidnapped."

"I didn't *cause* it."

"He wouldn't have been kidnapped if you'd stayed at home."

"No, Annalyn wouldn't have seen Nick, and we wouldn't have left him alone, and Robbie would have driven us nuts, but he'd have been safe."

"So it would never have happened?"

"I'm not sure. The police think he was being stalked."

"Then it would have happened anyway?"

"Maybe. I'm not sure."

"I wonder if it's possible to be vigilant every single minute of the time."

"Not every single minute. No."

When it was time to leave Dr. Connie's, it was like coming up for air from a deep dive. Becca had entered the office, noted new details, the handmade clay figure of a cat, how the troll dolls seemed to have moved from one place to another, as if this were their home and they had lives of their own. But then she would submerge herself in the process with Dr. Connie and be unaware of anything else for a whole fifty minutes.

When Becca got home, she was always exhausted. She'd collapse on her bed and sleep. Why these sessions with Dr. Connie should be so draining she didn't know. It wasn't as if she even moved, let alone did anything physically punishing, like the runs she took five days a week. She was tired after those, too, but oddly refreshed.

Dr. Connie's receptionist, Linda, greeted Becca with a little more chatter now. She'd look up from her work, saying, "Becca, there's a new teen magazine," flattering Becca that her interests were older for her age. Linda seemed as discreet as Dr. Connie, and Becca no longer felt threatened by whatever Linda's opinion of her might be. She worked for a psychologist, after all.

Becca never saw Dr. Connie's other clients. When someone was in the waiting room, Dr. Connie ushered the departing client out another door. Becca knew because she'd done the same to her. "Why don't you go out this way instead. Linda will call you about your next appointment." Becca had been surprised until she understood. Even the fact that she was "seeing a shrink" was confidential.

"So actually, Robbie wasn't kidnapped because you went to the park, but because you left him alone for a few minutes," said Dr. Connie at their next session.

"That's right."

"So that he'd be kidnapped?"

"Of course not! I never dreamed he'd be kidnapped."

"It didn't occur to you?"

"Of course not! Who even thinks that will happen? I went to the bathroom with Annalyn because she saw Nick and wanted company while she fixed herself up. That's the truth. I didn't even have to go. Back outside, Robbie was getting into the van."

"And you stood and watched."

"No, I ran after him, yelling and screaming."

"Did you run as fast as you could?"

"Of course I did." Now Becca was heaving as hard as if she were running after the van at this very moment, her last sight of Robbie in his red Pooh sweatshirt, waving to her and yelling something she didn't understand (although she thought it might have begun with, "We're gonna . . ."), platinum-haired Toyman looking back at her in his blue shirt, sleeves rolled neatly to his elbows, earring flashing in the sun, before he hopped in after Robbie, the door slid shut, and the van roared off.

"So you're telling me that Robbie was kidnapped because you went to the bathroom for a couple of minutes?"

"Yes."

"Not because of what Toyman did?"

"I shouldn't have let him out of my sight."

"No, you shouldn't have. But lots of parents and brothers and sisters do. Hasn't your mother ever let you and Robbie out of her sight, perhaps to answer the phone?"

"Well, yes, but then I'm always there to look after Robbie. And no kidnapper's in the house."

"True. But suppose I told you that I'd left my baby girl playing in the tub once to answer the door, just for a second, and she drowned. What would you say?"

"Oh, that's awful. Did that really happen to you?"

"Wouldn't you say I shouldn't have?"

"No, I don't think so."

"Why not?"

"Well, for one thing it would be rude."

"We're talking frankly here. Wouldn't you tell me I shouldn't have left my baby alone?"

"Well, yes, but —"

"But, what?"

Becca struggled for the words.

"It's not fair."

"Why not?"

"You made such a little mistake. And to lose your baby for such a little mistake . . ." Becca broke off, pounding the couch in wordless grief and fury all mixed up. Then she sprang to her feet and paced up and down, trying to get control of herself.

"You think I suffered too harsh a penalty for what I did?" Dr. Connie asked, showing no shock at Becca's behavior, eyes simply following her back and forth.

"Yes, I guess that's it."

"I was human, and I made a mistake?"

Becca took her seat again, leaning forward, twisting her hands.

"Did that really happen with your baby?"

"Not to me. But it's happened to other people. That and lots of things like it. Dads in cars accidentally roll over their toddlers. Mothers accidentally smother their infants in bed while nursing them. And yet, lots of mothers take their babies into their beds with no harm done. And lots of dads roll their cars out of the garage, and thank God, the toddler darts out of the way. Life isn't fair like the ideal criminal justice system, where if you rob a bank, you get ten years, and if you beat up somebody, you get twenty. Sometimes there's no punishment at all for the mistakes we make. Sometimes the punishment's much worse than we deserve."

Becca lapsed into silence, trying to sort it through. Everywhere her eyes wandered in this room, there was something pleasant, the vase of daffodils on Dr. Connie's desk, the yellow troll swinging on the pole lamp, and most of all the books in all their variety of bindings. Becca should try to make her life like that. Still, a result deserved or undeserved was still a result.

"You don't understand. It's just about killed my mom and dad."

"It? What do you mean by 'it'?"

"Robbie being kidnapped." Why did she have to say it?

"Hasn't it been just as bad for you?"

"It's been terrible. The worst thing that ever happened to me."

"Does your mom understand how awful it's been for you?"

"I don't think it's even occurred to her."

"What about your dad?"

"He didn't at first. Then he said they shouldn't have blamed me. I don't think he'd have said that if he didn't know."

"What about your school friends? Besides Annalyn, I mean."

"They haven't a clue. It hasn't happened to them."

"People realize how awful it is for a parent to lose a child, but they don't understand how awful it is for the brother or sister."

"Mrs. Bergmann, our neighbor, says kids are resilient."

"That may be. But it's a terrible thing to lose a brother or sister. They're like your other self. You can confide in them things you can't tell your parents. You live through them in ways you can't with others. You never thought about your own death before, but now, perhaps you do?"

"Every day," Becca said. "If he can be kidnapped, why not me?"

"Do you find yourself thinking someone's following you, perhaps? That you're in the same kind of danger?"

"How did you know?"

"You've mentioned several times that you're careful to always look around when you're on your way home or to the store."

"Oh, yeah."

"It's scary, isn't it?"

"Sometimes I'm scared, and I don't even know why."

"Perhaps you're scared for him. It's perfectly natural to identify with your brother. In a sense, what happens to a brother or sister happens to ourselves. We feel as though we're them. And if we had any part in it at all, we feel endless guilt. So I think it's perfectly okay for you to cry at home, whenever you feel like it. You have a *right* to cry. Those kidnappers took your parents' son, but they took your brother, too."

Becca kept swallowing hard.

"I really don't want to waste the time here crying. It's expensive. Dad says he's paying through the nose."

"Grieving isn't a waste. In fact, crying cleanses us, purifies us even. Research shows that crying helps us secrete the natural painkillers, the endorphins, in our brains."

"I'm still trying to find Robbie. Like looking in the places he might be."

"Do you look for him every day?"

"I did. Not as much now."

"Why is that, do you think?"

"I guess — Her breath was coming short again, a series of little heaves, threatening another downpour — "there doesn't seem to be much point. I mean, I've looked everywhere. He must be someplace else. Or," she stopped.

Dr. Connie nodded her head, a nudge to continue.

"Or maybe not."

"Then where would he be?"

"Buried."

"Somewhere else. Or buried," Dr. Connie said. "Both possibilities. The hard thing is not knowing which. If they found Robbie's body, at least you'd know he wasn't coming back. You'd stop looking for him. You'd have a beautiful service with flowers and music and lots of sympathetic friends. And then, eventually, you'd go on. Now, with this uncertainty, it's very hard to go on, because you don't really know which way to go."

Aunt Cordelia couldn't figure out why Becca slept so much. She kept after Becca to come in for beauty treatments, but Becca said she was headed home to collapse.

"You need a styling cut and a facial, a manicure, and probably a pedicure, too, although I haven't seen your feet. I'm only guessing from the rest of you."

Thanks, Aunt Cordelia!

Without knowing Aunt Cordelia's opinion, Annalyn shared it.

"You look like hell these days, m'dear" she told Becca at lunch in the cafeteria. Becca thought her black pants and gray sweater were fetching and felt hurt at Annalyn's criticism.

"Well, thank you, too," Becca said.

"Your hair's a sight. When last did you cut it? When last did you even wash it? Or your sweater, for that matter?"

She'd washed her hair this morning. It was only after she'd begun blow-drying it that she realized she'd used rinse instead of shampoo.

"What's wrong with my sweater?" The instant she looked down, she saw the spots. Only little ones. Pea soup drops. She simply hadn't noticed.

"I told you, I don't have time. With Dr. Connie and everything."

"And sleeping."

"I can't help it if I'm exhausted. Maybe I've got that chronic fatigue."

"I think it's more likely lazy fatigue. You're looking more and more like a sloppy mess."

"I don't care!"

"Now you've got it. Let's go see your aunt."

"It's Robbie's birthday." March 6.

Annalyn didn't know what to say. A rare occasion.

"Want me to come home with you?" she offered finally.

"No. I think I'll go see how Mom's handling it."

Predictably, Mom wasn't home. Robbie wasn't supposed to have ever existed. Becca opened the door to his room quietly, as if he were still in there, and she didn't want to disturb him. Perhaps asleep or talking to his blocks as he built his tower to the sky.

Everything was as she had left it the last time she'd been in here — was it in January, two months ago? A fine layer of dust had settled over the bureau, the desk, the red bedspread now graying. She ran a finger over the sailboat on his top bookshelf, and a gray spot coated her fingertip. All was decaying, particle by particle, even though she couldn't see it. Robbie's room was on its way to becoming a ruin, like that Greek or Italian town of Pompeii that Mt. Vesuvius erupted over and buried, where curtains and bedspreads had shredded long ago. All that would be left were the hard plastic things, the Legos. Even his blocks would splinter like the wooden beams of old ruins, perhaps new life springing from them.

She must get in here and clean. Clearly, Mom wasn't going to. Cleanliness preserved.

Robbie's room. Was it still? Would it always be?

More of a museum dedicated to the past. He was six, now. "Going on seven," he'd brag, as if talent or effort had led to this accomplishment. If he came back, would he love his room still? Or would he want to change his spread and throw out the sailboat because it was too "babyish." What of Robbie himself? Would he be a taller boy, more gangly, with longer hair a darker, dustier blond, with new words from the places he'd been? If so, Becca would help him catch up to the boy he'd grown to be in the six months he'd been gone. Or the year or two. Whatever Robbie needed.

Becca felt committed to whoever Robbie was. Wherever he was. If . . .

"How do you think you should have handled his birthday?" Dr. Connie asked.

"Maybe with some kind of memorial. Maybe if we'd all gotten together and said prayers around the candles on the cake and talked about him a little. Just sent our love into the air with the smoke. Of course, none of us would have eaten the cake. Or maybe all of us should have gone to church together. Except that would have been kind of hypocritical because we aren't that religious."

"Do you think that, if you were, it might help?"

Becca paused to give that possibility some thought.

"I think it might. It helps other people in trouble."

"And it's something you can do on your own, you know. Attend church services occasionally. You don't have to go with someone."

"I suppose I could."

"Where have you gone before?'

"St. James Episcopal."

"That's a nice one. Very positive in their outlook. Why don't you try it?"

"I might do that."

"As to Robbie's birthday, maybe your parents ignoring it was their way to stop blaming you."

They talked some more about what it should have been like until Becca felt as though she had memorialized Robbie just by speaking about him.

"What I don't understand is, how would you have protected him?" Dr. Connie asked, returning to the subject at their next meeting like a musical variation on a theme.

Becca frowned in puzzlement. How would she have protected him? That was obvious, wasn't it?

"I just would have."

"Let's go through it step by step. Perhaps it would help you visualize if you leaned back in your chair and closed your eyes."

Becca wasn't nearly as skittish about giving up control as when she first came.

"Feet flat on the floor, hands comfortably in your lap, that's right. Take a deep breath. And another. You're sitting at the playground talking to Annalyn. Where exactly?"

"On the bench at the edge of the walk, near the monkey puzzle tree."

"Is it a sunny day or a cloudy one?"

"It's a beautiful sunny day," Becca said, taking a deep breath. "That's another reason Annalyn and I wanted to go."

"And Robbie — where is he at this moment?"

"He's on the slide. He likes to climb the steps. Then when he gets to the top, he turns around and yells to the other kids, 'I'm king of the world.' They get mad and yell at him to hurry and go down, and he does."

"Landing in the sand."

"Yes."

"Okay. Now Robbie's playing on the slide. And then what do you think happens? Does Toyman come up to him and catch him coming down the slide maybe?"

"I don't know."

"Well, when he's contacted Robbie in the past, has he just come up to him while you were all together in the mall?"

"No. He waits until we're doing something else, maybe looking at clothes."

"And your eyes aren't on Robbie at that minute."

"That's right, because the next thing we know, Robbie's gone."

"Okay. So Toyman has some way of getting Robbie to come to him while you're not looking at him. Is that correct?"

"Yes. Probably he holds up a toy like the sailboat, and Robbie knows him and runs over to get it."

"That seems logical. Toyman's got a method that he knows works. It's only logical that he'd use it again. So on that day at the playground, you and Annalyn are sitting on the bench talking. What are you talking about?"

"Probably the same stuff. The boys we like."

"And neither of you is focused on Robbie."

"No."

"So then what happens?"

"I don't know."

"Well, what happens in the mall is that you look around, and Robbie's gone. Do you think it would have been like that at the playground?"

"Maybe so."

"Didn't you ever lose sight of Robbie there? I mean, he's on the slide one minute, and then you look, and he isn't there any longer — hasn't that happened?"

"Yes."

"What do you do?"

"I look around until I spot him."

"Do you get up and look around, or do you just stay on the bench?"

"I look from the bench at first. And then, if he's not around, he must be in a harder place to see, so I get up."

"Where is he usually?"

"On the swings, maybe. Or running around playing 'Monster' with the other kids."

"Anywhere else?"

"Sometimes he's run off to play with a dog. He knows he's not supposed to, but he does anyway. Or he's climbed into this pipe maze where I can't see him."

"So, on this day, you'd have seen that Robbie wasn't on the slide or the swings or the merry-go-round or anywhere else. Would you have seen him getting into the van then?"

"Not right away. See, the road's across the lawn behind the bench where we usually sit."

"Well, suppose, just suppose that you spotted him running toward Toyman who was waving a sailboat at him. What would you have done?"

"I'd have gotten up and walked toward them, I guess, calling Robbie back."

"Would he have come?"

"Not at that moment, no. He'd have been too excited by the sailboat. He'd have known Toyman was going to give it to him because he did in the past."

"So you'd have kept walking toward them."

"I guess."

"Or would you be running toward them as fast as you could?"

"No. I wouldn't know Toyman was going to take him."

"No, of course not. So where is Toyman now?"

"Maybe he's by his van. Or a little way across the lawn."

"And Robbie takes the sailboat from Toyman. Now he's looking it over. What do you do?"

"I call out to him that he's not supposed to take things from strangers."

"Call it out to him."

"Robbie, no, you're not supposed to take things from strangers."

"Is Toyman still standing there?"

"I don't know."

"Don't you think he'd have hopped back into his van and sped off before you could get a really close look at him? You see, he's been giving toys to Robbie for some time. He plans to snatch him one way or another, and he doesn't want you to get a good look at him. Does that make sense?"

"Yes. The police said it wasn't a random kidnapping, which was what they thought at first. It was planned. For some reason, they'd picked Robbie out, and they'd followed him at least several times before, waiting for their chance. Then they got it." Becca didn't want to say more.

"So let's say that they hadn't gotten their chance that day, because you were with Robbie, and you were watching him very closely. Or maybe you hadn't even gone to the playground. You'd have stayed home as you were told. Would that mean that Robbie would never have been kidnapped?"

"I'm not sure."

"Well, do you think they'd have tried again?"

"Probably. Yes."

"And do you think you and your family would have been vigilant enough to protect him every single time?"

"We didn't know anyone was after him."

"Of course you didn't. Do you think it's possible to be one hundred percent vigilant every single minute?" Dr. Connie asked.

"So what you're saying is, they'd have gotten him sooner or later. If not that day, another day?"

"Maybe when he was with Alex across the street, or with your mom and dad or in the mall."

"And maybe, after a while, they'd have given up and taken some other little boy."

"There's no way of knowing that, is there?"

That was the terrible problem that Dr. Connie couldn't help her with — what she called "closure."

When Becca got up to leave at the end of her fifty minutes, she was aware that Dr. Connie only had ten minutes between patients and might need to go to the bathroom or something.

"I have a question." Later, Becca would understand that that last question was her way of postponing the session's end, staying a minute longer, even gaining some measure of control over Dr. Connie, who had so much control over her. She would understand further that Dr. Connie understood. But now it was simply a question that couldn't wait. "Are you the one who moves the trolls?" It seemed incongruous that Dr. Connie might actually play with her dolls. And yet Becca couldn't imagine a patient having the nerve.

"Sometimes. I like to help Lizzie climb the pole lamp. She's not happy in one place for very long. Restless, I think." Dr. Connie had gotten up and was leading her toward the hallway. "Sometimes my clients move them, too. I have one who wants 'Sunshine' — that's what she calls him because he's yellow — nearby when the session begins. But someone else used to call him 'Scaredy Cat' and wanted him behind the books on the top shelf. Why? Did you want to move them?"

"That might be fun."

"Next time you're here, go right ahead."

17

"GOD, I HOPE HE didn't change the locks on us," Kenny said as he fitted the key into Carl's apartment door. He'd forgotten about this possibility until they'd arrived to pick up clothes and toys while Carl was at work.

As soon as they got inside, Kenny said, "You see, Damon, Carl still loves us. But what a mess!" Dishes encrusted with food, clothes in heaps, discarded mail still unopened, and garbage everywhere.

"Wow!" Damon was impressed.

"Carl never put anything away in his life. He has no idea that things go back into the places they were before. You know that old saying, 'a place for each thing and each thing in its place?' For Carl, there's only one place and that's the floor. Use and drop, use and drop, that's Carl. Things or humans, it's all the same to him. You didn't notice because I was always one step behind him. He needs a wife."

Now Kenny was carrying an armload of trash into the kitchen to dump in the can under the sink, but of course, this was full to overflowing, the garbage spilling out onto the floor, and Damon had to get out a clean bag for Kenny to use. Kenny closed the full bag with a plastic tie and was out the door with it to the alley.

When he returned, he said, "I swear, he'll never get anyone else. I was so good for him. He didn't appreciate all I did. I'll clean up and do our laundry while you run our bath. Now, make like a whirlwind and bring me your clothes."

After Kenny'd cleaned to his satisfaction and stowed clothes and toys in his suitcase, he wandered into the kitchen, saying, "Hmm, you know, Damon, our cupboard is getting kind of bare. What can we bring to eat?"

Cupboard? They didn't have one, and the closet was filled with paint stuff.

To Damon's look of mystification, Kenny added, "Cold cereal for breakfast and dinner is getting kind of old, don't you think? And money's in short supply right now. Besides, half of this is mine."

Damon had no idea why any of it should be Kenny's since they always bought with Carl's money, but he cheerfully accepted the cans of soup, lunchmeat, tuna, chili, and spaghetti and ran to dump them into a grocery bag. Next came crackers, macaroni and cheese to cook on Trent's camp stove, and a bag of corn chips.

"Oh, look, Carl's got rocky road ice cream. Too bad we don't have a freezer. Let's have some now."

Kenny provided each of them with a spoon, and they dug in and filled up. They were scraping the bottom of the container, when Kenny said, "We'd better leave some for Carl, or he'll get annoyed."

"Only two drops left," Damon said, then grinned and swiped his spoon across the bottom before Kenny could stop him.

"Oh, you little devil!"

Damon giggled, and Kenny started to toss the container into the garbage, then thought better of it and opened the freezer, saying, "If he spots it in the garbage, he'll get mad sooner. But if he opens the freezer, maybe looking for something else, he may think he still has some left. He may not get it out at all. Although if he does get it out and opens it up, thinking he's about to have a delicious treat, he'll get even madder. What do you think? Garbage or freezer?"

"Freezer."

"I agree." Kenny tossed the two spoons into the sink. "Carl can wash them. He's got the dishwasher." Then Kenny spotted the Brie cheese, "Oh, I just love Brie. Carl, that booger, he's eating Brie without me. How could he? Since we don't have a fridge, we'll keep it at room temperature for a day or so. It'll get nice and runny, and then it'll be gone anyway. Okay, I think we've got our share. After all, we're not taking anything from the freezer. Not that there's anything in the freezer to take except the ice cream."

"And not much of that," Damon put in.

"Correct. But if there were more stuff, we wouldn't be taking any, would we? 'Cause we don't have a fridge. Oh, and the bread. What a lovely loaf of sourdough!"

They rolled their load out into the yellow San Francisco sunlight that Kenny always said washed the streets clean, although this was a mystery to Damon because the sun wasn't wet. But the colors did seem brighter, the sky bluer, the stucco pinker, as Damon followed Kenny, lugging his net bag of blocks. People nudged each other and grinned at Damon.

Like a storm crashing and thundering with bolts of lightning, Carl descended on them that night.

"I'll have you both on bread and water, you twist. I leave the old locks, so you can get your clothes, and you rob me blind. I'm surprised you didn't take the cash."

"Oh, I forgot," Kenny said with the same dismay he showed when he'd forgotten the rolls. "Be reasonable, Carl. Money's kind of tight. I have two mouths to feed."

"I oughta kick you out of here. Into the street where you came from." His fists were balled up, his neck muscles knotted, and Damon knew Carl meant the word "kick."

"I don't think you'll do that," Kenny said calmly.

"I'll do what I damn please."

"Of course you will. I just don't think you'll please to kick us out, that's all. We're in transition, Damon and I. We'll get ourselves settled in the next month or two and won't bother you again."

"*Bother*! You steal from me and you call it '*bother*'?"

"We didn't steal. We took what was rightfully ours. I bought all that stuff."

"With my money."

"But I bought it. And I took it just to tide us over. Until my exhibit earns us some money. You're so stingy all of a sudden!"

"If you're so hard up, you know damn well what you can do to bring in the megabucks." Carl was touring the studio as he talked, pausing to evaluate each painting, and dismissing it with a snort as he moved on to the next.

"Oh, so that's why you're so upset. You figure I won't agree to let Damon be in your films until we're starved out. This is a siege you're doing. And after all I've done for you."

"All you've done! Who saved you from your ogress mother and supported you all these years!"

But instead of expressing his gratitude again as he always did, Kenny replied, "For which I've generously repaid you with the best years of my life — shopping, cleaning, running errands, laundry, massages, and all around psychotherapy. You'd be a basket case if it weren't for me."

"You'd be dead in the streets. And may be yet if you don't stop spoiling your little baby and let him get some real life experience."

"Out of the question."

"He only has to watch."

"Damon, you'd better go wait in the hall."

"The macaroni's ready," Damon said. It was boiling over.

"In a few minutes. Go."

Damon started toward the door, but Kenny didn't wait to say the rest as he usually did.

"He only has to watch?" Kenny repeated. "That's what you said about Damon One. He only had to watch. And then he only had to lie there while the other boys piled on with the pillow over his face, his little legs kicking and squirming slower and slower. And then you only had to keep the cameras rolling when Mickey took the pillow away. And then you only had to pan onto that poor dead boy's face."

"It was an accident. And it was our best seller ever."

"Where are your morals? No amount of money is worth a dead boy."

"Kept you in kimonos, didn't it? Besides, it's not as if I was responsible. Doc Phillip said it was a heart attack."

"That's what he put on the death certificate. Damon, out!" Kenny shouted as he spotted Damon lingering by the open door. "I don't even want Damon watching."

"No acting even? Martingale's crazy about him."

"You call that acting? I call it screwing. I'll get a job first."

"That I'd like to see. You've never worked a day in your life. Unless now I've kicked you into the street, you're planning to rent it out to someone else."

Damon could still hear them through the closed door.

"Carl, what a horrible thing to say!" Kenny's voice sounded tear-filled. "Living with you was hard work. Don't kid yourself. All your little hang-ups and phobias, and 'Ooh, somebody's out to get me.' And the mess, God! Without me, a health inspector's going to come through and condemn your place one of these days, mark my words."

Damon sat on the stairs, listening to Uncle Trent's puppy, Noodles, barking merrily above. Probably he sensed that Damon was there. Maybe he even smelled Damon. Dogs have a keen sense of smell, and since Damon's baths were irregular at best, he was pretty sure that his smell climbed up the stairs like a fog and drifted under Uncle Trent's front door. He could no longer get inside the apartment. They'd been locking up ever since the time they'd found him inside asleep with Noodles, and he didn't even remember how he got there.

The fighting began to fade. A few minutes later, he was asleep, although he didn't know this until he woke up. More and more lately, if he didn't like where he was or what was happening, he just blanked out. Ordinarily, this would have been a good thing. Trouble was, when he woke up, he found he'd done things in his sleep that he didn't remember doing.

The next thing he knew, Kenny was shaking him awake.

"Damon, haven't you heard a word we've said?"

To Damon's surprise, Trent and Barry were standing across the room, Trent in his silk pajamas carrying Noodles and Barry in his business suit.

"No. I was asleep."

"You were not asleep. You were sitting right here mouthing off. I don't know what's gotten into you."

Damon got to his feet, wiping his sweaty hands on his jeans.

"Now wha'd I do?"

Trent and Kenny exchanged mystified looks, while Noodles wagged happily in Trent's arms and tried to get down.

"About Noodles? Remember?"

To Damon's mystified look, Barry said, "Damon, you're not supposed to enter other people's homes. When the door's locked, it means no one is supposed to go inside. It's called breaking and entering."

"How'd you get in, anyway?" asked Trent.

"I told you, you forgot to lock it."

"Did not!"

"I know Noodles is a temptation," Kenny was saying. "You just wanted to play with him, didn't you?"

"I didn't."

"You see what I mean?" Kenny said, raising his shoulders with his hands spread wide to show how empty they were of solutions.

"You didn't come into our apartment and put Noodles in the dishwasher?" Barry asked.

Damon was astonished. "I didn't do that! I wouldn't!"

"Who did it then?"

"I don't know." Leroy? Gregory?

"Well, we think it must have been Damon," Trent said to Kenny.

"I'm so sorry," said Kenny.

"Noodles is fine. It's not as if he turned the dishwasher on or anything." Noodles had finally squirmed out of Trent's arms and made a dash for Damon, legs splayed and sliding along the floor.

"Noodles, you little sweetheart, I wouldn't do anything nasty to you, would I?" In his arms, Noodles wriggled with pleasure and licked his ear.

"He doesn't seem afraid," Kenny said.

"Dogs forget," Trent said.

"No, they don't," said Barry. "Maybe there's another explanation."

"Pleaser did it," Leroy whispered into Damon's ear.

"Leroy says Pleaser did it."

"What?"

"Who?"

"It's just a game he plays," said Kenny.

"When are you going to learn to shut up?" Gregory snapped. "We're inside you, just like your brains — so-called. They can't see us. They can't hear us. It makes you sound crazy when you talk about us that way."

"Nothing," said Damon. "I was just kidding."

"Well, we don't know if you did or didn't come into our apartment. And we don't know how you'd have gotten in anyway. We keep the place locked tight. Yet it was unlocked when we got home."

"Pleaser can unlock anything," said Leroy. "It's a natural talent he has."

Damon clapped his hands over his ears and squeezed his lips shut.

Damon lost a lot of time during the summer. Sometimes, he went to sleep deep inside himself, where Gregory told him to lie down and rest. He had no fear that someone else would "take the spot" for him. Like on a stage where an actor comes out into the spotlight, and the others fade into the background or even exit.

Damon began to see a little attic room inside his head, like Alex's, with a peaked roof and a window that looked out over the neighborhood, except that the leaves were turning already, and Noodles lay curled up at the foot of Robbie's bed.

One morning, Kenny dressed up in his spiffiest duds and went out, "Not to look for a job exactly. Just to check on what's out there, kind of get the lay of the land," and he'd giggled, stopped, and giggled again at some private joke.

He returned to find that Damon had taken the painting that Kenny was working on off the easel and substituted his own.

"Why would you do that?" Kenny gasped in shocked fury. "I didn't."

"Look, you smeared the corner."

"Didn't touch your old painting."

"Who else, then? Has anyone else been here?"

"Don't remember."

"I'll tell you who else has been here. Nobody, that's who. Nobody except you. I've told you a hundred times not to touch my paintings, especially when they're still wet. Now what am I going to do? My exhibit's in two weeks. You may think you're hot stuff because Carmine gave you fifty bucks. But let me tell you something, Carmine was just being nice. He gives to other charities, too."

"I'm not charity."

"You don't think your paintings are worth anything, do you?"

"Carmine says."

"He's just being kind. Don't you ever, ever, ever, touch my paintings again. Do you understand that? Well, do you?" Kenny had him by the shoulders and shook him until his teeth rattled.

"I didn't touch your stupid painting. I wasn't even here."

"Where were you then?"

"Asleep."

"That's always your excuse. You paint in your sleep then, do you?" Kenny was pointing at the unfinished portrait of Madam Adam on his easel.

"I told you, Leroy did it probably."

"Once and for all, there's no such person as Leroy! Leroy doesn't exist. And if he does, he's a lousy artist."

"Leroy says *you're* a lousy artist. A lousy retro artist!"

Kenny slapped Damon's face to the left and then to the right. Sniffling, Damon went to sit in the corner.

Before Damon knew it, it was August, and Kenny was talking excitedly about how well his exhibit had gone.

"Showed Carmine, didn't we?" he chuckled — many times, in fact.

Damon had a vague memory of a lot of people at the gallery, mainly because everyone liked Kenny and was kind enough to come. Also, Kenny cooked his special crab puffs and cheese roll-ups, and people love free food. Carmine supplied the wine.

Kenny didn't sell enough at his exhibit to support them, however. At least, this was what they told each other. Actually, Kenny didn't sell anything. They'd had to bring all the paintings back to the studio, but they didn't tell each other that. "Didn't sell enough" was the phrase.

So Kenny went looking for a job again. He found part-time work in a gallery three mornings a week and another job waiting tables in a gay bar. With free rent, they were suddenly living tolerably well. Carl told Kenny he'd let him stay in the studio, if Kenny would come by and clean once a week.

"I can stay in the studio as long as I want," Kenny said to Damon. "I don't have to clean. Carl will never kick us out. We know too much."

Damon had no idea what they knew, but it was fine by him if they stayed. He loved painting and sleeping, which was mainly how he spent his time. Trent and Barry had found a couple of army cots in their storage area down in the basement, and both Kenny and Damon moved "up" from the floor.

So once a week Kenny and Damon would trudge back to the apartment and set it to rights. "What would Carl do without me?" Kenny sighed as the door opened once again on an unimaginable mess. Could it be possible that Carl did it on purpose? "He needs me to help organize his life," Kenny would say. "I'm indispensable." And he'd put on the stereo, take Damon's hands, and waltz him around the living room.

They took the opportunity to have long, luxurious baths. The rest of the time it was sponge washing at the studio sink. The only food they took was what was rightfully theirs, and Carl stopped complaining.

"He can always cancel our service if he doesn't like it," Kenny told Damon. "Small businesses like ours have to put up with cancellations once in a while. It's part of the risk."

Damon noticed that Carl was stocking Crunchy Bunchies, rocky road ice cream, and Brie.

"Isn't that sweet," Kenny said. "You see, Damon, Carl still loves us."

"Time to enroll you in school," Kenny sang gaily one afternoon as he opened their mail. "Your forms came through." He laid them on the studio table. "You now officially exist."

There was a birth certificate with the name "Damon Warhol" on it. His father was listed as Kenny Warhol and his mother as Angela Martingale. He was born on October 20, half a year later than his old date, so he was mature for his age. "That will always be an advantage for you, Damon. You'll always seem a bit older and be better in sports and win class elections. Next, we have to take you to Dr. Phillip for your physical exam."

"No, no, not Dr. Phillip," Damon whimpered.

"Dr. Phillip isn't going to operate or anything. That was last time. This time," and Kenny sat Damon on his knee to illustrate Dr. Phillip's examination, "he's going to listen to your heart with his stethoscope. And he's going to say, 'Oh, what a beautiful heart our Damon has. So kind and so steady. Boom, boom, boom.'" He tapped Damon's chest until Damon giggled and squirmed away.

"Not like that," Damon said.

"And then he's going to put a band on your arm and blow it up tight, just like that, to see what your blood pressure is." Kenny squeezed Damon's arm, but not too hard.

"No, he'll take *your* blood, not mine."

"Not blood. Blood *pressure.* And you'll undress so he can examine you."

"Oh, no, not that again!"

"I'll help you. I'll be right there, and I won't let him do anything you don't want. Okay? All he wants to do is poke you here, and here, and there," and he poked and prodded Damon until he laughed again. "He wants to see if you're ticklish, that's all. And I talked to him this morning about all the sleeping you're doing, so he may do a special test on you called an EEG to see how your brain works. Doesn't hurt a bit. Not one bit. If it does, I'll sock Dr. Phillip POW right in the jaw."

At this, Damon went "POW" and socked Kenny in the jaw.

"Ow! Like that. The last thing he's going to do will hurt just a little bit, Damon. Just a pinch. But the school absolutely requires it. You have to have your shots."

"No, no shots."

"Only tiny ones," Kenny promised. "All the kids have them, so they don't give each other horrible diseases. You wouldn't want to catch a horrible disease, would you?"

"Yes."

"You would? You want to catch a horrible disease?"

Damon nodded and tried not to laugh.

"Listen, listen to me, Damon. Shots are wonderful things. They only hurt a minute, and then it's over. In the olden days, kids got these terrible illnesses that hurt and made their fever go way up, and they died even. Nowadays, for a prick that only takes a minute, you avoid all that. Don't you think that's worth it? I think it is."

"Then *you* have them."

"Silly, I had mine. You're the one going to school."

"No, I'm not. Gregory's going."

"I've got news," Dr. Phillip said to Kenny the third time he and Damon went to his office.

"Bad from the sound of it," Kenny said.

"No, not bad exactly. Puzzling. Very puzzling. To make a long story short, I've got two sets of results, and they're both completely different from each other."

"Different?"

"As night and day. You saw it yourself when I tested Damon's reflexes by giving him a knock on the knee. Remember that, Damon? The first time, his knee jerked hard enough to kick me. The second, there was hardly any reaction at all. Then there was his blood work-up. His red blood cell count was low and his white cell count high, so I did it again. Now, it's the reverse."

"Couldn't he just have an infection or something?"

"Wouldn't account for it. Both EKGs were different, too, one with a congenital heart murmur and one without. His EEGs were as different as if they were the brains of two different people. The second set of results is more normal than the first set."

"That's because I took over for the first set," mumbled Leroy in Damon's ear, "You were too scared."

"But Leroy isn't exactly normal," added Gregory. "So Pleaser gave the good doctor what he wanted."

"What's the matter, Damon?" asked Dr. Phillip, who seemed to notice that Damon was pursing his lips to keep from saying anything. "Have you any idea why this should be?"

Slowly, Damon shook his head "No." Maybe it wasn't a lie if he didn't say it.

"Even if he were putting on an act," Dr. Phillip said, turning back to Kenny, "he couldn't fake these results. No one can."

"What about school? That's the only thing we're interested in. Can you give him a pass on school?"

"You mean, pick and choose among the various results? I don't see why not. Mostly, they're interested in vaccinations anyway. But beyond school requirements, I should see him again, maybe call in a consultant. There's a medical mystery here. We should solve it, just in case Damon needs treatment."

"Things are a little tight right now. I don't see how I'd pay for it."

"We didn't sell enough at the gallery showing," Damon chimed in.

"Don't worry. I'll put it on Carl's bill. I'm sure he won't object."

They got back to the studio to find Trent at their door, cradling a very still Noodles swathed in a blanket.

"Did you do this? Did you put Noodles in the freezer? Do you know he could have frozen to death? Barry's on his way, and we're taking him to the vet."

"Oh, Noodles!" Damon exclaimed, reaching up to stroke his head as he peered down at Damon.

"Don't you touch him."

"I didn't do it, I swear."

"The dishwasher, the freezer. Why would you do such a thing?"

Kenny shook his head.

"I just don't believe Damon did it."

"Who else? That's how serial killers get started, you know. Torturing animals when they're young."

"Don't be ridiculous. Damon isn't a serial killer."

At that moment, Barry hauled up the stairs and said, "Come on. The vet's waiting." He scowled at Damon. "We'll deal with you later."

Damon was so upset that, as soon as they entered the studio, he said, "Gregory, I have to talk to you. I didn't put Noodles in the freezer. Did you?"

Kenny shook his shoulder.

"Stop talking to yourself, Damon. It's not cute or funny anymore. It's crazy."

"I'm not. I'm talking to Gregory." He ran to the mirror over the bathroom sink. "Gregory, I have to talk to you." Most of the time, Gregory was invisible, but now, perhaps because of the urgency of the situation, he appeared in the mirror in full regalia, black vampire coat, hat and pants, daffodil yellow shirt open at the throat with a Celtic cross. Beside him lounged Leroy in his paint splattered clothes. A slightly taller and gangly Pleaser with a belt of hardware smirked behind them, smelling as though he needed a bath. "There, you see," Damon called to Kenny. "There's Gregory, right in the mirror."

Kenny poked his head in the door and said, "I don't see anything except crazy Damon."

"How many times have I told you?" Gregory scolded. "And no, I'd never put a dog in a freezer."

"Me, neither," said Leroy.

"Or me," Pleaser added.

"Except he lies like anything," Leroy said, for which Pleaser poked him.

Damon felt it in his ribs. "Ow!" he said.

"Barry's right," said Gregory. "That's how serial killers get started. Pleaser, do you know anyone else who might have done it?"

"Why me?" Pleaser asked indignantly. "No, I don't know anyone except Robbie and Wendy, and they wouldn't."

"Leroy?"

"Nobody who'd do that, no."

"Leroy, I know you know some of the others that I don't," Gregory said.

"I thought you were the boss," said Damon.

"I am. But I'm pretty sure there are others I don't know. Leroy, you have to tell me. We could all be in danger."

Leroy stared out at Damon and shrugged his shoulders.

18

BECCA GLEANED THAT DR. Connie had two white cats, Glinda, named after the good witch of the South, and Glitz, signifying a personality trait — she dove after anything shiny. Silver-framed pictures of her cats decorated her desk. Later she added three more when a friend died, launching into a mini-disquisition on their care and feeding, what the vet said about Andiamo's arthritis, how Francesca hated her baths, her decision not to declaw Maria Callas, cat-scratch fever, and whether or not you should put a cat on a leash like a dog and take him for a walk. Did Becca think she wanted a cat?

"Instead of a brother?"

Dr. Connie complimented Becca on her new pink barrettes, as Becca returned the two books she had borrowed. She was wearing her pink sweater outfit, and Dr. Connie admired the color so close to that she favored, making more of Becca's looks than Becca felt was warranted. Dr. Connie herself always resembled a pastel angel, white-haloed and smiling. Becca felt she should respond with false enthusiasm. Her improved appearance was supposed to signal that she was feeling better. But she was feeling worse.

"I'm more depressed than ever," Becca admitted, ten minutes into a session.

"Why is that, do you think?"

"I don't know. I was hoping you would." A tad impatient. Must Dr. Connie always respond with a question? Couldn't she just once give her the answer? She had the right ones, of that Becca was sure.

As if in response, she said, "You know better. Think it through."

Becca sighed the objection she should not voice. "When Robbie was first kidnapped, I kept expecting that he'd be found."

"You thought he was coming home."

"It didn't really occur to me that he wasn't. Maybe I just couldn't face the possibility."

"And now?"

"Now, I'm not sure. It's been six months. There's no word. The police aren't working on it, I can tell. Oh, they say they're following leads in California beach towns, but that's just to give me an answer. Mom and Dad seem to have given up. Nobody ever talks about Robbie any more."

"To spare your feelings, perhaps."

"And Mom's. Everybody's."

"What about you? Do you talk about him?"

"I can't. Except here. It's like there's some conspiracy of silence. As if he'd done something bad. Or I had. Or I hadn't done enough. But what else can I do? I've done everything I can think of."

"And since there's nothing else, do you think that's what makes you more depressed?"

"I don't know." Becca subsided into the leather chair in despair.

"It sounds to me like you felt very effective for a while."

"I was," she insisted.

"Right. You were searching for Robbie, and you were doing a darn good job of it, apparently. Now, it seems as though there's not much left to do."

"It's more a matter of luck than anything anybody does."

"That's right. You don't have the control you thought you did. Even your mom and dad, who used to be all-powerful in your eyes, can't control this most important thing, the welfare of their son. We tend to get very depressed when we lose control."

"I thought I was supposed to be getting better by now. Everybody thinks I should. Aunt Cordelia — it's like she's saying, 'Enough is enough.' Fix my hair and I'll be okay."

"Everybody isn't you. While you were working with the police, making posters, and looking for Robbie all over Santa Cruz, you expected to find him, didn't you?"

"I was sure he was just around the corner. I could feel him."

"Now, a lot of time has passed, and you can't think of anything else to do. You feel helpless. I think feeling more depressed is natural, under the circumstances, don't you?"

"I guess." Becca was feeling more miserable by the minute. She picked up the Troll with the upswept orange hair, completely naked, but not seeming to mind one bit. Taking life as it comes. Easy for her! She hadn't lost a brother. "I wonder if any of them are only children."

"I think in a way they are, and in a way they aren't. They certainly act independently. And yet it's hard to believe they aren't family. They look so much like each other and different from everybody else."

"Who else would have such ugly children?" Becca laughed.

"Still, very lovable, don't you think?"

There was a lesson here somewhere. Ugly could be lovable. Was that it? It had nothing to do with how she felt. She didn't feel ugly or pretty. She didn't care. Did she feel loved? Not by the ones who counted. But had she ever? Not after Robbie came to them. Then she had been loved for what she gave him, and when he was gone, even that semblance of love was gone, too. If that was true — she couldn't follow the thought.

"How long will I grieve?"

"How long is a piece of string?"

"You know I hate that answer."

"It's one of my favorites," Dr. Connie laughed. "A piece of string can be any length, and so many of life's problems can last any length of time. The advantage is that you don't have to feel compelled to shorten it. You can let it take as long as it takes. And do it right."

"Annalyn says we grieve in stages. First, you get upset, and then angry, and finally you accept it. Except I never will."

"Those stages are sort of a myth. They've done a lot of research now and found that grieving is more cyclical. You can get depressed, then angry, then depressed again, then maybe you start to accept, and then get angry again. Everyone's different, and so is the loss. It's all normal."

"When will I feel better?"

"Depends on what you mean. If I could wave a magic wand and make you forget Robbie, would you want me to?"

"I never want to forget Robbie. Never ever."

"But remembering him means remembering pain. Which would you choose?"

"I always want to remember him." She loved him whether or not it brought love from her parents as well. "I even feel better here because I can say his name. Robbie. Robbie. My teacher at school, Mr. Fritz, says I have to move forward, but how can I leave Robbie behind?"

"It will get better," Dr. Connie promised. "Very gradually. You'll begin to remember the good things about Robbie, the things you loved and still do. Bit by bit, you'll think less about the way he left your life, the painful parts. Then you'll remember the kindnesses, too, your Aunt Cordelia, how understanding that officer was — "

"Officer Sam."

"Officer Sam, yes. And all the others."

"The neighbors. Some of the other kids at school. Annalyn, of course. Can't we speed things up?" Becca asked only half jokingly. "I mean, without having to forget?"

"I usually find that forgiveness speeds things up."

"Forgive who? The kidnappers?" The idea enraged her. She could never forgive them. Let God do it! It was *His* job!

"You could start by forgiving yourself."

"I don't know how."

"Then you might try to forgive your mother."

"I never blamed her. She blamed me!" And then Becca added, "Because she felt guilty herself. I know. I know."

Dr. Connie laughed.

"You'll make a good therapist someday. Start by talking to her."

"I do. She doesn't answer."

"Keep talking anyway. One day she'll respond, and you'll get back to some semblance of a relationship. You help her forgive herself that way."

"I'm the girl who lost her brother."

"But you're the girl who had one. Lucky you! Even if it was only for a few years. Aren't you grateful for that?"

"I'm not sure."

"Would you rather you'd never had a brother?"

"No! But then I was a sister, and now I'm an only child."

"For just a few months more."

"No! No, no, no! I refuse. The twins Mom's got inside her aren't my brothers. I'm still an only child. Nobody can take Robbie's place, nobody! They're probably rotten kids anyway, with a dad who doesn't even come around."

Dr. Connie didn't say anything at first. But Becca had noticed that often as the fifty-minute hour approached its end, Dr. Connie sought a way of giving it some kind of closure, or summing up, or pointing Becca in the direction she wanted her to go.

"Your identity is changing in a way you hadn't expected. But it would have anyway, you know. Life is a process of leaving the old behind, and you're growing new parts of yourself. You may find you like those new ones a lot."

"Like Billy Milligan and his multiple personalities?" Dr. Connie had loaned her the book.

"Well, we're more integrated than multiples are. A lot of psychologists and psychiatrists don't even think MPD exists. In fact, there's a big controversy about it."

"What do you think?"

"Oh, it's real enough."

"Have you ever treated any?"

"I have, not realizing what I was dealing with. When the personalities came out, I turned the cases over to experts."

Dr. Connie joined Becca as she selected two more books from her shelves. "For our next session," she said, "I'd like you to bring me a few of your poems, if you would."

"Why?"

"I'd like to see them."

But, of course, with Dr. Connie, it was never that simple.

A shock greeted Becca as she entered the garage to dig out her anthology. Robbie's things were packed into cartons, his blocks, fire trucks, Legos, clothes, his pajamas that she'd washed so carefully and put away in the chest, even his red bedspread, faded now. On top of one carton sat the sailboat from Toyman that the police had checked for fingerprints.

Becca noticed that Robbie's smell, which had always clung to his clothes and even his toys, was gone. Her fingers flitted lightly over his *Peter Pan and Wendy* book.

Becca ran upstairs to Robbie's room and found it empty and clean. Where was the bed? Someone must have helped Mom take it down and put it somewhere. A tarp had been thrown on to the floor, and a can of white paint with a roller in a pan and a wide brush lay there as clues to her mother's intention. White would hide the room's true color, yellow.

A few spring-like April days later, poring over her poems in the backyard and trying to select a few for Dr. Connie, Becca fell in love with them all over again.

Which was, of course, why Dr. Connie had given her the assignment.

19

"WHAT'S GOTTEN INTO YOU?" Kenny screamed, shaking the phone at Damon. Still dressed in his "gallery clothes," cerise silk shirt and wet black leather pants, and his fiery foulard that he claimed made him look "like Apollo, the Sun God," Kenny erupted, "I call home to make sure you got back from kindergarten and I get this message. I couldn't believe it. I figure I must have dialed the wrong number, except it's got all our names right. You'd better pray Carl hasn't heard it."

They were standing in the studio, homey with the odds and ends from other people's lives, Trent's and Barry's cots, sleeping bags, and smelly cushions, the red and white checked tablecloth with the brown stain like a centerpiece that Madison had bestowed on them, a few books from Jeff's book store upstairs from Carl's movie basement, Carl's bathroom TV that Kenny had managed to spirit off with the tray table, and his blue willow dishes besides. "I wouldn't have that green Melmac stuff — that's plastic," Kenny had said. "He got that before we were married. He had no taste then. I had to teach him."

Now he was holding the phone that their good friend Harmon from the art store had loaned them, the phone with the offending welcome message for all callers to hear.

"How dare you?" Kenny exploded again. Upstairs Noodles barked excitedly in a rare show of alarm.

"What does it say?" Damon asked.

"You know damn well what it says. You taped it, didn't you? Well, didn't you?"

Damon shook his head miserably, afraid to say out loud that he really hadn't, for fear that Kenny would blow up again. And, of course, so would Gregory.

"It's your voice," Kenny said.

Damon shook his head again.

"Listen, listen," Kenny shoved the receiver hard against his ear. "You're telling me that's not your voice?" before Damon had had a chance to hear.

Damon took the phone and twisted away from Kenny, trying to listen.

"Hello! You've reached the Warhol household. Leave a message for Kenny or Damon after the tone. You can reach that pervert Carl at his porn studio."

"That's not me," Damon said.

"Who is it then? Who else has your voice and access to this phone? Huh? Tell me who."

"That's Pleaser's voice."

"Pleaser! What kind of a name is that? Who is he? One of your new kindergarten friends? Pleaser? Or another imaginary chum of yours?" Kenny slammed down the receiver.

"He's not 'maginary." Damon had learned that calling someone imaginary was an insult. It meant they weren't real, that they were dead, even. He didn't want Pleaser mad at him, too.

"Why did you let him play with this phone?"

"I didn't let him. He does it when I'm asleep."

"So you just invite him into the studio when I'm at work, although I've told you a hundred times not to let anybody in. And then you go to sleep. Not very polite of you, is it, Damon? And meanwhile, this Pleaser changes the phone message? He knows just what to say because you've blabbed about Carl's studio? Even though —"

They were interrupted by the ring. Kenny picked it up and turned a sickly yellow above his red foulard.

"Yes, Carl, yes, you're absolutely right. I just got home. I'm having it out with him right now. I'll change the message immediately, Carl. Absolutely. See you in a few." Kenny hung up and said, "Carl's on his way over, and he's absolutely livid. I can't keep him from beating you up this time," Kenny shook his head ominously. "No, indeed, I can't. Whatever he does to you, you deserve it. You better hop out of your good school clothes fast 'cause it's gonna get bloody."

Damon didn't want to go to his new kindergarten in bloody clothes. Maybe he could say it was paint. He backed away from Kenny, as if he were about to beat him up himself.

"Now, see what you did," Damon said to Pleaser, although, of course, it seemed to Kenny as if he were talking to him. "I'm going to get beat up again and it's all account of you."

"I had nothing to do with it," Kenny said, then turned away and taped his own cheery message over Pleaser's. Finished, he added, "It's your own doing."

When Carl arrived, Damon tried to run past him into the hall.

"Oh, no, you don't." Carl caught his wrist in a bruising vise, twisting Damon to the floor, where he kicked him all over with his shiny brown pointed boots, while Kenny looked on.

"Who's a pervert, huh, you little cocksucker? Trying to get me in trouble with the cops, are you?" Carl stomped him in the small of his back, then stood on it while digging into Damon's ribs with his other heel.

"Ow, I didn't do it, please, Kenny, help! Leroy, oh, oh, you're supposed to take the pain. It's your job."

"Leroy! Don't start that with me again."

"Leroy! Leroy!" screamed Kenny. "You see what I have to contend with, Carl?"

Damon was trying to pass out. How had he done it last time? He'd prayed. "God the Father, God the Son, Our Father who art in Heaven —" he couldn't remember.

He was barely aware of the knock on the door. Trent and Barry entered in their matching yellow tennis-racket pajamas.

"We heard the noise. We just wanted to be sure everything was okay." Their glances took in Damon on the floor screaming in pain, Carl's boot in his back, and Kenny standing off to one side. At the appearance of Trent and Barry, Carl released Damon's arm. Damon lay crumpled on his stomach, face buried in the floor, trying to give up, trying to die.

"Kid needs a lesson," Carl was saying, out of breath.

"Punishing a kid can be quite a workout," Barry sympathized. "We had our own sessions with Adam, especially when he first came to us."

"Had to take turns," Trent agreed.

"Did you try to reach me on the phone earlier?" Kenny asked pleasantly.

Trent and Barry shook their heads "No," apparently mystified. "Why would we call you when we can just come down?"

"Oh, nothing, just wondering."

Carl nodded to Kenny, understanding the question. Who else had heard the message? The myth of Carl's occupation as producer-director of fine art films must be preserved.

Damon had rolled over toward Trent and Barry and was trying to get up, but his arm kept giving way.

"I don't know why you put up with him," Barry said, shaking his head sadly. "He's been terrible with Noodles."

"I mean, who would do that to a dog? Except someone who's totally psycho?" said Trent.

"We put up with Adam for as long as we could. Then we got smart and put him back where we found him. Things have been so much better since then, haven't they, dear?"

Trent nodded "Yes" with tears in his eyes.

"I mean, after all you've done for the little fella."

"What did he do this time?" Barry asked.

"Tried to turn me into the cops, that's what."

"Well, not quite that," Kenny said. "But he made a very serious mistake that could have gotten us all in trouble."

"I told you, I didn't do it."

"He claims a friend of his did. Have you ever seen anybody else come into the studio?"

"Never. Haven't heard anyone either. And our living room's right above you. Not to worry you or make you paranoid or anything, but we can hear quite a lot of what goes on down here," said Barry.

"When we're home, which isn't much," Trent added tactfully.

"He's not a friend," Damon cried. "Oh, oh, you broke my arm."

Roughly, Barry hauled him to his feet by the other arm. "You'll survive."

"Unless you don't, of course," said Trent. "Well, if you fellows need any help, you know where to reach us."

Damon tried to slip out with them, but Kenny and Carl called "Damon" in one voice. After the door closed, Carl stood poised to attack again, and Damon cowered in the corner, crying,

"Why don't you believe me?"

"Stop sniveling," said Carl.

"We don't believe you because your lies are so asinine," said Kenny.

"I can't stand snivelers," said Carl.

"But I'm not lying. Pleaser did it. At least, I'm pretty sure it was Pleaser. Gregory wouldn't, and it's not Leroy's voice, so it must have been Pleaser, he's got his mouth in the gutter," quoting Leroy. "Unless it was one of the others that I don't know."

Carl and Kenny listened to him with increasing hardness in their faces.

"You know," Carl said pleasantly, turning to Kenny, "I really do think he's nuts."

"You may be right."

"It's not your fault. You couldn't know. He didn't show any signs at first."

"What do you think we should do? Take him back? Like Adam?"

"Yes, yes, take me home."

"That's one possibility," said Carl, clearly in charge now. "Why don't you move in with me again, so we can discuss our options?" His face was mild when he said it, but as he turned his eyes toward Damon, there was lightning in them.

"Oh, no, please, Kenny, don't let's us go back. You know Carl will hurt me."

"That's right," said Carl grimly.

"Thanks for the offer, Carl. I'll think it over, really I will. This studio's a bit crowded. And camping out gets old."

"Of course it does," Carl nodded sympathetically. "And I really don't manage that well without you. You're so much better organized."

"Are you just finding that out?" Kenny laughed.

"Maybe I didn't appreciate it before."

"Better late than never! Let me sleep on it."

Carl's eyes traveled to their pathetic cots and sleeping bags, as if to make a point.

"Talk to you tomorrow."

After Carl left, Damon shuffled off to the bathroom. He'd wet his pants and had to strip and wash everything out.

Then, thinking to please Kenny, he began heating water on the camp stove for macaroni and cheese. A tear plopped into the water, but he didn't think it was unsanitary. Just a dash of salt, somebody told him once. Better not tell Kenny, though.

Kenny changed quickly out of his gallery clothes into his "costume." Somehow, Kenny's job as a waiter in a gay bar had evolved into a performance. "And why not?" he had asked Damon a couple of months ago when he first got the job. "We sing, we tell the customers out-and-out lies, but we do it so expertly they believe us. We help them choose the most expensive bar food, as if one tasteless tapas were better than another. It's all an act. If I ever decide to audition for a play, I'll put this job on my resume."

Now Kenny was saying, "I don't know what's gotten into you," as he pulled on his black polyester pants in the "dressing corner" of the room, where their clothes hung on rungs of the painting ladder.

"Gregory's gotten into me," Damon wanted to say. "And Leroy and Pleaser, and all their brothers." But Gregory was shushing him through gritted teeth. Damon felt assaulted from all directions, Kenny from the outside and Gregory from the inside.

Aloud, he said, "I didn't do it," which Kenny ignored.

"First, poor Noodles in the washing machine and the freezer and the oven, although, thank God, you didn't turn them on. Then the screws you hammered all over my 'Phase Ladder!'" Kenny blazed at the very recollection. Clearly he was more upset about his painting than he was about the dog.

"Whoever saw a ladder without screws?" Damon asked mildly, although actually this was Leroy's idea, not Damon's. "Even your painting ladder's got screws in it. See?" Damon ran to the dressing corner where the tall ladder stretched, spattered with the paint drips from 'Phase I,' 'Phase II,' coffee-colored 'Diversity,' orange 'Political Perspective,' and all the others. "Look, see them?"

"It's a work of art!" Kenny yelled at him. "You're not the artist. I am."

"Leroy's a artist, too. He says."

"Leroy doesn't exist! He's a stupid figment of your imagination."

"Will you shut the fuck up," Gregory ground out so loudly that Damon clapped his hands to his ears. Gregory had never been so loud, but nothing could soften him because he was inside.

"Leroy is not stupid!" Damon realized Kenny had used that nasty word "imagination" again, but he hadn't challenged it because he wasn't so sure about "figment." He waited for the rest of Kenny's rage over 'Diversity,' because Leroy had added yellow, white, and pink to it. "Diversity should represent *everyone,*" he said, "not just the darker races." It was a political statement. Kenny chose not to mention it again, although Damon knew he hadn't forgotten.

"And now this phone business! Either you're terminally idiotic, or you're just a malevolent child. A very malevolent child, Damon, a very malevolent child. That was a malicious thing you did, leaving that message. I know Carl's been strict with you, maybe a little stricter than he should, but you've got a lot to be grateful to him for. The clothes on your back, for instance, the food in your stomach, even this studio. It's his, you know. He doesn't have to let you stay here."

"But if he didn't, you'd do something to him, so he's just scared."

"I may not do anything to him after all."

Damon's arm hurt a lot, but it must not be broken because he could still scoop the macaroni and cheese into two bowls. How could

Kenny even think of betraying him like that? Kenny had seen what Carl did to him.

As if in answer, Kenny said,

"I'm getting awfully tired of macaroni and cheese."

"We could have franks and beans." They kept the franks in the cooler.

"I'd really like to make beef stroganoff."

"Okay, let's!"

"Heavens, no! We need a real stove and all those spices and a freezer for leftovers. I'll eat something at my place of employment. Come over here, Damon, I want to talk to you." Kenny was dusting his face very lightly with a powder puff to smooth away imperfections, just like other actors did. "I want the truth now. What on earth possessed you to leave that message on the phone?"

"Honestly?"

"Honestly."

"Honestly, I didn't do it, Kenny."

"Oh, if you're going to keep on with that," Kenny said, pushing him away in disgust.

"No, listen to me, Kenny, listen, okay? Listen. You know the people who live with you?"

"What people? There's just you and me, that's all."

"Well, you know how when you look in the mirror, you see the others?"

"Such nonsense! When I look in the mirror, there's no one except me."

"No, I mean the *other* people. Like, when I look in the mirror I see me, but I also see Gregory, and Robbie — "

"Robbie!" Kenny's mouth was a tight straight line.

"Uh-huh. He's off in the back, and he's either crying or playing with his blocks or asleep. And I see Leroy in his pants and shirt with all the paint stains on them, and Pleaser just moved in. He has a whole bunch of keys and lock picks and handcuffs and other stuff on his belt. There are some others, but they're kind of blurry. Come on, Kenny, let's look in the mirror. Let me show them to you."

"Okay, Damon, okay. Let's look."

They stood together in front of the bathroom mirror, and Kenny said, "I only see Damon and Kenny."

"That's because the mirror isn't big enough for all of us. But look up right between you and me, you can just make out Gregory's head, see?"

"I don't see anything."

"Then, move over so you're not in the mirror, and you can see him better."

Kenny moved to one side.

"Like this?"

"He can't see us, kid. How many times do I have to tell you? We're inside you. He can't see inside you."

"Gregory says you can't see inside me. But you could see inside you. I'll move away, and you stand in front of the mirror yourself. Now who do you see?"

"I see me. Look, Damon, this is getting us nowhere."

"But what about the others? Who do you got inside you?"

"There *are* no others!" Kenny shouted. "If you really think you see others, then you *are* crazy, just like Carl says." Kenny cinched his red plaid cummerbund around his waist and shouldered into his vest over his white shirt. "You've changed a lot, you know. You're not the same sweet boy I brought home a year ago. I don't know why I make all these sacrifices. Do you think I like living here where I can't even cook beef stroganoff? Do you think I like waiting on people and wiping their noses? The gallery's okay, but I'd rather be doing my own thing. I've sacrificed a lot for you, and how do you repay me? By getting into a ton of trouble. If it isn't one thing, it's another. Trent says little boys who torture animals are psycho. You sure act psycho. We should take you back like they did Adam. I don't know. We'll talk to Carl about it tomorrow."

Damon gave up in tears. Kenny didn't want to be poor and live in the studio any longer, that was it. And for a little more comfort and security, Kenny was willing to sacrifice Damon.

Kenny wouldn't protect him.

After Kenny left with Harmon, who'd been picking him up lately in his truck, Damon cleaned the studio, snuggled into his sleeping bag, and watched TV a little while. He tried to see his tree tower stretching across the ceiling, but it was just the shadows of trees outside waving in the breeze. He hadn't had any luck growing his tree since they got here. It was too afraid of getting chopped down again.

He was tired and achy but too scared to sleep. If he slept, someone would do some kind of mischief, and Damon would get blamed. It seemed like the mischief they did got worse and worse. So Damon lay awake, listening to the voices inside his head.

He didn't know what to make of Kenny's denial that he had others inside him, too.

"Of course, he does," Gregory assured him. "Probably some straight dude that Kenny can't deal with."

"Kenny's lying, then."

"Not necessarily, exactly. Just that he doesn't want to deal with them, so he pretends they don't exist. You see, Damon, everybody's a whole bunch of people. It isn't just you. Kenny's a waiter, and a gallery artist, and a gay boy with Carl. Only difference is, Kenny's the boss of them, and we're all independent."

They were sitting around a dining room table that Damon had only glimpsed vaguely in the mirror, but now it was as real and solid as anything outside. Someone had laid out a plate of cookies that smelled just like the ones in Kenny's kitchen when Kenny was gone and no one was there. A kettle whistled, the one he'd heard. "I'm boiling water for more hot chocolate," a girl's voice called. The pot of hot chocolate was covered with what someone called a blue and yellow woven "tea cozy."

Off in all directions, Damon could see doors and stairs, leading to the individual rooms where they lived, but their outlines were vague. The only pieces of furniture were the table and chairs with the carved crests on top of them like those in Alex's house. It was nice and warm and cheery, and Damon thought how cozy it would be to stay here and never go out again. Gregory could keep going to kindergarten for him. As it was, he and Damon each went part time.

"You look exhausted, kid," Pleaser was saying, holding his mug by the rim instead of the handle and slurping noisily. He smelled of metal like on the school staircase, and no wonder with all that hardware dangling from his belt and the rings in his nose, his ear, and his lip. "You need more rest."

"I can't sleep, or you or Leroy will come out and do things that make Kenny and Carl mad."

"That's their problem, not yours."

"I'm the one gets beat up. Leroy, you didn't take the spot."

"Your fault." Leroy spooned his cocoa, because it was too hot to drink, and helped himself to a dollop of whipped cream from a china pot that Damon hadn't noticed before. "You gotta give it up."

"I don't know how. I tried."

"He'll get better at it," said Gregory, who seemed to defend him the way Kenny used to. (Would Gregory ever insist they take baths together?)

"Now we're going back to Carl's," Damon said, "and it's your fault."

"I'd run away, if I were you," said Pleaser.

"Where can I run to?"

"He can't run away," said Gregory. "He's too young."

"That's right," Leroy added. "He'd end up in the streets."

"Maybe Mickey at the porn studio would take you in," Pleaser suggested. "He seems an okay dude."

"Are you kidding?" said Gregory. "He wouldn't keep it a secret from Carl for a minute. Use it to buy another ticket to Hollywood."

"Keep you in bennies and 'ludes, that's for sure," said Leroy.

"I don't know how to get to the porn place."

"Not far. If you walk up and down, you'll find it eventually. Go when Carl isn't there and see if you can get in without Paulie seeing you."

"Maybe he should tell Mickey he's coming first. That way Mickey can leave the door open or something."

"Where can he hide that Paulie won't find him?"

"Mickey would know."

"I don't think Damon needs to run away necessarily," Gregory said. "School's more important. Damon needs his education. We all do. I'm teaching him to read."

True. Every afternoon after school, Gregory sat Damon down on his sleeping bag, their backs comfortably to the wall, and they read one of his books. Like *Mother Goose*. Gregory would point out words, and pretty soon Damon would see them, too. "There's the word 'kittens' and there's the word 'kittens,'" and he'd go down the page pointing out a word. Then the word was "mittens." Even though Damon was only in kindergarten, he was going on seven already, and reading wasn't too hard.

"If Carl gives him any trouble, I'll take care of it," said Leroy.

"I don't think Kenny will put up with it."

"He put up with that beating."

"Pleaser, no more mischief out of you."

"You're not the boss of me."

A shadow of a young girl appeared at the table with a vase of bright yellow flowers, like the ones Becca and Mom picked from their garden. She put it down in the center.

"That's Wendy," Gregory said. "She takes care of us. When we're all getting along, she gets more and more solid until you can see her dress, her hair, her eyes even. All blue."

"Except her hair," Leroy smirked.

"But when we argue, she starts to fade. We don't know if she can fade to completely nothing. Hope not."

"Mainly, she takes care of the basement babies. We sure couldn't."

The shadow took the tea cozy off the cocoa pot to see if there was still more inside. Apparently satisfied, she put it back and spirited away the empty cookie plate.

"She looks like a ghost," Damon said, shuddering.

"Shhh, don't let her hear you say that," said Gregory. "She thinks she's just as solid as the rest of us."

"But ghosts have been alive," said Pleaser, "and now they're dead, although they may not know they are. Wendy hasn't been all the way alive yet, but if we don't fight too much, maybe she'll make it."

"How about Carmine?" Leroy suggested. "Maybe he'd let Damon sleep in back of the gallery. He likes little boys."

"He sure does," Pleaser said. "He's had his hands all over my sweet bod."

"Yuck!" said Damon. "I don't like him."

"I don't know how long I can hold him off," said Pleaser, grabbing a fistful of chocolate chip cookies from the full plate Wendy set down. "Oh, okay," Pleaser said, letting some of them fall back.

Which mystified Damon, because he hadn't heard Wendy say anything.

"I suppose Carmine's affections are better than being beaten," said Leroy.

"I'm not absolutely sure Kenny will move back in with Carl," said Gregory. "Sure he was mad about the phone, but he doesn't really want Carl ass-fucking Damon again. He still loves Damon."

"He sure wants to get back to more comfortable quarters though — a bed, a kitchen, a full bathroom, and a lot less work," said Pleaser. "No matter how he dresses it up — as Damon's fault or as love of Carl or what — I think comfort's gonna win out."

"Wants his old life back," croaked a teen voice, breaking between child and adult. To Damon it was unfamiliar.

"Breakout," said Gregory. "Or his twin brother Bounce. I can't tell them apart."

Suddenly, Robbie appeared beside Gregory, a red-eyed, sorrowful boy who said nothing, but just stood quietly until they acknowledged him. Damon felt odd, as if he knew him and didn't. Robbie didn't seem to notice.

"Robbie, would you like a cookie, huh?"

Robbie nodded and accepted one.

"Cocoa?"

He shook his head and went back to the corner of the room where he got down on the floor and, still holding his cookie, played with his Legos.

"That boy's going to starve if we don't get more into him," said Leroy.

"Just remember, Damon," said Gregory "we're the only ones you can count on. Kenny can turn at any time, Bec-Bec gave you up, Carl is cruel, and who knows about Mickey? We're your family. But you've got to do as we say."

When Kenny got back from his job, Damon pretended he was asleep, but apparently Kenny had heard him through the door.

"Who were you talking to, Damon?"

The next morning, Kenny awakened Damon who, in spite of himself, had fallen into a light snooze.

"Is everything okay," Damon asked anxiously. "Did anything happen?"

"What would happen?" Kenny asked him, pouring two bowls of Crunchy Bunchies and soaking them in dry milk and water. "When I got home, you were talking to yourself again."

"I wasn't talking to myself exactly," Damon said, raising himself up from his sleeping bag and getting out to pee.

"Whatever," Kenny said, seeming not to want to revisit the topic of the others inside Damon's head.

Damon sat in front of his bowl of cereal without touching it.

"What's the matter? Aren't you hungry?"

Damon shook his head.

"You don't have a fever, do you?"

Kenny lay a cool hand on his forehead, and Damon could imagine, just for a minute, that his Kenny loved him again.

"Don't be a fool," whispered Gregory.

"All you had was the macaroni and cheese last night. You didn't have anything else, did you? Did you have something else to eat after I left? It's all right, Damon. Really, it is. It's okay to have more food."

"Cocoa and cookies."

"What?"

"I had cocoa. With whipped cream. And chocolate chip cookies, so I'm not hungry now."

"Damon, you know very well we don't have any cocoa in the house. Cookies either. They're not healthful. Did Trent and Barry give you cookies?"

"No."

"Then where did you get them?"

"I don't remember."

"You're teasing me, aren't you. My Damon's such a tease!" he said, with a touch of the old pleasure in Damon's cut-ups. "I've been thinking. We should put off moving back with Carl."

"Really?"

"Oh, look at those wide saucer eyes!"

"Because of Harmon?"

Harmon had been visiting so much that Damon had begun to wonder if Harmon would be his new uncle.

"Of course not! Harmon's a friend, a good friend. Don't you dare say anything to Carl about him. You'll upset him. Understand? Yes, I think you do. I thought we'd wait just a while longer. If we make it too easy for Carl, he won't behave himself," Kenny said. "He won't appreciate me either. Let me see. What do I want?"

"New clothes?" Damon suggested.

"That's good. A bigger limit on my charge card. I have to buy for two now. And I think a new bedroom set. The one we have is awfully old. Cheap and old. Old can be good if it's expensive, but not if it's cheap. Remember that, Damon. And I think I'd like us all to go out to dinner once a week. Or maybe just Carl and me. We can leave you home. I do. And you don't run away. You don't run away from kindergarten. You come straight home. No place to run to, right?"

Damon hesitated, remembering the talk last night of running to Carmine or Mickey, until Gregory prompted with a poke in the ribs.

"Right!" Damon agreed. "How about a cleaning lady?" he suggested brightly. "So you don't have to work so hard."

"Excellent, Damon! Excellent suggestion."

"Or is that blackmail?"

Kenny frowned, and Damon was scared for a moment that he'd upset him. Then Kenny seemed to come to a decision. "It's not blackmail if it's a legitimate request."

Over the next few weeks, negotiations proceeded in a series of phone conversations with an occasional visit from Carl. Kenny was still hesitating.

"You don't want to live here in the studio forever." Carl pointed out.

"Oh, I don't know. The studio's not so bad."

Not what he said to Damon in private.

"I like my freedom and independence," Kenny said.

"You'll be even freer when you don't have to hold down two jobs."

"I like my gallery job. It keeps me up-to-date. Carmine always says I don't stay up-to-date. Now he can't say that."

"Give up the bar job then. You work too hard, Kenny. Your art is your career. You don't need to work, too."

What a change from his previous contempt!

"You've said some awfully nasty things to me, Carl. Especially that crack about selling my socks."

"You know I didn't mean it."

"It hurt all the same."

On these visits, Carl paid almost no attention to Damon. It was as if Damon didn't exist, which made him less nervous. Non-existence was good.

It was settled then. Kenny and Damon returned the cots and sleeping bags to Barry and Trent. Carl brought his van around and helped them load up their clothes and Damon's toys.

Gregory, Pleaser, Leroy, Bounce, and Breakout peppered Damon with so much advice on how to plan his escape that sometimes Damon couldn't hear anybody because they were all talking at once.

20

LEMME BREAK IN HERE a minute 'cuz I'm the Pleaser, and between Gregory, Damon, Leroy and the others you don't know about ('cuz they're scary), I never get a word in sideways.

So, where were we? Oh, yeah. Kenny and Damon did boogie on over after Carl met Kenny's whaddya call — "conditions."

Temporarily. Only to get Kenny back. Nothing like permanent. Kenny even knows this; you can see it in his eyes. But he's so hot to get out of that art studio where he feels he gotta paint and into a clean comfy bed and cook gourmet, he'll believe anything. As for Damon, he's a jittering mess.

Carl was polite to Damon the first fifteen minutes or so. That's how much he wanted Kenny.

Nah, I exaggerate. First ten.

At least, he *thought* I was Damon. Damon was so terrified he ducked out, leaving the spot wide open to anyone who'd take it.

YOU'RE NOT SUPPOSED TO DO THAT! Who knows who'd take the spot if it's just lying open like that? Maybe some demon. You're supposed to wait 'til someone takes it away from you. Fact, you're supposed to fight over it. That's the rule.

Leroy's too busy painting his "Great Heavens" mural (boy, am I sick of hearing about it), so good old Pleaser has to take the spot.

Not to worry. I can defend myself against Carl with one *cojone*. Got my ways. But that's why I'm the only one knows what happened after Damon ran. Leroy claims he knows, but he don't.

Damon's so scared that first night, he lies there waiting for Carl to come after him. Gregory kept telling him Carl wouldn't with Kenny there, 'cuz after all Damon was only a substitute for Kenny, and a bloody poor one at that. (Ha! Ha! Little joke there!) Leroy kept promising him he'd take over, but Damon didn't trust him. Leroy's hardly whaddya call — "reliable."

Carl didn't do nothing to Damon at first. 'Cept look at him. But only when Kenny's attention was elsewhere. He'd be in the kitchen cooking beef stroganoff with real sour cream, and Carl would turn to Damon and stare. Not angrily, or threateningly, or even mildly. Or Kenny would be on the phone with Tim, guiding him through his latest fiasco, saying, "Tim, I don't want to have to come up there again," stabbing terror like an icicle into that poor schmuck Damon's heart, and Carl's head would swivel away from Kenny to Damon, as if it were on a Mardi Gras stick, and he'd fix those flat black eyes on him, impossible to read. Carl was planning something. Something for Damon. But he wasn't about to share.

This freaked out Leroy. He didn't want to take time out from his newest masterpiece (if you don't believe me, ask him) just to handle Damon's pain.

"Damon, you gotta run."

"Run to the orphanage."

"Sure! Mick's your friend."

"Yeah, he gave you that little blue pill when you were in pain, remember?"

"He'll get lost," says Wendy. "He'll never find it."

"I'll show him," says I.

"The Mick'll give you a place to stay."

"Are you crazy? That's the first place Carl'll look."

"You've got your head up your arse."

"Up yours!"

"You wish!"

"You gotta travel nights and sleep days, so the police won't catch you."

"But the gangs will."

"Dopey, it's only a dozen blocks."

"A mile at least."

Now the voices in Damon's head are all arguing at once, so Damon can't tell who's saying what, who's insulting who.

"Damon, what did you want to say to me? Damon? Damon?"

It's Kenny, shaking him roughly. Outside of him. Not inside. Nobody's shaking him inside.

"Yes? Yes?" Damon replies frantically.

"Where were you?"

"Here?" In the sailboat room that Kenny insisted was Damon's, with no sign of the tree tower in the ceiling. Even the roots were gone, just stains where they had been. Kenny complained to the people upstairs, but they were as mystified as he was.

"I sorry, Kenny. It's just all the others. They're all talking at once."

"*I'm* sorry, not 'I sorry.' What do you want to go back to baby talk for?"

"I'm sorry. They're making such a racket, I can't hear."

"Well, Madam Adam heard voices, too." Which was the first Damon had learned of it. How did Kenny know? "He's in a mental institution getting shock treatments." Did Madam Adam tell Trent? "And Trent says they make him shake all over, and he screams. Is that what you want?"

"No."

"Sure," said Carl, lounging in the doorway and sucking on his pepperoni penis. "They tie him up with the vacuum cleaner cord, plug it into the socket and turn on the juice. Fries his insides crisp as bacon. Brains curl up like a worm on a hook."

"Maybe we should take you to visit him. So you can see for yourself. Do you want that?"

Damon shook his head No. He didn't say it aloud because if he said he didn't want something, Carl would find a way to get it to him.

"So what did you want to say to me?"

"Nothing."

"Nothing? You called me in here to say nothing to me?"

Had he called Kenny? Damon remained silent, trying not to look at Carl, but his eyes skittered over to him, like mice with minds of their own.

"Damon, you've got to understand about Carl and me. We're married. Anything you say to me you can say to Carl."

Carl gave a snort and pushed off from the doorway.

"Is that better?" Kenny asked. "Now what is it? I don't have all night."

"Carl looks at me."

"Of course, he looks at you."

"No, I mean, he stares."

"Carl stares at you? That's what you called me in to tell me? Really, Damon, we all look at each other. You should be upset if Carl pays you no mind. But he does. He has your best interests at heart. He wants to see that you're healthy, happy, whatever. Of course he looks at you. You don't want him to?"

"No."

"Well, if you're going to stay in this house, you'll have to look at Carl, and he'll have to look at you. He's put up with a lot from you, you know. Now, no more foolishness."

But when Kenny tucked Damon in, it wasn't like it used to be. He didn't tug the covers over him, up to his chin and tamp them around his neck, so he'd be nice and warm. He just kind of pulled them up absentmindedly, not even high enough, and left them there to do their own thing.

"You gotta run," the voices started up again.

"Run, run, run — "

Gregory's trying to calm Damon down, and Leroy swears on his mother's grave (like he can find it) that he'll take the spot next time. Gregory doesn't want Damon to run out into the night, 'cuz that'd put the whole family in danger. After all, what gets done to Damon might get done to the rest of us. Least, that's what Gregory says. Though I'm not quite clear on the whys and wherefores.

Anyways Damon sneaks out of the house. Doesn't even bring nothing with him. No food, no clothes, nothing. Any self-respecting runaway knows you gotta bring stuff in a garbage bag or a pillowcase. But Damon doesn't have the brains he was born with.

Or maybe he does, but terror just blew commonsense clear out of his head.

Damon don't know how to get to Carl's porn studio, but I do. A few blocks down, a few blocks over, and then a zig and a zag.

So he gets there, and it's all locked up, of course, this is San Francisco, not the South Seas like in Carl's flicks.

He knocks very softly so's not to wake up Paulie. See, knocking loud would wake up Paulie, but knocking soft would only wake up the Mick. Honest to God!

No luck. How to get in? This is where I take over again, breaking and entering being a specialty of mine. That's how I got to pal around with the cops.

See, it's a rule or a principle or something. People secure their most valuable stuff with the best locks. You see an old lady caning it down the street with a two-hundred smacker purse, you figure she isn't using it to carry bus fare.

So there's no going down the steps and getting in through the basement. Carl's got wood slats nailed across the windows and iron bars across those. The doors have three locks apiece, deadbolts even Brinks would call "awesome." Front and back doors are similarly "fortified," to quote Gregory, 'cuz they lead to where Carl's movie sets and equipment are. They're obviously the most valuable part of the building, being most expensive and hardest to replace.

Not like kids, who are a dime a dozen, coming in every day on the bus like they do.

Jeffrey's only got two locks on his bookstore front and back, and the windows have bars, too. One way or another, Jeffrey's always behind bars.

Ha! Ha! Little joke there.

But people get careless with upstairs windows. Figure nobody can get to them unless they take up flying. I'm betting Carl's got nails in the sash like at the art studio. Nail's what let's you open the window a little ways to get some air, but not enough so's people can climb in.

I shimmy up in the two foot space between Carl's building and the next, hanging onto things like bricks and sills and gutter spouts. Being flat as a board helps. Got muscles in my fingernails.

Sure enough, I ease open the window. If you know it's just a nail there, and if you're lucky enough to have something nearby to lever it up, all you need is strength. I use a bat that's just inside. Carl's got it to defend hisself against burglars like me. Hah!

I crawl into what's a storage area with lots of theater stuff, masks, props, curtains, costumes, cute little stage sets, the works — plenty of heavy material, like velvet for Damon to wrap hisself up in and fall asleep on a dusty old couch.

Me, I'm allergic to dust, but Damon isn't. So he's the one gotta take the spot.

He tries to get me to stay. "I'm scared," he whines. "Carl might come up and find me."

"No way I'm sneezing the night away," I tell him.

Next morning, just as it's getting light, he's starved, of course, and I could use a bite myself. He sneaks down the stairs, and who should he run into but Mickey darling coming out the bathroom in his red flannel nightshirt.

"Damon?" he guesses, peering nearsightedly into his face. "What are you doing here? Jeez, man, you're freezing, how'd you get in — "

"Don't tell Carl."

"'Course not, jeez Marie, you think I'm a rat fink or something? Come on into the dorm, and let's get you some warm threads."

The room's filled with snores and sweaty bodies tossing in their creaky bunks. Mickey's clothes are too big, of course, so he pinches some of Dickybird's, which are only a little big, and an old jacket, too. They bring the stuff into the kitchen so's not to wake the others.

"Dickybird moved out a couple months ago," the Mick whispers at him.

"Where'd he go?"

"Nobody knows. At least, not so's they're telling. We just woke up, and he was gone. We think he did a Damon One. Oops, sorry. He won't be back. That's for sure."

Mickey slaps together peanut butter and jelly sandwiches and hands Damon a carton of orange juice.

No worry about Paulie catching them. Turns out Paulie didn't come home last night, 'cuz like you probably guessed, Paulie's lazy. Gets the boys to do the cooking and cleaning (unless Carl's around, then he has to fake it).

Paulie's only real job is to deposit his cash! That's enough work for him.

See, Mickey gots this place in the basement next door. It's an abandoned brick factory with a faded white sign outside beneath the roof whitewashed right into the bricks — "UNeeda Biscuit" — in tall letters, real old time. You go up through the roof of the orphanage, cross over to the biscuit building, and take the old rickety stairs down. Careful not to step through the splintery ones and break your fool neck.

The Mick's got a thrashed couch, a lamp with a short in it, plenty of blankets and sleeping bags he pinched off bums sacked out on the street and too drunk to hang onto them. So what if they freeze to death? Not the Mick's lookout. Crackers 'n stuff in coffee cans to keep them from the rats and stacks of porn mags to give his pad some class. That's the Mick's stash.

"I come here when I need peace and quiet. And to rehearse for my auditions," he adds like he's important. "No one knows about this place, not even Carl. You're safe here, Damon."

Damon falls all over himself thanking Mickey.

"You're my best friend. I thought Kenny was my best friend, but he isn't. I'm gonna' tell you secrets."

"'Bout money?"

"Well, I don't know, I'm not sure, could be," Damon says, wracking his brains for some connection between Gregory and the rest of us, on the one hand, and a pile of dollar bills on the other.

'Cuz it's money the Mick cares about more than anything. That's all you gotta know about him. He wants to be a star, so everyone will tell him how great he is and pay him for it. You can't have one without the other, he thinks. If you got money, you can buy yourself a part in some movie, buy the movie even, become a producer. Mickey makes no difference between Hollywood and half a dozen bank accounts.

If you wanted to do him in, that's what you'd focus on. Not that you would. Or me. But some of the others hide their fury at Becca for what got done to Robbie. In a secret place.

Carl's in a rage, Mickey says. He comes storming in and demands to know where Damon is. But Mickey tells him he has no idea, and neither do the others.

"I covered for you, Damon, 'cuz I'm your friend. I'm no rat fink. You gotta think about what you're gonna do, though. Can't stay here forever."

"Why not?"

"'Cuz. I'm trying to make arrangements. How would you like to live with Mr. Martingale? I hear Dickybird's there."

The Mick's got it into his head to sell Damon, see? Only Damon don't suspect a thing. But I'm the Pleaser, and I know a grifter when I sees him.

Carl pleads and offers rewards. Says Kenny's beside himself. He'd give anything to have Damon back.

"I'm doing it for Kenny," Carl says.

Is not. Doing it for Carl. But Kenny brokenhearted makes betrayal a bit more respectable.

"Five hundred dollars I give up just for you," the Mick tells him, bringing him hot dogs and Pepsi. "Five hundred smackeroos for a stinky little kid like you."

'Course, he's holding out for more from Martingale.

Damon uses the toilet that doesn't flush down the hall and sneaks over to shower in their bathroom every few nights. It can't last. Somebody'll spot him.

"You can get to Hollywood and stay awhile for a thousand bucks," Mickey tells him a few days later. That's what Martingale has offered.

See, Carl and Kenny can't tell the police that Damon's missing 'cuz then they'd have to tell they took him. They've put out the word to their friends, but nothing's coming back. Trent says somebody locked Noodles in Kenny's studio, and he pizzled and plopped all over the place. They think Damon done it, but they haven't seen him.

Tell the truth, I'm the one done that, being the lock-pick. Noodles was a nuisance, barking like a mad dog and even grabbing ahold of my pants, while I was going through Trent and Barry's things. Not to take nothing. Just borrow. Everyone's got expenses.

Meanwhile, Damon's getting pretty sick of the basement — leaks through the walls when it rains, and smells of mildew. Rats with teeth the size of a dinosaur's. Has to keep them from chewing off his leg, his left leg especially — the soft and caramelly part. In the middle of the night, he can feel them. Big enough to ride on. When they're not chewing on him, they want to be his friend.

Besides, there's ghosts. He hears them creaking around and whispering late at night in the dark, even with the flashlight on.

Ask me, I think he's got the ghosts in his belfry mixed up with the rest of us. We all whisper. 'Cept when we're shouting at him 'cuz he won't pay attention.

Leroy says no such thing as ghosts. Gregory says there is, too; he's seen them. Me, I'm hoping the ones in the rage place are just ghosts, or they'll come out some day.

But the immediate problem is: Where's Damon going to run next?

Mickey solves it for him.

Late one night, while Damon can't sleep because of all our jabbering, he suddenly hears Mick's footsteps coming down the stairs. But there's another set of steps as well, heavy thumps. Damon springs to his feet and backs up against the wall. He knows those thumps. If he could melt into those bricks, he would. Too late. Flashlights blind him.

"Damon, I brought you a visitor," says the Mick cheerily.

"Hello, Damon," says Carl. Evidently, the high bidder.

"This is good, Damon. I done you a favor. No, really, don't have a spas', now."

"You caused us a lot of trouble," Carl says.

"Carl's gonna send you and me to Hollywood to meet with a

talent scout. He's sending me first. Then when I get established, you can come, too."

"Kenny's beside himself. But he forgives you. We both do."

"You're gonna be a star, Damon."

"Leroy!" Damon yells.

"Who's Leroy?" asks Mickey, 'cuz, even though Damon's told him about us, he only listened with one ear.

"Don't start that crap," Carl says, grinding his teeth and taking a step toward him.

"Leroy, come quick! Carl's gonna beat me."

"Don't you dare start with me!"

"Gregory! Pleaser!" Damon screams, trying to squeeze into the brick wall.

"Oh, them!" says Mickey.

Carl grabs his hand, not that roughly, just firmly. He's not about to show Mickey what he does.

Not that the Mick can't guess. He's been on the receiving end himself. Or rather, his end has. Ha! Little joke there!

So that's how Mickey turned us in. Like Damon says, "How could Mickey betray me like that? He promised. He lied."

"Rat fink" is the preferred term. We'll get him for it, too.

Carl yanks Damon up the stairs, across the roofs, and down to the orphanage. He cuffs him to the bed in the porn studio and locks him in for the night.

He has plans, you see. Plans that include Martingale and a whole bunch of other porn fans. Plans that are gonna keep me busier than ever, 'cuz I'm the Pleaser, 'cuz I know how.

Only people I don't please is my own family.

"Like the prophet," Gregory says.

Whatever.

21

EVERY TIME BECCA TOOK the twenty-four hour bus trip from Seattle to Santa Cruz, it was like traveling backwards through a time tunnel into her past. It was always like that, since the very first occasion when she went home to Dad's for Thanksgiving without telling her mother, because they'd had a huge fight, and she couldn't stand it any longer. She left a note saying only that she had gone. Well, Mom knew that by now, didn't she?

Seattle was a foreign land to which they'd moved to escape the past and to avoid nosy questions about the twins, who their father was, for instance ("mystery meat," Becca joked to Annalyn). A cluster of hills and valleys nestling communities of Scandinavians, Asians, Africans, factory workers, gays, students, protesters, student protesters, gangs, emerging computer cultures, and skaters around a lake named Green. Seattle's Broadway was hardly a "great white way," and it hardly featured great talent; rather, it was noted for its polyglot diversity of beggars from the world over, who assaulted passers-by with their smells and demands.

The whole was surrounded by water and steely-tipped snow mountains that glinted and threatened to erupt at any time. Strange wooden totems as tall as houses bore carvings of the Promethean

Raven, shape-shifter and trickster, that had stolen the light for humans and taught them how to survive; also eagles with healing feathers, whales as iconic intelligence with their protruding fins, frogs that peeked out from the mouths of other creatures, bears that protected warriors with their strength, and owls that assisted shamans and forecast death. Each totem pole had a story of a family that you had to learn if it was to mean anything — reminders that most Seattleites were strangers here, native peoples having lived companionably with the northwest spirits long before white arrival.

Not far from the lake, Becca's mother rented a duplex apartment for half of what it would have cost in Santa Cruz — a wooden structure, gray to match the sky, ramshackle once-green stairs to the front door, flanked with rhododendrons that dropped their blooms on Becca's arrival. Moss growing on the roof prompted one of their new neighbors to suggest that they put a goat up there to mow it like they did in South America. Probably an old Seattle joke. Becca replied that she didn't want to upset the crows that used the roof as their own personal toilet — they'd have to find a Honey Bucket. At which Mom glared at her unforgivingly. For a nurse and unwed mother, she was oddly prudish.

Inside, there were three small bedrooms with splintering windowsills, a kitchen with an ancient range that stood on legs, no less, double cupboards with steel handles that used to be an icebox, a leaded glass window in the parlor, a fireplace with the soot of generations on its bricks, and crickets which freaked her mother out but which Becca chose to think of as pets.

Twins Mike and Ike proceeded to scream as loudly in Seattle as they had in Santa Cruz. To herself, Becca called them the "stinky turds," appropriate monikers considering that they always had a full diaper, one or the other. As they grew, they sat and scrunched up their little faces threateningly at the least provocation. If yelling didn't get him what he wanted, big-shouldered Ike, the future football player and bully of the playground, pounded the floor, his square face inflamed. How dared they yank him out of that warm, wet swaddled place he'd demanded from the day he was born? Who gave them permission? Oh yeah? They'd pay for it, that was for sure.

Scrawnier and more wiry, Mike continued to go on breathing strikes. He twisted his wound-up little body and then let out a long lingering cry of protest against the world. It went on until you'd have thought he'd never breathe again. He'd be an activist, marching *against,* not *for,* eternal friends with other long-haired protest groupies who ate yogurt and wore homespun.

Both had been "beautiful" according to everyone in Santa Cruz. Here in Seattle, where no one knew about Robbie, they were just infants. Neither of them remotely resembled Robbie, thank goodness, probably because they had a different father. Mystery meat.

As they grew, Becca hardly noticed the changes in them. Only that they cried less now because they could use words to complain. Ike didn't like potatoes and gravy (tasted like barf), brushing his teeth (for sissies), girls (also sissies), his softball (didn't go far enough), and the boy next door (a different reason every time). Mike sniffed or sniffled that everything in his room was crooked, one sneaker was too tight, the music on the stereo was flat, his book had too much yellow in the pictures, and Ike was Mom's favorite.

After their move to Seattle, Becca made her escape every morning, and soon her mother did the same, procuring a nursing job at Seattle General Hospital and abandoning her precious charges to a day care around the corner.

In Becca's new middle school, everyone else knew each other, having attended the same elementary, and since they were unaware of Becca's "sordid past," they didn't remind Becca by being "supportive." A healthy identity change. Better than having to play the role of "the sister who let her brother be kidnapped." Becca decided that remaining silent was the better part of discretion. People like you better, anyway, if they can do most of the talking. They may even call you "cool" and "smart," because you're smart enough to listen to them. She never intruded and ate alone unless invited.

After school, she raced around the track until she began to float. No one could catch her, and she could catch anyone. Instead, she chose to pass them like the wind. People began to notice. The track coach invited her to try out for their team, but she declined, citing responsibilities for baby brothers. A computer geek, who fancied she had a crush on him, would lounge against the fence, grinning like a jack-o-lantern with his teeth leaning every which way, and yelling, "Hey, Rebecca, what are you running from?" Clev-er-r-r!

Run completed, she went home to study, and when Mom and the turds returned at five, she disappeared to the library, which was a godsend. Here she wrote Annalyn long letters of misery in return for long letters of gossip, always ending with the cryptic "I've got so much to tell you." Evidently something she couldn't write. Knowing Annalyn, this was about boys. Or sex. Same difference.

Bit by bit, the other kids began to talk to Becca, kids with names like Paige, Ashley, Brianne, David, Latisha, Kaitlyn, Ricardo, and Jakob. When they asked her if she had any brothers or sisters, she didn't know what to say. If she said "No," she was denying that Robbie would ever be found. She hated to acknowledge the turds, but it became the safest answer. Since a lot of them had turds of their own, they were understanding until they gradually realized Becca had no responsibility for them and didn't even have to get home to baby-sit. They grew jealous. "Oh, you don't know what it's like to have to babysit your brother (or sister)." Groans around the table. Becca said nothing.

Not a scrap of Robbie's existence remained. Even Crunchy Bunchies had been replaced with Sticky Wickets. All her memories, both precious and painful, must remain inside her head with this alien land superimposed over them. Day by day, she recalled her own house less, the windows where she awaited Robbie's return, the utility room where she washed his sheets and clothes, the linen cupboard where she got him fresh towels, the backyard for his softball practice with Dad, the tree to watch them from, the garage through which so much of their lives passed. Gradually, this awful Seattle house was replacing them. She could feel the danger that mountains, islands, waters, and totems would crowd out her memories of that beautiful golden blue and flowered land of Santa Cruz, and she'd lose Robbie all over again.

But she always knew how long it had been since Robbie was taken. Like the birth of the baby Jesus, Robbie's kidnapping separated all that had come before from all that came after. B.K. Mom and Dad had fought over "seriously ill" Grandma Emily and disrupted dreamy days of playing the piano and writing poetry. A.K. Grandma Emily had died, Mom and Dad now lived in different places, but Dr. Connie had appeared. Like the continental divide, her brother's kidnapping ran through her life, with people and events falling away to one side or the other.

When the bus rolled away from Seattle that November day and the many others that followed, traveling through lush Oregon to the Golden State, it grew already easier to picture Santa Cruz. As they dipped down Route 17 into the Scott's and Santa Cruz Valleys, the memories of the search intensified, ranging farther and wider than where they'd lived. In the redwoods over there, she had joined the grid search and petted Star, extracting a promise from the poor dog that he was unable to fulfill. At the bus terminal here, pictures of new runaways and kidnap victims crowded the wall, and Robbie's was no longer there. Santa Cruz was home, a haunted one, admittedly, where she still might meet Robbie coming down any street, at the amusement park, sitting on the floor in the library, or whizzing down the slide at the playground. Unable to retrieve him, she had returned to where they'd lived and played together. A poor substitute but better than the alternative.

In Aptos, Dad and his live-in girlfriend Lisbet were expecting her and welcomed her into a warm room of deep-cushioned chintz, glazed Cupid pottery, and watercolors, obviously Lisbet's handiwork. A lacy shawl lay draped over the back of the couch, Dad's sax resting beside it. Becca let her heavy backpack slide to the floor, as if it contained all her troubles. Hugs all around. Her Dad looked tons fitter, happier, younger even, the creases in his face relaxed while Lisbet's pale delicate beauty with the tendrils around her face remained unchanged.

"Your mom's frantic," Dad said perfunctorily. Both of them knew she wasn't.

"I left her a note," Becca said, neglecting to mention that it was contentless.

"We figured you'd taken the bus, and you'd be here about now," said Lisbet. "I've made cream of chicken vegetable soup, and there's bread and cheese."

A short while later, Dad excused himself.

"They need a substitute at the Cactus Club," he explained, rather proudly, Becca thought. He grabbed his sax, nestled it into its carrying case, and headed out the door.

"Your dad's had some success," Lisbet said, clearing and putting away. "Perhaps because he's so personable. The other musicians like him. He's got gigs planned for New Orleans, Branson, San Francisco, and Nashville." Lisbet paused to show Becca pictures of her Dad in local nightclubs.

"He's so old," Becca said. "I mean, most of them are like teenagers or twenty-somethings."

"I think that's one reason they enjoy taking him in. An 'old dude' — that's what they call him — who's actually cool makes them feel liberated."

Every time Becca returned to Santa Cruz, Annalyn took her to the UCSC campus Baytree Bookstore Café, where they ate sandwiches of eggs and alfalfa sprouts amid the redwoods. Probably Becca wouldn't have noticed the changes in Annalyn if she'd been growing up with her. "Budding," as the school health books liked to put it. Maybe that was what was getting her all hot. Becca had just itched. Long-waisted with hips and bosoms now, Annalyn's bushy brown hair flowed in straightened shiny waves, her teeth banded and encircled by a cupid's bow of wine lipstick. She favored silver rings with authentic turquoise stones on every finger to symbolize her spiritual connection with the southwestern native peoples (her family had taken to winter vacationing in Scottsdale, Arizona). She, in turn, admired Becca's shoulder-length bob with the streak across her high forehead and the dangling earrings.

During Christmas vacation, they wandered down Mission Street into an ice cream store for a cone, Becca saying,

"I remember Robbie and I used to come here. I'd spend my baby-sitting money." Annalyn put a silver-ringed hand on Becca's arm.

"But, Becca, this store didn't open until September, a few weeks after you left."

"You're kidding."

"You've never been in here."

"But I remember. Robbie'd order 'spistachio' — I think he just loved to say that word."

"That was another store. The one by the playground. We took him there a lot."

"It was here. I remember it," Becca said, growing upset.

"Besides, Robbie's favorite ice cream was chocolate."

"That was when he was three. Remember?"

But how could the image of these happy posters and these little round white tables and chairs be so vivid and not be true?

"Pistachio was his new favorite," Annalyn comforted.

"As soon as he learned the word."

Her mind was playing tricks on her. Were there any other "memories" that had never happened? She felt afraid.

"It's as if I'm losing Robbie all over again," Becca told Dr. Connie, who still saw her on occasional visits during her lunch hour, because her other times were full. "I keep forgetting who he was and making up someone else. And Dad's become a stranger, this skinny pot-smoking musician with greasy hair, eating greasy burgers on the road and talking their lingo. The only one who hasn't changed is dear Aunt Cordelia."

"It happens," Dr. Connie assured her in her office still peopled with trolls that other patients got to play with. "Very common, really. We're not sure how. But it's like the same creative process that makes us able to link two things to make a third. Like baking. If you've always baked pumpkin pie and made peach ice cream, you might make peach pie and pumpkin ice cream."

"Robbie's becoming something he never was, a little boy who went to a place that didn't exist. I even got his favorite ice cream wrong. Annalyn remembered it, and I didn't."

"But you remembered how he loved to say 'pistachio.'"

"Was it his favorite, though? What else am I forgetting about the real Robbie? And what am I making up?"

"Time has a way of changing our memories. Memory's never been as dependable as we'd like to think. What I suggest, when you get home to Seattle — "

"Seattle will never be home!"

"*Back* to Seattle, then. I suggest you write out a little memory book for Robbie. It hasn't been that long. You probably remember a lot about him that's true. Write it all down so you won't forget."

"A memory book," Becca repeated, enchanted with the thought. "That's what I'll call it. *A Memory Book for Robbie.*

"Is Robbie dead, do you think?" Becca asked Dr. Connie another time, as she finger-combed Wild One's hair.

"There's no way of knowing. But he's changing, just as you are. Even if he came home today, he wouldn't be the same Robbie you knew. He'd have grown. Being snatched from his family and what-ever else he's been through would have changed him. Then again, you know that he'd have grown and changed even if he'd stayed home. We can't hold our loved ones still, much as we might think we'd like to. You're growing and changing too. That's not bad or good — just life."

"Sometimes, I find myself praying to Robbie instead of God. I know that's a sin. But what's the use of praying to God anyway? He didn't protect Robbie."

"Do you think you'll always feel that way?"

When Becca got up to leave, she put the troll back on the shelf in front of *The Minds of Billy Milligan.*

"Why don't you take Wild One with you to Seattle?"

"Mine to keep?"

"Yours to keep."

Wild One! Naked and indecent. Mom would be appalled. The prospect immediately cheered her.

22

"2 x 2 IS 4, 2 x 3 is 6, 2 x 4 is 8, 2 x 5 is 10."

Damon sat on the stool in the kitchen, under the calendar picture of a naked boy skipping down the road among the trees, while Kenny prepared vegetables for his "Sudo Hot and Sour Soup." That was what he called it. He'd dumped four cans of chicken broth and a lot of water into his biggest pot and was now chopping green peppers as Damon recited his times tables.

They went through this routine every night at about seven o'clock, after Damon had finished his day at the private school Kenny was paying through the nose for, following which he'd run as fast as he could to the studio, where they were waiting to shoot him.

Kenny and Carl had made this deal. Carl let Damon go to school in exchange for acting services. Kenny said, "You got it backwards." Back and forth they went, while I explained to Damon that this was a power struggle, but Damon didn't understand. Finally, Kenny said, "I'm your agent, Damon. And you'll do as I say. You're a very lucky boy. It'll be your after-school activity. Some kids just play ball or go swimming. You get to act. Other kids would kill to be in motion pictures."

"I wanna play ball," said Damon.

There was never any question of Damon running away. If he ran, Carl would hurt Kenny. Damon believes this. Carl tells him and Kenny tells him. In fact, soon after he began first grade, Damon dashed into the studio to find Kenny naked and tied to the bed, with all the boys standing around in utter silence, as if they were witnessing an execution. Carl brandished a thick leather strap over Kenny, saying Damon was late, so Kenny had to take a whipping.

"Oh, no, Carl, no, here he is now. He's right here, see, he's only a little bit late."

Then Kenny howled and twisted to his side as Carl laid the strap to him, leaving an angry red mark across his hip and buttock.

Only later did I point out to Damon the whirring cameras. I didn't even have to appear in the mirrors; Damon was accustomed to Gregory's voice. It was all an act. Now, he stood with the other boys, watching in horror.

"Tell Carl why you were a little bit late," Kenny implored Damon, but Damon didn't know. He thought he'd run to the studio as fast as he could.

"The teacher made him stay," snorted Mickey.

"He had to say his times tables," Hank suggested.

"Is that what happened?" Carl demanded of Damon.

Scared of lying to Carl, Damon simply nodded. It could have been. The teacher could have made him stay.

"I don't believe you," said Carl, raising the strap above Kenny, who screamed as it came down on him once more, a thread of blood oozing from his blue-white flank.

"Leroy, Leroy," Damon cried out. "Come and take the pain for Kenny."

"Doesn't work that way, kid," said Leroy in his foghorn voice. "I can only take the pain for you."

Meanwhile, Kenny was protesting loudly, "Carl, that was too hard," and struggling against the ropes that tied him to the bed.

"Who's Leroy?" asked Flip.

"Yeah, who's Leroy?" asked Nate.

"His little imaginary friend," Mickey whispered loudly enough for everyone to hear and giggle.

Carl leaned over Kenny and untied the ropes.

"Okay, I'm letting you off easy this time, since Damon was only a little bit late. But let this be a warning to you."

Kenny rubbed his sore buttock gingerly.

"I think I need stitches," he said.

"Nah, just a nice disinfectant that stings like hell."

"Don't you dare hit me that hard again," Kenny warned, disappearing into the bathroom.

"Next time your teacher wants to keep you, you'd better tell her you have a dying brother at home," Carl said to Damon. "It'll be the truth. Okay, places everyone."

Mickey hadn't gotten to Hollywood yet. Carl was still making arrangements with a famous producer and a famous agent as the months slipped into a year and beyond.

"They're waiting for just the right role for you," Carl explained on one occasion. And on another, "I think it's best for you to have the right part rather than just any old thing, don't you?" And later still, "Which would you rather be, a minor character or a star? Your choice." Meanwhile, Damon's roles got bigger. Jealous, Mickey tipped over a rack of sex toys during one of Damon's scenes. Then Damon couldn't find his costume, not that there was much of it, but he had to have something to take off. At one point, Mickey was supposed to engage in a bit of horseplay with Damon and Hank. Mickey poked Damon's balls so hard he had to sit the scene out, Carl erupted in a stream of invective, and Mickey smirked at his double victory.

But, Pleaser and Leroy weren't exactly idle in spite of my dire warnings. They'd never forgiven Mickey for betraying Damon. This was why they were trapped here in the studio, after all, Pleaser to "act" and Leroy to take the pain. While they weren't big enough to do something major to Mickey yet, they were growing. During a hasty breakfast one morning, Mickey gobbled down his cereal before he noticed it was salty. The rest of the day, he alternated between mad gulps of water and mad dashes to the bathroom to the humiliating taunts of an increasingly frustrated Carl. Mickey blamed Damon, of course, but Damon had had nothing to do with it.

Then there was the endless hiding of Mickey's glasses, resulting in unsightly bruises when he wasn't on camera, because he'd bump into the furniture.

"Mickey! Glasses!" Carl would yell.

"3 x 5 is 15, 3 x 6 is 18, 3 x 6 is 24, 3 x 6 is 36."

Sometimes Damon went "off track" because he was tired, but mostly it was to test Kenny. Kenny didn't know his times tables. This was because he was "rusty." Rust is a beautiful color in art, as Leroy's often told us, especially when rusty metal oxidizes and streaks with yellow, but it isn't very good for times tables.

Sometimes Damon got just plain mischievous. "3 x 7 is 176, 3 x 17 is 6."

Kenny said "Um-hmm," but rarely corrected him because he didn't know the right answer, until Damon got too outrageous even for Kenny's rustiness.

"135 x 3,279 is 1,698,532 and a half."

"And a half! Oh, now my Damon's teasing me. There couldn't be a half because, well, there just couldn't be. You have to take your studies seriously, Damon."

Now came the "serious school speech."

"If I'd gone on with my education instead of quitting in high school — " Actually, he'd quit in the middle of ninth grade to run away from his mom who beat him with a pudding spoon, a broom, a rake, and a TV clicker — "I'd be a successful artist, eminent even. Do you know what 'eminent' means? It means very, very famous. Everybody looks at you and wonders what you eat for breakfast."

"You eat Crunchy Bunchies, just like me."

"Everybody doesn't know that."

"You want me to tell them?"

"They're not interested. Not yet, anyway. Because I'm not famous."

"Sometimes you eat eggs."

"Instead, I'm only a struggling artist, a promising artist."

"If you ask me," Carl said between phone calls, "you broke your promise."

"Well, I didn't ask you, did I?"

"Back to struggling," Carl taunted, but Kenny didn't think it was funny.

"Where were we, Damon? Were we up to the times sixes?"

"Uh-uh, times nines."

"Oh, I don't think we were that far," Kenny said, dumping chopped celery, carrots, and red and yellow peppers into the caldron of simmering chicken broth. Now, he was draining tofu on paper towels and opening cans of bean sprouts and water chestnuts. "We haven't tested your spelling in a while. How do you spell your name?"

"That's easy. D-A-M-O-N. How do you spell 'gefilte fish'?"

"Gefilte fish? What's that?"

"This boy at school eats it. His name's Aaron."

"Oh, I don't know, let me see," and Kenny pondered, while defrosting a bag of cut-up turkey to put in the soup. "Gefilter — "

"You've got to test him on the important words," Carl put in, roaming the kitchen and sampling soup ingredients — "like the stations of the cross," I inject into Damon's ear.

"What's 'stations of the cross'?" Damon asked Kenny.

"Sounds like a religious thing to me," Kenny replied. "Like a pilgrimage that you get on the train for."

"A food pilgrimage," I murmur. "Some people are very religious about their food."

"I think Dad was."

"Was that something you heard about in your old family?" asked Kenny, splashing vinegar into his brew to make it sour.

"How do you spell 'ball'?" Carl persisted.

"B-A-L-L."

"Oh, Uncle Carl's right. That is important. Very good, Damon!"

"Now how do you spell 'balls'?"

"B-A-L-L-S."

"That's right, Damon, you just add an 's' to it."

"What else does he need to know?" Carl asked. "How do you spell 'cock'?"

"Carl, that's not necessary."

"You'd rather I asked him how to spell 'rooster'?"

But Damon thought it was funny, and spelled it out, then asked Carl, "How do you spell 'asshole'?"

"M-I-C-K-Y," answered Pleaser brightly.

Kenny's jaw dropped and Carl looked thunderstruck.

"Mickey has an 'e' in his name," he said calmly.

"That wasn't me, it was Pleaser," said Damon. "He's a rotten speller."

"Pleaser doesn't please me," said Carl.

Damon felt himself in earthquake territory and sought to regain the gaiety of the previous conversation. "How do you really spell 'asshole'?"

"Easy. It's just two words put together, see? A-s-s and h-o-l-e. How do you spell 'fuck'?"

"How do you spell 'shit'?"

"He's got the idea," Carl nodded to Kenny.

"I'd rather he didn't take those words to school," Kenny said lightly. "Come on, guys," he added, sprinkling chopped green onions over the three bowls, "soup's ready. Damon, you carry yours in, Carl, yours, and I'll get the rolls."

"You forgot to forget them," Carl teased.

"Not this time."

At last, Mickey was headed to Hollywood on a one-way bus ticket. The reason Carl gave for this was that Mickey would become so famous he wouldn't return, or if he did, he'd be rich enough to charter a jet.

During Mickey's last few days at the studio, he dressed up in fancy period costumes with shirts opened to the waist that showed off his naked chest and Celtic cross, and he gave his hair a kind of spiffy pompadour. He stood by Carl as if he were the assistant director, holding himself aloof from the studio action, but occasionally deigning to correct one of the boys by moving the part of the body that he thought at fault. Carl regarded these directorial maneuvers with a clenched jaw, but remained in control, possibly because he'd soon be shut of the Mick for good.

When Mickey arrived in Hollywood, he'd be met by a famous director of art films, who would escort him to his own house in Malibu and put him up in a room on the top floor. A famous agent would meet with them at the director's home, and they'd plot Mickey's future over glasses of champagne, trays of caviar, crepes suzette, and gefilte fish. While Mickey was waiting, he'd hoof it down to the beach and spend his days sunning and ogling the tanned boys and girls as they played volleyball. Best of all, it was free, the pad, the champagne, the beach, the parties.

Mickey explained all this to Damon, Hank, Flip, Nate, as well as Pleaser, Leroy, Wendy, and myself (without realizing it, of course) over lunch each day, expanding on what Hollywood would be like, and promising Hank that he was undoubtedly next in line, the promise to Damon at his betrayal apparently forgotten. At least, by Mickey.

We didn't miss him. Not one bit. Mickey had outlived his usefulness to the studio and his popularity with the boys. No sooner had Mickey left than Flip came down with some horrible disease, and Carl had to shunt him off to a hospital, no one knew exactly where. When Hank asked to visit him, Carl told him Flip wasn't allowed to have visitors. Hank didn't ask again.

"I wouldn't talk about him if I were you," Paulie suggested to them one night.

"Like Dickybird?" asked Nate.

"Exactly like."

Ball and Shayne, a brother and sister act, joined our circus and made quite a splash in the acting credits.

One day, Kenny was getting Damon ready for Reggie's birthday party. Damon was excited. He wasn't allowed to socialize with his classmates; he might say something he shouldn't and get everyone in trouble. Carl and Kenny had disagreed over this policy, Carl thinking it would be nice to let Damon have his school friends over. Who knows, one of them might be talented. Kenny argued for caution. Maybe when Damon was a little older and better trained to keep his mouth shut.

No, Kenny and Carl kept Damon close to the nest, but Reggie was Trent and Barry's new boy, this was his first "birthday," and everyone was going to welcome him into the "family." Kenny had opened his own studio, so they had another area to put drinks, food, and party favors. He hardly used it for painting anymore, anyway.

"Isn't our Damon a handsome young man?" Kenny asked Carl, turning him around in his wine velvet suit with the white ruffles and fancy gold pocket watch.

Carl was on the phone, apparently an important call, because his jaw was working back and forth.

"How long ago? Everything? You just stay put, I'll take care of it." He slammed down the phone and jumped up. "That was Jeffrey. Cops raided our place a few minutes ago. We're closed down. Yellow police tape across the doors. Jeffrey's bookstore, too. The boys took off. We can probably round them up, but we'll have to suspend production until we get this mess settled. Got to get down there," he sprang up and grabbed his coat, dark glasses askew. "Maybe Madison can lend us his studio in the meantime." Then he turned to Kenny. "Somebody turned us in. I wonder who could have done that?"

23

POOR CARL!

You gotta feel sorry for the smarmy bastard.

He gets shut down on an anonymous tip. (That's me, A.N. Ony-mous.) Cops turn up at the apartment and haul him off to jail, where he spends the night in a snit. Fr. Martingale hisself comes to court. In a collar, yes. Oh, you didn't know? Jesuit, no less. They're just as sicko as the rest of the perv clergy, but they're very intellectual about it. He gets his lawyer to bail Carl out. Takes in some of the younger boys in return. Payment on demand, you might say.

D.A. tries to bring Carl to trial, but can't make it stick. No matter. Carl's out of business, at least temporarily. He's terminally upset, which I love. I wallow in his helplessness like a hippo in a mud hole. They're watching him, and he knows it. So do all his friends, who suddenly don't want him around. "Nothing personal," they say.

Cops try to stick Hank, Nate, Flip (back from the hospital) and the rest of the older ones with Social Services, but they split to the streets.

Paulie isn't at the orphanage at the time of the raid, of course, so he's in the clear. They try to charge Carl with neglect, saying he should have an adult supervising the children — that's a long one, since he shouldn't have had the children at all, but they're desperate. Carl tries to get Paulie to come in and tell them he's the orphanage headmaster or Dad or chaperone or something, but no way Paulie's making an appearance. He just got paid.

Damon sacks out with Kenny, who's taken a bunch of money and split again. Can't stand the disgrace.

Carl finally gets his place reopened, paying off the cops with Damon's sweet bod — that's me. A one-man sex industry, I am!

No sooner does he get the studio running at full capacity again than the earthquake knocks the whole building flat! Or pretty damn near. Boys barely escape with their shorts. Yellow tape's back up around the place, this time for keeps.

Carl can't even claim a business loss, because, of course, he can't claim a business.

With major assurances from Father Martingale, Carl moves the boys out to his "ranch" complete with a jerry-built studio. Carl and the good father work hand in glove, so to speak. Ha! As Leroy would say, "Little joke there!"

And now to the six o'clock news! Mickey's back from Hollywood, tossing pictures of himself in various poses around, labeled with movie titles you never heard of.

Ball and Shayne are actually impressed. As Gregory says, they're young yet.

It's been a whole year since the Mick went to meet with that talent scout. 'Cept he's just a director in another porn studio. Adult films, not child.

Mickey tries to pretend to himself and everybody else that he's come up in the world. He made these films, but he don't make the grade, ya' know? He don't cut the mustard. But no one's saying that. They're saying he's moving on to another phase of his career. Don't ask me how going back to what he done before is a step forward.

"Call him promising," Carl taunts Kenny who is busy making copies of gallery paintings of computers. Claims Carmine approves.

Mickey goes back to work in Carl's films, lying like hell about his Hollywood successes, only to find that Damon has eclipsed his star.

He stands around watching Damon do what he used to and not a bit pleased. Jealous as hell, in fact. Damon's cock's gotten bigger. It used to be average, I'd say a Medium, if you use the same sizing method as tee shirts. Didn't matter too much in a child. Now it's longer and thicker, maybe on account of all that use, like when you're at the gym pressing a hundred pounds, and then you get so's you can press one twenty-five. Like that.

Mickey plays adult to Damon's young sweet innocent pre-teen, and the cameras are on Damon. Mick complains. Carl tells him, "Shut the fuck up, or I'll turn you out."

Don't need the Mick anymore. Plenty of other out-of-work adult actors, that's for sure. Not much call for extras in porn films, as you undoubtedly know.

We're all pleased with the Mick's misery. We still remember what he did to Damon. And we're bigger and stronger now. Now we can take our revenge.

Against Gregory's advice, of course. We don't tell him what we're up to, but he gets wind of it and calls a family council to tell us to lay off the Mick. What a wuss! All he cares about is family security. He's afraid we'll end up in jail. Maybe him, not me!

If he does, I won't even visit him.

Not often, anyhow.

And, of course, you know what they did to the Mick. No? Can't even guess? Well, I don't know much more than you do.

I know what happened, just not how. I know the result, you might say. If you as me, Leroy knows, but he's not talking. You can be sure where Leroy's involved, though, it's something hideously horrible. Not that Leroy does anything hisself, mind. But, like me, he gots friends, he —

Pleaser wants I should tell ya' what happened to the Mick

He don't know shit except he knows I know 'cause I'm the one what done it or rather   saw that it got done.

I was in Kenny's studio painting a study for my "Great Heavens" mural which is the most magnificent painting ever seen by human eye

makes the Sistine Chapel look like graffiti

I been painting it over Kenny's "Political Diversity"
that coffee-colored monstrosity don't deserve to live   'Scuse inter-
ruptions
Gotta get this color just right   this line   this shadow — —
Now Kenny, he don't hardly come to the studio no more
since he moved back with Carl he keeps planning to and says he's
gonna but one thing and another
He's making copies of paintings in galleries   not   museums
mind you not the "Mona Lisa" well he'd have to go to the Louvre for
that
don't even know it   had a fit when he seen what I done to his
"Poli Di" blamed Damon. His tough.

"Great Heavens" is cerulean blue that's what cerulean blue means
sky blue and the more you look at it the more you see   like
Tchelitchev's "Tree" —
the gardens with the celadon greens and a touch of verdant and
roseates incarnadine   and saffrons   of sunrise and just a hint
of burnt ocher where the galleries of gods and saints and angels rise
higher and higher.
Get so excited just thinking about it
            I'm out of breath this is the
                        greatest painting anyone's ever done I
had a vision of heaven see and I been working on it ever since.
I been working on my masterpiece for fifteen years.   That's longer
than I been alive.
Carmine's excited about the sketches I showed him although
he's excited about what that shit Pleaser does for him and that
kinda' spills over into art appreciation
            or maybe it's the other way around "Great Heavens"
turns him on and Pleaser finishes the job like he's the sorcerer's apprentice or something.
                        See, Carl promised
Mickey a crack at crack Hollywood.   Ha! "Little joke there."
So Mickey showed Carl where Damon was and Damon,   that   poor
excuse for a
      schmuck,

starts yelling for me to take the spot for him but I'm into painting much more than pain

although pain inspires visions in me.

        I saw "Great Heavens" while Carl was tearing open my bum, for me so I guess one's gotta put up with anything for one's

        art still Carl wasn't actually hurting Damon yet. He had plans for him or rather he had Fr. Martingale's plans,

        so I went on working until Damon just LEFT THE SPOT!

        All kinds of characters rushed in like something's gotta fill a vacuum, and you never seen such weirdos! I didn't know half of them myself I swear.

        Gregory thinks I know everybody in the family, and I do know more of the others than he does, but I don't know'm all.   Just a minute.

That's Gregory trying to horn in again, but he can't have it both ways either I do my chores that the family's assigned and have my say or I leave the spot and don't do any more goddamn ass-pains-taking ever again

        their choice!

So Mickey that no good rotten rufous ratted out Damon and sent him into conniptions, so I had to keep going back and forth between my art and Damon's screams, and an artist needs   tranquility to paint   don't need a lotta ear-splitting squalls!

        Finally that little worm Pleaser done his bit for family and country

     by getting the cops to shut down Carl's studio, and I have to hand it to him, and I don't hand much to the Pleaser

       believe me but we was all

        free to do our thing and it was a relief let me tell you

    Mickey's so jealous of Damon at Father Martingale's studio and mean to him

People are always mean and jealous when they done you wrong.
That's when I called on my cousins go by the names of

    Vigrid the Avenger   and Mefisto.

Vigrid the Avenger's the brains of the outfit and Mefisto's the brawn
 doesn't get   as much action as he'd like
        Vigrid ran the operation on account of going for his A.A. nursing
degree while Gregory studies computers   got no idea why
he's missing classes
one minute he's sitting in front of a computer the next he's standing
over a dogfish in the lab or something
        Vigrid's mostly self-taught   studies the anatomy
of pain
 which nerves work with which nerves to cause the most intense agony
possible
that's his specialty making people wanna die but keeping them alive
for more of it
        I help him from my own experience
He's getting plenty of practice though I don't know where
animals I think   some humans   street people they say
                but he's gotten very good and he and Mefisto are a team
whatever he can't do 'Fisto does and he guides 'Fisto on where to hit
and how to damage
tear arteries
                        Smash kidneys to a lumpy pulp
rupture stomach and spleen
            but leave the nerves and genitals to Vigrid
His specialty   and Mefisto loves him for it.
Truly truly adores him for it.

    Getting the Mick was easy.   Ask yourself
            what's the Mick's weakness? Fame and fortune, right?
 That's how you get people
                        their dreams   tell him there's a
 producer waiting for him in a photography studio tell him
            they want to cast him in a brand new film by some great
director but he's got to get his portfolio up to date none of
                        those old pix of his cock in various positions this
is the real Holy-wood so show up for the photo shoot at midnight

they're on a tight schedule and have all these other candidates coming in before him so be on time   or else.

Mickey walks in.

First thing he hears the locks click makes him jump

it's dark makes him stop and call out you want him spooked but not spooked enough to run

not yet anyway   there's a light on in the inner sanctum of the photo place   he figures

that's where the action is and a voice tells him sit in front of the cameras the photographer will be there in a minute and he checks himself in the mirror with his glasses on   with them he can see

without them he looks better

Runs a comb through his curls powders his face again lightly maybe thinks pock marks aren't as deep as they used to be but that's okay 'cuz scrof isn't "in" scrof's out besides who ever saw scrof in Holywood so takes off his glasses,

sits down in the chair noticing   the camera isn't on and waits a few   fidgets   picks a piece of lint off his pants like it's all he needs to be perfect.

Gets up and feels the camera   cold   which is puzzling what about all those other candidates they interviewed?

maybe this is a different camera   that's right they have several photo rooms not just one.

Then who should walk in but Vigrid the Avenger only 'Fisto's taken his glasses and Mickey thinks it's Damon see the Mick's half blind and they look   alike.

And what does that poor little pimple Mickey know?

"Damon, what are you doing here?" the Mick asks

"Are you auditioning for the movie?"

Then in his very sweet nursey-nurse voice, Vigrid says to Mickey "I'm not Damon." "Course you're Damon" says Mickey and Vigrid turns the camera on and starts taking stills and Mickey immediately puts on his best poses as Vigrid tells him to laugh

now cry   now look mad

but all the while Vigrid is saying "Damon's not here" and

then this rough voice that sounds like four-wheel drive crunching over a gravel road says "You betrayed Damon"   and they're throwing their voices around the room so it sounds like there's a lot more of them

bouncing off the walls and into the corridors

and you can see the Mick's real spooked but the camera's clicking so he stays rooted doesn't bolt not then anyways.

Besides it's just Damon what can he do?

"You turned Damon over to Carl that's not nice" Vigrid says sweetly

"Especially you promised jeez Marie you wouldn't fink   on him I know I was there.

"Did you really think you could sic Carl onto Damon?" I say

"and we'd do nothing about it?"

While the Mick's saying "We who's we?   Who else is here? What the hell's going on? Is the producer coming or not?"

"I've been watching you," says another soft poetic voice that I swear to you I

don't recognize and Vigrid and 'Fisto look kind of startled who's this new guy anyway and what's he doing here?

Now all our voices are echoing across the room and bouncing off the walls again and Mickey's saying, "I'm getting outta here" "Then you won't get the part," Vigrid warns sweet

as pink spun sugar that you buy at the circus and it melts in your mouth because it's nothing.

"The Hell with the part I don't think there even *is* a part."   "Oh, yes there's a part just for you," says Vigrid the Avenger.

"Promise promise promise" say the voices echoing.

"Time to go into the darkroom and see what we've got so far," says Vigrid but Mickey's out the door into the waiting room already so Mefisto grabs his arms

twisting them all the way back

his hands on Mickey's neck you can hear it crack and Mickey yells, "Ouch, Damon that

hurts" and tries to pull away but 'Fisto twists again and says "We told you we're not Damon   now you heard us

"Into the darkroom with you."

Mickey's breath's in gasps and his heart hard beating gives 'Fisto a
    boner just to feel it
    how he gets his rocks off and even Damon says "Isn't that enough
what are you going to do to him?   I'll take the spot
now"   "Oh no you won't you   gave us this job for men if you
can't stand to watch go sleep with Robbie."

The dark room is ready oh yes we've prepared the dark room in advance
                    with special chemicals in the sink that have nothing to
do with developing fluid   nothing whatever to do   one chemical
doesn't hurt nor the second nor even a few drops of the third but
                    Put them all in together you better watch it don't splat-
ter up on your skin your face your eyes.
Good deal you poured them in with rubber gloves that reach to your
elbows   and a rubber mask   and welding goggles.

"Now, stand on this stool here and develop your pictures we'll see if
they're good enough for the director   if not we'll take more"
    "I don't know anything about developing pictures"
                            "That's what we're here for to help you."
    Mefisto lifts him up by the arms so his body has to follow. "Now
put the negatives in"   "Shouldn't I put on gloves first?" hanging on
hooks over the sink "If you want to protect yourself but you see you
don't"
    "Don't want to protect myself sure I do — hey wait"
                    as Vigrid the Avenger drops the negatives into the sink
"Are they any good? I can't see"   "Then I'll help you" and Mefisto leans up against him forcing his arms down into the solution like
a puppeteer moving a doll's arms by hand that easy
                    and Mickey screams then Mefisto thwacks
him upside the head so Mickey collapses into the acid that eats away
his face melting like wax he can go stand in the Holy-wood's Wax
Museum all by hisself no one will know the difference and his
    head too not that it matters — Mick's not going anywhere. Vigrid

yanks the stool away and Mick slides still breathing to the floor because   death would be too kind to Mickey he needs

to live with what he done to Damon and the rest of us and what he thinks Damon done back to him   but we're all well out of there.

The photographer finds the Mick the next morning and what a surprise!

I can't resist I   put my study for "Great Heavens" aside and paint a portrait of Mickey melting   Carmine says it has the veracity of appearance over substance or something and

sells it for enough money to keep us all in thongs for some time

The police are hot on our tails of course except they think it's just one tail.

They get Damon's fingerprints   off   the   camera and whatever and match them to a burgeoning file that Pleaser hasn't quite been able to cop

Gregory's in a state when he finds out so we tell Damon to offer to take a lie detector test which the chief gives 'cause he thinks they're buddies and Pleaser gets Breakout to take the spot. If we can get him away from the ball court long enough and Damon gets away scot free.

PART II
1998

24

THERE'S NOTHING FOR IT but to call a family council.

Which isn't easy. First of all, I don't know everyone; second, I can call them, but they won't necessarily come; third, I have no evidence — I only suspect that at least one of us is implicated in the recent tortures of street people reported by the press. Three have involved razors; in fact, the ever-creative press has baptized the torturer with a soubriquet. They call him "Razorman." But it's the acid burning of a woman's face that alarms me more, the similarity to what got done to Mickey that gnaws at me. The gratuitous pain.

I get home from my job as a computer programmer. After hanging what Damon lovingly calls my vampire coat in the hall closet, I take the stairs two at a time to my gorgeous Victorian sanctuary with its high carved bed, inlaid marquetry tables, Wedgwood lamps, Aubusson carpets, and ceiling panels painted with cupids looking down from the heavens — a little banal in their eroticism for my taste but classic in their composition. Here I change out of the black pants, shoes, purple shirt and tie that the mirror approved just this morning. I learned that mirror approval thing from Kenny, of course. On me, it doesn't approve those wretched geometric scarves of his. So pretentious! Into jeans and tee shirt I wriggle, pondering the question. When you're the head of a family, many of whom you suspect you don't even know, it's a challenge.

Damon has no idea that there are other rooms. He lives in public housing — a studio apartment with linoleum floors and one wall devoted to a two-burner range, an oven, a cooler, and cabinets across the top. Better than Carl's apartment where Damon was always terrified every time he and Kenny went back; or the art studio with only a cot and sleeping bag; or the orphanage where Mickey welcomed him and hid him in a basement until he betrayed him like Judas for thirty pieces of silver which was about what he figured a career in Hollywood was worth. Well, the Mick paid dearly for what he did. That acid attack was purely horrible. Now only the pervs will have him — the ones who get off on beating freaks because they deserve it. So their consciences are clean.

But I don't criticize. In fact, I don't say anything about it to anyone. One of us did it, but I never found out who. I hoped that would be the last such incident, but I knew it wouldn't. Perhaps I'm over-vigilant, seeing our involvement where none exists. But it's the cruelty of the techniques . . . Pleaser gives us the bloody details supplied by his cop friends, occasionally supplemented by whatever Damon has gleaned from TV.

This poor little corner of the San Francisco tenderloin, where the windows look out on the alley with its dripping dumpsters, drunks, coke dealers, and whore bashers, is still better than the porn studio to which Kenny finally abandoned Damon, saying "You've changed so," allowing his wrists to be cuffed to his bed, not even letting him out for school. Better than the places men took him when Carl rented him out after he got sick and had to close the studio for good, places where men did agonizing things that Damon had never imagined, keeping Leroy so busy he couldn't paint, and boy did he bellyache about that! Better than the shelters and the streets where guys dumped him after he was used up.

Here Damon has his very own bed — a "reconditioned" saggy thing with stained ticking — and a rickety night table on which previous owners have scratched their initials (desperate to *be* someone), a "haunted" lamp that goes on and off by itself, a bookshelf with paperbacks lifted from garage sales, odd dishes, what he likes to call his "silver," and a ceramic Labrador puppy that reminds him of something he can't quite remember, but he thinks maybe he had a dog when he was a child growing up on a farm like the one in Kansas, where Dorothy and Toto were blown away. All of them bits and pieces of other people's lives that he tries to make his own.

Damon makes up his childhood as he goes along. Just like the rest of us.

Damon isn't clear on how his apartment gets paid for. He always thinks he's behind a month or two on the rent, and then he finds out he's up-to-date and has money in the bank, thanks to my computer skills. He doesn't remember buying the fancier food in his cabinet, courtesy of Pleaser, so he thinks he's just absent-minded. This much is true; he's absent from his mind often and long enough for the rest of us to take the spot.

We, of course, have to have our own rooms to come and go as we please. Otherwise, we'd be on top of and all over each other. Not a pretty sight. There's an upstairs, an attic, and a basement for the babies.

I go hunting for the others in their rooms to tell them about the family council meeting. Usually I post a sign as well. I've found that the more methods of communication I use, the more members attend. Some of them tune me out. Others don't read, even if they can.

I don't go into their private quarters. I knock or stop on the thresholds; otherwise, they'd rise up in revolt against me again — me, Gregory, the one who saved them from Carl and gave them some semblance of a decent life after he turned us out.

Leroy isn't home. He might be at Kenny's old studio, painting another study for his "Great Heavens" mural. Or he might be somewhere else, in a coffee shop or at a public dance, studying how to socialize.

"You learn to socialize the way you learn to paint a picture," he tells me, "by doing it until you get it right." Socializing, he's discovered, is the best way to learn how the faces of other people express their emotions. He needs to paint them in the great throngs below his Heavens. The people in Leroy's mural have a universal range.

"It's not that I myself need people," Leroy's been saying lately.

This was after he met a woman named Dessa at a nightclub. She started to dance with him, then told him he stank of paint. And she's not into housepainters anyway.

"*Housepainters!*" he explodes at me. "She thinks I'm just some housepainter."

Leroy tries not to let on how much it hurt him. Is there some other aspect of Leroy that's evolving?

"If you took longer showers," I suggest.

His bedroom is more of a studio, a riot of paintings, mounted, stacked, and stored, closets so crammed that additional space is just beginning to extend out the back across the alley — you can see the outline of it, although it hasn't solidified yet. (Admittedly, solidity is a relative term in our family.) Drawers of oils and acrylics like those at Harmon's art store sit back to back at the foot of his bed so as not to take up wall space. The place stinks of paint and Turpentine. No posters of rock stars like you'd find in a normal kid's room (Bounce and Breakout's, for example), no plates of moldering pizza or bottles of Coke spilling over the carpet, or ashtrays with half-smoked butts, no basketballs or footballs or skateboards or other sports regalia like the twins have. No stereos or computers or dirty magazines concealed under the mattress. Just art, on the ceilings, beneath the bed, even in the bathroom, where Leroy makes his showers rare and short, so he doesn't steam up his masterworks and peel them. I've always suspected that the stink of his paint conceals more personal aromas — purifies him, you might say. Evidently, Dessa didn't think so.

Leroy ages so slowly I sort of envy him. He was eight when he began, and he's only about nine. I think it's the painting that keeps him young, the creativity of it. Besides, he doesn't have as much pain to take as he used to — only when Damon's absent-mindedness gets him fired from his job *du jour* as dishwasher, dirt hauler, moving man, gofer, garbage helper, sweeper, assistant baker, or asbestos remover ("no mask needed, just a short job"). There's a rhythm to his hirings and firings which happen every week or two, a few months at most. Even then, Damon doesn't suffer when he's fired like he did before. "Practice makes perfect," he reminds me. In fact, he's gotten downright philosophical. "Another day, another pink slip," he jokes.

Me, I have a birthday or two every year, my last was my twenty-second. Not that I really know. Like most kids, I don't remember my early childhood. Someone told me I was named after the Gregorian chants and that I'm ages old in universal time. But I remember bits and pieces of Robbie's life better than my own. Isn't that funny? Everyone gathers around the cake and candles and congratulates me for growing older because I'm the only one who can, but at this rate I'll be dead someday, and they'll still be young or middle-aged. Who'll take care of them then?

Until Damon goes, of course. One reason I'm so anxious to keep him alive and out of jail — although Breakout or Pleaser can always get him free, they have before, Breakout with his technique, Pleaser with his winning ways. Getting free has always been more important to us than anything.

Damon rarely sits in on family councils. Can't stand the noise, for one thing, everyone talking at once, and the kids in the basement screaming. He tells us to shut up. Sometimes he does this in public. "Shut the fuck up," he yells and covers his ears, on the street or in the fast food joint or on the assembly line, where he's sticking widgets into whatchamacallits. Gets us weird stares from people.

Also, Damon rarely attends because, except for me, he tries to ignore us. He tells us we're just "figments" (Kenny's word). He found out (from some counselor, probably), that not everybody has a bunch of alters living inside his head, and he wants to be like "Onlys." One person, one body. "Normal people." Favorite phrase. Fat chance!

Robbie, of course, we never call on. We all protect him, though, except for Damon, who says he's dead. Carl told him. Robbie's still five, and he still cries for his Bec-Bec, but not as much as he used to. We tell him Becca's fine and maybe we'll see her again some day, instead of telling him how we really feel about her. We give him blocks and trucks to play with. We play ball with him when we have time and Candyland, and Fish upstairs in the attic with all the windows looking out onto his trees where it's always autumn. We let him sleep as much as he wants, round the clock sometimes. He never takes the spot. What would be the point?

Pleaser will probably show up just as soon as he gets back from wherever he's gone, probably donating sex to his favorite charity, the cops such as Blake-on-the-Take, so they won't bother us. He can be a twelve-year-old flat-chested girl or a fifteen-year-old boy, depending on what they want. He's versatile that way. He calls it "gender bending," which I think is a masterpiece of understatement for the complete transformation he undergoes.

Or Pleaser might be servicing some old lady who can't get it anywhere else. In return, he'll come back loaded with his "gifts," tins of gourmet food, cream cheese, lox, and bagels, pot, macadamia liqueur, lobster, crab mousse that Damon finds in his cabinets, and other stuff we can't afford on my salary. Don't knock it. Pays the rent.

No one's home. I post a notice in the kitchen. "Family Council Meeting," it reads. Usually, I post the topic, trying to word it seductively and draw as many members anxious to have their opinions heard as possible. This time, I'm not sure.

"Street tortures the work of a family member?" Everyone who has any knowledge whatsoever will stay away, maybe out of loyalty to whatever secret pal might have done it. Like Leroy, I suspect,

"Family may be in extreme danger?" I'm always pointing out that what one member does affects the rest of us, our safety and existence, although I'm not altogether sure of how and why this should be so. They hate it when I say that. They think we're a commune of unrelated individuals leading independent lives. I'm an alarmist, they say, and they never believe me.

Best not to say anything at all.

Because there are the others, you see, the ones I don't know. That's the most frustrating part of my job. I can sense them, even though I can't see or hear them. Leroy, Pleaser, Wendy, the twins Bounce and Breakout, each knows some alters whom I don't, and they're very secretive. Otherwise, the other alters wouldn't tell them anything. It's like a brotherhood or a code of honor or something.

It's Tuesday night. We're gathered here around our dining room table with the lacy white plastic cloth, the cobalt blue glasses, and the blue and white willow pattern china. I picked everything out, and it all matches. Damon doesn't have a dining table because he doesn't have a real dining room. He has a rickety tray beside his stuffed chair — well, partially stuffed — where he watches TV.

Wendy's making us banana berry milk shakes. I suspect she laces them with vitamins. Some people come just for those — a bribe of sorts, as a favor to me. If Damon wants one, he'll have to join us.

Wendy's a shadow, and sometimes when she's pleased with us, she becomes more and more solid until we can see the embroidered flowers on her pink or blue or white frock. But if she's upset with us, she fades until she's just a silhouette moving across the dining room wall. Then you can see her milk shake going down her throat, with an occasional bubble. Sometimes we're afraid she'll fade away altogether, so we try to do as she says. We eat our vegetables and clean up after ourselves. (At least, I do. Not Pleaser. He wallows in his own filth.) Wendy hardly speaks, and when she does, her voice is a breathy whisper. Pleaser says it's sexy, but he says everything is.

Wendy's main job is caring for the basement kids, the babies and toddlers. I've never seen them. There are ghosts down there, so I'd never go. But I've heard the children wailing, giggling, fighting mostly. They do other things with each other, too, things they shouldn't, but they're quite innocent about it. When they crawl up the stairs, Wendy sets a gate across the top, so they can't get out up here where they'd wreck the joint. They play with their pets a lot. There's a whole mini-zoo down there, and sometimes the stench gets annihilating. Wendy makes them clean it up, though.

"I called this meeting because — because —" I break off. Quite unbusinesslike. Still can't figure out how to word it without offending someone, either here or somewhere else.

"Spit it out, Gregory," says Pleaser, sucking noisily on his shake.

"I'm afraid this family may be in danger."

"Not that again!" Groans around the table.

"Hah! Some family!" says Pleaser.

"Family's not so bad," I say. "We have a lot of advantages compared to *Onlys*. We live our own lives and other people's besides. We remember each other's experiences, sometimes. *Onlys* don't. Like a whole bunch of karma in one lifetime. We don't have to wait for another. But we've got to stick together and not do anything that could endanger the others."

"Would you get off that family kick?" says Bounce. The twins wear matching sports jerseys.

"Yeah, we're not family," says Breakout.

"I don't even like half you guys," says Bounce.

"We don't like you either," growls Leroy.

"Well, I sure don't like you," says Pleaser.

"Family members don't necessarily like each other all the time." I'm being as diplomatic as possible.

"Would you all shut the fuck up!" Damon yells from his chair in front of the TV, where he's watching a crime program.

"We're having a discussion, you twit!" says Leroy.

"I can't hear!"

"Why don't you join us," Wendy suggests sweetly. "We're having your favorite banana berry shakes."

"Would you bring me one, Wendy?" Damon's never so polite as when he's asking Wendy for something.

"Uh-uh, rules are you have to eat at the table. *Our* table. Too much gets spilled over where you are."

"Like it doesn't get spilled where you are? Honest to God, Wendy, we're all here."

"I think we should listen to Gregory," says Wendy. "He's been right before."

"When?" Pleaser challenges. "When has Gregory ever been right?"

"I don't quite remember. But I know he has."

"Could we get on with it?" Bounce asks. "We're missing the ball game."

"Yeah," echoes Breakout. "Could we get on with it?"

"Yeah," says Bounce. In their hurry to agree with each other, the twins sometimes forget that they already have.

"State your case," says Pleaser, licking his fingers as if germs were chocolate sauce. Hanging around police stations has given him an occasional pseudo-legal view of things, with which he bullies people when it's to his advantage.

"It's these street tortures," I say. "Horrible things being done to these young boys. Girls, too."

"Only a couple of girls."

This makes it okay?

"A lot of cutting," Bounce says, swallowing a glob of ice cream because he's a growing boy and needs to fill out those shoulder pads.

"Nerves, mostly," Breakout adds.

"Acid too," Damon calls in from the living room. "Like what got done to Mickey."

"Oh, the Mick — that's ancient history."

After the Mick's unfortunate accident, the cops came around to Carl's when Kenny and Damon were there. Mickey had accused Damon. Damon didn't hide his anger at the Mick very well. Said he got what he deserved. Not a good move. Cops probably don't remember, but who knows what they've got in their computers. After Damon screwed up, Pleaser handled them, of course.

They sure know a lot — these guys. I'm not telling them anything new.

"Yet they're left alive in that condition," says Pleaser, and you can't really tell if he's horrified or enjoying the spectacle in his head. He's the only one of us who's been to the hospital with his cop cronies to "interview" the poor human remains. At least, the way he tells it.

"That's terrible what happened to Mickey." Leroy shakes his head seriously, and Bounce, Breakout, and Pleaser erupt into guffaws, while Wendy looks grave.

"Is not," yells Damon from his living room. "That fucker got what he deserved for what he done to me."

"Only kidding, Damon," says Leroy.

"God," says Pleaser, "when brains were handed out, Damon must have been in the can."

"Pleaser, you yourself said the cops are still holding Mickey's case open," I remind him. "They have some DNA they found under his fingernails."

"Just don't know what to do with it. Besides, the Mick told them such a crazy story about a gang of invisible people — " Pleaser breaks it off to give everyone a chance to laugh, "they half think he did it to himself."

"If they get the same DNA from torture cases, even from one victim, they could come after us."

"Only if they've got DNA from one of us, which they don't have. None of us did anything serious enough to get into their files." Pleaser scoops out a piece of banana with his incredibly dirty fingers. I see Wendy notices, but she's not about to say anything. She doesn't want to run the risk of someone leaving the family council. Few enough here as it is. "Besides," he adds, cheeks bulging and mouth offering an occasional inside glimpse of his masticatory process, "they can't keep up with all the DNA they got. Lab's way behind."

"Techniques are antediluvian," someone heretofore unheard from growls.

"No money or time to process it," Pleaser finishes.

"What if they catch up?"

"We'll all be dead by the time they catch up. And our children."

"Children?" The possibility of one of us having children and complicating our lives exponentially was a thought I tried to avoid. The kids downstairs aren't direct descendents of ours, more like brothers and sisters. Wendy's a virgin, and she's not solid enough anyway, and the only one of us messing around with people on the outside is Pleaser, who favors men. Too, any children on the outside would be on the outside. One of the many advantages of being a closed-door family.

"And besides that, if one of us did the dirty deed, he's the one to go to jail. Nothing to do with the rest of us."

"I've told you over and over, we all have Damon's DNA, and that's what got found under the Mick's fingernails."

"Did not," replies Bounce hotly, thrusting his empty glass toward Wendy without so much as a "please."

"I didn't do anything," Damon shouts from the living room.

"I have nothing of Damon's," says Breakout.

"Me neither," says Bounce.

"Or me," says Breakout.

"I don't even want anything of his," giggles Pleaser.

"Too clean for you?" sneers Leroy.

"Well, I don't want anything of yours either," yells Damon from his living room.

"How many times do we have to tell you, Gregory?" Leroy asks rhetorically. "What does it take to get it through your thick noggin? DNA is like a fingerprint. It's not the same for any two people. If any of us did these tortures — and I'm not saying any of us did — "

"That's why I asked you here," I say, seizing my opportunity. "If any of you knows anybody who might have done these street people — Mickey, even —"

"It's irrelevant," Leroy's voice rises to a roar. "We all have different DNA."

"I don't think so," I say calmly, although the tension is making my heart do somersaults. "We share Damon's body, don't forget."

"Only when we take the spot."

"Haven't you heard a word we've been saying? We couldn't have Damon's DNA because we're totally different people," Leroy explodes.

As their voices rise, the voices in the basement grow louder as well.

"Yes, but we're very closely related, even closer than other families, I think. We use Damon's body at times, when we take the spot, and —"

"Too many people taking the spot lately," Damon pipes up angrily.

"We're not talking about that right now," I tell him, pathetic little wimp with his blond hair died black and pasted to his skull, so he won't be recognized on the street like other "stars." I have this moment sometimes where I see Damon as others see him, but it passes.

"Why not? Why don't we ever talk about what I want to talk about? I say we talk about it. Too many people taking the spot. I can't remember what I did or what I'm supposed to be doing from one minute to the next. I start to load the dishes onto the tray, and suddenly I'm in a alley miles away dickering with some heavy duty type looks like he'd as soon shiv me as give me the time of day. Which I got no idea about, by the way. And when I get back the boss says I'm fired for leaving a full tray on the table and just taking off. No wonder I can't keep a job."

"I agree," I say to Damon. "And I think we need to have a whole family council about people taking the spot and what the rules are. What they should be."

"You're acting like an adolescent," says Leroy to Damon in disgust.

"I am a adolescent."

"Sure, he's eighteen."

"I mean, they can't just barge in on me like that. It's my body, not theirs."

"It's my body, too, and I can visit when I please," says Pleaser.

"You can't have it both ways," I tell him. "You either have your own body with your own unique DNA and just visit Damon, or you share his." A coup! But sophisticated reasoning never has been Pleaser's strong point.

"Yeah, and I end up in jail with no idea how I got there." Damon rarely wins a point, and when he does, he presses it.

The squabbling downstairs is becoming a series of screams.

"I can't stand it," Damon yells. "I can't hear myself think."

"It thinks it can think," says Pleaser in a truly vicious and malicious manner. But the others snort in glee.

"I'll go quiet them down," Wendy says.

"Gotta go," says Breakout. "The Yanks are playing the Boston Red Sox."

"Hey! There's been another acid attack!" yells Damon.

"Yeah, the Sox," says Bounce as both get up from the table, unconsciously flexing their muscles.

"Woman named Dessa Clark," says Damon.

Dessa Clark. Wasn't she the one Leroy romanced at the club? Said he stank and called him a housepainter?

Pleaser has started up the stairs with Leroy following. Wendy is clearing the table. Leroy pauses midstep, then comes back down to watch the TV account with Damon, a rarity in that he stays as far from Damon as he can, for fear he'll get co-opted into some disagreeable task like pain-taking that will steal time from his work.

He glances at me sideways. Slyly, almost. Finally, he goes up to his room.

Afterwards, they've gone to bed, and I'm the only one in the dining room, the lights turned low. It's a peaceful moment in my day. The smells of the evening — Wendy's banana shakes, Leroy's paint, Pleaser's dirt, Bounce and Breakout's sweat, Damon's frozen dinner, and others less distinguishable — are fading away. Soon the air will be clear, unbreathed.

But I'm frightened.

This fear has been coming over me more and more often lately. I'll be on my way to my job or sitting at the computer or rinsing out my coffee mug when all of a sudden, out of the blue, I'm terrified, and I don't know why. I begin to sweat, my hands are clammy, my heart races, then jumps and jerks. Maybe I'm having a heart attack. It's as if I'm in extreme danger, and I have no idea from which direction. Anything I do may kill me. I feel as though I'm going to die. And there's no reason for it.

Oh, sure, I can *assign* reasons. Like what happened to Dessa Clark. Or I can say it's because I'm coming down with the flu, or I'm worried about my boss, or I don't like the way Pleaser's taking the spot. Much too often. Damon's right. What got done to the Mick still haunts me. The exquisite torture of allowing him to live like that. And what about the street people, fallen prey to a sadistic psychopath? Are these experiments, perhaps, undertaken to refine the cutter's skills? It's completely beyond my control. And that's the worst of it. The best I can do is to negotiate with Leroy, who I suspect knows the cutter and the acid thrower. If they're not one and the same.

I'm sitting here in a puddle of fear in the dim light of the dining room, and I begin to get that creepy feeling again that I'm being watched. Someone else knows my terrors. Is maybe enjoying them or is concerned about them or is even planning to get rid of me because

I'm no longer good for the group. If I go mad, what will happen to the rest of them? I'm the only one who takes responsibility in this family.

Except for Wendy, and let's face it, she's just a shadow of her unborn self.

Our boundaries are so fragile, even porous in places, that something of us can run out like water.

I don't trust Leroy.

I look across at Damon's little lamp. Suddenly, it dips — once, twice, three times. I still don't know what these numbers mean. But then it stays on. It's a sign. This is why I call it haunted. Whenever I'm in crisis, which is more and more often lately, Damon's lamp starts acting up. If it goes off, it's a sign that whatever decision I'm making is not a good one and that I won't be supported in it by the other side. But if the lamp dips and stays lit, it means encouragement and help from the spiritual world that surrounds us.

Tonight, the light stays on.

25

ON THE SAD OCCASION of Dr. Connie's death, Becca took time off from her Graduate Studies to fly back to Santa Cruz and attend her funeral. Annalyn had spotted her picture in the *Santa Cruz Sentinel* and phoned Becca with the news.

At the funeral home, most of the mourners greeted each other with quiet welcomes, murmurs, kisses, and hugs. No one whom Becca recognized. The air was smotheringly warm with a whiff of incense, as if to take away the breath of the survivors — thus allaying their guilt. Incense concealed the smells of death, real or imagined — embalming fluid, decay, the stench of roasting flesh.

The chapel was filled. Becca slid into the back row. As she did so, she noticed a man across the aisle, not staring exactly, but showing interest, thirtyish, blue eyes softened perhaps by the occasion. She dropped her own, and he turned away. As the service proceeded, he looked around at her several times, and their eyes met, unintentionally on Becca's part. Downright embarrassing! She had no interest in new social encounters over the body of her dead therapist and friend. She was, after all, trying very hard not to cry.

After the service, he disappeared, but, as she moved toward the door, she heard a voice behind her.

"Excuse me, you're not Becca Merrow by any chance?"

And she turned to find him, taller than he'd appeared while seated, solidly built in his navy suit, shoulder-length light brown hair tied back at the nape of his neck, very Santa Cruz. She tried to say she was indeed Becca Merrow, but the words wouldn't come, so she nodded instead.

"I'm Dr. Craig Austin," he said. "I believe Dr. Connie mentioned me to you?"

From Seattle?

"Oh, yes, she did, last year, in fact. I wasn't sure —" if it was for therapy or a professional contact, she finished to herself. What was wrong with her today, anyway? Not that there was any connection, she was sure there wasn't. She must be more upset than she had realized.

"You weren't sure?" He cocked his head, inviting her to finish the thought. Typical psychologist! She didn't like it.

"Not — nothing — important." she murmured.

"I was wondering — would you like to stop next door for coffee?"

"Coffee's good." Away from the funeral home.

He pushed open the cafe door for her, holding it in that awkward demonstration of politeness that men feel obliged to show new women acquaintances. Would his colleagues in Seattle consider his pony tail professional? Would he care? As she slipped past him, she felt acutely aware of the faint scent of aftershave at his neck, his lips slightly parted but not fleshy like those of her geologist lover, Hugh.

Well, didn't that beat all! She'd returned to the Santa Cruz of her childhood tragedy, attended the funeral of the woman who'd mothered her through her grief, and now she was attracted to her protégé!

No need to take it seriously. She'd studied enough psychology to know that a strong emotional arousal was apt to become sexual as well. It wasn't real, and it certainly wasn't serious. Her romance with Hugh, while stuck in missionary, wasn't threatened.

He selected one of those tiny tables meant to discourage paper work, held out her chair, and, after consulting her, ordered lattes for them both and a large chocolate chip cookie. For her part, Becca sat with determined composure.

"So, I understand you're in practice in Seattle, Dr. Austin?"

"Craig, please. We're almost colleagues, after all," he said, relieving anxiety about their relative status. "Yes, I'm attending at Seattle General and have a private practice a few blocks from there. And you're in Graduate School at the UDub, Becca?"

"Yes."

"Any specialty in mind?"

"Did Dr. Connie tell you why she was seeing me?" The question was freighted with more emotion than she'd anticipated.

"It wasn't a referral, so, no, she didn't." He broke off a bite of cookie, pushing the plate toward her, but she shook her head.

Not a referral. That was a relief. She didn't want to go back to being treated as the girl who'd lost her brother. She'd left that behind.

She hadn't meant to tell Craig, but her question had obviously tipped him that her concern had something to do with the traumatic experience for which she had consulted Dr. Connie. So she told him very briefly about her brother's kidnapping and her desire to help other siblings who had experienced the loss of a brother or sister. When he leaned forward slightly, showing strong interest in what she said, even though she knew this was a therapeutic technique, she told him a little more, then broke it off, feeling as though his eyes could see through her to her brother, where he lived in her memory still, and asked,

"What's your specialty?"

"General practice, but like you I'm concerned with impact of traumatic events on families. Particularly the families of the mentally ill. And like you, that came about from my own experience. No one seems to realize how tough it is on the families when there's a mentally ill son or sister."

Becca decided not to ask him what his family experience had been. Before she knew it, they had slipped into an easy discussion of psychology — he favored biological approaches because of the heavy genetic components in many mental illnesses, like his father's bipolar disease, while she pointed out how greatly talk therapy had helped her. That led them to reminiscences about Dr. Connie, he under her supervision when he was an intern at the University of California, San Francisco, and she as a ten-year-old in crisis.

"She had an unusual technique that a lot of people criticized, but I've found invaluable," Craig said. "As with psychoanalysis, she began by helping the client with review and abreaction of all the horrible things that had happened to him and how he felt about them, but at some point she believed it was time to stop. She'd switch to what he loved and have him concentrate on the positive in his life, rather than the negative."

"Pretty difficult to do if they're depressed."

"Right. There's nothing positive in a depressed person's life. The things that used to give them pleasure no longer do. So she had them remember what they had loved in childhood. Usually, that's a tip-off."

"Yes, she did that with me, too," Becca said, recalling Dr. Connie's encouragement of her poetry. When Craig paused so she could tell him what this was, she hesitated. "I've been reading her book on grief counseling. I was surprised to find how much she relied on prayer."

"Yes, she told me that, if I was ever stuck, I should pray for help."

"Do you?"

"Occasionally."

"Does it work for you?"

"Either that or I'm deluding myself," he laughed

"Not very professional of you," Becca teased lightly.

"Don't tell my colleagues." He gave himself a generous few sips of latte, then cocked his head to one side in question. "And you?"

"I've used prayer in volunteer counseling with adolescents several times. Not that I believe in it. It just seems like a secret weapon that I take shameful advantage of."

"Your motives are pure, I take it?"

"Absolutely," she laughed. "I can't help wondering if she was praying while she was listening to me."

"I'm sure she was while she was listening to me. Only prayer could have saved me and my clients from the stupid counseling mistakes I almost made."

He was pushing cookie crumbs on the plate into a little pile, one at a time. He caught her staring. "Does this indicate perfectionist tendencies, do you think?"

She laughed, saying, "Or a passion for making mountains out of mole hills."

"In order to knock them down," he replied, scattering them apart.

"Only to start over, I'll bet."

He sat on his hands, saying, "I'm not going to do it. I'm not going to do it."

"With a touch of obsessive-compulsiveness," she teased.

"Ah, you've learned your field too well. A pity I have to interrupt your diagnostic expertise to catch a plane. When are you going back?"

"Tomorrow."

"Here's my card. Are you in the book? Let's get together for lunch. I'll show you around Seattle General. Have you been on the psychiatric ward? We're pioneering a lot of its treatments and techniques."

26

BECCA WAS BURIED IN *Psychopathology*, the *DSM III-R*, *Cognitive Behavioral Therapy*, and her smart young geologist, Hugh, who kept his finger on the seismic pulse of Seattle over dinner at Cutters Bayhouse in the Pike Place Market, with a sunset view of the Olympics beyond the Sound. Smacking his thick lips over the excellent Dungeness crab, he pictured for her in detail Mt. Rainier erupting and spilling lava into the valleys below, just as Mt. St. Helens had done eighteen years before. His lovemaking was as stolid and reliable as he was.

Then there was Craig. He asked her to lunch at the Seattle General Hospital cafeteria, not exactly Cutters Bayhouse, but he wanted to give her a special tour of the psychiatric unit.

Becca paged Dr. Craig Austin at the reception desk, experiencing an unexpected jolt of excitement, as she spotted him in his white coat with the obligatory pens staining his pocket, striding toward her, shoulder length hair bound at the nape of his neck, Santa Cruz style. She'd taken uncommon care with her appearance and wondered if he had done the same. She wore gray slacks and a taupe suede jacket over a red angora sweater that showed off her breasts to advantage, should she have occasion to lose the jacket.

Pleasure at seeing her lit his face, and she had to stop herself from embracing him. They shook hands instead, Becca fearing that her own trembled or, worse, felt clammy. Suddenly not hungry, she chose salad, noting his hearty stew and biscuit entrée.

"I don't cook so this is my main meal," he explained.

"I don't cook either," she said mischievously, just to see his reaction.

"You're not supposed to admit it," he laughed, implying a feminine rather than a professional standard of conduct.

He sketched a few of the major players at Seattle General and said he hoped to introduce her to Dr. Bernie Leonard, the Chair of the Psychiatry Department.

"His specialty is dissociative disorders, so you'll want to bone up. The DID unit is his pride and joy, one of the best in the world, as he'll tell you himself if you give him half a chance. And even if you don't. A good person to know," he added, although he didn't expand into respect or liking or anything else about their relationship. Becca noted the absence with interest.

Becca expressed her skepticism about dissociative identity disorder, more popularly known as multiple personality. It had just been renamed in order to stress the identity and dissociation aspects over the old overly dramatic image of a bunch of people inhabiting one body, as in *The Three Faces of Eve, Sibyl,* and *The Minds of Billy Milligan.* Before going further, Becca checked Craig's face to see how he felt about the controversial diagnosis. If he felt it was legitimate, she didn't want to antagonize him. He nodded, agreeing that many psychologists shared her viewpoint but not disclosing his own. Becca went on to say that, while she had not yet made up her mind, she was leaning toward the view that a multitude of personalities constituted a throwback to the time when devils had to be exorcised by a priest. Positively mediaeval! They both laughed over the portrait she painted of horned demons with pitchforks and tails.

They were interrupted by one of Craig's white-coated colleagues, Dr. Noel McKay, an attractive woman of about thirty with features that Becca thought of as classical Roman, long wavy auburn hair, and a body whose parts seemed at angles to each other. But then, Becca often got these intuitive impressions of people that had no basis in fact; they turned out to be true in some other way. Doctor McKay proceeded to ask Craig if he would look at a patient of hers, sketching the problem and what she hoped he would do.

When they'd finished lunch, he put a hand on Becca's shoulder, saying, "Come on. Tour next."

Seattle General had a psychiatric floor for patients that included those who might be a danger to themselves or others, with a large proportion of depressives on watch: high schoolers who had attempted suicide in despair over the ending of a love affair and in the certain knowledge that they would never find another like it; college students who had ruined their lives with a B on a transcript of A's; others so severely afflicted they couldn't get out of bed. Bipolars needed stabilization on their medication. Schizophrenics, too; they heard voices either cursing them from some TV tower in the distance or reminding them that they were God. The organically impaired were a generally older population, requiring careful testing because apparent senior cognitive decline may mask a plethora of conditions, including depression or over-medication.

As Craig conducted her around the floor, he introduced her to nurses, residents, and doctors. Becca didn't see her mother, nor did she expect to. As a nurse, Mom would be working in OB-GYN. The Psych Unit seemed well staffed and cheerful in decor.

"And this is Doctor Bernie Leonard coming toward us."

A tall, fleshy man with a triangular patch of black hair beneath his thick lips that gave him a Machiavellian air, his black eyes immediately pinned Becca, as he stopped to ask,

"Craig, who have we here? Dr. Merrow, is it? Splendid!" His flattery felt oily to Becca, but she smiled obligingly. "Have you seen my pride and joy yet? Our Dissociative Disorders unit? No?"

"We were just headed over."

"Let me join you."

Becca thought that Craig might have been planning to skip it in view of her skepticism. She wasn't about to insult the Chair, however, who might let her do her practicum here next year, so she went pleasantly enough, Dr. Leonard taking her arm, which Craig, who walked on the other side of her, had yet to do.

Dr. Leonard seemed under the impression that he was irresistible to the fairer sex. With a proprietary nod, he greeted by name each woman they passed in the hall. A form of bragging, Becca felt. They simpered but was it her imagination, or did they give him a wider berth than customary? With his power, the Chair was probably in the habit of getting his way. Sexual harassment policies would mean nothing to this man. He probably served on the committee. In her wanderings, Becca had learned that many of the most egregious offenders guarded the roost. Mentally, Becca reviewed other hospitals and clinics available for a practicum.

Dr. Leonard was babbling away about alters — they'd had a patient here with over a hundred. And switching — that patient could switch among seven of his personalities at the rate of once every second. And integration, truly the best treatment, he opined. He'd begun a research project to determine how long integration of personalities was effective. Did integrated patients suffer relapses? Rarely, he thought. His was a world-famous unit, and they were hosting the annual conference of the DID Association in the spring. He'd be sure she got an invitation. She must give him her address. Her phone number? She gave him her campus address and department phone number because "it's easier to reach me there. That's where I spend all my time," she finished with a deprecatory laugh.

Craig had her home number.

As for her practicum, it was almost a year away. Who knew what might happen during that time? Dr. Leonard could drop dead. Tragedy happens. In the meantime, she had Craig to think about.

When they said goodbye, Craig asked if she liked opera, and she said she did. This was true, although she'd been too poor to attend in recent years. Her last opera had been *Aida* in San Francisco with Aunt Cordelia.

Three weeks passed, during which she thought of writing Craig a note to thank him for his courtesy. It was the professional thing to do, but she didn't do it. Instead, she wrestled books, classes and exams, and ran around the university track or Green Lake to work off the tension. Then Craig called and invited her to *Eugenie Onegin* on a Thursday night. He had season tickets for two. She couldn't help wondering who the second persons usually were, or was there just one? Had Dr. Noel McKay ever accompanied him? She knew she was being silly. Her relationship with Craig was early stages yet.

Becca had forgotten how much pleasure the opera afforded her. Emotions in the opera were acceptably primal, but cloaked in both visual and aural beauty. Afterwards, they ducked into a Lower Queen Anne bar, where Craig ordered a Scotch on the rocks for himself, a martini for Becca, and also hot wings and biscuits with plenty of butter for them to share. The bar was unpleasantly smoky, so they sought escape in a booth luxuriously upholstered in leather that invited closeness. Craig sat beside Becca rather than across from her, an indication of interest, according to the romance research.

Their conversation eased into mini-biographies. Becca gave him the short version of what happened after Robbie was kidnapped — the search, the family split, the twins, the move to Seattle, as Craig devoured hot wings and a biscuit. While Becca picked at the nuts and pretzels, having been too excited to eat dinner before their date, Craig described a family where mental illness was in the genes, handed down from generation to generation like a set of fine china.

"Lots of stories about crazy Aunt Delilah," he said. "In those days they didn't put too fine a point on diagnosis. If you didn't do as Mom's parents said, you'd end up like crazy Aunt Delilah. On Dad's side, there was 'Grandma Oreo' — that's what they called her because cookies were her favorite food. Her only food, actually. Ate nothing but and lived to ninety-three. How she kept regular was the mystery of the medical field. Maybe she sneaked prunes the way some people sneak cookies. There are other possibilities not appropriate to mention while we're eating. They'd have to call me 'Uncle Sausage'," he laughed.

"They'd call me 'Aunt Brie'."

"Brie and Sausage. That's a combination! Anyway, Grandma Oreo was wild about knives. Had them tucked into her reticule, her bun, the sofa cushions. Used them to scrape cookie crumbs off her TV tray and food off her set as well, clean her nails, comb her moustache — at least, according to some." He paused to scrape butter on his biscuit with a grin.

"And you take after her?"

"My father does. Bipolar. Used to chase us around the dining room table with a carving knife. Picked it up from his mother, I guess."

"Never caught you?"

"We learned to run fast, change directions, crawl under the table, and scream to attract Mom's attention. Which it didn't, but he thought it would. When he wasn't chasing us, we'd walk on eggshells through the house trying not to incite his paranoia, which could quickly turn violent."

"It's a wonder your mother stayed."

"She had agoraphobia. Afraid to leave the house."

"Wasn't she worried about you kids, though? The effect he was having on you?"

"She was in conflict about it. Several times she was on the verge of going out for a loaf of bread and forgetting to come back. Whenever she left, my two sisters would scream. It was a contest between them as to who screamed louder. Mom never understood why, but at some level they knew the reality."

"But she would have taken you all with her, of course," Becca prompted, having heard in his words a lone woman fleeing.

"We were never sure. That's why they screamed. She stayed because the minute she opened the front door, she was seized with terror. She described it as a smothering other world that just kind of descended like a black curtain over the real one. Another excuse was that she was worried about Dad. How would he survive? Who would make sure he took his medicine? He used to hide it. God, he loved to play that game. Or he'd pretend he'd taken it when he hadn't. But he'd get this cat-that-swallowed-the-canary smile on his face, and she could tell by that. You haven't had a hot wing. Too messy?"

Becca smiled at the good guess, and he returned it, moving a hair from her cheek like a caress, then taking his hand away.

"Ah, the rules of dating," he sighed. "I hope you won't feel bound by them. Here, I'll butter a biscuit for you, so you can eat it without oily fingers."

She took it from his hand, laughing. "What if it drips?"

"Let it drip, Becca. Enjoy."

She couldn't help thinking that sex with him would be a lot drippier, so this was good practice.

"Good practice," he said.

Becca gaped at him, then bit into the biscuit in a hurry. Could he have actually meant what she was thinking?

As he was driving her home to the apartment on Capitol Hill that she'd been able to afford after her father's death, she asked where he lived.

"I have a house in Green Lake," he told her, "stuffed with books and manuscripts and CDs and foreign films and an outsized black labrador that must have some St. Bernard in her."

Odd that he hadn't mentioned it when she told him she'd lived there with her Mom and the twins before moving out. Perhaps, she'd been too caught up in what she was saying for him to interrupt. Nor did he say she must see it some time.

"You cocoon a lot, then?"

"That I do. After the stresses of the day, it's good to get home."

His kiss goodnight was friendly but uneventful. She inhaled his breath, but he didn't try to prolong it, and he didn't ask to come up. Becca had been getting ready for passion.

A few weeks later, Craig called and suggested a walk through the arboretum the following Sunday. Why did he always ask her out on a weeknight or an afternoon, but not on a Saturday night? Never mind that she usually had a date with Hugh. She'd break it in a heartbeat for Craig, although she'd hate herself for doing it.

Crisp gold and red leaves still clung to the trees, and they kicked eddies of them as they talked about their week. They stopped to admire an adorable baby bundled up in her pram. It was then Becca learned of his own sibling tragedy. Miranda, his baby sister and "wonderful to behold," had died when she was only a year old.

"How?" Becca asked, with that puzzlement in her voice so common on learning of a death that is off-time.

"We're not sure, actually. I was only eight. Mom said it was SIDS, and another time she said it was 'just one of those things,' and a few years later, that God took her because she was too good to live, and He wanted her with him. Boy, did that make me mad at God! My older sister, Dani, said she'd died in a ritual murder by Satanists — ritual murders are Dani's thing. Like I said, I come from a crazy family. I don't think we ever really found out."

An odd coincidence to be talking about the loss of siblings among the brilliant fall leaves that always marked her own loss.

Craig delivered himself of a scholarly mini-essay about the research on almost every topic they touched, and she was beginning to suspect that he might be a genius in disguise. Society wasn't kind to geniuses, and they usually learned to cloak their gifts in acceptable presentation. But Craig seemed to open to Becca more and more, perhaps because he found her receptive. For her part, Becca couldn't be certain if she was enjoying his mind or the prospect, however faint, of his sex.

Taking a deep breath on the Azalea Walk, unaccustomed as she was to an aggressive approach, she said, "I was thinking. Perhaps you'd like to come to dinner next Saturday night?" Surely he wouldn't have anything planned a week away, would he? If he did, at least she'd know.

"But you don't cook," he reminded her teasingly. He turned to her on the path, his hands thrust into his jacket pockets against the cold.

"With one exception. I make a mean lasagna. Lots of sausage," she added.

"I love lasagna, especially when it's mean." His eyes that were sometimes blue, sometimes green, seemed to look deep inside her, and the erotic overtones were unmistakable. Then he added, "Unfortunately, I can't make it Saturday. Wish I could." He didn't suggest an alternative or even a rain check.

The next time Becca saw Craig was on a Friday night. Some friends of his were celebrating the birth of their first child.

She enjoyed sprawling over their furniture with a cup of mulled cider and discussing a murder case with an attorney, the intricacies of breast feeding with the hostess, the cramped space in the new art museum downtown with a curator — "not worthy of Seattle's cultural milieu, simply not worthy," and a doctor couple's adventures in caves worldwide. Amateur spelunkers or "spieleologists with an i," the woman joked, rather than speleologists. "We tell tall stories about caves."

But Becca and Craig didn't have much time alone together, whether by accident or design. She watched him across the room where he sat, with his legs spread apart and his wonderfully long trim thighs that hinted at power. When he brought her home, he kissed her lightly on the lips and left her at her door. Again, no attempts to coax her into letting him in.

27

NOT THAT I THINK any of us had anything to do with Carmine's ghastly murder, the reports of which are all over the San Francisco city papers and the tabloids. Even those who did Mickey and the street people and Leroy's trial girlfriend, Dessa — even they couldn't have done Carmine. The escalation in brutality is too appalling.

As I hang my coat and hat in the hall closet, Damon gets home from his job *du jour*, says to me, "Hi, Gregory! I got fired today," and turns on the television set, where the reporters compete to give the goriest accounts.

I run upstairs to change, increasingly aware of a stone in the pit of my stomach. Could the murderer be one of us after all?

"They say there must have been two of them," Damon turns to tell me when I come back down. "A gang, even. Two to lift him to the wall and another to drive the bolt through his chest and make sure it didn't hit his heart. They wanted him alive."

He's such a child, Damon is. Takes everything without questioning. Even at eighteen, he's underdeveloped.

"You don't know anything about it, do you?" I ask, more out of a duty to the process of elimination than any real suspicion.

"Me? How would I know?"

"Okay." I open our refrigerator door. "Why were you fired, by the way?"

"Somebody painted this naked man boinking a woman on the bathroom wall. Anatomically correct," Damon giggled. "They think it was me."

Silence. We both know who it was. Then Damon says — whines, rather,

"Tell Leroy to stop taking my time."

I'm sure he was just doodling.

"I'll talk to him."

"You always say you will, but you never do." Petulant, unattractive with his small pasty face, his hair hanging limp over his forehead, dyed black because he thinks he's in disguise, some people having recognized the porn star on the street. He's seen it in their eyes. "You like him better than me. You say you don't play favorites, but you do."

Damon can't help what he's been through. I have to keep reminding myself of that.

I consider whether Damon is right as I grab an apple, part of Wendy's campaign to feed us healthfully. "If I don't have any temptations in the house, you'll eat raw veggies and fruit," she says. Unless we buy hot dogs on the street. I conclude that I like almost anyone better than Damon — sniveling little runt that he is. I can only abide him when he's acting, when he's somebody else. Even though Leroy is my rival and perhaps my enemy, at least he's interesting.

"It's good you were fired," I say, trying to make peace with the truth. "Now you have more time for acting." We pretend that acting is his occupation, because it's the only trade he ever really learned. But for Damon, his acting now consists more of backstage volunteer work, painting sets at the Golden Mission Community Theater, so maybe he'll get a part that isn't porn someday.

If any of us killed Carmine, one of the others knows about it, not Damon. I post the notice on the corkboard in the kitchen.

"Council Party, Tuesday, 7:30 p.m. Agenda: Carmine murdered. Should we run?"

The promise of a gory discussion should get out the vote.

Then I go to search their rooms without their permission, because the circumstances are dire and desperate.

What am I looking for? Long thick nails or bolts or hammers, perhaps, to affix Carmine's revolting tub of lard to the wall? I wonder idly — did they use a stud finder to prevent the whole lathe and plaster structure from crashing down?

Halos surround the lights in Leroy's room when I turn them on. I'm getting a migraine again, and I'll be no good to anybody. Better take a pill.

Leroy has lots of reasons to hate Carmine's guts enough to pierce them. The better he got at his craft, the more favors Carmine demanded and gave him precious little gallery space as recompense. Leroy was discovering with Dessa that he was straight, so Carmine's demands were particularly odious. Pleaser subbed for Leroy, who had to do him favors in return, mainly in the form of providing secret information that I know exists, but of whose shape and substance I have no idea. That last time, Leroy took Carmine to the studio to view his masterpiece study in process. Carmine promised him a showing but then got pissed about something Pleaser did, although he didn't know it was Pleaser, of course, and Carmine told Leroy that "Great Heavens" was garbage, and all he was good for was painting signs.

Painting signs!

Leroy was devastated until Pleaser gave him the word that Carmine was selling his work at fat prices and giving him diddley. He didn't believe it until Pleaser showed him a receipt he'd lifted. Even so, I don't think Leroy was capable of what happened. He wouldn't have the strength. I need to question him, though, to be sure he doesn't know anything about it. Thing is, I'm pretty sure he knows some of the more unsavory alters that I don't. With all we've been through, it would be natural to have the fury stored in a vault some place. Not all of it in the basement children.

Leroy has a hammer and nails to put together frames and stretch canvases when he wants to, but the nails are too small for hanging a ton of flesh.

There are plenty of other suspects — artists over the years, gnashing their teeth about what Carmine said of their work — very like Milton's or William Blake's descriptions of Hell. Carmine had a way with words; he could prick the balloon of an artist's pretense or expose the one weakness that the artist was trying to deny, even to himself. Like when he said something new was "retro." He did that to Kenny, who didn't even know he was denying. But Kenny wouldn't kill him. Not in his nature.

Kenny looked up to Carmine as a mentor. When Carmine betrayed him, Kenny finally gave up his art and helps out in someone else's gallery. At least, he gets to talk that phony language he learned from his mentor, which is all Kenny understands, never having gotten the real art education that Leroy says he needs. And not being the genius that Leroy is. (If you don't believe me, ask him.)

Carl would be more likely, such brutality easily in keeping with his character, although in his present weakened state I don't see how he could have lifted Carmine's not inconsiderable bulk to his wall of crosses and nailed it there, still writhing through the night as the coroner speculates (according to Pleaser), blood dripping over his masterworks until it was a small pond on the floor with the mosaic fish rippling through, and Carmine had no blood left inside him to keep his heart beating. "Exsanguination", they call it.

What would be Carl's motive? It's been a dozen years since the first time Kenny left Carl because of what he did to Damon, and while Kenny's gone back periodically, out of love or pecuniary need (both so confused in his mind that even Kenny couldn't tell which was which), most recently to care for Carl during another bout of what will probably be his final illness, that bond was never as strong again. Carl broke it when he raped Damon and then put him in his films.

Pleaser? Pleaser wouldn't do Carmine that way. His sense of mischief is more antic. He'd report Carmine as a drug dealer, so the cops could shoot him. Not that Carmine was into anything stronger than pot, but Pleaser would report that he was. Like the raid he staged on Carl's studio. Not subtle, but effective.

If one of us did Carmine, they probably left clues, and I don't think all Pleaser's "charity work" with the cops will save us.

Killing Carmine by hanging him on one of his own oversized crosses just isn't the jock twins' style. Bounce and Breakout are more into sports and brawling, not mutually exclusive activities when you include soccer, boxing, and ice hockey. They'd have snapped one of those heavy gold gallery frames and used it like a golf club or a bat to beat Carmine to death. Or slammed that gorgeous melty blue Chihuly bowl to the concrete floor and stabbed him with a piece, twisting it in his gut for as long as he screamed, then laying off when he passed out because where would be the sport in that? They don't get their pleasure from refinements. No, Bounce and Breakout didn't do Carmine. Lord knows they're strong enough, just not quite imaginative enough to make sure he was kept alive for his entire execution. Besides, what had Carmine done to them? They don't care about Kenny and Leroy and Damon. Not altruistic at all, I don't think. Well, maybe they care about Leroy.

As I say, a lot of suspects, far more numerous than I can name. Carmine was more feared than loved, his power making it dangerous to show him anything other than devotion. But I can't believe such brutal cruelty exists in any of us.

We're gathered at the kitchen table, where Wendy is serving us her cookie dough treats. She discovered these accidentally, having put a cookie sheet full of dough in the oven a few months ago, or maybe it was a few years — I have trouble remembering times — and she forgot to turn the oven on. Pleaser hauled them out, and we all helped ourselves. It's no good for her to simply leave the cookie dough on the table, though. We're nothing if not creatures of habit. She's got to put the cookie sheet in the oven, so we can discover it for ourselves. Even better if she exclaims, "Oh, I forgot the cookies."

Now we grab the soft globs of peanut butter, nuts, and chocolate, and we stuff them, unsticking them from the roofs of our mouths with the milk on which Wendy insists.

Having found nothing incriminating in their rooms, I survey those at the table. But it's those who aren't here that worry me. They know me, and I don't know them. It's creepy, unnerving. Leroy's present, of course. He's the most cooperative, because he's planning to take over some day. He doesn't think I know. He'd be a disaster, no organization, no tact, not an administrative bone in his head — it would be chaos. Even if I gained some satisfaction out of the mess he made, I'd also have to live with it. Unless I found a way out.

Which would be a way out of Damon and into someone else. A kind of emigration. There must be others on the outside who could use my services. Leroy insists I'm paranoid, as if it were a genuine diagnosis. But our house is expanding, there's a new bridge across the alley that leads to a blank wall, and a new staircase to doors I can't unlock, and a tower on the roof with no entrance that I can find. Lots more people live here than I know.

"They tortured Carmine first," Leroy tells me, stuffing a fistful of dough into his mouth.

"With knives," says Breakout.

"Yeah, knives." Bounce makes a slitting motion across his throat.

"Nuh-uh, razors like last time," Pleaser says. "Cops told me. And they showed me the body while the coroner was doing the autopsy. Razorman's work. It looked like every single vein and nerve was nicked. You can tell the difference because the veins bleed more. His kidneys, his balls. They said he felt every one. Died slow as mud."

"Wild!" says Breakout.

"Double wild," says Bounce.

"They didn't say 'mud,'" I argue. Whoever heard of a doctor de-scribing death that way?

Wendy's shadow starts to fade, the flowers in her hair withering like time-lapse photography. She doesn't like hearing about violence.

"Shhh," I tell them. "I called this meeting to find out if any of you knows anything. Or if you know anyone who does," I add.

"Razor nicks all over his body, so the blood would ooze slowly," says Pleaser and giggles.

"I don't remember that being on the news," says Leroy.

"Leroy did it," suggests Pleaser in his pleasant fashion, squeezing a mound of dough into this mouth with his truly filthy fingers that have been in the locks of half the buildings in San Francisco.

"Manners," Wendy whispers.

"Nuh-uh, Leroy was here minding his own business," Bounce says.

"That's right," says Breakout, giving double weight to their argument, because you have to remember that, as twins, they're not quite separated. They were born conjoined, one person, really, but gradually a rift began to show up like an amoeba pulling apart into two that you watch through a microscope. Everyone knew it was happening, except Damon, of course. While they've managed to complete the split, they often communicate without words.

"How could I do Carmine?" Leroy demands. "But, if I had, Carmine got what he deserved."

"And after I gave him everything he wanted for years," says Pleaser. "Shame on him." He's wiping his filthy fingers on his filthy shirt. Idly I wonder if the fingers make his shirt dirtier or vice versa.

"Do any of you know anything about this at all?" I ask as delicately as I know how. "Do you know anyone who knows about it?" They're so sensitive.

"If I did, I couldn't tell you," Leroy says, building a dough fort on the table until Wendy deftly slides a plate under it.

"It had to be somebody who knows just where to cut nerves to cause the most pain," says Pleaser. "Cops say whoever did it knew his anatomy."

"That's justice," says Leroy. "Carmine's been nicking us for years."

"Hoist on his own petard, as it were."

"What does that mean exactly?"

"What goes around comes around."

"I need to know," I tell them, trying to bring them back to the focus of the meeting, "if we might be in trouble. I understand you're all loyal to your sources. And you should be. But this is a matter of the whole family's safety. If one of us goes, we all go. You know that."

"Gregory, you're such a hardass."

"Nerd."

"I'm the hardass nerd that keeps this family together." I'm trying not to raise my voice and incite the basement kids.

"Well, I didn't do it," says Breakout, then gulps the last of his cookie dough. "And as long as I didn't do it, I can take the spot for whoever did, with different symptoms and everything."

"You can't change Damon's fingerprints," I argue. "You can't change his DNA."

"How do we know that?"

"We haven't tried."

"Use your heads. Our fingerprints are Damon's. So's our DNA."

"Who says?" asks Leroy.

"We have different brains, different medical conditions. Who says we don't have different DNA?" Pleaser argues.

"Because we have one body."

"Who says?" asks Leroy.

"Different people have different DNA, any dope knows that," says Pleaser. "Coroner says," he adds for authority.

"If I have to have Pleaser's dirty body, I resign right now," says Leroy.

"Go ahead! Get the fuck out!" says Pleaser.

"Leroy, Carmine did awful things to you, so if you wanted to get revenge, it would only be natural." I feel guilty about such crass manipulation, but ends justify means, and I'm scared for all of us.

"Aw, come on, Gregory," says Pleaser, "Does this puny little bundle of putrefaction look like he could lift Carmine's belly?"

"Or his right nut?" adds Bounce to Breakout's guffaw.

"I'm not saying that."

"Then what are you saying?" Leroy flames, hot tears running down his cheeks. "The bugger had it coming. I wish I'd done it, but I didn't."

"I'm simply saying you might know someone," another family member, perhaps. "Someone who knows anatomy, for instance."

"Oh, sure," Pleaser says. "Leroy hired a hitman, and then I paid him off with my delicious bod."

"That's not what he means," says Bounce seriously.

"He means, another one of us," says Breakout.

"Someone who isn't here."

"Who? Who else is there?"

"We don't know everybody."

"Gregory does."

"No, unfortunately I don't."

"Well that makes me feel nice and safe."

"Oh, bugger off. Gregory does the best he can."

"Want me to wash that shirt?" Wendy asks Pleaser. She's been standing around, dying to ask.

In answer, he tears it off and throws it at her, then sits there, as if he were proud of his bare concave chest with the ribs stove in. What his lovers see in him is beyond my comprehension, but then I don't know much about it.

Now the little tantrums in the basement force Damon to cover his ears, yelling, "Shut the fuck up!"

Someone who knows anatomy, I think. Whenever one of us gets seriously ill, we all lose time, and somebody else comes on the scene and tends us expertly. As if it were a profession. Then we all wake up, and the sick one is better. Could one of the others be a nurse? If I could get a computer degree in community college, another could get one in nursing.

There was the time I had the flu, and someone made chicken soup. Wendy swore she hadn't. And that poultice for Pleaser's knee after he got into that scrape spiriting off crack from the evidence room. There was the new cortisone ointment on the night table for Bounce's jock itch and drops for his eye, when he looked like he got the worst in a sports bar brawl, but as Breakout said, "You should have seen the other guy." And our medicine cabinet is a hospital pharmacy's dream.

Someone changed a bandage on my arm — good thing I wasn't awake. Even my family's touch spooks me. I try not to show it. As if touch hurt me a long time ago, although I don't remember. I say to the doctor, "You can look, but don't touch." Joking, but the minute a hand starts palpating my throat, I turn the spot over to Pleaser, or maybe Bounce or Breakout because they're cleaner. How do I know the good doc won't forget himself and begin to squeeze? I can't remember when someone throttled me before, but they did. What's the point of remembering?

The doctor complimented me on the bandage, and I took the credit. What was I going to tell him? That we had a resident nurse in Damon's head?

Leroy's EKG shows a heart rhythm disturbance, whereas the rest of us are normal. Breakout himself has an abnormal EEG, which accounts for his seizures. None of the rest of us have them, and when Breakout starts to fall and thrash and foam, Bounce takes the spot, and Breakout gets to his feet, asking, "What happened?" The doctors attribute these cures to their treatments, like the arrogant sons of bitches they are. We're damned if we're going to pay for it all. Not our fault there's so many of us!

"I think we'd better get out of town — fast!" I say, interrupting another brawl. "And hope the DNA from the Mick and Dessa and Carmine and the street people doesn't follow us."

"How about Portland?"

"Oh, goody, Timmy's there."

"How about Boston or New Orleans where we could 'rouler' with the good times?" It seems as though we could lose ourselves in any of those places, especially if our appearances kept changing.

"How about Seattle?" I suggest. "I found Becca there on the Internet."

Mouths drop open. For an instant, the entire table is a still life.

"Found Becca? In Seattle?"

"What's that broad ever done for us?" Pleaser demands. "Not one fucking thing." His hand is a claw, scooping up more cookie dough.

"That's right," says Breakout. "She wasn't supposed to take Robbie to the park, but she did. She's the one got him kidnapped."

"That's right," says Bounce, nodding vigorously.

"Kenny said she gave him away," says Leroy, contributing to the family mythology. "Becca didn't even care."

"Oh, I don't believe that," says Wendy.

"I'm a liar?" Pleaser's about to shoot up and sock her, but Bounce and Breakout leap to her defense.

"Of course, you're not. Just that there's a misunderstanding somewhere."

"That's always your excuse. 'A misunderstanding,'" Pleaser simpers. "Ask me, you need a good lay. Without any misunderstandings."

"Nobody asked you," says Leroy.

"Show some respect," says Breakout.

"Yeah, respect."

"Thing is," Leroy says, "She's to blame for all we been through. She got us into this survival mess we're in today."

I know these aren't Leroy's words. He doesn't use phrases like "survival mess." Who has he been talking to?

"I don't think we're in such a mess," I say. "If Robbie hadn't been kidnapped, maybe we wouldn't have split up and become a family."

"Some family!"

"Let's not go through that again."

"You don't get to decide what we go through."

"She coulda found us if she tried," Pleaser says. "The kids downstairs would have parents," instead of being the little bundles of orphaned fury that they are.

Would there even be kids downstairs? As if they've heard their names mentioned, their voices begin to rise.

"I beg your pardon," says Wendy, "I'm a good parent to those children. You could all help if you really cared."

"Who, us? We don't know the first thing about children."

"I could teach you."

"So, Damon," I call over to him where he's watching TV. "Should we contact Becca?"

"You mean, Robbie's Becca?"

At the mention of his name, Robbie appears in the doorway.

"Did someone say Bec-Bec is here?" he asks, rubbing sleep from his eyes. "I wanna see Bec-Bec."

"That's your vote," says Wendy, shutting the basement door behind which the kids quiet down after she throws them a few boxes of animal crackers, appropriately enough.

"Where's Bec-Bec?"

"In a place called Seattle. Far away from here."

"Seattle!" exclaims Pleaser. "We can't go to Seattle just to have a head-to with this broad."

"I wanna see Bec-Bec."

"But does she wanna see you?" Pleaser inquires nastily.

"There are some reasons to see Becca," I suggest tentatively.

"Name one!" Bounce challenges.

"Better yet, name a hundred," giggles Damon, grabbing the last of the cookie dough.

"Help yourself," says Bounce. "Want what's left in my mouth, too?"

"If we contact her, we could find out a lot more about our family," I say. "Where we came from. What our roots are. Our history, our genealogy. Like that."

"I don't think it's a good idea for us to see Becca." Leroy's deep voice is chilling. Whose opinion is he voicing? "I think it's dangerous."

"How dangerous?" I ask, sounding fainter than I mean to.

"Me, I wouldn't mind," says Leroy. "Especially if Pleaser's against it."

"Suck my cock, asshole."

Leroy retches in reply, then turns back to me. "There's some of us, at least, I hear through the grapevine, that are very, very angry at what Becca did. Selling Robbie for money to buy clothes."

"She did no such thing," says Wendy.

"What else might be done to us?" I ask.

"Us?" asks Leroy.

"You said it might be dangerous."

"I meant, dangerous to this Becca."

After they've left and the dining room light has dimmed, I sit in my crested chair watching Damon's haunted lamp for a sign. If it stays lit or dips and then lights again, we'd better go. Of course, I'm the one who set up this code, as a kind or programming, and I could be wrong; in fact, it could be the reverse. I'm feeling more and more panicky, as if every moment we spend here exposes us to increased danger.

It occurs to me suddenly that all the victims have done something to Leroy. Mickey, Dessa, and Carmine. Never mind the street people. Could Leroy be the hidden connection here?

As if reading my thoughts, Leroy is suddenly standing by my chair. He'd gone upstairs, and I hadn't heard him come down again. He smells perpetually of oil paint and turpentine. It's in his clothes, his hair, his skin, his voice. I hate to think of what his liver looks like — the fumes must have curdled it.

"Something," Leroy says. Not exactly good with words. Leroy talks okay in a group, but going one on one gives him trouble.

I look up at him questioningly. "The others?"

He takes a deep breath into those paint-saturated lungs of his, and his mouth is a thin line at first, but then he talks again.

"I'm worried."

"About what?" Pulling teeth, that's what it is to have a conversation with Leroy, he has so many loyalties and conflicts.

"Things may be getting out of control."

"Who?" I ask, seizing my opportunity. I want to know what "out of control" means, but I want to know who they are first. It's unusual for Leroy to be this thoughtful about anything except his work, and confiding in me is possibly unprecedented.

"I can't tell you."

Then why are we here?

"Does your source know you're talking to me now?" I glance around into the shadows and beyond the blinds, sensing danger.

"I don't think so. No, offense, but they hardly know you exist."

They. More than one.

"They live in their own little world. Don't even tune in on me that much. When I have trouble, I have to go ask them for help."

Leroy slips into the chair at the head of the table and picks at his paint-encrusted fingernails.

"You asked them to torture Carmine?"

"Not exactly."

"What then?" I try to pretend I'm a model of exquisite patience.

"You gotta understand." No, I don't. "I was upset." This is new? "'Great Heavens' is my whole life." True, I've never been able to understand this. "Without it, I might just as well not exist. I was — well, I was bawling about what Carmine said about me sign painting, and I just happened by their lab when they were there, and they didn't ask me what was wrong, but I told them anyway."

"Them? How many?" Is it my imagination, or is the lamp dipping ever so slightly, lighter then darker, then lighter again. I believe that there are spirits on the other side who are communicating with me, who protect me for the family's sake. But they might be other entities whom I don't know. When he doesn't reply, I add, "Maybe I can do something." Now the light is flickering like a mad thing.

Leroy says, "Bulb's about to blow."

"What? Oh, yes." I'm not insane enough to tell him the truth. "How can I get in touch with them, get them to stop?"

"Thing is, I don't think you can. They're not in touch with you, and they don't want to be. You have to go through me."

So that's all this is — a power play? What would be effective? Letting him think he has it? Resisting? Answer a question with a question.

"Why are you telling me if there's nothing I can do?"

"They're getting stronger. They've got the scent of blood now. They like it. Love it, in fact. They're talking about who else to do. They'd do Carl, but he's too weak to have much fun with. He'd probably consider it a favor."

"Who else are they talking about then?"

"They haven't told me. But I hear them whispering a lot."

So do I. I hear a lot of whispering, but I don't tell him this. Damon complains about it. He thinks we're whispering about him. "Thanks, Leroy. I'm glad you told me. Let me think about it."

Leroy's out of his chair and has a foot on the staircase.

"Seattle's a bad idea."

I feel a stab of alarm. The lamp's going on and off like crazy, but I realize in dismay that I haven't been keeping track to discover the pattern.

28

All this no-talent garbage on his gallery walls
　　　　and he says *I'm* a no-talent?

Don't take no artist to paste sequins, Hell

　　　　　　　　　　　　　　even *you* can do it!
　　Don't take no steady hand to glue a feather
　　　　　　and perspective's　　　　　　as you see it
Color
　　　　　　　you can

argue.

MeFisto wore gloves but
　　Vigrid the Avenger took his off I couldn't tell Gregory about
　　　　　　　　　　　　　　　　that part he'd
have a
　　　　　　fit with his fingerprints and his DNA　　　　　Gregory's
such a wuss
　　　　　　　　Vigrid he loves
the raw contact with the flesh and skin he tortures

feels throbs of pain as nerves contract and scream
"I'm an artist of pain" he shouts with glee
"Torquemada's apprentice"
"I will perfect what he left undone."
So he searches new and more creative methods.

He uses blunt instruments
sometimes
for Carmine a pallet knife
"rough justice" he calls it the
blood carmine like his name.

Wendy would be all shocked and say they "shouldn't."
"Little Miss Shouldn't" we call her now but not to her face she
might fade away

29

WHEN KENNY OPENED THE door, Damon almost didn't recognize him. It had been months, or maybe years. Damon wasn't good with time. Kenny's thinning hair was now just fuzzy scalp on top with white on either side. He wore a loose-fitting lilac cotton shirt over matching drawstring pants. And they were stained. Kenny had never worn anything stained in his life. If he couldn't get it clean one way or another, he gave it to the poor people in the Tenderloin or the Mission District who didn't have anything to wear. They'd be glad for stains that didn't show that much, just a variation in the weave, really. Happens with hand-dyed material all the time. Why not factory?

"Well, if it isn't the prodigal son!" Kenny exclaimed with a touch of bitterness, although Damon was at a loss to understand why. They'd talked on the phone several times, Kenny had invited him to come by, and now he was here. He couldn't remember when last he'd visited Kenny. Summer was it? No, spring. Maybe last year. He kept blanking out, so his memory wasn't as dependable as it had been. Not like when you have an experience, and then you remember it. Sometimes it was one of the others who had the experience, and Damon couldn't remember those.

Besides, truth to tell, he'd wanted to be absolutely sure that Carl was too weak to attack Leroy. Or maybe it was Leroy who wanted to be sure. Damon knew Kenny would just stand and watch, maybe tell him he'd brought it on himself. Not that Damon actually remembered the attacks or what it was that Kenny stood and watched. These were mostly Leroy's memories, and those that weren't, should be. So Damon blocked them out as best he could.

"Come on in and see Carl," Kenny was saying, as if it were a genuine invitation, although it sounded more like payback. "Carl," Kenny went singing down the hall with a trace of his old self, "guess who's come to visit."

As Damon stepped into the dining room, where the phone still threatened him from the table, then turned past the parlor into the hall, the smells assailed him — incense, pot, pine freshener, ammonia cleaner, and under these, the stench of urine, feces, vomit, and decaying flesh. Not all at once, but in successive stages, as if the very air itself were undergoing metamorphosis from artificial freshness to putrefaction. He held his breath, inhaled in short shallow gasps, then held it again. If he could have masked his nose with his hand without offending, he would have.

Surely, that wasn't Carl lying gaunt and shriveled like a dead brown leaf on the very bed where he'd done the nasty to Leroy so long ago. On the night table, a glass of water with bubbles of long-standing replaced the keys to his handcuffs. No whip waited obediently over the bedstead, where the unused cuffs hung in chains. But these were just images, and Damon wasn't even sure why he had them. It wasn't as though he remembered what Carl did. Just that he did something.

"I remember," Leroy whispered.

As for Carl himself, his eyes were sunken in deep purple sockets, but at the sight of Damon, they glittered like those of the Beast. He was not wearing his dark glasses. In fact, they lay dusty on his bureau. His proud curly hair, now gray and dyed only at the tips, poked out all around his head like a nimbus of iron filings, and his beard was a darker unshaven stubble. Lesions masked his face. Only a sheet covered him.

"He has such fevers, poor thing, and he can't bear anything heavier on him," Kenny said, raising the sheet to neaten it and exposing only for an instant the purple creeping over Carl's feet and ankles. "Of course, it's his own fault, as I've reminded him many times. If he'd been faithful to me instead of howling around with all his protégés, he wouldn't be in this predicament. But I imagine he's sick of hearing me scold, aren't you, dear? And yet, there's nothing you can do about it, is there? Well, is there?"

A cough from Carl could have been interpreted as any response.

Damon should say something. "So, Carl, how's business?"

"The business isn't what it used to be," sighed Kenny.

"All Internet chat rooms nowadays," said Carl hoarsely.

"Only Carl calls them 'shat rooms.'"

Carl broke into a coughing fit, and Kenny had to suction him.

"Now, I'm HIV positive, too. That's the thanks I get." Kenny turned to Damon. "Have you been tested?"

"Yes." Gregory had insisted. "I seem to be okay." If he wasn't, he'd have to give up the spot permanently so the others didn't get sick.

"So far," said Kenny. Was that a wish or a promise? He fluffed the sheet up and out again. "Oh dear, did I accidentally cover your face, Carl baby?" Kenny asked in mock concern. "Wouldn't want to do that. He can hardly breathe as it is. You might smother to death and miss all the yummy experiences to come. Don't think I'm not tempted," he said as an aside to Damon, obviously well within Carl's hearing. "But he wants out, and I wouldn't give him the satisfaction."

"Die, Carl, die," said Leroy.

Kenny pulled the sheet down, checking to be sure it hung evenly on either side, although Damon was sure Carl cared less. Kenny left the bottom loose and untucked. "Did you come to help me? The hospice volunteer canceled at the last minute. They're a godsend when they're here, but they have so many emergencies, there aren't enough of them to go around. And they figure Carl has me, so what does it matter if I work myself to exhaustion? I don't count, do I? You only count with those people if you're dying."

"What about Barry and Trent?"

"Oh, they came by when Carl first got sick. Token duty. Even brought old Noodles for a visit. That was before they found him crushed in the dumpster. Every bone in his body, the vet said. What could have done that? A car, probably. But how did he get out?"

"That stinky little runt bit me," Pleaser growled in Damon's ear.

"Did he bite somebody?" Damon asked.

"Whatever are you talking about?"

"I don't know," Damon answered truthfully. Had he said that? How much else had he said that he hadn't heard. Panicked and confused, he did as Gregory had instructed him in these situations, picked up the conversation where he remembered it had left off. "Did Trent and Barry help out?"

"Good boy," said Gregory.

"Didn't do much but gave lots of advice to make up for it. That's the only thing people are generous with. Advice. Have you noticed? Come into the kitchen. I have to whip up Carl's milk shake. Bring that wastebasket, will you? Put on a pair of gloves, first." The dispenser was nailed to the wall.

"But there were so many others. Jeff — "

"Jeff, oh, Jeff!" Kenny threw back his head, his mouth a rictus of a smile, but he didn't laugh. "Jeff got awfully mad when the cops raided his bookstore. Blamed Carl's sloppy business practices. You still have no idea who tipped them off? We figure it was one of the boys. We knew it wasn't you. Don't have the balls, do you? Maybe Mickey, he was growing too old for the business, and he resented being pushed out. Well, he got his. Carl swears he didn't do Mickey. One time I believe him. Acid simply isn't Carl's thing. Whipping, that's his thing. Or used to be. Not much into it now, are you, Carl?" he called across the dining room.

"He didn't hear you," Damon said.

"Hearing's perfect. Only thing that is. Anyway, Jeff moved to Chicago. Last I heard, he's in books again." Kenny was mixing frozen strawberries, bananas, and milk in a blender.

"But what about Torq and those guys?"

"For that matter, what about you?"

"I'm working all day." Probably some of the night, too.

"Death duty isn't as much fun as partying," Kenny said bitterly.

"Oh, we have other volunteers, college kids who are *so* sincere and want to make Carl's last hours a glorious transition from this world to the next. We have a flutist who plays music from heaven, as if she knows what heaven sounds like. And the candle lighters! Death-junkies, the lot of them. Easy for them — they're in good health. The knitters spend hours on shawls he can't use. They'll go to the AIDS thrift shop eventually, won't they, Carl?" His voice rose loud enough for Carl to hear, "Your shawls will just go to the thrift shop, won't they?" Kenny laughed and turned on the blender. "Get out a joint," he said, indicating a wooden box with a picture of some heavy metal band on the cover. "Light up, will you? We have to get his stomach in shape to keep some of this down."

"I can't," Damon said. Robbie complained that pot made him loopy, Gregory warned him against smelling of contraband and getting them all in trouble, Leroy said it made his paintings too Rothenberg-ish or even Lichtenstein-ish, God forbid, but Pleaser loved the stuff and supplied the eye drops and breath mints. "Pleaser?" he called the alter mentally. No answer. The Pleaser was otherwise occupied.

"Don't tell me you're clean," Kenny said. "I can't keep lighting up eight or ten joints a day, pot zonks me out, and I have to take care of Carl."

"Why can't he do it?"

"Bug's in his lungs. Hard for him to inhale enough to get it started. Jeez, Damon, this is just a little thing you can do for your Kenny."

The phrase echoed unpleasantly down the corridors of Damon's mind. "Just a little thing you can do for your Kenny." Where had he heard that before? Kenny had said it to him many times, but he couldn't remember what the little thing was. The image of the bath-tub flashed through his mind.

"Die, Kenny, die," said Leroy. Leroy remembered.

"I'm sorry," Damon said. "Maybe I'd better go."

Kenny's face fell, and he tried to compose it into a mask of tranquil friendship. "You only just got here," he said lightly.

"This isn't the right time."

"Well, there's never a right time when someone's dying, is there?"

Carrying the smoothie and the joint, Kenny bustled into Carl's room, put them on the bureau by the photo of the older and younger women so full of themselves, and raised Carl's pillows, supplying another so that he was on a slant to keep the liquid down.

"What do you think, Carl? Is there ever a right time to visit a person who's dying? I don't mean anyone particular, just people in general."

"Asshole," croaked Carl.

"Oh, you're the asshole expert. I defer to the asshole expert." He lit the joint from a matchbook with the picture of a naked man on the cover. "You know, I don't think that's very nice of you, Carl. Calling me names when I do so much for you." Carl watched greedily as all that good pot went up in smoke. "All my loving care and you still call me names. Say you're sorry." He held the joint to Carl's lips, then snatched it away. "Say you're sorry, or you won't get any."

"Asshole!" Carl yelled, his voice cracking.

"I guess you don't need it. Come along, Damon."

As Kenny started out of the room, carrying the burning joint, Carl gave a horrible groan.

"That's better," Kenny said, putting the joint to Carl's mouth. Carl took a deep drag.

If pot had had calories, Carl would have been plump. He held the smoke in his lungs and asked Damon, "So what's up with you?" as if Damon could supply a change of scene. Damon wracked his mind for harmless details of his life.

"Nothing much to dishwashing, actually. Sometimes they don't get clean. The boss just brushes them off with his elbow."

"What about painting? Are you doing any painting?" Kenny asked.

Damon was tempted say that he never had, that it had been mostly Leroy's doing, but of course, he knew better. Keep the conversation clean of the others. So he said, "A little," pretending that he was Leroy. Of course, Leroy did A LOT, but Damon felt it was better not to explain too much. Like Leroy's "Great Heavens painting", for instance. Kenny would call the whole idea "retro," and Leroy would explode, maybe even get some of those secret friends of his to do something horrible.

"Answer a question with a question," Gregory told him patiently for the umpteenth time. "When someone asks you something you're not comfortable answering, give them just a tiny answer and then turn it back on them."

"What about you, Kenny?" Damon asked. "Are you painting?"

"Where have you been?" Kenny demanded sarcastically. "Caring for Carl's a full time occupation. Absolutely full time. When could I paint? You tell me."

"Did you see Carmine before — before —?"

"I saw him. He didn't see me. He called me one of his 'former artists.' How do you like that? 'How's my former artist?' he asks. Like I deliberately gave it up. I tell him I have to take care of Carl, and he says, 'Real artists don't make excuses. They do their art no matter what.' Well, he got his. Too bad I don't know the killer."

"Killers, they say," Leroy corrected.

"Killers, then. We'd invite them to lunch, wouldn't we, Carl? Wouldn't we invite Carmine's killers for a toke and a poke?"

"Bastard!" screamed Leroy.

Kenny appeared stunned. "Well, yes, Damon, he certainly was. So I'd say, maybe he'd like to come by and help with Carl. He says he's got too many real artists to bring forth into this world. God, I hated him. Still do. I'd say, 'I'll get back to my art just as soon as — I can.'"

Damon was pretty sure that Kenny had almost said, "as soon as Carl's dead," and Carl gave him a look that would shave glass, then took another breath of his joint. The breath of life. Kenny held a half a teaspoonful of smoothie to Carl's lips, so small it seemed like just pretend to Damon. He had a sudden intense image from Robbie's past, Becca in her pink dress with the embroidery on the collar, dark, shiny hair hanging over her cheeks, concentrating on feeding her doll with a miniature plastic spoon as she crooned a tuneless lullaby. He rarely got those flashes now.

Carl took a big hit of nirvana. Hit, hit, hit, sip, hit, hit. Carl was dying, but at the moment he didn't care.

"Oh, Carl, if you're not going to drink it, what's the use?" Kenny set the glass aside by the stale water and got up from the bed. "I'm wasting my time. Damon, come along, I'll show you your old room. I'm in there now."

Showing Damon his room was just an excuse, however. As they went down the hall, Kenny said loud enough for Carl to hear, "I can't do this. This isn't how it was supposed to be. The smells. I'm not cut out to be a nurse. I'm simply not cut out."

Damon's old room was a mess of dirty clothes. The bunk beds had been replaced with a single twin. Damon searched the ceiling for any signs of his tree, but the ceiling was water-stained, otherwise bare. Not even a bump to signify that a tree once grew up, out, and through, killed as finally as if Carl had applied bleach to the roots, then burned them. Damon struggled to remember what it was Carl actually did to it. The boats were gone, from both the curtains and the shelves. Party trinkets had replaced them, bits of sequined things, mirrors, feathers, painted cardboard, beads, tinsel, and foil. A Mardi Gras party mask hung from the bedstead. He turned to the mirror where he first saw Gregory, with Robbie crying in another room off to the side. They weren't there. That was because he no longer needed to see them. They were inside him now.

"I came by to tell you something," Damon said, as he and Kenny sat side by side amid a pile of smelly clothes on the bed, Kenny's shoulders sagging in defeat. How could Kenny live this way? It wasn't like him. "Gregory found Becca."

"What!" Kenny had stopped questioning Damon about Gregory and the rest. Kenny just assumed that the other names were Damon's way of talking about himself. Pursuing the subject had been too frustrating.

"Gregory works in computers — "

"Computers! You don't have the brains."

"Gregory does, and he got on the Internet and found Becca."

"You're Gregory!" Kenny exploded. "For Chrissake, you're Gregory."

"I understand you think that," said Gregory tactfully. "Whatever. Anyway, Becca lives in Seattle."

"This is insane," said Kenny. "Are you sure it's the same one? There are a lot of Beccas."

"Becca Merrow, right?"

Kenny flinched, but didn't say yes or no, seeming afraid of betraying too much.

"We've been having this huge fight," added Damon. "Some of the guys want to meet her and ask her about our family. Others hate her guts for not trying hard enough to get us back home. Thing is, we may move up there."

"What do you mean, move up there? Why would you do such a thing? That's crazy."

"What did I tell you?" Gregory nudged his ear. "He hasn't changed. You don't owe him anything."

"Don't tell anyone. It may get hot for us around here."

"What do you mean, hot?"

"Something to do with Carmine's murder."

"Well, you didn't do it. That's for sure."

"I have no idea what's coming down. Pleaser says we'd better get ready to skip town. Fast. Leroy seems to know something about it, but he's not telling. I came to say goodbye."

"Damon, you're making no sense whatsoever. I need you here. Look, Damon, I've been thinking. Wouldn't it be nice if you and I found a little place for ourselves and moved in together?"

"But I already have roommates."

"You mean these?" Kenny prodded Damon's forehead. "The ones in here? They can come, too."

"I'm not sure they want to."

"Remember the fun we used to have in the studio?"

"That was fun?" asked Leroy.

"We can do that again," Kenny went on. "Thing is, I need you to help me take care of Carl. And then we can find a place of our own."

"We have to go to Seattle."

"But what about me, Damon? What about your Kenny?"

"You're not my Kenny anymore. That was a long time ago."

"I'm HIV positive, too. Who'll take care of me when my time comes. Could be any day, now."

"Carl?"

"Carl! He'll be dead, you —" Kenny bit off the rest. Nitwit?

Ninny? "You've got responsibilities here, Damon. Friends take care of each other. Those imaginary playmates of yours are just an excuse to do whatever selfish thing comes into your head. Selfish, selfish! And after all I've done for you." Kenny was up from the bed, slashing away at the trinkets on the shelves, so that they glittered and jingled to the floor, fists clenched like Carl's. Would he tie Damon to the bed and beat him?

"I know, Kenny," Gregory said in his best business manner. "I knew you'd be upset."

"Die, Kenny, die," said Leroy.

"What about hospice?" Damon suggested.

"They only come for an hour or two a day. What about the rest of the time?"

"Your friends?"

"What friends? They send Christmas cards. That's what my friends do. Or maybe you'd like to see me in the grips of those sanctimonious college kids, eh? Who get their jollies out of watching someone else buy the farm. Knowing they're a hundred years away from it, and everything will be cured by then. That would be revenge all right."

Revenge? For what? Oh, yes, it was just on the edge of his mind.

"Farm?" he asked.

"Buy the farm. You know, kick the bucket, croak, pop off, bite the dust, turn up the toes, go to the happy hunting grounds — DIE, for God's sake."

"Die, Kenny, die."

"Maybe I can come back," replied Damon to this attack of death imagery. But he didn't want to come back to Kenny, did he? He wasn't sure he even cared about Kenny any longer. "It's like we all have a vote, see?" Damon tried to explain. "And I'm the only one who voted to stay here." Not really, but how would Kenny know? "Everyone else thinks we should go, especially since something's coming down, and we could be in big trouble."

"No, this is just some scheme you've cooked up —" Kenny broke off again.

"I'd better go," said Damon. "I promised I'd get back."

"Promised who? Oh, where are my manners. I haven't even offered you tea. Come along into the kitchen, and I'll make us some. We'll discuss it better over a good cuppa." Going down the hall, Kenny called to Carl in passing, "Carl, do you want tea?"

"Yes," came the weak, scraggly voice.

"I can't hear you," Kenny sang as they reached the kitchen.

"He said 'Yes,'" Damon told him.

Kenny winked.

30

LATER, THEY ASKED BECCA when she had received the first phone call, and she had to admit she didn't know. There had been hang-ups.

The first time someone actually said something, it was a young man asking for Ms. Becca Merrow.

"Did you have a brother named Robbie?"

Becca's legs turned to rubber.

"Who is this?" she began, but in a sudden attack of hoarseness, she lost her voice and had to clear it.

"Was he taken from the playground?" But this was another voice entirely, coarse and gravelly.

"Unless you identify yourself —"

"Were you in on the deal? We want to know. 'Cause some of us think you were."

"Not all of us."

"Did you sell Robbie to Kenny and Carl?"

"Did you try as hard as you could to find him?"

"Did you try even harder?" A giggle in the breaking voice.

The questions were tumbling over each other now, as (she imagined) one man or boy after another snatched the phone from an unwilling hand. Becca felt her own receiver shake. She tried to hang onto it, but then, why should she? Some sick bastard who got his kicks from hounding others about the tragedies in their lives. Very softly she hung up, as she had already done on her past, and when the phone rang immediately afterwards, she ignored it.

Becca contacted the phone company and the police, who labeled the calls "crank," not worth the time and money to trace. No threat to some sensitive body part, no snide reminder of endangered loved ones, certainly no blackmail demands. Mere feelings of threat didn't warrant more than superficial commiseration.

Becca tried to forget. Her enjoyment — pleasure even — at being twenty-three, alone in her apartment, and dateless on Saturday nights caught her by surprise. Hugh disappeared from her life on the night she asked him what he'd think of "doing it" in a cave, and he responded, "Why?" It was a test question.

She sat at her used spinet with a glass of merlot on top, playing Chopin, Beethoven, and Rachmaninoff. A baked potato topped with broccoli, onions, garlic, and melted cheese, a broiled steak, and a chocolate brownie served as her dinner, while she watched a video.

Then she curled up on the couch, cozy under her winter green fringed throw, reading a mystery and drowsing to New Age music on her stereo, music that ran through her like a Santa Cruz waterfall into a brook.

At eleven p.m., she roused herself to tour her little haven of safety, checking the front door and the kitchen burners. Hers was a top floor apartment in a Victorian brick building shaped like an "H." Front and back stairs divided the two sets of three floors, with no one on either side of her, yielding plenty of privacy and quiet. The back stairs and porch were not enclosed, however. Anyone could go up and down, and occasionally did, leading Becca to question her landlord's claim that this was a security building. Nor was her kitchen door a thick wood panel; rather, half of it enclosed a pane of supposedly shatterproof glass through which she could see clouds schussing across the sky, towering pines that bred Christmas cones, and her neighbor's garden below. Because of this view, she refused to curtain it for privacy. Once she'd watched the locked-out tenant next door swing himself over the porch railing to lift open his kitchen window and climb in. That had taught her to nail her own window to the sash. In hot weather, she could remove this homemade lock and open the window six inches, slipping the nail into corresponding frame and sash holes. She told herself that she was too security conscious. Robbie's kidnapping had left its indelible mark.

In the tiny square hall with a door each to the kitchen, the bedroom, the bathroom, and the dining room, Becca's gallery of photos radiated from the central portrait of Robbie, the one from the newspapers. Borrowing the original from her mother, she'd had an enlarged copy made. Everyone asked, who was that adorable little boy in the red bear sweatshirt with the blond hair swept across his forehead, and the chubby chipmunk cheeks? (Well, they didn't say "chipmunk.") Becca told them he was her brother, but she never told them he was gone. Most didn't ask, assuming growth like Becca's into work, sports, women, and bars — secure in confinement.

Surrounding him were other family pictures — Mom and the twins — their school "angel pictures," and their most recent photo at age twelve, clowning around an old truck wreck that Ike was fixing (was love of trucks genetic?) Mike pretended to help, but he hadn't a clue, being much more inclined toward astronomy books. There were several pictures of her dad in the band, Santa Cruz, Branson, San Francisco, and his beloved New Orleans, so similar that they could have been snapped in the same place, always with grinning fellow musicians, their arms around his shoulders. The one of him and Lisbet on the beach betrayed his missed chance at love, she thought. But then, Lisbet hadn't missed.

Aunt Cordelia marched triumphantly across her little square of wall in a Planned Parenthood parade. A rare photo showed Dr. Connie as she sat beaming in her office, surrounded by her trolls, and then the one in the paper at her death, a much younger Dr. Connie looking to the future in the halo that professional photographers use to such idealistic advantage. More numerous were the photos of Annalyn, from childhood to her most recent full maternal glory beside Jim, the latest picture of baby Nita appended.

On the largest wall, Becca had begun what she was sure would be a lifetime "album" of those she counseled, photos of street kids, students, and others. There were, of course, ethical questions about taking pictures of patients in long-term therapy with her, but she wasn't at that stage yet. These were brief interventions as a grad student during which Becca worked hard to bring them back from wherever in their minds they had gone. The street kids showed no attempt to please, no smiles or gaiety. Rather they stared into the cameras as themselves — depressed, defiant, sultry imitations of Madonna or a rapper whose fashionable rage had brought him fame and money. They saw no difference between themselves and the celebrities, partly because a hallmark of their illness was their fragile and uncertain identity. Becca had deliberated where to hang them, not in her bedroom to haunt her dreams, not in her living room to bring her work home with her. The hall with her family, where she would see the lot of them only in passing, seemed just right.

Beyond Becca's living room bay windows, the Seattle night skyline gleamed and glittered on the horizon. Red lights on high-rises winked warnings at low-flying aircraft. On her tables and bookshelves, her new plants and flowers thrived — globus, marantha the praying plant, ivy, schefflera from Hugh, dieffenbachia, a rare begonia from Craig, and a collection of violets.

Having performed her cleansing ritual, Becca opened a window, breathing deeply of the night air that always reminded her of something nameless, bearing messages from alien yet familiar places, calling her to another life beyond herself. Finally, she climbed under the covers — alone. The last thing she remembered was an odd sound, a "click," before she tumbled down the rabbit hole.

She was awakened by a sensation of weight pressing down on the corner of her bed, as if someone had come to sit beside her while she slept. The odor of something pungent like ether smothered her. She wrenched her head away from the cloth over her face, eyes clenched shut, measuring each movement of the mattress as the weight shifted. Closer? Farther? Up? Back down again? The news had been filled with stories of "home invasions." She took a deep breath, opened her mouth, and began to scream.

She screamed and screamed in that way we do when we are trying to rouse ourselves from a nightmare, forcing the air through paralyzed vocal cords, groans not formed into words. At last, her screams awakened her, even though she'd thought she was awake before. She switched on her night lamp. Of course, no one was there. But at the corner of her bed she thought she could see the imprint left by the sitter, just as she'd seen imprints from police officers on her childhood bed so long ago. The mattress sagged slightly in that corner, and the white duvet cover gathered in tiny wrinkles. The odor lingered in her nostrils, with a burning sweet taste in her mouth.

Someone had been here.

Rationally, Becca knew this was improbable.

Still terrified, she lay listening. No one knocked at her door, front or back, to ask if she was okay. Apparently, no matter how loud a noise she had made, no one heard. "The penalty for privacy and quiet," she told herself grimly.

At last, Becca swung out of her bed, drew her robe around her shoulders to keep out the cold, and made the rounds of her apartment, opening the walk-in closet to peer behind boxes and clothes. The square that led to the attic appeared sealed tight. What could be up there except empty space and mice? The noises she made during her search both frightened and comforted her.

"I make a sound, therefore I'm still alive," she paraphrased Descartes over the drum beat in her chest.

The floor creaked as she padded across the kitchen threshold and paused. The back porch bulb cast a pattern of light and shadow through the window in the door, but the shape was not quite right. Part of it curved. Why would that be? It should be angles. Had her neighbor put some object on the porch, a sack of garbage perhaps, as he did occasionally? No, that sack would barely reach the bottom of the window.

As she stood still, trying not to breathe, telling herself this was a game, that she was over-dramatizing, part of the shadow detached itself and, still hunched over, descended the back stairs noiselessly. Since whoever it was tried not to make a sound, it meant that he knew she was there. She rushed to her bedroom window to see who it might be, but her view was obstructed by the building corner, the bay windows, and the branches of the Douglas fir that screened the sidewalk below. She waited a long time and never saw. He could have ducked around the back instead. He could have climbed the short fence into her neighbor's yard. He could still be there, watching her.

Even tension gets tiring. Tiptoeing to the back porch door again, she peered out the shatterproof pane and froze. No trash, no person, nothing. Her window was still nailed shut, her door locked, but she was startled to discover that she'd forgotten to slip the chain. She was sure she remembered sliding it into its groove. Maybe not. She'd been pretty relaxed, half asleep actually, when she made that final tour of her apartment.

A ladder led from the back porch up to the attic trap door, which was always padlocked, although she couldn't see this from her present vantage point without stepping outside. Probably it was the sound of the back porch creaking that had awakened her. A homeless person seeking a scrap of shelter, she told herself. She'd become more familiar with their habits as she'd worked with the street kids. Taking a few deep breaths, she resumed her review of her apartment. The ceiling had been "lowered" when the apartment owners renovated it, which simply meant that a false ceiling had been installed below the true one, as in many of the older buildings here. This was considered to be an improvement over the original high ceiling, which might be too difficult to fix properly, with moldings and decorative trim half disintegrated.

The living room felt chilly but undisturbed. Seattle lights blurred in the now foggy distance. A plane rumbled overhead amid a sprinkling of stars. The front door was bolted.

It was five-twenty in the morning. The lingering odor, whether imaginary or real, made her feel a bit sick. She wouldn't sleep again. After turning up the heat, she brewed herself a cup of coffee and began work on the Sunday Crossword Puzzle. She couldn't remember being so terrified since she was a child, and indeed, she recalled little of that. At least, that was what she told herself. Her life had started the day Robbie disappeared.

For no good reason, her nightmare led to thoughts of the other frightening thing that had happened to her in the last few months. Perhaps, the phone calls had laid the groundwork for her nightmare. As she filled in blank squares, a problem she could solve, she was busy at work on this other one as well.

31

THE fIRST TIME DAMON saw Chloe, he stood riveted to the basement floor in the old wooden building that housed Seattle's Phoenix Community Players. A red paisley scarf protected the yarn that was her hair from spatters of the green paint that she was applying to the flat. He couldn't have said what color her hair was naturally. Wisps of blue, fuchsia (Leroy's word, not his) and doll yellow escaped the scarf, below the edge of which silver ear cuffs clustered. She straightened up her little boy body with the adorably tiny breasts like points of light beneath the denim shirt, her hand still holding the brush, not delicately between three fingers like Kenny, but clenched in her fist, as if it were a knife.

"Well, don't just stand there," she said with a sly grin. She knew very well why he was just standing there. "They're not paying us to stand around." Of course, "they" weren't paying the two of them at all. Theirs was a labor of love, in addition to many other labors, in return for which they got small parts as townspeople in *Our Town.* "Grab a brush! Here, take mine. We have this whole flat to do, and there's just the two of us. We'll be lucky if we get out of here at all tonight."

What then?

There was something flirtatious about how she extended the brush, cocking her head to one side, judging him as many girls had done, but not finding him wanting, not in the least. As he reached for it, he heard a growl, and saw for the first time the little white dog no bigger than a minute, standing on her paint-spattered tennis shoe.

"This is Go-Go," she said. "He's Maltese. Mostly. Father was a St. Bernard." St. Bernard? "He won't bite. Probably. Go-Go, don't frighten the nice man." She scooped him up and hugged him to her chest. "Can't you see you're scaring him?"

"I'm not scared," Damon maintained valiantly. Truth to tell, he'd been nervous around dogs ever since his misadventures with Noodles, although they weren't his misadventures exactly, more like Pleaser's. Still, he never knew what he'd done, so he had no idea what he'd do. He reached out a tentative hand to pat Go-Go, who seemed unsure as to whether this was friend or foe. Above them, they could hear the voices of the director and the players on the stage rehearsing.

"How old is Go-Go?"

"A year. I have him around for protection."

"Protection?" Damon asked dubiously.

"Sure! Go-Go'd never let anything happen to me. He's saved my life dozens of times, haven't you, sweetie?" she said, nuzzling his dirty fur, in response to which he licked her nose. "It's the St. Bernard in him. I had a fella once grew garlic in Gilroy. That's in California, you know. Said he was the garlic king. Or maybe president, I guess, since this is a democracy. Anyway, he was wearing his sandals around the house one day, just normal like, and Go-Go got hold of his big toe and wouldn't leave off it."

"Why?"

"Reached for me, I guess. And that just goes to show, because, you know, when you grow garlic, you smell like garlic, taste like garlic, you even spit garlic, and Go-Go wouldn't let go even though that toe must have tasted real bad. 'Course that was a few years ago when I was fifteen, and Go-Go probably figured I couldn't take care of myself."

"But, you said he was only a year old. How could he have saved you a few years ago?"

"How old do you think I am?" Chloe drew herself up to her full height and looked upset.

"Very young," Damon said quickly.

"I'm Chloe, by the way, Chloe Lippincott. And you're —?"

"Damon Warhol."

"What kind of a name is that?"

"I'm going to change it."

"I'd do so quickly if I were you. Pick something aristocratic. Damon Hemingway would be nice. No? How about Damon Morgan? Damon Chase? Damon Hearst, and you're a distant cousin. They can't prove you aren't. I was Chloe Hearst for a while, but I like Lippincott better. How do you do, Damon Hearst."

She held out her hand to shake his, and he quickly switched the brush to his left so he could take hers, which he held a second too long apparently, because her mouth curled in a little laugh. It was a gamin mouth with the ends turned up.

"Don't they have a rule against dogs here?" Damon asked.

"Sure, they do! Well, back to work," she said, dumping Go-Go unceremoniously onto a red velvet jacket in the corner, which he circled several times before he lay down. "You paint those ladders over there for Emily and George to stand on, and pretend they're on the second floors of their houses. I'll paint the trellises with phony flowers winding up them."

Ladders again! Was this the symbol of his life? The meaning, even? Damon climbed a real ladder and set to work on the fake one.

"Have you done this before?" she asked approvingly.

"I've watched others do it."

"I had a fella once in Albuquerque. That's in New Mexico. The state, not the country. So scared of ladders, thought he was going to fall. Lost his job because of it. He was a judge, and he had to climb ladders to crime scenes. Couldn't do it. Went back to hanging wallpaper. That's when I met him."

"You have to climb ladders for that, too."

Chloe shrugged. "Must have had an assistant."

"Maybe Albuquerque has short walls."

"Short walls, that's it."

Who knew what they had in Albuquerque?

From the top of the stairs, someone yelled, "Amy, Bebe, what's her name again?"

"Chloe," she yelled back up.

"Whatever. Come up here a minute."

Chloe dropped her brush, saying, "Oops, casting call," and hustled her sweet booty up the stairs, leaving Damon to paint, hoping Leroy wouldn't try to horn in.

"Are you kidding? I wouldn't paint a set if my life depended on it," said Leroy scornfully. Had Damon said it aloud, or was Leroy reading his mind again? "Even painting signs is more creative. *You* have to paint sets for a part. How humiliating! *I* don't even want a part. Shit brown, here mix some cerulean blue in it."

"No, no," Damon said. "That's the brown they want. Don't mess me up again."

Left to himself, Damon finished the top rung and, uncertain as to whether or not to proceed to the others in the same color, wandered around downstairs, into the prop room with all the furniture and then into the costume closet and finally upstairs to watch the wedding scene. Theater was tame compared to porn.

Chloe was arguing with her father, saying she didn't want to get married, acting the part of someone who hadn't shown up, projecting her voice into the farthest reaches of the theater dramatically with a lot of hand gestures.

"That's good, Amy. How would you like to be second understudy for the part?" Apparently the first understudy hadn't shown up, either. Chloe responded with equal drama, "Yes!"

When they knocked off for the night, Damon said "Goodbye" to Chloe just outside the stage door. He started off one way, and she the other.

Until now, Damon's sex life had been chaotic — quick couplings with young women when he thought Leroy wasn't around to ogle and Pleaser wasn't around to steal the spot from him. He found he preferred women over men, partly because he was strong enough to be on top. For Damon, arranging a tryst was a complicated affair, because he was at the mercy not only of the girl's fits and moods and desires, but those of his family as well. Once he'd awakened to find his girl bloodied and bruised; someone he didn't know had taken the spot and made no difference between anger and sex. "Rough sex," they called it. She was furious at him, although too weak to do anything about it. Gregory got her to a hospital and faded out of the picture fast.

Gregory tried to keep the rest of them away when Damon had a girl, saying that this was Damon's private moment, and he was entitled just as they all were, "boundaries" must be preserved, etc. (He'd learned about "boundaries" during his occasional visits to the college counselor for his panic attacks). The only safe way for Damon to achieve relief was to beat off on himself, or "spank the monkey," as Pleaser delighted in calling it. Beating off bored the others "to smithereens," just like going to the toilet did, and so as soon as he began, they left him in peace.

When he reached the street corner, Damon remembered he'd left his script backstage near the curtain controls. He wanted to study it, just in case any opportunity for second understudy came his way, as it had Chloe's. The theater doors were locked, of course. Under these circumstances, he'd call on Pleaser, but if Pleaser wasn't in on Chloe yet, Damon didn't want to alert him. The longer he kept Chloe a secret from the rest, the better. Pleaser would check all windows first to see if one was unlocked, then use a skeleton key, or shimmy up between two buildings to the second floor.

To Damon's surprise, he found the back basement window open, airing out the paint smells. He climbed in. A faint light beckoned from the prop room, and there was Chloe, reclining on the couch underneath an old velveteen curtain, eating dinner with Go-Go at her side.

"Back for refreshments?" she asked. If she was surprised to see him, she showed no sign. On the couch was an assortment of cheese squares and the rest of the donuts that Damon recognized from the morning coffee break. "Have some cheese. I think it's wasted on the mice around here myself. Mice will eat anything. Practically. You don't have to use perfectly good cheese. Go-Go's gotten nipped by a trap several times. I think that's cruelty to animals, don't you?"

Damon had been about to take a square, but when he grasped where it had been, he paused.

"Go on, go on," she urged. "Gotta eat when the food's there, know what I mean? Not just when you're hungry. 'Cause there may not be any food around then."

"Don't mice make you nervous?"

"No, there are always animals where I live — spiders, roaches, rats. All God's critters."

Damon was growing hungrier by the minute.

"I was just about to get a cheeseburger and fries. How about letting me treat you?"

"Well, that's sweet. I'll get changed. Don't want to embarrass you in front of your fast food friends."

Was that a nick? Should he have offered to take her to a chandelier sit-down-place? Probably. That was what girls expected. They expected you to treat them nice if they were going to treat you nice. Except that he didn't have that much money on him. Jobs were even tighter in Seattle than San Francisco, and Gregory was creating a whole new résumé for him.

Chloe slipped off the couch, and Go-Go took the opportunity to dive into her share of the spoils. She flipped through the trolley of costumes off-stage with practiced motions, commenting to herself about the regal lace and velvet gowns, the long-sleeved crepes for old women, the maids' costumes for naughty scenes. Among them were scattered her own clothes. She chose a number of items, holding them out to examine them, then replacing them or keeping them.

"No one knows the difference," she said. "In fact, sometimes they think my clothes are the costumes. Isn't that a hoot? I don't mind. I borrow theirs, they borrow mine. Fair's fair. I'll just be a minute," she added, closing the door to the communal dressing room

Minutes later, she emerged in a black leather skirt, leotards, a pink fur vest over her top with lipstick to match, a chain around her waist, a leather collar, and her yarn hair released from its scarf, poking out all over her head.

"Why did they call you 'Amy'?" Damon asked her as they headed up the street. "Is that your stage name?" Like "Clint" was Mickey's stage name when his name still mattered?

"Oh, Amy was here before me. Bebe, too. They forget and call me that."

"Don't you mind?"

"Amy, Chloe, Mauritania, whatever it takes. You be sure to let them call you what they want to. They don't like being corrected."

"You live in the theater?"

"As good a place as any. I have to take the chairs off the couch at night and stack them in the hall and put them back in the morning, so I can get the door shut. It's like making your bed, really. The curtains smell of dust, and they're full of holes, but warm. I'm saving for a sleeping bag from the Salvation Army."

"Does the director know you sleep here?"

"Hasn't a clue. Wonders why the heating bills are so high," she giggled. "But that place is an igloo. Cold air blows in everywhere, through the walls practically. Have to keep the heat up. Not enough meat on my bones to keep me alive."

At the fast food joint, Damon got in line to order, but Chloe shook her head, as if he were a hopeless case.

"Not that way, silly. They make the burgers ahead of time here, and then they throw them out after ten minutes. They're still perfectly good, if you're not fussy about whether they're singles or doubles. And they get a good deed on their karmic record, go to heaven and all that. We're doing them a favor."

She went to the counter where the manager greeted her cheerfully and watched her hands in fascination as she spoke.

"I called ahead? For my friend and me?" So the rest of the line wouldn't catch on.

"Right!" the manager smiled back at her, grabbed up a few burgers and tossed in an order of fries.

"Good on you, sir!" Chloe blessed him.

"What about the shakes?" Damon asked.

"Those you buy."

They got back to the theater and feasted on the couch, Chloe breaking off bites of meat for Go-Go, and putting aside a bite of each item for breakfast. Damon contributed to the pot from his meal as well.

After they'd finished, Chloe excused herself for a few minutes, returning in a slinky nightgown and peignoir set. She climbed onto the couch, pulling the curtain over her and stretched out, saying, "I'm pooped. You can get in, too, if you want," she added, tossing the cushions off so there was more room.

"So you sleep here?"

"It's not bad."

It wasn't, actually. Piled high around them were the elements of a real bedroom with phony curtained windows looking out on a phony balcony, sky, boats in a harbor, phony pictures on the walls, phony lamps that lit or didn't, little tables with phony glasses of colored water that simulated liquor, and phony books in a bookcase. This couch was another place for the actors to move to when stage left or stage right got boring. Damon had noticed that the less action there was in a script, the more there was on stage; in fact, the moving around could get quite frenetic if the story was wordy and slow-paced.

Damon should leave, but he didn't want to. Who knew how long he'd have his privacy with the girl of his dreams? Well, maybe not the girl of his dreams, exactly. He liked to talk the way other people did.

"So what do you do when you're not in theater?" Chloe asked.

"All sorts of things," Damon said, racking his brain for the most acceptable job he'd ever had. That made a difference to girls, he'd found. "I had this job as assistant manager of a restaurant once."

"Really?"

"'Course it was only for a few months." Actually, one.

"I don't like to stay in jobs too long," said Chloe, squirming around under the curtain.

"Me, neither," said Damon.

"A few months is just about my speed."

"Mine, too! Weeks, even."

"Jobs get so boring."

"You're so right!" Why hadn't he thought of that? He changed

jobs not because he was fired for incompetence or laid off in a reces-
sion, but because he was bored. Why didn't he recognize this as soon
as it happened and just quit? Usually, he hung on as long as he could,
trying to exceed his record of six weeks and three days and one and
one-half hours and seventeen minutes at a car body shop, counting
from the time he actually left rather than the time he was let go. It
made no difference; he got canned sooner or later, so why not take the
initiative and quit *before* it happened? In gratitude to Chloe, he bent
closer to her, gauging whether or not she'd let him kiss her.

"I had a fella once," Chloe was saying. "Sold brassieres door to
door."

"You mean bras?"

"He called them 'brassieres'. Classier, he said. Anyway, he was
selling them in this little town in Vermont. In the dead of winter, so
they had to invite him in."

"But nobody sells brassieres door to door."

"This fella did. That's what made him such an en-tre-pre-nure,"
she pronounced each syllable distinctly to get it right. "Nobody else
was doing it."

"But when he came to the door, didn't women think he was getting fresh?"

"That's why he wanted me to go with him. Said women would
trust him even more. He had this whole case and everything. And
he'd open it, and let them step into the bathroom or someplace to try
them on."

"Well, I wouldn't think they'd try them on in front of him."

"You'd be surprised. When they got comfortable with him —
'cause he had this way of making people real comfortable, just something about him — why, they'd even let him adjust the straps."

"I'll bet some husbands got home and beat him into the floor."

"You'd think, but then he'd show them his case, and sure enough,
they'd end up buying presents."

"You tell real tall stories, you know?"

"They're true, though. Now why was I telling you this one? Oh,
yes, we were talking about boring jobs. He said he was never bored."

"I'll bet!"

Chloe turned toward Damon and closed her eyes.

"You sure you don't want to join me?"

"Thanks, but I have a place to sleep."

"Are you for real?"

Damon thought about it. Why did he have to go home? Of course, Gregory would worry, and Pleaser and Leroy would look for him, and Wendy (whom they'd taken to calling "Little Miss Shouldn't") would scold.

A night away from the family, a night of privacy, maybe even sex! Damon lifted the curtain and crawled under, while Chloe snuggled up against him.

"Mmmm, you're warm, you know?"

The next morning, Chloe told Damon to make the coffee and rinse out the cups before the director and the rest of the crew arrived. Damon did so with a light heart. Chloe was so adorable, with those freckles scattered kind of like fleas across her nose; how could anyone even think of refusing her anything? For her part, Chloe contemplated the mostly brown flat and began touching it up with yellow and a spritz of orange. Then she'd stand back, paint some more, stand back, paint some more.

"What do you think, Damon? Having it all brown was kinda boring, don't you think? I mean, it takes place in a country town."

Damon stood back, but since he wasn't sure what he was looking for, he said,

"I think it looks pretty real, don't you?"

That could be said of anything.

"You're right. Set that ladder over here at the other corner and paint the sky, will you?"

The crew arrived, and the director descended to see how things were progressing.

"Not bad, Amy," he said, munching a cruller. "Come on up for breakfast, kids."

They'd already eaten their "bites" from the night before, but Damon was hungry again.

Once more, they ascended into the rarified air of the stage. Damon chose a sugared donut because there were more of those, and no one would mind. Chloe took a cruller and an apple fritter "for later."

"Take one for later," she whispered to Damon, nudging him.

"Well, where have we been for the last three days?" asked Gregory, using the word "we" more accurately than hospital nurses.

"As if you didn't know," said Damon, who had finally returned to keep Leroy and Pleaser from looking for him.

"Are you going to bring her home to meet the family?" Gregory asked archly. He was under the impression that he headed up a family just like a godfather in the Mafia. Damon knew it was in his best interests to play along.

"When I know her better," he suggested.

What would it mean to bring Chloe home to meet the family exactly? It didn't have to happen at home, after all. It could happen anywhere. Any of the others could snatch the spot away from him at any time, a situation Damon deeply resented, and now feared as well. He finally meets a girl he really likes who'll let him do it to her, and he's in danger of losing her to his own brothers.

"Our family's a bit much on first acquaintance, eh?" Gregory was saying. "Hey, I've been minding my own business, and I've kept the others minding theirs."

This wasn't exactly true. Damon had felt Gregory spying on them, but he hadn't tried to grab the spot.

"Thanks, Gregory," Damon said.

"I only got a peek," Gregory confessed, maybe because he knew Damon knew.

"I didn't even get that," said Pleaser, who appeared as if by magic on the threshold of Damon's living room. "Did our Damon snag a hag, eh? Shag a snag? Tell us, tell us."

"Now, Pleaser, Damon will share when he's ready. It's his business and none of ours."

"It's all our businesses. Damon don't even know what part of a frail he's supposed to put it in."

Damon felt the heat rise to his cheeks. "You see? That's why I never tell you."

"His colors are retro, I can tell you that," said Leroy.

"They're not my colors."

"Painting? A theater, eh? Which one?" asked Pleaser. "Never mind. We'll find out at the most appropriate time."

The threat was clear to Damon. The most appropriate time would be when he was inside Chloe, making her little booty squirm with pleasure. All of a sudden, Pleaser would grab off the spot and kick Damon out. Then Pleaser'd do things to Chloe that she didn't even know were possible, and she'd beg Damon to do it to her again, and he'd be unable because he wasn't the Pleaser. He'd lose her for sure.

That evening, Gregory posted his new set of rules.

1. No snatching the spot away from someone else. Once a person has the spot, he or she (a politically correct reference he'd learned in college that could apply to Wendy, who never took it) — gets to keep it until they give it up.

2. If they keep it too long, like more than a day, we hold a community council meeting to see who gets it next.

3. Give up the spot when you're sleeping or doing something unimportant, so the rest of us can have a turn.

4. No spying on each other during sex. That's our special private time that nobody's supposed to watch unless they're invited.

5. Everybody be polite and civil to each other. We're family, after all, and there's been entirely too much fighting. Fighting's dangerous for our family. It can break us up or even cause us to do horrible things to each other.

Reactions to The Rules were not long in coming.

"When I need to paint, I don't have time to wait for Damon until he's finished whatever stupid dishwashing or sexing he's up to." (Leroy)

"That's my best time, when he's having sex." (Pleaser)

"When someone's in trouble, we need to take the spot fast to bail them out." (Bounce)

"That's right. You need someone on the spot, fast!" (Breakout)

In response to these criticisms, Gregory added a sixth rule.

"When someone's in trouble, whoever can help him gets the spot fast."

"But they'll take advantage," moaned Damon. "They'll say they thought I was in trouble and grab it off."

"You're such a baby. Learn to fight for yourself. Keep your damn spot!"

"Out out damned spot!" said a voice they didn't recognize.

"Life's a brief candle."

"Blowing in the wind" someone else chimed in.

32

THE MOMENT BECCA OPENED her front door that Thursday evening, she knew something was wrong. Carrying her groceries into the kitchen and peeking into her bedroom and bath, she tried to figure out what it was.

Slowly, she toured her living room, surveying her books and plants, her sheet music left carelessly on the piano's music stand, the pile of mail on her little desk in the alcove, her small vases and memory icons on the mantel above the "seduction fireplace." (Fat lot of good *that* had done her!) There had been a real fireplace once, but it was now screened by a hammered metal scene of a knight on his steed, bending to bid farewell to his lady, she handing him her scarf to carry as his colors into the fray. Above the fireplace in the mirrored mantel, Becca caught a startled glimpse of herself, dark hair straggling at her shoulders, dangling art fair earrings now awry, "rosebud" mouth open, eyes wide with alarm. I look scared, she said to herself, and the mirror agreed.

She sniffed the air. Nothing out of the ordinary. Perhaps, it was just below her level of consciousness, or perhaps the remembered odor of ether from her night visitor, now dissipated into doubt. On an impulse, she opened the walk-in closet that had once stored a Murphy bed behind the mantel, after the fireplace was torn out — a succession of "improvements" in this old brick Victorian that did not bode well for the future. Her clothes appeared undisturbed, as did the little square in the ceiling that led God knew where.

"What is it, then?" she asked herself, moving from room to room. "What's different?"

After stowing her groceries, she set about cleaning. Craig was coming by tomorrow night to pick her up for dinner, and she didn't want him to see her place like this. Besides, she needed physical movement to release the tension.

As she dusted, she fell into her customary erotic daydream of a night with Craig. Supposedly, it was men who thought about sex all the time, and while she had once worried that she was over-sexed, in her recent years of confidences with Annalyn and other women, she learned she was hardly exceptional. Sex was never far from *anybody's* thoughts, although she knew of no research on ninety-year-olds. As for the so-called frigid women who haunted TV-land, probably some of them were merely mismatched or indulging in a passive-aggressive act of revenge against their mates.

Was it possible that her erotic dreaming over Craig made her function like the dreamer rather than the real Becca and respond to him that way? Wasn't there a danger in treating him like a dream lover? That it created a false relationship rather than nourishing the real one?

Her dream progressed from a detailed night of passion, uninterrupted by sleep or even bathroom breaks, to a breakfast of scrambled eggs and bacon in their house on Queen Anne Hill, she and Craig scanning the newspaper before driving to work together, and their children dawdling over their Crunchy Bunchies before heading off to daycare. Sometimes, her dream children numbered two or three, sometimes only one, but that one was always the blond five-year-old boy intensely concentrating on the milk carton, as he fed an occasional spoonful to his imaginary companion. "I could be his friend," he was saying. Robbie would come back to Becca one way or another, although his name would be anything but her brother's. Sometimes, she wondered if that was why she dreamed of marriage and children in the first place, to create a substitute at long last.

It was while Becca was dusting in the living room that she noticed her potted schleffera on the windowsill had been moved about a quarter of an inch to the right. This was embarrassingly easy to see. A ring of gray dust surrounded the outline where the pot had been, like a child's fairy ring, she thought. She checked the other plants on her shelves set into the south bay window to catch as much light as possible in the drear and foggy fall days. The rare begonia that she had grown from Craig's cutting, the prayer plant, the ivy, the pink polka dot, and one of the violets — all had been moved as well, some to the right, some to the left, so that they were not aligned at the same distance from each other as they had been. They were either too far apart or too close, a shaggy line rather than her customary straight one. It must have been this overall effect of skewness that had registered on her subconscious mind when she came home.

Becca moved soundlessly through the apartment, so as not to disturb some unseen presence. She checked her vase collection in the bedroom and on the mantel, her curios, the books on her shelves, her desk. Some objects had been moved, some not, the dust always a telltale sign. Further, the lack of dust inside the circles showed that the movement was recent. It was as if someone had entered her apartment and wandered about, picking up and examining at will. Perhaps to test how well she cared for them? A silly thought that slid unbidden across her mind! There were a lot of these unbidden thoughts lately. As far as Becca could see, nothing was taken, not the costume jewelry in her chest, not even the extra hundred dollars in her nightstand. These seemed undisturbed. Feeling ridiculously paranoid, she looked under her bed, her couch, and other places where a person might be lurking. No one was here.

But about a week ago, while dashing for the phone, she had accidentally knocked askew the hall photograph of Robbie. She was always meaning to straighten it, but every time she thought of it, she was in a rush, and when she was on slower time, as now, she didn't think of it. His photo was now perfectly positioned.

Without realizing it, Becca put her hand to her chest to keep her heart from beating through. Had she absentmindedly repositioned it herself? Had she nudged her plants and forgotten? To what purpose? Not to dust! No, someone else had shifted them. But, again, who? And why?

She thought of calling the police, of course. It was the first thing she thought of. And tell them what? That she'd been receiving odd phone calls about her brother who had disappeared many years ago? That she'd awakened one night to the smell of ether and felt someone was there, only he wasn't? That an intruder had sneaked into her apartment and moved her plants and straightened her brother's picture? And, no, she was sure she had not done it. No, she would have remembered. Yes, she realized it was nonsensical. What would be the purpose? In her mind's ear, she heard them labeling her a "crazy lady" — "you know, a psychologist."

She decided it wasn't worth it. She would have to wait until something else happened. Maybe a threat or an attack. Or her death, she concluded grimly. That would get the attention of the authorities.

She did the next best thing to reporting her experiences to the police. She reported them to Annalyn.

"Look at it this way, Becca. Either someone is invading your apartment, or you're going crackers. That's the technical term."

"I know, you learned it in med school."

"Psychiatry 101."

"I can't be going crackers. For a psychologist, that's unprofessional," Becca joked feebly.

"So you're being stalked."

"Don't say that!" She hadn't even used that word to herself.

"You have to face reality here, Becca. Your life may depend on it."

"I called you for comfort, and I'm getting scareder by the minute."

"Of course, you are. That's why you don't want to go to the police. It'll make the whole thing more real. I don't count the nightmare; in fact, I wouldn't tell them about that. But your things moved? Now that's real. You have to report it."

"But they'll say people break in to steal, not to admire someone's plants."

"Who says they're admiring them? Maybe they're criticizing. Burglaries get reported to the police. Have you had your locks changed?"

"No. This only just happened. I have to notify the manager."

"Do it first thing tomorrow, and tell him it's an emergency. Tell him someone's getting in. That'll show the police you're serious."

"But what if they just dismiss it?"

"They probably will, at first. The thing is, you have to report it. Go on record. And maybe the sixth time you report something odd, maybe even with a little proof or a witness, they'll start taking you seriously."

"Either that, or they'll dismiss everything I say as loco-no-motive. They'll see me coming through the door and assign the rawest rookie to take my report."

"You have to make a beginning. Go on down and get to know them."

Annalyn had treated Becca's concerns as perfectly reasonable, so she fell into the trap of new hope that someone else might see them the same way. After informing the manager that her locks needed changing immediately, Becca walked into the police station for what she feared might become one of many visits.

It was surprising how like the Santa Cruz station it was, so many years ago, even the sweaty metal smells. No wonder she'd dreaded coming here. Their evaluation of her appearance, and their judgment, disbelief and hounding returned unexpectedly, and she almost wheeled around to walk out. Instead, she was passed from the desk officer to Officer McNalley who was not Officer Sam or 'Slewski or even T., but someone else entirely. He seemed more neutral. But then, this wasn't about a kidnapping.

He began scribbling notes on her complaint. At some point, she noticed that he was just asking questions and no longer jotting down her answers.

"Signs of a break-in?"

"No. They must have had a key."

"Nothing taken?"

Becca shook her head.

"Nothing else moved besides the plants and the picture?"

"Books pulled out and only partially put back."

"That's all?"

"That's enough, don't you think? It means somebody was in there, somebody who had no right to be."

"Have you given anyone else a key to your apartment?"

"No."

"Never? Maybe an old boyfriend?" Eyes slid down to her breasts, evaluating their boyfriend potential, then hurriedly back to her face.

Hugh? "Never. But the previous tenant could have a key. The manager has one. He keeps them hanging up on a keyboard in the basement behind a locked door. Who knows who else might have one? I've left him a message to get the locks changed today."

"Good move. You didn't notice if your door was unlocked when you got home last night?"

"I'm pretty sure it wasn't. I'll pay more attention from now on."

"Thing is, Ms. Merrow — you're not Dr. yet, right?"

"No, not yet."

"Thing is, Ms. Merrow, sometimes I'm wandering around my own apartment, and I'm thinking about an important case, and I pick up something and put it down again; I don't even know I did it. It's just a natural, normal thing to do. We all do it."

"I didn't. I haven't dusted in three weeks. The dust rings are there. I don't pick up my plants when I water them. And what about the phone calls?"

"The calls are weird, no question. Of course, there may not be a connection." Except in my own mind, Becca thought. "If they continue, we can have a trace put on the line." He didn't say it as if he were suggesting it. It was more of an offer to mollify her or to hold out hope of future action than a recommendation he thought important to follow. He sat back from his intake form without bothering to complete it. "Thing is, most crimes are kind of predictable. The perps want money to buy crack, so they steal VCRs and jewelry. If you'd been robbed, it would be different." Becca found herself almost wishing she had. "But for a perp to walk in and move your plants, just a little bit — why? To get your attention? He couldn't be sure you'd even notice a little thing like that. He could have made his presence more obvious, don't you think? Thrown your plants around. Trashed your fridge or something. Used your living room for a — you'll excuse me — a latrine. I don't want to alarm you, but anyone who'd just get into your apartment to move your plants around —"

"And the picture."

"And the picture — has got to be psycho."

"Like the phone calls."

"Yes," he nodded grudgingly. "From a whole bunch of different males? School kids, maybe?"

"No, older. I was wondering. Wouldn't it be possible to check the plants and the picture for fingerprints?"

The officer stared at her steadily. "Because someone may have come in and touched them?"

"Not 'may have.' Did! And it's not the touching that I'm worried about," Becca replied hotly. "It's his being there."

"You don't even know it's a he. I'm sorry," said Officer McNally, but he didn't sound sorry at all. "Our resources are stretched to the limit." Canned speech. Your fault. Vote the levy next time. "We don't have probable cause to fingerprint your plants."

Becca heard how ridiculous it sounded as he said it. She gathered her things. It was just as she'd thought it would be. He was brushing her off. Her complaint was inconsequential. She wondered why he hadn't reminded her of the *real* crimes they had to deal with, the rapes, murders, arsons. Why hadn't he played the guilt card?

"There's something else," she said in a last ditch effort to get taken seriously.

The officer lifted one eyebrow, as if he were thinking, "Now it comes."

"The picture that was straightened was my brother, Robbie. He was kidnapped when he was five and I was ten. They never found him."

"Your point?" said McNalley, the last veneer of official politeness falling away. "If it had been a different picture, you wouldn't be upset? I don't get it."

Then, Becca had to admit to herself that she didn't get it either.

At least, not so she could explain it. She had established a record with the police, as Annalyn suggested — a record of nutsmanship. She thanked him and left. They were adding her name to the list of the neighborhood crazies even as she exited the door.

By the time she got home, Frank, the manager, was supervising the replacement of her locks. Unable to stifle his curiosity, he asked the cause, but she was as vague as she could be with him.

"I've just had the feeling someone's been in my apartment. Do you ever get that feeling?"

"All the time. I live with George, remember?"

When Craig arrived to take Becca to dinner, she offered him an unwinding glass of wine first — something they both enjoyed while talking about their week.

"And yours?" Craig asked. They were sitting side by side on the couch in the west bay window, half turned to the sunset as if in toast.

I've been having some rather strange experiences, and I don't know what to make of them, she thought of saying.

Instead, she joked about being overworked and underpaid, and they exchanged vignettes of incidents with patients and staff. The case managers assigned the practicum students all the patients that the senior staff didn't want, usually the depressives.

They ordered pad thai and chicken curry at their favorite restaurant, Thai Hai, with the gilt Bodhisattvas in attitudes of welcome, the dainty pewter dishes of hot mustard and chili, and the parasols hung from the ceiling.

"Becca? Becca!"

Becca started. "Oh, I'm sorry, Craig. What was that?"

"I'd thought I was a fascinating conversationalist," he joked, and she assured him he was. "You seem tense tonight. Is something wrong?"

"No, it's nothing important."

"It must be important if you won't tell me."

The tension of the last days welled up into her eyes. She absolutely hated that she was such a pushover for tears. She told him, grateful that he listened intently with his therapist's ear, only interrupting to ask a couple of questions. She told him about the phone calls, the plant and picture movements, the new locks on her doors, even the nightmare, as well as Annalyn's reactions and the police officer's.

"The police have way too much to do," Craig said, looking grim and settling the check for both of them, as Becca was too tightly wound to think of offering her share. "They don't even pay attention to car thefts anymore, and certainly not break-ins and other vandalism. Come on, I'll take you home. I'll stay with you, if you want. You don't have to be alone with this. You're obviously pretty shaken up. Why didn't you call me?"

When they got back, he asked her, "Which plants were moved, exactly?" And she showed him which and how. She tilted Robbie's picture, then straightened it.

"You don't think gravity could have done that?'"

"It hadn't for a week."

"Entropy?" The gradual effect of gravity building to a sudden result?

"That doesn't explain my plants and books."

"No, it doesn't."

"Or the phone calls."

"Who do you think would be doing this, I wonder?" He added "I wonder" as Dr. Connie had.

"Some pervert. Some stalker." She shrugged her shoulders.

"You don't suppose it could be Robbie himself? That he's finally found you?"

The tears flooded Becca's eyes again. Damn! She hated being such a crybaby.

"It occurred to me."

"Of course, it did. But in that case, why would you be afraid?"

"I don't know."

"I mean, if it were Robbie, and he'd found you at last, I'd think you'd be glad, wouldn't you?"

"I don't know. I mean, of course, I would, but . . ."

"Adopted kids and their natural mothers are reunited all the time. It usually works out. Sometimes it doesn't. But most don't regret it."

"Do you think it could be Robbie?"

"It's what you think that counts."

"Why wouldn't he just call and say, 'Hi, this is Robbie. Let's have coffee.' Why would he have a bunch of his friends do it, like a gang, almost, and then come in and poke around my things when I'm not here?"

"Getting to know you, maybe. Who knows what his life's been like? Then again, it might not be Robbie at all. That might just be your fantasy."

"Is that what you think?"

"Becca, you know better. Show me the books that were moved."

"In my bedroom." He hadn't been there before, although he could glimpse it from the hall that also led to the bathroom, dining room, and kitchen.

"All poetry?"

"Some of them were put back with my psychology books in the living room."

"Quite a collection you have here."

"I seem to have picked up one book and then another, mostly at garage sales and bookstores."

"So the poet in you hasn't quite died."

"No, but it's become more practical."

"How about some hot chocolate?" Craig suggested.

She let him make it for them both, noting that he remembered where she kept the box. He wanted to do this for her. She got out the whipped topping from the fridge and spooned it into their mugs.

"This is the door where you saw the shadow move?" he asked, walking over to peer at the back porch. "I agree, it's probably some homeless person. Pretty good shelter from the storm if you have to stay outside. Cold, though."

They carried their mugs back into the living room and stood staring out at the Seattle skyline, the top of the Space Needle.

Something drew Becca's attention to the house across the street, its porch flanked by bushes waving from side to side in the brisk wind. Suddenly, a shadow moved.

"Did you see that?" she asked Craig.

"What, the shadow? Sure, I saw it. I don't think it has anything to do with you. I want to ask you something. Would you be so spooked if you didn't think it might be Robbie, returned from wherever he's been?"

"I'm not sure."

"Well, would you have made a connection between the night-mare, say, and the telephone calls?"

"I don't think so."

"Or between the calls and the plant movements?"

Becca shook her head.

"You see, I really don't see a connection between prank calls and plants that get moved around and a nightmare. I wonder if your fears might not be based on your whole terrible experience of Robbie's kid-napping that you're reliving because of these odd occurrences."

"Threatening occurrences, Craig. Somebody came in here and moved my things."

"Yes, well, we'll get to that."

What was there to get to?

He sat her down on the couch and continued earnestly in the lamplight. "That kidnapping changed your life, after all, changed you from a sister to an only child, from a daughter to an orphan perhaps, when your mom blamed you and your dad left, from a poet to a psychologist." This was true, her own personal continental divide. "If you didn't think it was Robbie, who would you think was doing these things?"

"I probably wouldn't connect them."

"No, I don't think I would. They're separate events. So let's look at them separately. Who would you attribute the phone calls to?"

"Just crank calls that everybody gets, I guess."

"What about the plant movements?"

"Trucks going by, shaking the building. Except, I'd think it would shake them all in the same direction."

"I would, too. Still, we have to live with the unexplained every day. And when is a nightmare just a nightmare?"

Becca laughed, as they both drained their cocoa at once. Her at-traction to him was returning, but, at the same time, she was thank-ful for such a good friend. It was true. Everything that happened to her in the least bit out of the ordinary she connected with Robbie's disappearance. It was *her* connection, not the events themselves. And yet. . .

"Do you want me to stay over on the couch?"

She understood that he wouldn't take advantage of her crisis to seduce her, which she would have loved under any other circumstances.

"Thanks, Craig. I have to handle this myself."

"Okay. But be sure to call me if you need to, or even want to, any time day or night."

He leaned over and kissed her forehead. As he left, she recognized that he had provided therapeutic first aid. Had he realized all along that she was not who she thought she was? That she had been blown off course when she lost Robbie? Perhaps he'd sensed that she was headed for just such a crisis, although he couldn't have known what form it would take. Perhaps this was why he'd hung back, reluctant to get involved with someone whose core issues were still so open and unresolved. In any event, if she wanted to preserve even the chance of the relationship she envisioned with him— at least she *thought* she envisioned it — she needed to get herself to another therapist and then tell Craig that, naturally, she couldn't talk with him about it anymore.

Becca listened to his footsteps going down the stairs, heard the front door open below, and watched him cross the street toward Broadway. As he did so, the shadow detached itself from one of the rhododendron bushes that flanked the porch across the way. It followed him.

33

NOT THAT CHLOE AND Damon were the only ones working on the *Our Town* set. Often, they discovered that others had hammered or painted sections, sewn a curtain, or set up a prop. But Damon was accustomed to the work of invisible family members. Things appeared and disappeared so easily.

Weeks of cuddling and labor flew by. As Damon nestled with Chloe under the curtain, he could feel the whole damned family gathering around him.

"I love that nose," Leroy said loudly into Damon's ear. He tweaked it gently, and Chloe giggled. "That's a classic Jewish nose she's got, you know that? The aquiline Greek with the delicate little hook. I want to paint her. I'm going to paint her. When you bring her home, she can see herself."

"That's all you'd know how to do with a frail," Pleaser taunted.

"Better than you," snapped Leroy. "Go play with your blow-up dolly."

"What's the matter?" Chloe asked Damon. "You seem tense. Not like usual."

"Usually, I feel freer. It's weird, you know. It's like we're being watched. Do you feel watched?"

"Don't be silly. Even if we were. Even if there were a whole audience out there that we can't see because of that black velvet curtain between them and us, so what? Let's put on a show for them," she said, squeezing him.

"Oooh, you little bundle of pleasure," said Pleaser, squeezing her breasts in return.

"Shut the fuck up!" said Damon, in his head he thought, but Chloe said,

"What?"

"Not you."

"Who?"

"The audience," Damon giggled. "They're not supposed to applaud and yell 'Bravo' until the scene is over."

She laughed. "You're weird, you know? I don't like you when you're weird." She rolled away from him. "I don't feel like doing it anymore. You can go home now."

"Oh, Chloe, please, I was just kidding."

"No woman likes to be told to 'shut the fuck up'."

"It was the audience. I just got carried away."

"Half the time, I don't know who you are. First you act this way, and then that. It's as if you're rehearsing for a bunch of parts or something," she said, sliding out from under the curtain to pace from the prop room into the hall, her pink satin and lace peignoir floating after her, somewhat grayer for wear. She picked up a maple bar from the table under the balcony window. "I had a fella once. An actor. Walked around rehearsing different parts in different voices and accents until he drove me crazy. Finally, I say to him one day, I say, 'Rupert, can't you act yourself, just for a few minutes?' And you know what he says?"

Damon figured he was supposed to answer, although for the life of him he couldn't imagine what Rupert said.

"No, what?" he asked finally.

"He says to me, 'I don't know who I am.' Just like that. He'd acted so many parts, he was no longer himself. That could happen to you if you don't watch out."

"Don't worry," said Gregory. "I won't let it."

"Well, you don't necessarily have control," said Chloe.

"I have perfect control," said Pleaser.

Someone else said, "All I have to do is hit you upside the head, and I got control."

"Damon!"

"That wasn't me!"

"Go."

"Can I come back tomorrow?"

"I'll decide then."

"You're absolutely adorable, you know?" said Gregory.

"Well, thanks. I still think you should go."

"I'll never let anyone hurt you."

"Hey, you promised you wouldn't take the spot."

"I'm helping you."

"Don't help," Damon said irritably, hustling into his clothes and exiting through the stage door.

The trouble was, they all wanted Chloe — Leroy to paint her, Pleaser to sex her and show Damon how it was done, Bounce and Breakout to cheer everyone on. As for Gregory himself, he'd never seen such a charmer as Chloe. She electrified him. He wanted a valentine romance, plain and simple.

That night, Gregory called a meeting to review the spot-taking rules. Pleaser and Leroy were yelling at each other, interrupted by gay insults from the others. Leroy spat at Pleaser, who tried to deck him, but Leroy got Pleaser's arms behind his back and held fast until Pleaser wriggled away and twisted his fist into Leroy's gut, all to shouts of encouragement from Bounce and Breakout, who were forsaking their usual Monday night game for this real live in-house grudge match. Gregory tried to break it up, yelling at the twins to help him, but both combatants evaded him, Pleaser faster and more wiry, Leroy landing clumsy but solid blows to Pleaser's hip and shoulder. Wendy was fading fast, the kids in the basement were screaming at the top of their lungs, and Damon had his hands clapped over his ears to no avail. There'd never been such a family fight.

Suddenly, Leroy went into a frenzied maelstrom of solid blows, beating Pleaser to the floor, while the others gaped. Gregory suspected he was seeing someone else in action, some friend of Leroy's, but he didn't think the twins realized it. Wendy screamed and knelt across Pleaser protectively. The rain of blows abruptly ended. Pleaser struggled to his feet a bloody mess, crying "No fair," although he probably had no more idea of what had happened than the twins did. Wendy hustled him off to apply iodine. By the end of the evening, the half of them that weren't fighting, weren't talking. Gregory feared that Chloe would break up the family. A plan began to form in his mind. Perhaps, if she were one of them, they wouldn't fight over her. Would it work?

On the following Sunday, at Gregory's suggestion, Damon brought Chloe and Go-Go home to "meet the family." Chloe didn't see anyone, of course, but she carried a big bouquet of flowers that she'd rescued from a florist's dumpster.

"Perfectly good," she said, trimming the stems over the sink. "They throw them out for no reason, just like the fast food places. Do you have a vase? Never mind, I'll use this pitcher," a green glass monstrosity that Damon had picked up from the Salvation Army because it was the only one that wasn't chipped. Wendy had whispered that unchipped glass was classy. "I thought your family was going to be here?"

"They'll be along," Damon said, as Gregory, Pleaser, Leroy, Bounce and Breakout crowded around her, touching her yarn hair, her scrawny little shoulders, the nape of her neck, her bony shoulder blades under the thin silk blouse from the costume trolley. Go-Go made a little circle for himself on Damon's bed and promptly fell asleep.

Damon hadn't planned to bring Chloe home at all. But it was the holiday season, and she said it was about time she saw his pad, and he couldn't get out of it. Gregory emphasized in family council that no one was to interfere with Damon's love affair.

"Not even if we can make it hotter?" asked Pleaser pointedly.

"Stay out of that theater," he'd ordered them.

"Or what?" asked Pleaser.

"Or you'll find out," said Leroy, eager to fight Pleaser again at any cost, even an alliance with Gregory.

"You want her for yourself," Pleaser sneered. "Not that you'd know what to do with her."

Gregory figured he'd worship her to begin with, but he must concentrate on Damon's welfare. That was his job, his responsibility. Someone had assigned it to him, although he couldn't remember who.

Finally, Gregory had struck a bargain. They could all meet Chloe at Damon's apartment, if they promised to stay away from the theater. But Gregory himself was hardly to be trusted. Even now, his hands were stroking her arms.

"Oooh, you're all hands today, Damon Hearst."

"Sorry," he said, apologizing for the lot of them.

"What's to apologize?" she grinned up at him. "So, this is your place," she said, clicking around the room on Amy's four-inch heels and trying not to stumble.

"They're called stilettos," murmured Pleaser to Leroy. "All the better to stab you with."

"Pleaser! Enough!" said Gregory.

Damon had cleaned madly, but the brightest and best thing was the bouquet Chloe'd brought.

"Could use a little decorating, y'know? I have just the throw for that ratty old chair." Probably from the prop room. "Do you like purple? When we get tired of it, we can get something else. No law says you have to stick with one thing forever, is there?"

"Or for very long."

That was what Damon loved about Chloe. Stability wasn't her cup of tea. Staying in the same place, the same job, the same furnishings and clothing — staying stuck sucked. His lifestyle was one she actually admired!

"That's it, Damon, old cock," sang Pleaser. "She's planning to trade you in."

Ignoring him, Damon motioned Chloe to his TV chair, the best place in the room to sit, Gregory's dining room being invisible to her. He'd invited her for dinner, and he tried to open a jar of caviar that Pleaser had ripped off from a gourmet store in Bellevue. When it wouldn't budge, Breakout bulged his muscles long enough to loosen the top for him, and he set it down with a box of crackers on the TV tray next to her.

"Aren't you glad you brought her here instead of trying to feed her caviar at the theater? You'd never have got it open by yourself."

Unless you were waiting in the wings, Damon thought.

"Didn't you hear Gregory? We're not supposed to be there," Breakout said virtuously as Bounce guffawed.

Bounce popped the cork from a bottle of champagne, and Damon poured her a glass. She drained it and held it out for more, then promptly devoured the caviar, pausing only to offer him a cracker generously spread.

"You eat it," he said. "I love watching you eat."

Damon followed with a roast chicken from the supermarket and a plastic container of ready-made potato salad, which he peppered generously. "My very own recipe," he said. He knelt beside the chair to share it with her. They had only the one San Francisco souvenir spoon between them, his other spoons having gradually disappeared, along with much of the rest of his "silver." But that didn't slow them down. They took turns, and that spoon was never still.

"I must say, you set a wonderful table, Damon Hearst," she said through a mouthful of chicken.

"Figuratively speaking," said Gregory.

"You could at least give me some credit," said Pleaser. "Without me, they'd be eating cat food."

"Shhh," said Gregory. "He'll do you a favor one day."

"Sure, he will! A turn in the hay, or in the prop room as the case may be, would be sufficient."

"Pleaser, you've got plenty of action on your own. What do you need to horn in on Damon's for?"

"Because she's Damon's, you boring clod of sod."

"Cool it," Gregory replied. "She's not yours," although Chloe was so electrifyingly adorable that he could hardly keep his own hands off her. Thank God this conversation was happening in Damon's head — at least, so far — and she hadn't a clue.

Chloe was discussing the various plays she'd been in.

"I was in *Who's Afraid of Virginia Woolf* once," she said. "The girl who played the new faculty wife sprained her ankle, and I got to do it one night. I could be Martha. Or Virginia Woolf, even."

"*Be* or *play*?" asked Gregory.

"What's the diff?" she asked, meeting his eyes earnestly.

"That's what I want to know," said Damon.

"You tell me," Chloe responded, not realizing she was addressing two people. "Your point?"

"Chilling," thought Gregory.

"Martha comes home and says, 'What a dump.' Only she says it like that. She should say it like this: '*What* a *dump!*' Elizabeth Taylor does it that way."

"I'd play George, except I'm no good at playing a drunkard," said Damon.

"I was Jellicle in *Cats*." She stuck out her tush and danced around the room.

"Mostly I've been in the chorus," said Damon. One chorus. "How about dessert? I have a decadent chocolate cake just for the two of us."

"If the others don't show."

"Even if they do."

"Decadence is good," said Chloe. "If I'd known you were serving decadence, I'd have worn my feather boa, my long pearls, and my cigarette holder."

"Silly! You don't wear a cigarette holder."

"You do if you're not smoking. It's part of the costume. Silly!" Her mischievous smile was absolutely captivating.

"That nose, I can't get over it," chortled Leroy as Damon served the cake. "A classic Jewish nose. I've got to paint it. It could be on an angel in my 'Great Heavens'."

"I'm not Jewish," said Chloe chattily. "I'm Irish. I'm supposed to be Catholic, but it didn't take. I had a fella once, he was a priest —"

"I don't like priests," said Damon, flashing back to Father Martingale. In the next instant, he realized with alarm that Chloe had heard Leroy. Leroy had broken through! In his mind, he shook both fists in exasperation at Leroy and gave Gregory a pleading look.

"He wore skirts he called 'cassocks,' and you know what he had underneath them?" Chloe was asking. "Damon?"

"Trust you to find out," Pleaser sniggered.

"Shhh," said Gregory. "She's an Only."

"Damon Hearst, that's not very nice."

"That wasn't me, that was Pleaser," said Damon, clapping a hand to his mouth.

"Pleaser?" Chloe echoed. "Pleaser?"

"The priest you know," he said, encouraging her to take up the tale again.

"There's nobody here but us."

"What did the priest have under his skirts?"

"As if I couldn't guess," added Pleaser.

"Not that. I'm not talking about that. He had absolutely nothing on, no boxer shorts, no briefs, nothing."

"Doesn't sound very sanitary," said Gregory.

"It just flopped around in every direction when he walked, only you couldn't see it because it was covered by the skirt."

"Then how did you know?" Damon asked.

"Did you crawl under his skirts to take a look?" leered Pleaser.

"Pleaser, enough! He couldn't have been your fella, Chloe. He was a priest."

"That's what I love about you, Damon. You're such an innocent."

Was he? The hell of it was, Damon seemed to remember less and less. He didn't think he was an innocent, but then . . .

"Of course, he was my fella," Chloe was saying. "Priests have lovers same as anybody else. They're just more discreet."

Damon thought he knew a little about the discretion required. He was no innocent, after all. The men to whom Carl had rented him out, when he got sick and had to shut down the porn studio, were always nattering on about secrets, although he couldn't quite remember them. Bizarre predilections, especially. Hose or hosiery? Dog or doggy style? They escaped him again.

"My fella was always saying to me, 'God told us to suffer the children,' which meant that suffering children were supposed to love God and his priests."

Chloe carried the dishes to the sink and prepared to wash.

"Wrap up the rest of the chicken, so we can take it back to the theater for later."

"So you can have it later, you mean," said Pleaser.

"We'll share," she said indignantly. "I've shared plenty of my food with you, Damon Hearst."

"Mouse food."

"Pleaser, get out of here, you're wrecking it. Gregory, please."

"Yeah, get the fuck out of here," said Leroy.

"Asshole!"

"Butt breath!"

"Finger-lickin' poop-plopper!"

"Damon, what's got into you?" Chloe paused, glass in mid-air, mouth agape.

"It isn't me, please, Chloe, it's them. Gregory's supposed to keep them in line —"

"I'm doing the best I can," replied Gregory with uncharacteristic heat.

"What's with all the different voices, all of a sudden? Are you re-hearsing for different roles? There's nothing in *Our Town* that sounds like those people you're playing. You're not helping out at another theater, are you?" Chloe's idea of loyalty restricted her to one stage.

"Chloe, there's something about me you should know."

"Don't do it," Gregory warned.

"Don't do what?" asked Chloe.

"Shut the fuck up, the lot of you," Damon yelled.

"Damon, I won't be talked to that way."

"Not you, Chloe, not you, the rest of them. You see, I don't know how to explain this, but I've got a bunch of people living in my head."

"Oh, that, well, we all hear voices occasionally," she shrugged, turning back to the sink.

"We do? You, too?"

"Sometimes, when I'm alone in the theater, I'll hear my mother yell at me. Just once. 'Inger!' she'll yell. Like that."

"Inger?"

"The name she called me by. I never paid much attention. I was better at thinking up names. Then there's the alligator. At least, that's what I call him. He doesn't yell or even talk, just heaves a big sigh. Like he's about to become shoes. And my dolls, after I went to bed, when I was falling asleep, they'd start yammering and gossiping like a bunch of ninnies. They didn't think I was listening. So you see, dear Damon, you're not the only one hears voices. Even Joan of Arc. I was third understudy for her once."

"Do you ever see them?"

"You mean, like the alligator? No. That would be crazy. I'm not some crazy person sees things that aren't there."

Damon felt his legs go wobbly and suddenly he had to sit down. He'd seen plenty of crazies waving their arms down the street and yelling curses at people who weren't there, and sometimes at people who were. But he'd never thought of himself as one of them. No, he wasn't crazy, he couldn't be. Chloe just didn't understand, that's all. She was an Only, and no one knew why some people were Onlys and others had whole families living inside their heads. He'd thought the reasons might be similar to why some people got married and had kids, while others remained single. It had to do with your character, or how easy you were to live with, or what you wanted out of life. Except that he hadn't chosen to live with a family, and sometimes he felt as though he'd rather be an Only. Although he wouldn't hurt Gregory's feelings by telling him that.

"It doesn't look like your family's coming," Chloe said, drying the spoon.

"Oh, they're coming all right," said Damon.

"I'm coming," chortled Pleaser.

"Might as well go home," said Chloe. "I think the theater couch is more comfortable. When we squeeze, it's big enough for two." She gave him a coquettish little smile straight out of *Carmen*.

"With me, darlin', you only need a twin bed because I'll be on top of you every minute."

"Sounds nice and warm."

"Pleaser, if you don't shut up, I'll tell Leroy to sic his buddies on you."

"They'll do you the way they did Mickey and Carmine," Leroy's voice rose menacingly.

"Damon, you're scaring me."

"Pay no attention to them."

"You haven't the balls!" Pleaser yelled gleefully. "I know a few things about what got done to Mickey and Carmine that nobody else knows. Dessa, too. I'll tell the cops. I'll turn the lot of you in."

"You know we didn't kill Carmine."

"Doesn't matter. They'll believe anything I say."

"Nobody turns us in," said Gregory sternly. "That would be treason. We stick together no matter what."

"Who's Carmine?" Chloe asked, her breath a series of ragged gasps.

"Stop it, both of you," said Gregory. "You're scaring Chloe. Pleaser, Leroy, I've had it with you two."

"Damon, stop talking that way. Take me home. Now!"

Gregory's anxiety was peaking. He needed to visit a therapist again, but he was new to Seattle, and he'd graduated, so the one at the community college was out.

"I may have to forbid you to see Chloe again," he told Damon regretfully, because Damon was the only one he could control. "She's too disruptive. We can't chance it."

"Disruptive! They're the disruptive ones," Damon cried, gesticulating at Pleaser, especially, but also Leroy and even Bounce and Breakout.

"*Now*, Damon!" Go-Go was peeking out of Chloe's backpack, as she held open the door. "Unless you want me to walk back alone. If you do, don't bother showing up at the theater tomorrow."

"Of course, I want to walk you back. Gregory, get away from me. The rest of you, too. I'm taking Chloe home."

By the time they got outside, it was dark, and the smell of night was like a thousand cars that had been caught in a traffic jam.

"You need help, you know?" Chloe said, taking his arm and tucking it under her own.

"I don't know where to get it," Damon said miserably. "Gregory got us help a couple of times, and things were better for awhile. But they gave him medication, and it made Robbie loopy and Leroy throw up."

"Gregory — he's one of the voices in your head, right?"

Suddenly, Damon heard the most soul-wrenching shriek.

"Oh, my God! Something's happened to Leroy. What is it? I don't know. Gregory says Pleaser spray-painted graffiti all over Leroy's 'Great Heavens'. Oh, oh, oh! That'll just about kill Leroy. Oh, oh, oh! Oh, no, the others heard it, too."

"Others?"

Damon had stopped dead under the street lamp, breath coming in ragged gasps.

"You see, there's Gregory and Leroy — of the ones I know — but then there are the others, and we think they're the ones did Mickey and Dessa and Carmine."

"You mean, *murdered* them?"

"Yeah. They're Leroy's friends, and they're coming after Pleaser."

"You've got a bunch or *murderers* living inside your head?"

"I've never seen them, but I can feel them. The whole house is shaking. Chloe, I've got to get you out of here. It could be dangerous. Now Pleaser's yelling. Oh, my God, Gregory, you've got to keep them under control."

"I can't. I can't keep control any longer. The light's going on and off like mad, and they're coming. I think it's Leroy's buddies, Vigrid the Avenger and Mefisto."

"Vigrid? Mefisto?" Damon was hearing their brutal names for the first time.

"The kids are ramming the basement door," Gregory said. "They're going to break through. Wendy's screaming. They're going to kill Pleaser and then the rest of us. Leroy, for God's sake, call them off. You're the only one who can stop them. For the sake of us all!"

Damon broke into a run. "I don't want to hear it. I don't want to know."

Chloe ran after him, pulling him toward the theater as if it were a refuge.

34

ROUSED BY A GENTLE voice, at first Damon thought it was Chloe crooning to him, as she had through much of the night, trying to shut out Pleaser's agony. But it was Gregory, saying,

"Pleaser won't steal your spot when you're with Chloe ever again."

"Is he dead?"

"No. Just gone. Now you have Chloe all to yourself."

"They castrated him," said Bounce with mock solemnity, flickers of mirth at the corners of his mouth.

Damon shuddered, and Chloe stretched closer, beginning to waken. "I was afraid that was what it was," he said.

"You might say he's not himself," Bounce added.

"Not funny, boys," said Gregory.

"If he ever takes the spot again," said Breakout, "you won't be able to do it."

"Do what?"

"Get it up."

"The old fuckeroo."

"Not even choke your chicken."

"Or flong your dong."

"So don't let him take the spot."

"Gregory says he's gone."

"Oh, he'll be back."

"That is, most of him."

"Not all."

A brotherly competition of titters ensued, except for Gregory who scowled.

"What about Leroy's painting?" Damon remembered suddenly. "Is it absolutely wrecked?"

"Damon?" Chloe raised her tousled head, as Go-Go squirmed between them and licked both their faces "Good morning. Talking to the guys in your head again?" She looked around, as if expecting to see them. "Introduce me, why don't ya'?"

Damon named them off quickly.

"I got most of it cleaned up," said Leroy.

"What's that smell?" asked Chloe. "Like paint thinner."

"Must be a whiff of our sets," said Damon, although Leroy truly reeked.

"I was up all night painting it out. It was yellow he threw. Can you imagine? Sun yellow! I mean, a *primary color*, for God's sake! His lack of artistic sensibility was staggering."

"I think he's lacking a couple other things as well," Bounce joked, and the twins high-fived in merriment.

"I'm taking Go-Go for her walk," said Chloe, scrambling into her jeans. "Don't eat all the breakfast."

"But, it turns out," Leroy went on as if he hadn't heard any of the others, "that particular yellow was exactly what I needed in this one tiny spot, so that was good. That worked out okay."

"Are you going to do a great painting of the scene?" asked Breakout. "Say, 'The Renunciation of Pleaser's Pleasure'?"

"Yeah, like the ones in your art books?"

"That we've never seen 'cuz you don't let us into your room," Breakout reminded his twin pointedly.

"'Vigrid Parting the Red Balls?'" suggested Bounce.

"'Penis Rising from the Dead Sea.'"

"'Pleaser in Hell,'" said a gravelly voice from nowhere, "after Blake."

"Boys, boys!" Wendy remonstrated softly, her presence a mere outline shimmering in the air, through which they could see the prop windows and chairs piled on top. "So cruel to each other! He was your own brother, after all, your own flesh and blood."

"He had it coming," said Breakout.

"Not coming anymore," said Bounce.

"Damon couldn't live his life. It's the duty of brothers to protect each other," Breakout added, showing a concern for Damon that his former disdain apparently had concealed.

"And that includes the Pleaser."

"What's he have on you, Wendy?" asked Bounce. "Did he teach you a few things you hadn't known before?"

"Enough!" said Gregory sternly. "Can't you see how faint she is? Do you want to lose her entirely?"

"Think of the good Pleaser's done for us," said Wendy. "He got Carl's studio shut down and freed us."

"You're making us feel guilty," said Breakout, although he didn't look guilty — not one bit.

"He brought it on himself," said Leroy.

"No! *You* brought it on him."

"He wrecked my painting," Leroy exploded. "Blame the victim, why don't ya'?"

"I might just go somewhere else," said Wendy.

"You can't abandon your children."

"Lots of women do. It's the new feminism."

"You're not a woman. You're a girl."

"I have a woman's responsibilities. But don't worry. Someone else will keep house. One of the children is old enough. Her name's Hellion, but she knows what to do."

"Does she make blueberry shakes like you?"

"Or calm us when we're upset?"

"Can anyone really take your place?"

"Especially a 'hellion'?"

"We're the lost boys. Only Wendy will do."

"You should have thought of that before."

"Where would you go?"

"Some other warm, loving family that needs me, whose members are kind to each other. Considerate of each other's feelings."

"I can't stand this," said Damon. "Our whole family's splitting apart."

"I don't think you can leave," said Gregory. "I mean, I don't think you can go somewhere else. You're part of us."

"Pleaser left," she said defiantly. With that, she disappeared in a shower of white sparks.

"She'll be back," said Bounce. "She doesn't know anywhere else."

Damon couldn't believe that his troubles with Pleaser were truly over. Could he love Chloe with no threat of interruption, no fear that Pleaser would take over? He kissed her goodbye, when she got back with Go-Go, saying he'd left all the cheese squares and crullers for her. He'd eat when he got home.

To reassure himself, he went in search of Pleaser's room, just to see if he'd really packed up and left. He was becoming more and more adept at nosing around Gregory's house, although it was a warren of forbidden rooms amid a maze of passageways, stairs, bridges, towers, and the like. He felt as though he were lost in a puzzle and couldn't get out. As for finding someone, it didn't do him much good just to walk by a door, which might or might not be closed.

The door to Pleaser's room was open, but it was impossible to tell if he was still living there. The contents of a dozen dumpsters piled toward the ceiling, so that even if Pleaser's body had been present, it could very well have been hidden. This was the place where Pleaser camped out, when he wasn't with cops or other sex partners. Evidently, he built a bower of trash the way some hikers lost in the woods lay a bed of pine branches.

Damon was tempted to walk in against Gregory's express command, but to do so would mean to crunch and wade through pizza crusts limed with the mold of years, roaches that scuttled among the dirty socks, paper plates, satin panties (several pairs), padded bras of various cup sizes, cardboard containers, empty tuna cans, police bulletins, and rats that scavenged among the smelly jeans, smellier boxer shorts and thongs, tattered porn magazines with voluptuous women in chains, used condoms, cuffs, dildos and other sex "toys," and Damon's "silver." The room seemed to await Pleaser's return.

The Pleaser himself had gone somewhere to hide out like a dying animal. Or lick his wounds until he recovered.

Gregory had promised he wasn't dead.

A week later, Damon's crappy TV broke down. Who knew if it was fixable? Even if it was, he didn't have the money. He was reduced to reading a mystery he'd swiped from a garage sale. As he read a sentence, he could hear the words in his head, so he thought he knew what it said. Then he reread it, and it didn't say anything like that at all. He reread it a third time and didn't know how he got the first meaning. Where were the words "home" and "family"? Not on the page. They must have been inside his head.

Damon had to face the fact that things weren't going so well with Chloe. She wasn't around the theater, and no other bits of fabric and prop dishes for his apartment miraculously appeared, scavenged from behind scenes. One night, he turned up to sleep with her, but the prop closet was locked. Where could she be? Even some of her clothes were missing from the trolley. He counted them over, smelling them for her sweet body scent, but the leather skirt and the velvet jacket — even some costumes — were gone. Although she herself had observed that it was hard to tell her stuff from the theater's.

Most of the last-minute painting and hammering fell to him. When she did show up one morning, he asked if he'd offended her in some way.

"What's to offend?" she shrugged, her body concealed in bib overalls, her hair beneath a red paisley kerchief. "I'm moving on, that's all."

"Where? Another theater?"

"Just on, Damon. We always knew we would."

"Was it because of what happened to Pleaser?"

At last, she gave him a hint.

"I don't know what's gotten into you, Damon." She was standing with her hands on her hips, one hand holding the brush for a touch-up carefully away from herself. "You're just not as sexy as you were. It happens. Frankly, I'm not enjoying you as much. I mean, you're nice and warm on a cold winter's night. But spring's coming."

He grabbed her then and there and tried to kiss her, but she squirmed away and ordered him to "Get to work."

So now Damon was sitting depressed and hopeless in front of his broken TV, eating a frozen pot pie. Their store of gourmet foods had diminished since Pleaser's disappearance. He could watch the TVs in Bounce and Breakout's room, but then he'd have to settle for sports. That reminded him how clumsy he was, how the kids had made fun of him when he was little, and he always got picked last for teams. Even girls got picked before he did.

"You have to do something," Gregory admonished. He missed Chloe as much as Damon did, although he didn't let on.

"What can I do?"

"Find out where she is. Look for her. Don't just let her go like this."

It wasn't good for Damon to be so depressed. He'd needed medication for depression some years ago, and that had upset everybody else. Robbie got loopy, Bounce and Breakout hurled the ball viciously at each other, and Wendy got flirtatious with Pleaser who was reading the newspaper, of all things. No one was himself.

In the midst of Gregory's fretting, the phone rang, rescuing Damon, who wouldn't have answered it otherwise.

"Hello, Damon? This is Timmy, you know, Kenny's heir? He wants you to come home."

"You mean, Kenny's brother?"

"What I said."

Damon could feel Gregory stiffening to alert status. Kenny hadn't called since Christmas, and only once before that since Damon had visited him last summer while he nursed Carl to death. Or was it the summer before last? Or before that, even?

"I *am* home."

"He means *here* home," said Timmy. "*Your* home before you took off and left him in the lurch. That's just where you left him. In the lurch," he repeated with satisfaction. "Kenny's sick. I'm taking care of him, but I can't be here all the time."

"Why doesn't Kenny call?"

"He don't feel so good. He's busy upchucking right now. As usual. Told me to call you and say to come down and visit him."

"You mean, take care of him," said Damon.

"He says 'visit.'"

"I can't just drop everything."

"Damon," came Kenny's voice on the phone, followed by a cough that sounded as though it began in his stomach. "If you ever want to see your Kenny alive again (cough cough), you'd better come."

"I can't come. We're in crisis here."

"You're always in crisis. Come down here and forget about crisis."

Forget about Pleaser and Chloe?

"What's wrong with you?"

"I told you I was HIV positive. Now I'm dying." He said it with a wobble in his voice.

"Oh, Kenny, you always did have a flare for the dramatic."

"This is Jenna Dooley," said a perky young voice. "I'm a volunteer with Transition Services. Kenny really is very sick. He wants you to come."

Very sick. A euphemism?

"Come and save me (cough cough) from these do-gooders. They'll be my death."

Damon could hear Jenna protesting in the background, saying something like "Now, now. We're not that bad." But Damon knew how Kenny felt about the young saviors, who weren't sick themselves, but were working out their own salvation by volunteering to wash disgusting bodies and give plentiful advice, because when a person's dying, all their store of knowledge and experience magically evaporates, to be replaced with the knowledge and experience of whoever's caring for them. Receptiveness is the least the dying person can show in gratitude to his caretaker.

"I don't have to go," he said to Gregory when he got off the phone. "I owe him nothing, absolutely nothing," in an unconscious parody of Kenny talking about his mother. He only realized it after it was out.

"Kenny stole me away from my family and then left me with Carl. I don't remember it, but it was horrible."

"I remember," said Leroy.

"Kenny loves you," whispered Wendy breathily somewhere in the air, although no one had seen her since she poofed. "At least, he thinks he does, which is the same thing. Dying's a lonely business, I've heard. Never done it myself." Positively chatty!

"He has the volunteers. Beggars can't be choosers."

Then he went upstairs to pack.

Leaving Gregory alone with his increasingly terrifying thoughts. Those who tortured Pleaser wouldn't stop with him. There was going to be another victim. Before Pleaser, there'd been Mickey, Carmine, Dessa, and the nameless ones. And after Pleaser, there'd be someone else. They had a taste for blood now.

35

BECCA TRIED TO PROVE to herself that there were no further intrusions into her precious sanctuary. Without thinking, she must have left her Norton and Oxford poetry anthologies mixed in with her psychology books. Although she could have sworn they were on her poetry shelves in her bedroom when Craig had examined them. Maybe when she moved here, she'd forgotten to sort them? Or had the evidence of a stalker made her more careless than usual?

Apparently, she'd watered her plants absentmindedly, some of them too much. A leaf on her rare begonia was yellowing. The constant disorder of her sheet music on her piano could be attributed to her new tendency toward distraction. She'd begin one thing and then jump up to check the back door or make a note on her dissertation. She resolved to put all her music away every night. But she kept forgetting. As for the bagel she'd planned to eat for breakfast this morning, she must have eaten it yesterday; no, she'd had hot cereal and that overripe banana. Must have been the day before. Or had she thrown out the banana in what her father would have called "a criminal waste of food"? She'd been tempted, but she was pretty sure she hadn't.

Thus, as Craig had suggested, she tried to come up with alternative explanations — a good experimental tactic. But it was almost as if she had an invisible roommate.

Nor were her days at the clinic any easier than her evenings at home. Class work had begun teaching her how to diagnose and treat, but sitting with too many patients over days too long only faintly resembled theory. Interviewing a patient with her supervisor in a clinic one morning, she was trying to make sense of his utterances to no avail. His words just spewed forth incomprehensibly. She attributed his behavior to anxiety. It was only after their session had ended that her supervisor commented on the patient's "word salad." Word salad! So that was it! She'd gotten high grades in Abnormal Psychology, but when faced with a symptom of schizophrenia, she didn't recognize it.

Later, she spotted this same patient walking down the hall with a cell phone pressed to his ear. Enterprising of him, she thought. This way, no one would be concerned that he was talking to himself!

As to her dissertation topic, "Bereavement and Grieving in Siblings," she hadn't yet come up with the esoteric title that should obfuscate the subject; this was required for success in academia. Too late she learned that death was not a popular topic, ever since a famous psychiatrist had spent a semester in Seattle garnering so much publicity and student praise that there was precious little left for colleagues. Jealousy had split departments into factions and these into elements of one. Nobody was anxious for *that* to happen again.

Had she removed the pile of scrap paper on which she jotted such notes from the middle left drawer of her desk? Had she absentmindedly put it on the kitchen counter? To what purpose? Well, that was what "absentminded" meant, wasn't it? Done without purpose?

Time fractured. Becca planned a New Year's Eve get-together for hospital and graduate student friends. She shopped for Craig's Christmas gift, picturing him as overjoyed or disappointed with a tie, a game of Go, something impersonal like aftershave lotion, something personal like a sweater. A perpetual motion doodad might drive him nuts, reflecting as it did the state of his life. How in the world could she get his shirt size without tipping him off? A CD? Craig was an expert on classical. How could she hope to select something critically lauded? A bookstore certificate? Trite. Besides, they agreed that they both read too much.

"Impersonal, definitely," counseled Annalyn. "Something he can return."

"Sentimental, aren't we? There's a linen sale at the Bon." Becca knew it was wrong the minute she said it.

"Get your *head* out of his *bed*."

Her gift should reflect the exact degree of their relationship, no closer, no more distant. Nor should she spend more or less than exactly what she should spend. She settled on two artsy mugs and a pound of coffee from the Public Market.

On Christmas night, Becca and Craig returned from a bizarre celebration with his family, and Becca invited him up for coffee. But as they climbed the stairs, she found her dread mounting as well, taking up what seemed like permanent residence in the pit of her stomach. Was it something she smelled? What would they find up there? What strange new invasion of her home? Was this the real reason she'd invited him?

As they stepped into her apartment, relief swept through her. It seemed just as she had left it, Moonlight Sonata on the music stand, plants undisturbed, the pattern of her books unchanged since Craig had picked her up four or five hours ago. Her apartment even smelled safe.

Relief was an aphrodisiac. She turned to him, longing for his arms around her. Was it true that men preferred women to take the initiative? That being seduced by a woman was a turn-on? Or perhaps that was after the first lovemaking session? Craig didn't exhibit a need to prove his manhood, but on the other hand, like a tai chi expert foiling his enemy's arrows, he had guided her advances to one side of him or the other. Uncertain, she offered him coffee, whiskey on the rocks, a liqueur, or a diet soda.

"How about whiskey in the coffee?" he suggested. "Make it Irish."

With a growing sense of confidence, Becca bustled about the kitchen. Nothing gone from her cabinets, her refrigerator, her counter. In the hall, her gallery of family and client pictures hung untilted. All seemed normal. She hadn't told Craig about the latest incursions — more poetry anthologies mixed in with the psychology books, the over-watered plants, and the music on her dining room table. She hadn't told him partly because she'd rationalized some of them away, and partly because she sensed some strange reaction on his part that he wasn't sharing with her. Not doubt, exactly.

Doubt?

Tonight she would try to seduce him into taking her to bed, and if not, she would follow Annalyn's suggestion of months ago and ask him why.

"I hope you weren't too put off by the family dynamics at dinner," he said, leaning against the kitchen counter and watching her preparations.

He followed her into the living room, where she settled their mugs on the coffee table in front of the couch.

Craig stood by the bookcase, smashingly attractive in his gourmet blue sweater and shirt that matched his eyes, hair ready to be unloosed in a night of passion — strong, vulnerable, and appealing all at once. The next instant, she was staring at Craig incredulously. He was holding the flame-haired troll doll that Dr. Connie had given her. It was supposed to be in her hospital office, where it leaned against the box of tissues, inviting patients to play.

"Wild One! What's she doing here?" she asked.

"You brought her home?"

Becca paused, uncertain how to answer. She should claim that she had forgotten.

"Where did you find her?" she asked instead.

"Right here between Jung and Kierkegaard. Didn't you put her there?"

"I must have." She knew very well she hadn't. She kept Wild One in her office for therapeutic reasons, just as Dr. Connie had.

"You look frightened."

"Oh, no, just that — I don't know."

"Have there been other incidents, Becca?" Craig asked, moving to the couch and sinking down beside her, "There have been, haven't there?"

"No, not really. I seem to be more preoccupied than usual lately, that's all. Does your coffee need more whiskey? I've been thinking about the possibility of a patron saint of the mentally ill in the chapel for them to pray to."

"Changing the subject on me?"

"You changed the subject on me, remember? Anyway, some people were in there praying. Caroline," of the endless tears, "and some relatives worried sick over their loved ones." Craig had put the troll back on the bookshelf, but she couldn't keep her eyes off it, as if it would explain its presence momentarily.

"Yes?" Craig pressed. "The worried relatives?"

He'd followed her eyes. He knew very well what was distracting her. She pushed on.

"It occurred to me that there are patron saints for a lot of other situations," she went on quickly. How had Wild One gotten here? "Sailors pray to St. Elmo; actors to St. Genesius; travelers have the protection of St. Christopher, or at least they did until he was de-beatified." Could she have scooped it up with her books and papers last night? "But the mentally ill don't have a saint. At least, not that I know of." No, it was too bulky, she would have noticed. "I asked Chaplain Meyer. He said he didn't think so either. Said he'd look it up. I'm thinking it might help the mentally ill and their families to have a patron saint to pray to. What do you think?" Her stalker had been in her office as well as her home.

"If there were one, I should think we'd have heard. I don't know how you'd go about creating one if there weren't," Craig observed.

"Maybe, we could sort of adopt one." If she kept her eyes off the troll now, she could sort out how it got here later. "It's right in line with what Dr. Connie used to say about the role of prayer in therapy."

Craig didn't answer at first. The wind rose outside, and a gust blew through the crack between the window frames, rattling them. He just sat there studying her, his face shadowed with concern, until she asked, "What's wrong?" Had he been ready to make his move?

Had she, like a dummy, forestalled it by telling him her stupid idea? Or was he still focused on that stupid troll that she, like a dummy, forgot she'd brought home.

"I hope you know that you can come to me, no matter what kind of trouble you're in," he said finally. He leaned over and took her hand in both of his, resting it chastely between them. She'd noticed he took her hand in public, rarely in private. In private, it could lead to more.

"Craig, I don't want you for a therapist. I want you for a friend," Becca said. And then, in a blaze of courage that she would brag about unendingly to Annalyn, she finished with, "And a lover."

Craig leaned over and kissed her, his lips just grazing hers. But when she caught her breath, her mouth opening to his, he stood her up, wrapped his arms around her, and pressed her to him.

"Are friend and therapist mutually exclusive states?" he asked.

"No. But therapist and lover are."

"I'm not your therapist, Becca. You think that way because we're both in the business, so you're sensitive to even normal concern. But you're wrong. I'm your friend, and as your friend I'm quite normally concerned that you're not telling me everything."

"I'm not."

"Don't you tell your friends everything?" He held her hands down at his sides, as if to take that defense away from her.

"Friends and therapists, not lovers."

"That's a helluva note. You mean, if we hit the sack together to-night, you'll clam up on me even more than you already do?"

Becca laughed. "You don't tell me everything," she reminded him, taking her hands from his, vaguely aware of the night shadows behind him, punctuated by splashes of light from streetlamps, stores, and occasional car lights. It would have been romantic — if it *had* been.

"I took you to my family's for Christmas, for God's sake. I thought that was pretty revealing."

"Yes. Why did you at this particular juncture, I wonder?"

"That's easy. To have a friend and ally with me in the family wars. Besides, I thought you ought to see where I come from. It's not a pretty picture."

"It's what you've become that counts, Craig," she said, kissing him.

"So what haven't I told you?"

"If you want to sleep with me. If you're sleeping with someone else."

"Yes, I want to sleep with you. No, I'm not sleeping with anyone else right now. There. You tell me what else is going on."

"You always seem to pull back."

"That's true. What do you make of it?"

"I thought maybe you have a foot fetish or something that you're afraid to show me."

Craig laughed, his hands squeezing her shoulders. She loved his laugh, hearty but not raucous.

"I have a lot of fetishes, and I'm not afraid to show you any of them. In fact, I plan to."

"I can't wait," she said, turning her body into his. "I promise not to tell."

"You must think they're pretty wild."

"Am I wrong?"

"I'll let you be the judge. Now, answer my question," he said somewhat sternly. "Tell me what else has been going on."

"I don't want to tell you. I just want to kiss you."

"We psychologists call that 'resistance.'"

"Who's resisting who?" she teased. "I want to explore your fetishes, that's all."

"You show me yours, and I'll show you mine?" he asked, brushing her hair from her face, then trailing his hand down her cheek and resting it lightly on her chest like a preview.

"I have to go to the bathroom. Is that resistance, too?" she teased as she turned toward the hall.

Becca washed her hands. Should she whip off her sheets and pillowcases and put clean ones on? Or should she lay clean over soiled? If she asked him to help, so there was less time for their ardor to cool, could they make it part of their foreplay?

She switched on the light in her bedroom, contemplating a

night of passion. At long last! It was then that she saw the giant troll, propped against her pillows. A low scream escaped her.

It was two feet tall, at least, wearing a pink-checked pinafore and a white apron, its blue hair combed back and up, tied with a pink bow. But it had been altered, or one might say adulterated. The necklace of tiny beads at its throat, and the ankle chain and bracelet were unusual for trolls. The dangling earrings that Annalyn had given her in Santa Cruz were pinned voodoo-like beneath its ears.

Most frightening: never in her life had Becca set eyes on that troll!

Craig was at her side.

"The doll?"

"I've never seen it before."

"Are you sure?"

"Of course, I'm sure! Don't you think I'd know if I'd seen a doll that size?"

"Yes, yes, you would." His hands on her shoulders suddenly seemed false. "Only that sometimes we do things without thinking," he went on. "We buy one thing when we mean to buy something else, for instance."

"You mean, I went out for a loaf of bread and came back with a giant blue-haired troll?"

"Haven't you done that kind of thing before? I know I have."

"When? When did you buy one thing when you meant to buy another? And then forget you'd done it? Name one time." Becca twisted away, furious at his attempt to manipulate her. It was standard operating procedure for therapists with patients, getting them to admit to something by saying they'd done it themselves. Effective at puncturing defenses. Police officers did it with perps, too. Only, fellow therapists weren't supposed to be doing it to each other. They did, of course, but they weren't supposed to. Who did he take her for? An idiot? He didn't believe that she had an intruder messing with her things. He believed she was doing this to herself!

"I can't remember exactly," Craig was saying. "I'm sure I have, but it was so unimportant. Come on, Becca, let's go back to our coffee. I'll reheat it."

"You think I'm doing this myself, don't you?"

"No, no," he said, hands on her arms, steering her into the living room.

"You think I moved my own plants? And left my music a mess on the piano? And straightened Robbie's picture? And messed up my books? You think I did it all? You do, don't you? Only I didn't."

"I didn't know about the music."

She felt tricked into having told him. "You think I'm dissociating. Maybe a fugue state. Maybe even your beloved dissociative identity disorder."

"That's Bernie's beloved, not mine."

"For your information, I am not losing time. I am not blanking out. I am not waking up in a strange place, wondering how I got there. I do not hear yelling at me or even whispering," she said, naming some of the more prominent DID symptoms. "A stalker's coming into my apartment and messing with my stuff, and now even leaving something. He's been in my office at the hospital. I know because he got hold of Wild One and brought her back here. Despite the fact that I've had all my locks changed. He knows when I'm gone. He's creepy, and I want him to stop," Becca finished in tears.

"Of course, you do." Craig's hands still firmly on her shoulders pressed her to the couch.

"I don't want to sit. I want to stand." It was easier to fight while standing, which, of course, was why he wanted her to sit.

"If this is really happening to you —"

"*If* it's happening. *If!* You psychologists are all alike." She ignored the hint of a smile. She, too, was a psychologist, after all. She was accusing her own profession. "You attribute everything to the mind. Well, I've got news for you, *Doctor* Craig Austin. Crimes happen, too. Break-ins happen, stalkings happen, and they're not all imaginary." His hands came up to grasp her arms in a calming gesture, but she brushed them aside. "People get attacked and get real bruises and real fractures, and sometimes they get really murdered. It isn't always a head trip."

He hesitated, seeming to search for the best response. "Do you want to call the police?"

"And tell them what?" she burst out. "That someone gave me a troll doll with a lot of jewelry on it?"

"They broke in to do it." The argument she'd made to the police herself.

"The cops don't see that as threatening."

"What about tomorrow? Why don't we go to the police station together tomorrow and report it again? Sometimes they pay more attention when a man's along. Now don't get defensive; it's just a fact."

"It would help if you believed me."

"Becca, I'll tell you honestly, I don't know what to believe. But I'm in this with you for the long haul, whatever it is. And I think we should cover all bases."

"You mean I should go directly to a therapist and get diagnosed with dissociation?"

"It wouldn't hurt to check in," he conceded, "for a tune-up," using Dr. Connie's phrase. "I've felt all along that you might be suffering from post-traumatic stress disorder. Becca, Becca, Becca, you had a terrible experience when you were a child, and I don't think you've ever gotten completely over it."

"No one gets completely over a trauma or a loss. You should know that."

"Right, but — and it's just my intuition — with you, I've felt there were more tailings somehow. You wanted to know why I hesitated to pursue a romance with you? Even though I knew you wanted it — we both did. And still do," he stumbled and caught himself. "To tell the truth, that's why. You never got over the loss of your brother, and in some ways, I don't know how, but I suspect that I remind you of him. That may be why you care for me."

"I want to sleep with my brother?"

"No, no, just to be with him again. Becca, it makes emotional sense. You've been drawn to me ever since we met. The only other meaningful relationship with a male that you had —"

"What do you know about my relationships? I haven't even told you about Hugh."

"Do you want to?"

"That is just so stupid!" Becca yelled at him. "You're not my brother. You're my lover, damn it. At least, you were. I thought. You're the one who's hung up on what happened to me, not me. Get over it! And get out of here."

"I don't want to leave you like this."

"Leave me like this," she said, jumping up from the couch. "Get out."

He'd stood up, and as she pushed him to the door, he lost his balance.

"First, let me be sure there's nobody here. Of course, there isn't, but you'll sleep better knowing we checked the place out."

She joined him without a word, not thanking him but feeling relieved. Together, they searched everywhere a body might hide, no matter how unlikely — in the kitchen cabinets, on top of the closet shelves, under the couch, and behind the sink, incidentally giving Becca a chance to calm down (which was why he had suggested it). They didn't find anyone. Nor did they find other trolls.

"Why don't I reheat our coffee, and we can talk about this some more," Craig tested.

"Thank you for helping me search," Becca said stiffly, with very little gratitude in her tone. "With my paranoid ideation and obsessive compulsive personality, I'd have imagined every noise was an intruder."

"Now, Becca, I never said that."

"No, you said I was dissociating."

"We all dissociate — on the freeway, while watching TV — you know that." He picked up the coffee mugs but paused to gauge her reaction to his offer.

"Please leave now."

"Come back to my place and spend the night with me," Craig said. It sounded not so much like an invitation to a night of sexual delight as an offer of asylum.

"No. I won't. Now go."

Craig put down the mugs, grabbed her arm and pulled her toward him. "Come and spend the night," he said. "Please. You'll feel safer with me. Tomorrow we'll go to the police together." He drew her toward him and tried to kiss her. It felt to her as though he was offering the possibility of sex in order to gain her admission of mental illness. She slapped him away.

"Leave!" she repeated.

Looking drained, Craig picked up his coat from the chair. But there was something else in his face as he turned back to her.

"You really are being unreasonable, you know," he said tightly.

"You'd tell a woman who's been raped that it was all in her head."

"Those who need the most help delude themselves into thinking they don't," he snapped.

"You're so smug, you're not the last authority, you know," she spat. And then, the clinker. "With a family like yours, you're hardly in a position to judge someone else's delusions."

He looked as though she'd struck him. Which she had. He slammed the door.

Becca watched him head toward his car. Craig couldn't have been the one who smuggled two trolls into her home. She had been with him the whole evening. The errant thought shocked her. Why was she even making excuses for him?

As he unlocked his car, he looked up toward her windows, but she was pretty sure he couldn't see her. This time, no shadow disengaged itself from the house across the street. Maybe even shadows had Christmas off.

36

WHEN DAMON AND I arrived in San Francisco, we found Kenny dying in the very same bed where Carl had croaked his last. Kenny refused to go to the hospital, so he had a suction machine to get rid of the mucus that oozed miraculously from his lungs into his bronchial tubes and took his breath away. His linens smelled of dead fish.

"I sweat so," Kenny said. "My bed needs changing every day. They'll do it. You don't have to," he added as Damon lifted the sheet.

Damon did so on the pretext of evaluating whether or not he could lift Kenny for the change, but actually, he wanted to see how much of Kenny was left. Not much. Kenny was a rail with stick arms and legs, just like those family pictures children draw that tell the therapist they've been abused. His cock and balls were shriveled to the size of a child's, the size Damon's had been when he first came to stay. Why, Damon could do anything he wanted to Kenny right now, if he had a mind!

What a strange thought!

The room's decor was now to the taste of his caregivers, mainly white and gray, with lots of steel things like kidney bowls and bed-pans. Not unlike Vigrid's operating theater, Damon thought, where he'd emasculated Pleaser. Someone had replaced Carl's masterpiece with macramé.

"For God's sake, take that rope thing down. The Transitioners brought it."

"What shall I do with it?"

"Put it in the trash. Down the alley so they think it's gone."

"They'll say I stole it."

"Blame it on Timmy."

Damon tossed it, then flung open Kenny's closet and extracted his red dragon duster from clothes that looked as though they should be destined for charity. And most likely were. No stairs led to the attic where Robbie was. Damon had taken things so literally in those days.

"Oh, that?" Kenny exclaimed when he spotted the red dragon. "That's ages old!"

"Still wearable, and the color suits you."

Kenny no longer had any hair for contrast. His pate was bald and bumpy, and the circles around his eyes were the color of ashes. But Damon raised Kenny up on his pillows and slipped the duster around his shoulders, remembering how it used to float behind him as if he were flying.

"There, that's better."

"Does the mirror approve?" Kenny asked as he drew the duster around his shoulders with a touch of the old vanity.

"Of course, it does."

"Let me see. Where's the hand mirror?"

"Don't you believe me? I tell you, the mirror approves. It wouldn't dare not to. How long have these dead daffodils been here?"

"Oh, Timmy got them for me before he left last week. He had to go back. He has a kid now, you know."

Damon didn't ask where the kid came from. He was pretty sure he knew. It seemed to run in families, this arrogating of other people's children to themselves. He threw out the dead daffodils, saying, "I'll get you fresh."

He thought of offering water to Kenny, or better yet, that puree concoction that Kenny'd made for Carl. He guessed that was what he was supposed to do. But any food or drink would only prolong his condition. He compromised by asking if he was thirsty.

"God, no! Those volunteers push water at me every five minutes."

"They think they know everything."

"They know NOTHING, absolutely NOTHING. They call me *their* patient — THEIRS — as if I belonged to them. As if I were their possession, like their pants or their cars. They're so smug. That old biddy nurse even had the nerve to ask me if I was at peace with my God. If I wanted a priest or a minister or something."

"The nerve! For all she knows, you're an atheist."

"I'm not. But I could be for all she knows. I wish *I* could be around when *they* croak."

"That'd teach them," said Damon. "Maybe you will be."

"I hope Carl's not around here."

Why? Because Kenny wasn't very nice to Carl toward the end? Damon couldn't remember exactly how, but already, Damon was nicer. Not that Kenny deserved it.

"I'm going to make tea."

He made a cup for Kenny just in case.

They chatted for fifteen or twenty minutes, just like old times. Damon found he couldn't remember much, but he followed my advice and went along with whatever Kenny said until Kenny began to fade.

"I have so little energy. How long can you stay?" Kenny asked anxiously. Which was all Kenny needed, companionship that wasn't bent on his salvation.

"A few days at most."

"Don't you want to be with me when I die?"

"Of course," he lied. "But I have a job to get back to. I'm a restaurant manager now." If it was good enough for Chloe, it was good enough for Kenny. "And I have a major part in a play." Second understudy for the third lead counted. "I have to get back to rehearsals."

While Kenny slept, Damon wandered around the apartment of his childhood. No sweet potato vine climbed the dining room blind. The porn pictures of children were long gone from the living room.

Damon found them packed away in the closet of his old bedroom. They were, after all, art.

In Damon's old room, a single sailboat sailed on the shelf of the bookcase. He thought it had been his. The beveled mirror that had seemed so beautiful in its carved frame, where he had first spotted Gregory, was tarnished and needed re-silvering. The bed where Kenny had slept while he nursed Carl was now neatly made up and empty of laundry. The odd, irregularly shaped water stain in the corner of the ceiling had been a tree tower breaking through the sky. Painted over now, but we could still see the outline. Oh, it was a beautiful tree, its roots hanging down like a ladder, with someone — a girl — beckoning to him from the top, and when he climbed it, he was safe, although he couldn't remember what from. Nor could he remember what had happened to it. Had it fallen or been chopped down?

"I remember," Leroy whispered in his ear.

Damon felt the branches poking into his side.

That night, Jenna Dooley came by and was so cheerful it was no wonder that Kenny puked his guts out! Damon announced he was going for a walk.

"Don't leave me alone with her," Kenny pleaded.

"Now, now," said Jenna, "Damon needs his break," presuming to speak of his feelings, when he'd communicated nothing to her. The arrogance! Giving him permission!

Damon wandered the neighborhood past the fast food restaurant doing as much business in French fries as ever. Snap! "Stop!" Snap! "Stop!" The tattoo parlor was now an art gallery with nude body parts in the windows. The building that had housed Kenny's art studio, as well Trent, Barry and Madam Adam's apartment, had been razed and replaced with pseudo-Victorian condos. Carmine's gallery was a furniture store, but the mosaic fish still swam through the concrete floor.

"Where did they hang Carmine?" Damon asked the salesman, who favored black pants and a red cummerbund, just like Kenny's when he was a waiter. His eyes widened with shock. "A few years ago, when he had his art gallery here?" Damon explained, as if he were trying to be helpful.

"I have no idea what you're talking about. You'd better go." Would he be pushing Damon out the door if he didn't have a very good idea indeed?

The next day, Kenny was worse. Before Jenna left, she gave Damon a whole list of instructions on when and what and how to feed and force fluids; a nurse would be by with shots, but here were his pills. The Transitioners had done a good job of keeping the place clean and bringing in extra food, so Kenny really didn't need Damon for anything except company, and the Transitioners could supply that, too.

"Pay no attention to her," said Kenny after she'd gone out the door, heading for her college classes. "Except for my pain pills and I can take those if you mash them up."

Damon helped him swallow them, while saying that he had to leave soon. Anticipating tearful objections, he got an early start on them, so he could finish in time to catch the bus.

"Damon, I have to ask you something," Kenny said weakly. Then he clenched his mouth in a white line.

"Ask me what?"

"Tomorrow I'll ask."

"But I'm taking the bus back to Seattle tomorrow."

"I have to ask."

"What then? Go ahead. Ask away."

Kenny turned his head to the stale water bubbles on the night table.

"Have you forgiven me?"

What was that about? Damon thought he had known once, but damned if he could remember now. He knew he should play along, as I had taught him. But for some reason he didn't want to this time.

"You know, Kenny, my memory's so odd."

"What are you talking about?"

Damon sat on Kenny's bed. How could he explain? "I forget things I should remember, and then I remember the oddest little thing. Is your memory like that? Sometimes I wonder if mine's normal. There are these huge patches of nothing, and then I seem to remember something someone else did that I didn't do at all."

"You've always been a strange kid," said Kenny, breaking into a wracking cough. Damon sat him up and suctioned him.

"That's better. So. What's the answer? Don't tell me you've forgotten."

"Damon forgives you," he said.

"Why are you talking like that?"

"Like what?"

"Like you're someone else. You've done it before."

"I'm trying to tell you. Damon forgives you. But Robbie never can."

"Robbie! You're Robbie!"

"You said I was Damon. I used to be Robbie."

"What's he got to do with anything?"

"He's the one you stole. He can't forgive you for that. He still cries for his Bec-Bec up in his attic room. Although he spends a lot more time sleeping than playing or crying these days."

"Oh, don't start that crap again. I meant, have you forgiven me for what Carl did to you?"

"What did Carl do?"

"You really don't remember?"

"I told you, I have this memory problem."

"You don't remember Carl hurting you?"

"Leroy remembers, don't you, Leroy?"

"I do. He did it to me, not to Damon," Leroy rasped.

"Now, stop that crazy talk!"

"I'm the real painter. You're just a dilettante. An amateur. A pretender. A *poseur*. You don't even know about consistent light sources."

"Damon, stop talking to me that way."

"What way?"

"You sound different, that's all. Like you're a different person, or something."

"I've tried to explain."

"You scare me when you talk that way."

"Leroy won't hurt you. But his friends would if Leroy had a mind. They'd do you like they did Mickey and Carmine."

"It was you!"

Damon disregarded this. "But I don't think they'll do you. They didn't do Carl. They watched him suffer and die instead."

The comparison wasn't lost on Kenny, who burst into tears.

"Don't go, Damon," said Kenny. "I always loved you."

"I know," Damon said.

"Can't you bring yourself to say you loved your Kenny? Just a little bit?"

"Of course," he lied.

37

WHEN WE RETURNED TO Seattle, Damon found the stage set for the soda fountain love scene, with a board across the tops of two chairs for a counter, and two stools for Emily and George behind it. A strange girl was second understudy for Emily, and no one seemed to know where Chloe was. Didn't Damon? His denial got him a roll of the eyes heavenward.

I was devastated. I'd fallen completely in love with Chloe, so much so that I wanted to marry her. I dreamed of buying her a little cottage in the West Seattle area with a view of the Sound and the Olympics. I'd let her choose the furnishings, drapes, fabrics, and colors — how she'd love that! She could spend her days in the theater doing whatever she pleased. Modest benefactor gifts to help support the theaters would get her auditions and an occasional role, I was sure of it. On weekends we'd visit cheese shops for tastes, and I'd massage her feet, kissing each tiny pink toe with its seashell nail, caressing her so completely that her desire mounted until she begged for it, as Pleaser had instructed. Only then would I enter her and pleasure her over and over. We would be one flesh, one soul.

I'd never made love to her, of course. She was Damon's, and I was a fairly upright sort. With one exception: occasionally, filled with a voyeur's guilt, I watched. I felt Damon's hands caress that fragrant skin, felt Damon's lips kiss that honey rosebud mouth, tangled my fingers in Chloe's hair, pushed my thighs against hers. When it got too intense, I went away. How dare Pleaser do what I myself had virtuously refrained from doing? That it was Pleaser Chloe missed (although she did not know this, of course) was the ultimate betrayal.

This was why, to my everlasting guilt, I'd made no attempt to interfere with Vigrid's and Mefisto's reprisals, not that I'd realized until near the end what they were up to. When I did, I was overwhelmed with horror. These were the same psychopaths who had tortured Mickey and killed Carmine and Dessa.

What do you do when you discover that two members of your own family are sadistic murderers? For one thing, you hope you don't offend them. The more prudent course of action seemed to be to find out as much as I could about them. Maybe meet to arrange terms for a truce.

Meanwhile, Damon was left with the responsibility for the *Our Town* sets, props, and costumes for just a few more days, supposedly. In a kind of mourning, he slept on the basement couch that still held Chloe's smell. When he squeezed his eyes shut, he could imagine she was with him. The days stretched to ten, and the director said he would have to "hire" someone else soon if Chloe wasn't back. He seemed certain that Damon knew where she was, but Damon had heard not a word from her.

We set out together to search for her, hitting all the little theaters in Seattle. When we didn't find her, Damon sank into a depression so deep that I worried he might need shock treatment.

Mefisto's and Vigrid's laboratory was at the end of the bridge, the door thrown open ever since that unending night they castrated Pleaser. It was said that a secret panel opened on stairs leading to a dungeon far below. But I had no idea who had said it.

The implements of their trade hung on walls; jarred body parts were shelved neatly in legal bookcases; and extensive torture notes in three-ringed binders detailed their results. The account of Pleaser's castration lay open for anyone to see in a spiral-back five by eight notebook, pages on pages of Vigrid's neat printing with an occasional cramped note from Mefisto. There was, however, not a hint of their next victim.

Behind the lab was Mefisto and Vigrid's library of torture that any master librarian would have praised for its rare editions and its comprehensiveness. I scanned *A History of Torture*. I knew of desultory tortures, but not as a history down through the ages. *The Body in Pain* had probably not been written with Vigrid's purposes in mind, but the corners of pages were turned down. The *Malleus Maleficarum* of 1486 was a witch-hunting handbook describing what witches did, drinking the blood of children and the like, and how they must be tortured until they confessed. I shuddered at the images these words called up. *Medical Torture* like the book next to it, *The Nazi Doctors*, described both the physical and mental tortures at Auschwitz. I felt too nervous to thumb through these but noted that there were lots of bookmarks and checks in the margins.

As I turned to examine the rest, my eyes snagged on *The Spanish Inquisition, Orgies of Torture and Brutality,* and *Rack, Rope, and Red-Hot Pincers: A History of Torture and its Instruments* by a man named Geoffrey Abbott. Thinking Vigrid and Mefisto wouldn't miss this latter among hundreds, I borrowed it.

I tore out a sheet of paper from one of their binders and left them a note.

"Dear Vigrid and Mefisto,

I came by to meet with you, but as you know, you are not here. I feel it is imperative —" I crossed this out and substituted "important that we meet. Please contact me in my room at your earliest convenience." Of course, I had no idea if they knew which room I was in, Leroy having said they didn't know I existed, so I added, "It's the Victorian room with the carved, wood-paneled door on the third floor overlooking the south gardens.

Thank you,

/s/ Gregory"

I thought of signing it "Your brother, Gregory," but for all I knew, they did not acknowledge our relationship.

Back outside their laboratory, I noticed for the first time that stairs led up to a trap door in the ceiling. There could be nothing up there that I was entitled to see, but frankly curious, I climbed the stairs.

The door was padlocked. I felt around the little crannies surrounding it, hoping to find a key. Finally, I went back downstairs and found that the twins had returned, so I prevailed on Breakout to assist me. He was thrilled at the notion of helping me do something evil, especially since the twins' last attempts to get me to try pot were met with non-stony silence and what must have seemed to them like a sickeningly staunch and virtuous decline. The door gave, and I climbed the last stairs to the top.

I stood in the middle of a spectacular roof garden. An arbor of wisteria vines shaded a gazebo; sumptuous baskets of fuchsias hung from the eaves; window boxes nestled in the shade of the trees with flowers labeled purple adjuratum and white alyssum, lobelia, pansies, helvetica, tulips, and hyacinths. A collection of yellow, pink, red, and white begonias, hung from the railings, while potted red lace-leaf maples, azaleas, bougainvillea, ferns, frilly hibiscus, and *bauhinia purpurea*, the purple and cream buds of the tulip tree just bursting from its branches, seemed affected by neither cold, nor wind, nor rain. This would be a wonderful roof garden for us all, I thought. And who was the talented caretaker here? I had no idea.

Peering through the window of a shed, I spied an army cot, a portable clothes closet, a stool, a sink, a row of bookcases, and a four-drawer filing cabinet. The door was open, and I left it so, as I tiptoed toward the files, which was ridiculous because no one could hear me. Whoever lived here was gone, although he could return at any moment. I noticed that the bookcases were filled with poetry anthologies from top to bottom.

The file drawers were not labeled, although the files were, the names including members of our family. Suddenly, Chloe Hearst's name leaped out at me. My heart beating so hard I thought I would pass out, I opened it and found it stuffed with dated reports. I tucked the file under my shirt and hurried out the door.

38

LOVE IS JUST AN overactive imagination!

Fueled by engorgement of the genital blood vessels during arousal to carry on the species, even past the years a woman can conceive, which in itself makes no sense. Nature is brutal in her insistence that the species continue. Profligate in her breeding attempts. She loses enough generations to pestilence and pesticide as it is. Those that survive must propagate.

Well, they don't *all* have to. Becca doesn't.

"He keeps calling and leaving messages, of course," she told Annalyn over the phone, as her friend burped her baby. "He didn't mean to imply that I was stark raving insane." Becca mocked Craig's apologies. "The presence of someone uninvited in my apartment isn't really my imagination."

"I've told you to date around," said Annalyn. Burp! "A lot of my friends are meeting people on the Internet in chat rooms. They kiss a lot of frogs, but some of the guys have potential."

"If they aren't serial murderers or rapists."

"Try women friends. They're great at swapping boyfriends. Hit the museums. I met a potential there once. Go to bookstores for readings. I won't suggest church, but maybe? When a fellow in the market's bread section asks your advice, for heaven's sake, make eye contact and smile. He's not really interested in your opinion."

"How does an old married matron know so much about it?"

"Honey, I did it all. I didn't just kiss a lot of frogs. Hell, I slept with them to make absolutely *certain* they weren't my type."

Toting the big troll doll in a shopping bag (she was darned if she was going to walk down the street clutching it to her breast), Becca entered the police station that by now looked too familiar.

"I want to report a home invasion," she said to the desk sergeant.

"What was taken?"

"Nothing. This was left." She pulled out the troll and set it on the window counter. The officer looked from her to the troll and back again, as if she were crazy.

"Well, if that don't beat all. Do you have kids in the house, Ms. — er —"

"Merrow. And, no, I do not. I've complained before, and it's getting worse."

After the sergeant took her report, she was passed along to another female officer who passed her again to Lt. McNalley with whom she was speaking now. He didn't seem enthusiastic about renewing their acquaintance.

"Boyfriends?" he asked.

She told him about Hugh and Craig and admitted she'd broken up with both.

"But I didn't break up with Dr. Austin until after the doll appeared and the other incidents too."

"Why did you break up with him?"

"Personal," replied Becca. She wasn't about to tell him her psychologist boyfriend thought she was crazy.

"Do they have keys?"

"No, and they never did."

"You work with mental patients, right? As I said last time, it sounds as though you might have a squirrelly admirer on your hands. He doesn't sound dangerous. I know — I know —" Officer McNalley raised his hand to ward off her interruption, "you feel threatened by his being in your apartment. And you're right, of course. You should be able to live in privacy. I'm just saying he sounds more like an admirer, admittedly a squirrelly one —"

"We call them psychopaths," said Becca acidly.

"Whatever. You might consider a self-defense class — not that you need one, but it would just make you feel better."

Becca thought it would make her feel worse. No way did she believe that she could get herself in strong enough condition to fight off an intruder. And she didn't want to have to think about it all the time, which she would if she investigated classes, visited a few, scheduled lessons, took them, needed to plan the rest of her life around them. She'd be thinking about what had provoked the need.

"Some people get themselves a gun," Officer McNalley went on, "but we don't recommend it."

Perplexed, Becca tried to divine his meaning from his face. Was he suggesting that she do so, and covering himself in case she shot the intruder? Or was he really recommending against it? The idea of a gun was repugnant. She didn't mind if other people like the police used a gun to protect her, but she didn't want to touch one herself.

"You could hire a P.I."

"Thanks, but I'm being watched enough as it is."

"We'll send a car around to check on your building occasionally."

Band-Aid!

Becca was spending as much time as she could at school and in the hospital, returning home only to sleep. Home was too uncomfortable. Hypervigilant as she was, she saw suspicious circumstances all around her, but at home she was alone, whereas elsewhere people might come to her aid.

"You could at least return my calls," said Craig angrily, barging into her office and shutting the door. The room really had been a broom closet in a previous incarnation, and Craig had to stand so close to her desk that she could feel the anger fumes peeling off him like condensation off the sidewalk in the wee hours of a winter morning.

"I don't want to talk to you," Becca said in her steeliest voice. He really was beautiful when he was mad, his lips sensuous in anger, long arms skirting his hips, eyes piercing points of black in blue. "Please leave. I have another patient," in an hour.

"What's happening? Did you go to the police? Have there been any new incidents? Becca, you owe it to me to let me in on this."

"I don't owe you anything!"

"Shh, don't make a scene. For your own sake."

"Why? Do I remind you of your family? Is that what draws you to me?"

He opened his mouth to say something, then closed it and banged out.

"Good one!" said Becca to herself. At the same time, she couldn't help feeling sad. Craig had been her friend and confidant, her last connection with Dr. Connie, but he had betrayed her by not believing her.

St. Dymphna, patron saint of the insane, is pictured as a young maiden with a crown upon her head, indicating virginity. Bearing a sword, she stands with the devil in chains at her heels. She has not slain him, but she controls him so that he can no longer possess us, which makes sense because St. Dymphna lived in a time when people believed that lunatics suffered from demonic possession. The devil must be rooted out with exorcism, stoning, and burning.

Her father reigned as a pagan King over Ireland in the thirteenth century. Her mother, a Christian queen, died when little Dymphna was very young. As she grew, the king perceived the increasing resemblance between her and the beloved wife he had lost. The accounts put it genteelly: he wanted to marry his daughter.

Dymphna fled her father with a loyal priest, Gerebernus, and they settled in Gheel near Antwerp, a hundred miles north of Brussels, Belgium. Enraged at her disobedience, her father stormed across the sea after her and beheaded them both. Angels made their bodies whole again, and the two were buried by the townspeople, their names inscribed on bricks above their coffins.

The citizens prayed at St. Dymphna's tomb and began to notice relief from mental disorder and epilepsy. According to one account, five naked lunatics, chained to St. Dymphna's shrine one night, had completely recovered their wits the next day. A night of cold terror in a graveyard might indeed restore one's sanity, thought Becca. Or end it!

The people of Gheel built a hospital for the insane, and St. Dymphna's shrine became a pilgrimage destination. To this day, rather than practicing NIMBY politics, the citizens of Gheel invite recovering patients into their homes when they are ready, thus helping to mainstream them in the community, all except those deemed pedophiles or otherwise dangerous. Gheel's reputation for enlightened professional treatment of mental illness persists to this day.

To Becca, that St. Dymphna should be the patron saint of the insane made perfect sense, as she told Dr. Bernie Leonard over lunch — at his invitation. He wanted to ascertain how things were going in her practicum.

"Don't you see?" she pressed him over her salad and his salmon and noodles *alfredo*. She was much more comfortable now than she had been, mainly because she felt he would not force her to do anything she didn't want to. "St. Dymphna was really a victim of incest, at least, attempted incest. When she wouldn't sleep with her father, he killed her. Many of the mentally ill are victims of sexual abuse, including incest. Your DID patients have a ninety-eight percent rate —"

"Not just my DID. Also my PTSDs, my depressives, and my alcoholics. There really is a much higher incidence of sexual abuse among the mentally ill population as a whole than among the healthy."

"I didn't know anyone was healthy."

He wiped *alfredo* sauce from his pointy little beard, not because he could see it, but because long experience had taught him that it was there. He could hardly expect to manipulate other people with a drip of sauce in so prominent a position.

"You and I are, aren't we?"

"I'll tell everyone you said so," said Becca. "So Dymphna's the perfect patron saint," she continued. "Isn't it just like the male hierarchy to eliminate the saint that tends to women's main problem? But I suppose that makes sense, too. The men caused it."

"My, my, we are in a feminist snit today, aren't we? Many men are victims, too."

"Well, you don't seem very enthusiastic."

"You don't know if she even existed."

"What does it matter? Who of us exists, at least for any length of time? We're always changing every minute." Becca loved to switch the level of discussion when the argument wasn't going her way. It was so satisfying to see the opposition falter.

"Oh, if you're going to get existential on me —" he laughed, shoveling a hurried forkful of salmon noodles into his mouth in order to be done with it and make his escape.

"Seriously. I think it's important for the mentally ill to have someone to pray to. I don't think it matters if she's a myth. She's shown how belief is power."

Dr. Bernie didn't think so. Scraping back his chair and rising from the cafeteria table, he looked down on Becca from his Promethean height, which originated in his departmental status, although he obviously preferred to think of it as a physical attribute, saying,

"The mentally ill don't need gods or religion to help them overcome. *We're* their gods," he grinned, licking his lips, rather salaciously, Becca thought. "And don't you forget it."

"So you wouldn't object to having her painting, say, in the chapel? Perhaps with a little printed history beside it?" And a dedication! But she mustn't move too fast.

"If you're serious about this, Becca, there's a problem," he said, walking her past Craig and an admiring Dr. Noel, as Becca looked up fondly at Dr. Bernie. Let Craig think they were having an affair. Serve him right! "Who's religious and who's paranoid?" Dr. Bernie proclaimed the metaphorical question sonorously. "Joan of Arc heard voices. They call her a saint. If I had her in my clinic, I'd probably call her schizophrenic. You would, too. Moses heard a voice in the burning bush that he attributed to God. Half the long-term patients on wards around the country think either that they've heard God or that they *are* God."

"You just said yourself that you are," Becca teased.

"Yes, good point. But what's the difference between me and a patient?" he tested.

"The difference is that you *are* God."

"Excellent! You'll go far. So all this mystical mumbo-jumbo is really just that. If we encourage it, we may be encouraging our patients' pathologies. We're saying 'Yes' to those who claim they killed Mom because God told them to."

"Then you wouldn't mind if St. Dymphna appeared in the chapel?" she pressed.

"As long as you don't start hearing her," he joked. "So how are you getting on, Becca?" he asked, an arm around her shoulders and a squeeze that veered dangerously from the professional toward the personal.

With Craig out of jealousy-provoking range, she made her tactful escape.

Later that evening, Becca slipped into the chapel to hang up her portrait and one-page biography entitled, "The Legend of St. Dymphna: Patron Saint of the Mentally Ill." She concluded the history with a prayer.

"St. Dymphna, helper of the mentally afflicted, pray for us!"

The Feast Day was in a few weeks, on May 15. She mounted the history on the wall just at the chapel's entrance in print large enough for troubled or medicated eyes to read and even a fancy font for the title.

Becca slid into a pew at the back of the chapel and knelt, noting how plain the altar was, how denuded of the beauty of stained glass windows and Madonna statues, wood carving, and even a velvet altar covering. It resembled nothing so much as one of those modern movie houses. She missed the beauty of gilt and sacred images, pillars and pilasters, and ceilings rising to heaven, all of which both consoled and con-souled.

She was about to rise when the most exquisite soprano voice rose through the chapel softly as if it were an exudation from the very walls, a hymn in Latin, then soared to the unadorned ceiling. She knelt transfixed, her eyes straining in the dimness to catch a glimpse of the singer, but she could not tell where the voice came from in the shadows. After a few minutes, it subsided and died away. She waited for it to come again, but it did not. Who could it be?

She got up and turned to leave. It was then that she saw what looked like the shadow of a teenaged boy slipping among the oddly irregular shadows that bore no resemblance to the chapel's structures, and he was gone

39

RACK, ROPE AND RED-HOT PINCERS was an encyclopedia of tortures, such as pressing with stones during our own witch trials, the boot, the lash, the pendulum, mutilation, and spiked effigies (the most impious of which was named "the Virgin," who clasped the heretic to her deadly bosom). Included was a brief history of those who suffered — puritans, priests, Protestants, and other heretics, as well as lords and ladies, martyrs, criminals, and revolutionaries. It might be Vigrid's manual. One Sicilian artist created a brass bull into the belly of which the condemned was placed, a fire lit beneath, and he slowly roasted to death. Ingeniously, reeds in the snorting nostrils converted his screams to music. Evidently possessed of some sense of justice, the ruler used the artist himself as a demonstration!

So this was Vigrid's mindset! Could we expect modern versions as Vigrid became more proficient? Here in my Victorian sanctuary, I felt chilled, but whether it was the room or the text, I could not tell. I got up and lit the fire on the grate.

In the still of the night, I examined the file on Chloe. The dated entries were in English mostly, much of it poetry. Occasional lapses into Latin compelled me to consult my old Latin-English dictionary.

These passages contained more details of Chloe's activities. In addition, I found brief passages in code. I assumed that these must be the most informative sections. But what code was the mystery spy using? Would computer cryptanalysis reveal its nature?

I turned to my computer to attempt a "differential diagnosis." After many nights of work, my computer eliminated some codes and showed increased probabilities of others. I began to understand why only sections of the files were encoded. The encoder did not possess the sophisticated skills I had attributed to him. On the contrary, he had chosen an old reliable cipher, used by Benedict Arnold, but almost impossible to break unless you knew which book was the "key." For example, if it was the Bible, and you wanted to use the word "she," you had to look for the word "she" in the Bible, and then write down the page, line, and number of the word, 28-1-1. It was also very time-consuming both to encrypt and to decode. There were no patterns that a computer program could pick up, even very simple ones, that "ones" were "a's" and "two" were "b's" for instance. I began to suspect that the "key" book might be the method, when after hours at my computer, nothing else worked. But I had no way of testing my theory, because of course, you need the "key" book itself. How could I ever figure that out?

I could translate the Latin words and phrases interspersed throughout, however, and this helped. Latin is a comparatively easy secret language, because most people don't know it, and so both coder and decoder can communicate quite safely. My guess was that Vigrid knew some Latin. It's the root of many a medical term, after all.

My own two years of the language in the private school Kenny sent me to (until he got disillusioned with me) began to pay off in revelations. The most important information I gleaned was that Chloe was at the Fulcrum Theater!

The sign-off was "Submitted," indicating that the report was destined for someone. Apparently, the keeper of the files made regular entries. Whether or not these were for his own uses, I could not be certain, but from such notations as "I'm supposed to. . ." I gathered that he submitted the originals of his findings to his employer and that these were his own copies. I guessed that the originals went to Mefisto and Vigrid, although I couldn't be sure. There might be someone else whom I didn't know.

As soon as I could, armed with one of Breakout's many skeleton keys, I sneaked back upstairs to the tower. I chose nighttime, because it seemed that the keeper of the files was out and about his nefarious business more often at night. But it was spooky as hell up there, with the wind susurrating through the roof gardens, all sorts of odd noises like the clatter of a spoon to the floor, the sounds of someone grinding his teeth, whines, squeaks, and whinnies, and I couldn't be sure there weren't hidden cameras tracking my every movement. The reporter was a spy, after all.

Armed with a mini-Cameramatic, I photographed a page or two of each file and then came back for the ones that seemed more interesting. For hours, I read in my own room which also might have spy equipment in it for all I knew, cameras squirreled among the curlicues on the ceiling, perhaps, or nestled in Cupid's bow or soundlessly clicking in the ornately carved bedstead or even microphones in the Tiffany lamp or the library shadow box, picking up my throat-clearings and private exclamations.

There was the thick file on Mickey, detailing every moment of his wretched life — his early nose-picking and prick-greasing and attempts to rub out his pockmarks with a variety of creams, his grapplings with a barmaid that ended in shame, and his tricking Dickybird into joining the "acting" troupe. With simple Latin phrases inserted among the English, the reporter described Carl's suggestion that Mickey cover Damon One's face with a *pulvinus*, and when they all piled on, no one would know who did it, and no one would suffer *culpa* for what was apparently only one of Carl's several snuff *picturae*. There was a section in code that I couldn't read, of course, not having the key. "So it was Mickey who killed Damon One!" I exclaimed before I remembered the microphones.

Another report detailed Mickey's negotiations with Carl over Damon's whereabouts, Carl's sleazy promises (that a man with bifocals smeared in Vaseline could see through), and Mickey's leading Carl down the steps to where Damon cowered in the dark *cum cratererae gelatus*, calling on Leroy to rescue him. Near the end, the mysterious words "referred to action." The account of Mickey's subsequent fate included ominous references to his *lavatio acidus,* and the attacks by a succession of perverts that followed, pervs who made him do disgusting things and then reviled him for them, punctuated by Mickey's *desiderium mortis* in tragicomic conflict with his *timor mortis.* The file itself was marked CLOSED in red capitals on the front. No more could be done to Mickey.

The file on Carmine was thinner than his corpulence warranted, including his grand *vexatio* of a succession of little boys over the years, as they evolved from touches *furtivus* to open gropings to *fellatio*; his snipes at his artists, his wondrous changes of mind over the quality of the works submitted to him which transformed the paintings from brilliant evidence of genius to unsaleable retro dreck once Carmine had no more use for the body behind them; his devastating put-downs of Kenny preceded, Gregory learned, by little *tête-à-têtes* with Carl at which *gratia* of Carl's *pueri* were exchanged. Carl wanted Kenny home, just as many husbands want their wives where they "belong." Carmine's ending was graphically described, including even the investigation. As with Mickey's, Carmine's file was stamped CLOSED.

A page that I'd accidentally grabbed in my haste was one of a whole report in front of a file drawer. The contents of the page, part of them in poetry, indicated that someone, a woman apparently, had brought a man up to her apartment at nine o'clock on Christmas night. The visit ended in disagreement ascertained by microphones.

The reporter's signature appeared throughout his files, as the single word "Watcher." Whether or not he had another name and this was just his code, it was impossible to tell. Pleaser, Bounce, and Breakout had names that reflected their more salient characteristics. So it's reasonable to suppose that, like them, Watcher calls himself by his main activity. Does he watch us as well? Probably so. It would explain my feelings of being spied upon when the hairs on my neck stand at attention, and I begin to panic. These panic attacks aren't neurotic after all, but based on legitimate animal instinct. If he's always watching, none of us has the privacy I've tried to ensure; all of us are exposed to this Watcher's contacts, whoever they might be. The traitor thrives inside the walls like a disease that creeps up on its prey and destroys before he or she has a chance to recognize it and prepare for combat.

After making copies, I returned the reports and searched in vain for one on myself.

What reward or payment does this Watcher receive for his assiduous attention to the affairs of others? He has room and board upstairs in the tower, of course, his trash revealing yogurt cartons and little else. Not that I'd stoop to snoop, just that I happened to be passing by in the roof garden one day, enamored with the views of Puget Sound, the Olympics, the Cascades and the city itself, when I noticed the trash container lid off, and a simple inclination of my head revealed Watcher's main diet. He has his garden and his poetry.

Why else does he do it? Possibly, he's compelled to spy by the very people to whom he reports. If so, what is the threat? The unwanted ministrations of Mefisto and Vigrid, perhaps, who might cut out his tongue, so he could no longer speak in verse?

But, no, I don't think it's a threat that keeps Watcher at his post, night after night. I think that he betrays a sense of deficiency; he seems to yearn to know how "normal" people live. He, like many Onlys, is under the delusion that there's such a thing as a "normal" person with a "normal" family. As if he's been only half-created but abandoned with parts missing.

The next night, we were sitting around the dining table eating a healthful vegetable and cheese casserole that Wendy, still invisible, had prepared. We were discussing Chloe's disappearance, where she might be, and what we could do to get her back. Suddenly, a high falsetto voice rose up like an ethereal emanation above our heads, singing *Jesu, Joy of Man's Desiring*.

"What's that?" Leroy asked in amazement, looking heavenward in the direction from which the voice came.

"It's Pleaser," I said, wondering, as I often did, how I knew such things.

The voice had moved on to an *a cappella* rendering of the entire violin and piano accompaniment.

"Oh, my God," said Leroy. "That's the most beautiful voice I've ever heard."

Still clinging to the thin hope that I could figure the code key book, I visited Mefisto and Vigrid's lab again. If they were there, I'd tell them that I'd come to see them about what they'd done to Pleaser and to plead with them not to hurt any of the others in our family — or our friends. I planned to do this anyhow, since Leroy wasn't much help. But, as usual, their lab was empty. Either they existed on another plane, where I had no access, or they were there during the day, when I was at work at my computer company.

Intent on returning *Rack, Rope, and Red-Hot Pincers,* I headed for the bookcase. This time, I noticed something odd. The whole section was about torture, of course, classics in the field. But pushed right in among the middle of them, between *Torture down the Ages* and *The Art of Pain,* was *The Oxford Book of English and American Verse.* What would Mefisto and Vigrid be doing with a book of poetry? My memory flashed to all the poetry books in the Watcher's bookcase. Could this be the key?

I didn't take it. Instead, on a piece of paper, I listed the name, editor, and edition, so that my record of the pages would be the same. I could get a copy from the local library. As I wrote, the ceiling light flickered several times, and I knew that those on the other side were aiding me, because my cause was just.

Back in Watcher's tower room, I noticed for the first time that there were section dividers among the files. Whether they were new or had been there all along, I simply could not recall. To my horror, I realized that Chloe's files were new and in a section labeled ACTIVE. My heart shivered, and my hands shook so hard I could barely work the camera; I photographed the latest entries. There was a whole bunch of active files on Becca Merrow as well, but I wasn't nearly as concerned about her as about Chloe. Why was the Watcher reporting on Chloe? Could she be their next victim? I returned to my room to read.

Everything about Chloe's adorable little life was in there, the "fellas" she'd known, her love of cheese, her secret rehearsals early in the morning before the cast and crew arrived, her long practice make-up sessions, her work painting sets, ironing costumes, selling tickets — a one-woman stage-crew was Chloe and a boon to this small community theater that couldn't afford to pay. Her sweet love-making with Damon, her extravagant care of Go-Go, and her disappearance from the theater, leaving Damon devastated, were also chronicled. But there was more. After the Fulcrum Theater, Watcher had tracked her to another, Pioneer Square Community, where she had a small part in a play and was involved with the director. I resolved to go and see for myself.

What earthly reason would Mefisto and Vigrid have for selecting Chloe as Watcher's assignment? If that was how this worked. It wasn't as if they were involved with her. They could care less if Damon's heart was broken. Or my own, for that matter. Leroy was enthusiastic about painting her nose, but its disappearance wouldn't incite his wrath and, by extension, Mefisto's and Vigrid's. What possible interest could these two brutal brothers have in sweet Chloe? Then again, I couldn't be sure this Watcher reported to them. There might be someone else entirely. Another brother, perhaps? Perhaps even God?

Speak of the devil, here came the Pleaser shambling into the dining room for dinner.

At first, I didn't recognize him. Thin, gaunt even, his hair disheveled about his shoulders, a musty fusty smell about him, his frame was clothed in a loose shirt and baggy "harem" pants that made him look more like a girl than a young man who had driven cops and old ladies to sexual ecstasy in his younger years. At least, he was cleaner than he had been, his shirt washed, his hands positively scrubbed.

Leroy looked abashed at his entrance, Wendy bustled to set an extra place, Damon exclaimed, "Pleaser!" as if he were actually glad to see him, Bounce and Breakout smirked to each other but kept their smart remarks to themselves, for once.

"Pleaser!" I greeted him, trying to inject a little warmth into my welcome as was my duty, although I had no idea to what extent Pleaser blamed me for his catastrophe.

"I'm not the Pleaser anymore," he said, his voice more vibrant than I remembered. "I pleased a few cops since it happened, but of course I get no pleasure from it, and they tired of that pretty quick. I miss them," he added, his voice choked off. "But I have a new life now."

"That's the spirit," I said lamely, then trying to bridge the awkward moment. "Good to see you again, Pleaser." I bit my lip, but I didn't know his new name.

The boy previously known as Pleaser didn't return the compliment. Instead, he helped himself to Wendy's green bean and corn salad with capers and vinaigrette. He stared at it, as if he were casing it, and finally balanced a kernel on his knife.

"As I said, I'm not the Pleaser. I assumed you all guessed that."

A flurry of nods and murmurs, with a snicker from Bounce echoed by Breakout.

"What are you?" Bounce asked brashly.

"He doesn't have to say," said Wendy.

"That's okay. I'm the Singer now."

"The Singer!"

"As in soprano?" asked Breakout.

"As a matter of fact, yes. Don't knock it. Young boys, before they change, have beautiful soprano voices, in case you didn't know. In ancient medieval times, they cut off their balls to keep those voices. It was an honor. They were known as the *castrati*."

"But," Bounce argued, "you'd already developed."

"True. For some reason, I got my voice back anyway."

"That's wonderful," breathed Wendy, setting a blueberry banana milk shake in front of him, the first we'd seen in weeks. "I hope you'll sing for us sometime."

"In fact, I think we heard you the other night," I said. "Really, a tremendous voice. Really. Tremendous."

"It takes a lot of practice," Singer said, slurping appreciatively. "I spend my days learning how to breathe."

"Breathe?"

"Breathe."

"You mean, like this?" Bounce and Breakout heaved their chests alternately, each one more dramatic than the other.

"No. Like this."

Singer didn't breathe any differently that I could see, but there was now a chorus of deep breaths until Wendy said, "I'm getting dizzy."

"Wendy, are you making shakes for us, too?" Bounce appealed.

"In honor of our brother's return," Breakout added.

"A celebration. Yes, indeed."

"Then I have to read the music and attend rehearsals," Pleaser continued. "Don't ask me to demonstrate. I'm in a choir now. We're traveling around to various churches, hospitals, and senior and community centers, and we lighten a lot of lives."

"How brave!" said Wendy, her arm around Singer's neck, now that no one could misconstrue her actions (and the neck was clean). I'd always suspected she had a thing for Pleaser. Maybe she hoped he might still have a little of his special talent left, although it was incestuous and totally wrong, and "Little Miss Shouldn't" wouldn't. Girls don't understand what happens to a boy when he undergoes Pleaser's type of metamorphosis. They don't get the specific biology of it.

"It's my choice. One must sacrifice for one's art," he said, dipping a clean finger into the shake and extracting a morsel of banana.

"That's right," said Leroy. "Sacrifice. That's what it's all about."

"And that's what I did."

"You didn't exactly have a choice," said Bounce.

"Neither did you," said the Singer cryptically.

Neither Bounce nor Breakout recognized it for the insult it was.

"I'm sorry for what happened," I mumbled to him at the door. Was I truly? This Singer seemed easier to control, his rebellion nipped, so to speak.

"Leroy isn't."

"What? Sorry?"

"Do you think?"

"I'm not sure."

"Anyway," Singer said, "like a lot of disasters, it may be for the best."

I tried to nod, as if I fervently believed it might be so. Singer had never been given to trite homilies, and this additional change in him was disconcerting.

"I'm late for rehearsal," he said.

He'd be back. A constant reminder of danger. But where else could he go? It was this family or none at all. Pathetic, really.

What should I do about Chloe? Damon kept bemoaning her absence, but I wasn't about to reveal her whereabouts. I told myself that it was to protect her, that the fewer people who knew where she was, the better, that Damon couldn't protect Chloe the way I could. None of this was true, of course. Obviously, the Watcher knew, as well as whoever hired him.

Later, when Damon had given up on Chloe and found someone else to love, I'd take her away to that safe beach town in Oregon, where I'd marry her and give her babies, and she'd be the star of the tiny theater on the pier, and dare I dream it, we might even live in a little house with a white picket fence, the seagulls screeching and diving as I fed them stale bread crumbs.

But now, I had to save her. Should I pay her a visit and warn her that she's in danger? Tell her to flee, that I would join her in this little beach town later? Would she believe me? She'd think I was Damon, after all, a tad changed in appearance, but once I introduced myself, she'd begin to see the resemblance. She was accustomed to thinking of Gregory as one of the voices inside Damon's head. She'd think he was crazy again. "Weird."

With a library copy of *The Oxford Dictionary of English Verse*, I reread Chloe's file. The broader decoding supplied me with a chilling motive for Mefisto's and Vigrid's interest. As Watcher wrote in code, they'd only "done" one other *femina* before. I read the sentence several times before I grasped the full implications. Chloe or Becca. I am ashamed to relate that I'd rather it was Becca, rather a stranger than a person who was practically a member of the family. Torture took the place of sex in Vigrid's and Mefisto's lives, and to torture a woman seemed preciously exciting to them.

First, extracting a promise of secrecy from Leroy, I told him that Chloe was in danger from Mefisto and Vigrid, and no, I couldn't reveal how I knew.

"They've been talking about doing another woman for some time," Leroy says. "Apparently they didn't learn enough details on Dessa. Hadn't proceeded slowly enough. But I had no idea they'd gotten this far. That's a shame. Chloe's a cute little baggage, that one."

"You love her nose, remember?"

"Indeed, I do. But I never did get to paint it, did I? Had to do it from memory. Not as effective."

"You have the influence with Mefisto and Vigrid that I don't."

"Matter of fact, I don't either, not like I used to. I tried to keep them off Pleaser at the last minute."

"You did! Why?"

"Don't know, exactly. God knows, I was mad enough. But the remedy seemed excessive. I asked them to just beat him up. They wouldn't even listen. They were so excited about what they were going to do to him. 'We have this new operation we want to try. It's you or Pleaser, Leroy. You get to choose.' Well, naturally. . ."

"I've gone by several times to talk to them. They're never there."

"That's funny. They're always there when I need them. As for your talking to them, I wouldn't advise it, even if you can find them. Fact is, they're not in a talking mood. They say Chloe's been unfaithful to Damon, and what gets done to one gets done to all."

"That's just an excuse."

"Maybe so, but they say she's got to pay.

"Becca's another top choice."

"Becca! How do you know that? Maybe we could convince them to do a stranger."

"What exactly is it that they do?"

"I don't want to know. Do you?"

This can't go on, this threat to family members and friends. As the responsible member of this community, I've got to do something. At least, I can try. I love Chloe enough to take the risk.

In broad daylight, I climb the stone steps to Mefisto and Vigrid's lab and torture chamber. I knock, and the door swings open. I call, but no one answers. I can't reach them. They're still unavailable to me.

Another thought bangs around in my head that I'd discarded numerous times.

I could turn them in. How would I do that, exactly? And to whom? The police wouldn't believe I was Gregory any more than Chloe would. And Vigrid and Mefisto might communicate with me at long last. In horrible ways.

40

I AM THE WATCHER.

Look out your window
To the doorway across the street
Sunken in darkness.
    Like a bruised eye,
         I am.
You do not see me until I move,
Then only my absence.
The door is simply
Shut.

Or you may catch me as I steal the light
Beyond the branches, maple or magnolia,
Gesturing in the wind, like a mad mother
    Over her "disappeared."
Among the black reflections on the lawn,
I am the still one.

I stand and watch you. Why?
It's what I do,
My job — I don't know how —
I didn't interview.
You think I'm but a shadow.
    You are right.
            I shadow you.

            I watch to see what you do
And how.
    I envy your "normal life,"
            Almost.
Watching's better.

Me?
I come from a distinguished line —
Those who report on what's been seen
By others like myself
On the ten o'clock news.
    You watch.
You savor other people's memories
To forget your own.

I was born immaculate, they say,
In a book with others like myself. God
Kept me in secret places
So no one knew.
Concealed in night, like Him
I watch over you,
    But not to save you.

Damon does not remember what Carl did.
    Why would he want to?
            There is a shadow where the memory lived.
Leroy disguises pain with cerulean blue,
    Creates of it a Heaven,

Just as the old masters hid
    A true painting that betrayed them
With a false, more pleasing to the eye —
    False memory.
Robbie has been cast out
For images that others do not want.
And Gregory? He's terrified
Of shadows flickering from light to dark
    With messages from the front.

I prophesy.
They will lay waste the places that I live.
Sky shatters into shards that fall to earth
    And splinter trees.
Which memories will survive?
    Which crucified like Carmine?
Blood runs in rivulets incarnadine
    Across mosaic fish.
    They wriggle into concrete, seek escape,
    Their creators killed.

The Fury and the Torturer of Nerves
Tell me to watch her.
    It's what I do.
I keep her dossier like a proper spy
Coded against your knowledge in files organized
To conceal. You are no one
Unless there is a file on you.
    (Is there one on me?)

I am the cloud of all-knowing,
Remembering nothing.
    Why would I want to?

41

THAT NIGHT, TO SAVE Chloe's life, we approached the Pioneer Square Community Theater, an unprepossessing old brick edifice flanked by art galleries and guarded by twenty-foot-high totem poles on which the homeless regularly relieved themselves. The marquee advertised *The Crucible* as the theater's next production. We slipped down stairs as steep as a ladder to a basement that must have been part of the underground. Rebuilding Seattle after the 1889 fire had been a simple matter of erecting the new over the old. Entire banks, bakeries, barbershops, haberdasheries, fabric emporiums, pharmacies, cobblers, hatteries, whorehouses, and vaudeville theaters were bricked in, their history sealed. We nearly smothered in the dank air that had been stuffed between these walls for more than a hundred years.

Crews were painting scenery and sewing costumes, a step up from Chloe's team of two and assorted visitors at the previous place. But Chloe wasn't there.

Upstairs, we discovered her on stage among a group of pilgrim girls, dancing near hysteria around a forest fire, while Tituba swung a rubber chicken over her head. Chloe'd been promoted to the cast and was no longer obliged to do scut work. We sat in the back of the darkened theater. The rehearsal was kind of tedious, actually, the director breaking it off every few sentences to block the action with "cross downstage," and the like, which the actors dutifully recorded on their play scripts.

When they took ten, Damon and I stole backstage and approached Chloe, who sat with a lot of other cast members in front of a long mirror. Squeezed into a black leotard, tights, and a short skirt, an inch bustier than I remembered, her yarn hair lightened to platinum, a dot of red on each cheek like Raggedy Ann, her sweet-smelling mouth pursed over her script, she picked up a powder puff.

"Oh, Damon, is it you? You startled me! What are you doing here? How did you find me?"

Go-Go, looking as though he was getting plenty of cheese, recognized us immediately and waddled over for a pet.

"Gregory found you, actually."

"Not that again!"

"Why did you leave me, Chloe? I thought we had a thing going."

"Don't start with that," I hissed at him.

She shrugged her adorable bird shoulders, studying him speculatively in the mirror, her eyes darkly circled.

"Nothing personal, Damon."

"I thought we were very personal. I mean, having sex, that's personal in my book."

"It's just sex," she shrugged again. "Time to move on. You said yourself you don't like staying in one place for long."

"I was talking about jobs."

"You said so yourself. You never get anywhere if you stay in one place. I've got a part in this one. I'm a pilgrim. They weren't getting anywhere in Europe, so they moved on, see? That's the way it goes."

"I'll take over now," I said to Damon. "Hi, Chloe, I'm Gregory, Damon's brother."

"Now, Damon, no more of your stupid weird stuff."

"Samantha," a man with a beard and sideburns down to his moustache butted in, carrying a clipboard, "We need you to read Ronnie's part. Who the hell are you?" he demanded of me in a heavy accent.

"Damon," said Chloe.

"Gregory," I said at the same time.

"Damon Hearst, this is Fyodor Tchelichevsky, our director."

"Hearst? Her brother? In that case, I won't throw you out on your ass if you're gone two minutes ago."

She was Samantha Hearst now? The next instant, I forgot.

"Chloe, I have to talk to you," I said.

"No, you don't."

"No one's allowed back here during rehearsal," said Fyodor.

We ducked outside and waited for the rehearsal to end, hugging the bricks so we didn't have to mingle with the smells of cheap wine, urine, and vomitus a few yards off. The totems could not protect us from these, having grown tall in an age when the dangers were merely wild animals and tribes — their spirits at war with others you couldn't see. Although, come to think of it, unseen spirits might help us now. Occasionally, I caught a glimpse, just at the corner of my eye — a shadow humping the night wind like a kite and then folding into itself. I could no longer tell myself that it was my imagination.

The time passed quickly as Damon and then I took the spot, and then both of us fell into reverie while others had their chance, Singer perhaps in his choir or Leroy in a gallery or Bouncer or Breakout at the stadium bar or even the Watcher on his appointed rounds. Before we knew it, the troupe was pouring out of the theater, Chloe in her white ermine jacket, her cute little booty encased in gold lame spandex, and a string of pearls studded with an occasional diamond hastily twisted through her hair. She floated like a movie queen on Fyodor's arm, which imprisoned hers. Even now she might be spinning a story about Damon, a "fella I knew once." At present, except for the oddly moving shadows, she seemed safe.

"Chloe," I said, planting myself squarely in front of them. "We have to talk."

"Damon, I told you, no."

"Is he bothering you?" asked Fyodor, whose every feature, every pore, in fact, ran to oil so that he looked incapable of physical defense. Probably the *raison d'être* for his facial covering.

"No, no. Okay, one minute, Damon."

"I'll be right over here," said Fyodor, posting himself beside the totem in a puddle of urine unaware, while a raven piled onto a bear on an Orca to escape the bums' most recent outpourings, and frogs peeked out all around.

"Chloe, I don't want to alarm you," I said. "There's just a possibility that you may be in danger. You remember what they did to Pleaser," aware that I was sounding disjointed in my haste to get everything in before Fyodor interrupted us for the final time.

"Silly! I'm not scared of your imaginary friends." But she seemed to cringe into the ermine as she said it. That was the change that had come over her. "I had one when I was a child even," she went on. "You're supposed to outgrow them."

"They're upset with you because you left Damon." Their socially desirable excuse. The real reason, that they were psychopaths looking for a woman on whom to experiment, was too grisly to tell her.

"Damon, if this is your way of trying to get me back —"

"Couldn't you move somewhere else for a little while? The Oregon seashore, maybe? A little beach town? I don't think they'd find you there."

"Damon, you really are crazy, you know?"

"I don't like being called that," Damon burst through. "It upsets me when you call me that."

"Haven't you heard the saying, 'the show must go on'? We open in three weeks. I have to help Abigail bear witness against the witches. They aren't really, you know," she confided. "And that's an important lesson."

"I'm talking about your survival," I insisted, trying to impress her with the urgency of the situation.

"This is my big break."

"You can't catch a break if you're dead."

"Someone's been following me. It wasn't you, was it?"

"No, but that's what I mean."

"What do you know about it?" Fyodor demanded, striding up to us and thrusting his oily pores into my face. Evidently, his hearing was acute.

Was there any way of putting a normal spin on 'Fisto and Vigrid and Watcher?

"And there was this dead mouse in my bonnet, all bloody and

matted and gutted like a fish," Chloe said, shuddering as Fyodor put a comforting hand on her arm.

"One of your pets?"

"Poor little thing. They trusted me, you know?"

"You took their cheese," Damon observed rather dryly for him.

Chloe either didn't hear or ignored it. "Jealousy, probably."

"Are you responsible for that?" Fyodor demanded.

"No, Damon wouldn't hurt a fly," Chloe protested. "He'd up-chuck first."

I supposed I should feel flattered, but I didn't.

"And the cheese covered with ooky stuff."

"Don't forget Go-Go," Fyodor reminded her.

"What happened to Go-Go?" I asked, suddenly nauseous. Shades of Pleaser with Noodles a long time ago. Singer wouldn't, would he?

"Cut in the belly."

"Sliced," Fydor added.

"We had to rush him to the vet, who sewed him up, but he's still bloated."

"Drags his intestines around like a luggage cart. They scrape the floor."

"That was when we moved in with Fyodor. Fyodor, just give us another minute." Chloe turned an enticing smile on him under which he seemed to melt.

Fyodor returned to his post, thrumming his fingers on a frog's head, but I reminded myself that Fyodor could still hear us.

"Do me a favor," I said hurriedly. "Don't go anywhere alone."

"I don't. I'm always with Fyodor now. Aww, Damon, never mind him," she whispered intimately. "He's nice for a director. No need for you to be jealous. We sleep together, he's got a king bed and ev-erything, but we don't sleep together. We're just trying to figure out what turns him on. For me, it's missionary work." He'd never heard it called that before. "Not even." She leaned over and whispered into what she thought was Damon's ear. "He can't even come when he's on top. Like this fella I knew once —"

"Samantha, we have to go." It sounded more like an order than a suggestion.

"I can't sleep with you, you know. Pilgrim girls are supposed to be chaste."

"You're not on stage now."

"But I'm getting into the role. See? I even wear a white cap, all modesty like," she said, digging into her fake leopard skin purse and extracting it. "'Bye, Damon. Be well."

So Chloe thought this Fyodor could protect her against the likes of Vigrid and 'Fisto! She had no idea of how brutal they could be. Damon and I had never told her about Mickey and Carmine and Dessa. Oh, she'd heard the names, but we hadn't told her the gory details. When she held me to her bosom on the horrible night of Pleaser's operation, she endured my agony but heard nothing herself. Besides, she was moving up in the theater world. She wanted to believe it was malicious jealousy or her imagination, and not really threatening, and that Fyodor, that poor excuse for a celebrity, could save her. How could I? I couldn't bear the thought of dear, sweet Chloe —

"Maybe it isn't as bad as you think," Damon said, ever the great denier.

"I've seen the files," I reminded him.

42

"GREGORY! GREGORY! YOU'VE GOT to come!" They were shouting themselves hoarse up the stairs.

Bounce and Breakout's gymnasium-sized sanctuary of brilliant primary colors was a shambles. Appalled, I surveyed the wreckage as the twins picked their way through it, a shredded basketball net, posters of rock stars hanging in strips, unidentifiable yellow and green splinters of furniture, slashed red and blue sofa cushions, crumbled CDs — not just broken in half but shattered. They held up each object and rotated it to see if any piece could be salvaged, then hurled it across the room. Barely recognizable TV parts crunched beneath their sneakers. Uncharacteristically, both twins were in tears.

"'Fisto broke in while we were playing basketball," Breakout sniffled, wiping his nose on his sleeve. "It bounces against the walls sometimes, y'know?"

Sometimes?

"Doesn't make *that* much noise."

Typically, there wasn't a tissue to be had, so I gave them my packet.

"We had the TVs on, too, don't forget."

"All of them?" I asked, trying to gauge the intensity of sound from a dozen TVs.

"No point in playing just one. It only shows one game at a time."

"We like to sort of coordinate."

"There's a rhythm to them."

"What happens in one game sort of gets repeated in the others."

"Or the opposite of that," nodded Bounce sagely.

"And the radios and CDs. 'Fisto just barged in and smashed everything with a baseball bat."

"Said if we didn't keep it down, he'd flatten us so we'd never get up again."

"Didn't ask first?"

"Hell, no! They do it for kicks. 'Fisto was giggling like a madman. He yanked our TVs from the ceiling and had at them with his bat."

"We tried to stop him."

"Had him down."

"Didn't whack him hard enough."

"He apologized."

"So we let him up. Fair play and all."

"Shouldn't have done that."

"Knocked us loopy with the bat."

"Smashed our goal posts —"

" — Just for spite."

"He's that strong."

"Tore our baseball mitts with his teeth."

"Have you seen his teeth? *Wolf* teeth."

"Stomped our baseballs until they're mush. Look, see?"

I'd never seen the stuffing of a baseball before — a mess of latex-coated rubber, wool, and polyester in which I could barely spot the cork.

"We tried to stop him, we knocked him to the floor and pinned his arms —"

"But he's an animal."

"Stronger than the both of us put together."

"Just roared and tried to poke my eyes out."

Both twins hyperventilating.

"Stomped my stomach with those hambone legs of his."

"Said if he had to come down again, he'd bring Vigrid with him, and Vigrid would take us apart."

"Bone by bone."

"Wait a minute," I said. "They can hear you way up there in their quarters? The floors are stone a foot thick at least."

"Heard us going up the stairs."

"They're scary, man," said Bounce, and I'd never been so aware that they were still fuzzy-cheeked teenagers, barely eighteen and wet behind the ears, probably virgins except for what they did with each other, which I wasn't sure counted.

"It's not an even playing field when they're around."

"You gotta take control, man."

Why me?

"We've been thinking of moving."

I kept quiet again about the fact that they couldn't. Not permanently. They needed to feel free. Even if they got another room, they'd lose more time than they'd gain peace, what with the commute between their dream home and this, their real one.

But the worst was yet to come.

Was it my imagination, or was that an alarm ringing in my head? I'd never heard it before and didn't know what it meant. Was it a fire? A burglar? The police finally coming to arrest us for Carmine's murder because the evidence had exposed us, and without Pleaser, we had no defense?

I dove down the stairs, Singer and Leroy meeting me half way, then Damon. In the babel of voices I made out, "Wendy." "They did it." "Fading fast."

Did what to Wendy?

I'd never been to Wendy's room before. It hadn't occurred to me. In all my searches, I'd missed it somehow. I think I'd assumed that she didn't have one, perhaps because she was always in the kitchen or the dining room. *They* were her home, an assumption I now realize was politically incorrect.

The door to the basement stairs hung open on one hinge. Of course, that was why I'd missed it. I'd never thought of going down there.

First, the caterwauling of the children. Damon and I both clapped our hands to our ears. As we descended, the stench became unbearable, and we tried to move one hand to our noses. Back and forth, ears and noses, finally we buried our noses in our shoulders, making our descent unbalanced, precarious even, especially since babies swarmed the bottom steps.

A thin layer of carpet coated the cement floor, where babies and toddlers writhed in diapers that leaked feces out the sides over rashes on their pathetic little thighs, as they screamed red-faced, tears drooling down their cheeks to their bare chests, hair wet with grieving, shaking their pudgy arms in helpless frustration, some crying rhythmically, "Na, na, na, na." No wonder I'd never been down here! It was cold, and baby blankets piled unused in little mounds among bottles of curdled milk strewn about the room, because Wendy wasn't around to tend them. One toddler picked up a bottle, sucked a minute, then hurled it with a cry, hitting an infant who set up a squall of breathless rage.

Leroy and Singer led us to the open door of Wendy's room. We paused uncertainly. On the virginal single bed, beneath the blue statue of her Blessed Mother, our Wendy lay naked and shivering in a spreading red stain around her young girl's hips, the blood far brighter and more real than the haze of her. Forcing myself to enter the room, I picked up a blanket and covered the cold nakedness of her little boy chest.

"Sweet Amanthus," she said so lowly I almost couldn't hear her.

"Her doll," Leroy explained.

Then I noticed for the first time that her room was a virtual doll collection torn limb from limb, their heads twisted around their shoulders. It would be impossible to figure out which was the one she wanted.

"She needs a doctor," I said.

"Well, we got a nurse in the house," said Singer. "Course, he's the one did her."

"Is that true?" I asked Wendy.

She whimpered, saying, "They had to learn my body. They put things in. They cut me inside. It hurt. I begged them."

"Maybe to know more about the woman they're going to do," suggested Singer. "When they were doing me, they'd say things like, 'In a woman you do it this way. There isn't any whatever to do it that way.' I knew they were planning to do another woman. They're quite excited about it, actually. They'll get us all eventually. They'll even get caught and put in jail, and we'll have to go with them."

To what extent his words were motivated by truth and to what extent by revenge, I couldn't judge.

"I'll take her to the hospital," I said, wrapping the blanket around her and lifting her, surprised to find her weightless.

"They're not going to be able to see her," Leroy reminded me.

"I'll bring her in and let her take the spot," I told him, forgetting that she'd never done that before and might not know how. But I was desperate not to lose her.

At the hospital, a doctor found her bleeding and unconscious on a gurney in the hall.

When I got back, I said to Leroy, "You've got to get me a meeting with Mefisto and Vigrid."

"I don't even know how to do that."

"Maybe we could go up together. Maybe they'd see me if I was with you."

"Who the hell are you?" 'Fisto demanded, appearing at the entrance in biker leathers and nail heads and acknowledging Leroy. The lab was in full production — pots and beakers with different colored liquids bubbling away, acrid smells, autoclaves, and steel bowls of what looked and smelled like rotting liver, kidneys, intestines, and other entrails. I struggled not to faint, deep breaths of clean, sweet air unavailable to me.

"What you did to Wendy was horrible," I said, barely controlling my anger. "You raped and tortured an innocent virgin. It's inhuman. It's got to stop."

"Yeah? What are you gonna do about it?"

"I'm telling you. The family won't tolerate it."

"Family be damned! We're just a bunch of strangers live together. You like to think you're the godfather. You're the head of nothing," Fisto spat.

"We need the body parts," Vigrid spoke up for the first time. "This is science we're doing. Most people don't understand science, but you look like an intelligent fellow."

"We don't like meddlers. Tell him what we do to people don't mind their own business," said 'Fisto, nudging Vigrid.

Vigrid had been sizing me up, cocking his head to his right and then to his left like a hawk, as if he might be able to read me, my thoughts and character. Finally, he said,

"You might like to try it."

"Try what?"

"Why, torture, of course. You're in complete control, you know. You put a nerve on a slide and — take a look through the microscope. You prick it with a pin, and see? It wiggles. You burn it with a lighter flame, it contracts. In fact, it gets to the point where it contracts before you even burn it. The mere heat of the flame, the mere lighting of it. Now, that's learning. Nobody can say different. Here, you try," he urged as I backed away. "See if you don't like it. People get pleasure out of hurting others. It's the great equalizer, the ultimate persuasion tactic. Madison Avenue would love it if they could find a way to torture us into buying their products. 'Buy *Zissiziliquium* or we'll stick pins in places you don't even know you've got'."

"They already do. They hammer our heads excruciatingly."

"Exactly. Greater men than I have said it." Vigrid was stirring a pan of something that sounded like popcorn but smelled like a pigsty. "Adler, for example. People want to be powerful. Power is the great motivator. And what is power? I ask you. What is power?"

I stared at him blankly.

"The power to cause pain, of course. The more pain we can cause, the more important we are. We want to feel significant. You're no different. You want it, too. How do you want it? Let me count the ways," he giggled far beyond what might have been the humor of it. 'Pain, holy pain.' That's De Sade."

He was quite mad.

We should hold a council meeting and take a vote. "Resolved: That 'Fisto and Vigrid cease and desist from torturing anyone else, either in the family or out of it." But what weapons would we have to enforce it? What leverage? How could we pain them enough to obey? We had no jail or even halfway house. We were a community without a system to enforce justice. We'd always been dependent on each other's good will. Now we were at the mercy of an evil far greater than normal human failing.

We could remain vigilant and try to prevent them from taking the spot, someone always awake. But one little slip, and they might wrest it from us. In fact, they might do so anyway. Who of us was strong enough to oppose them?

How many votes could such a resolution get? Mine, of course, and Singer's. And Bounce and Breakout's with their sports home in shambles? Damon would vote, if I could persuade him there'd be less taking the spot. Maybe I could maneuver Robbie into voting for it. He'd do so, if I reminded him that Becca was also in danger. "My Bec-Bec?" he'd ask. Then he'd want to see her and I didn't know what I'd do about that.

Would Leroy vote to restrain Mefisto and Vigrid? They've been pretty good to him, in a manner of speaking. Leroy might want to abstain. Any chance of getting the Watcher with us? He might have an ethical conflict, considering his job. Were any of the children old enough? Hellion, whom Wendy had mentioned? We couldn't ask Wendy.

Of course, anyone who voted for such a resolution put his own life in danger. Or hers. We could end up with a massacre of our entire household. But we could end up with that anyway.

I left a note for Watcher, saying, "Because of your work, Chloe and Becca are in mortal peril. What happens to one of us happens to all. Please rethink your priorities and your relationship to the rest of your family."

Eventually, I got a short poem back, left in the message pocket beside my door.

"The mundane is not my task. It's yours."

The Nuremberg defense.

We all visited Wendy at the hospital, except 'Fisto and Vigrid, of course. Maybe Watcher. Leroy had found Sweet Amanthus, a cloth doll with embroidered blue and pink flowers over her chenille dress, and he had had her mended before bringing her in.

"Gregory, I have to ask you something," Wendy whispered one night, so faintly I could barely hear her.

She lay thin and pale in her hospital gown with the IV bottle of solution measuring her life in drips. I had to bend close to hear her.

"What is it, Wendy? I'll answer if I can."

"Am I —" she broke off, seemingly unable to finish.

"Are you what?"

"Still a virgin?" she choked out.

I struggled to answer and nothing came.

"The Virgin Mary. You see, I've tried to do what she wanted. My whole life. She came to me once."

I must not let the shock show on my face. "You had a vision?"

"In blue." Wendy was in so much pain that she had to struggle to get the words out. "A crown of thorns."

I'd never heard of her appearing this way, but now was not the time to challenge Wendy's experience.

"I can't believe she'd desert you because of something you couldn't help," I said, trying to dig up memories of what I thought might have been my religion once, before I'd been forsaken. "It wasn't your fault."

"Maybe — I tempted them?"

"No, you didn't."

"Never made them shakes. Blueberry. Jealous?" her words great efforts between gasps for breath.

"Wendy, *they* did this, not you."

"My fault. Somehow. I've prayed. The sweet Virgin Mary doesn't come."

"Jesus felt deserted, too," I reminded her. He did, didn't He?

"You didn't answer my question. Am I?"

"I'm sure you are," I told her finally, lying being another of the increasing accomplishments of which I am not proud. "Still a virgin. You're a martyr to her cause," I added in sudden inspiration. "She must be proud of you."

"Not safe anymore. Make it safe, Gregory."

Why were they always telling me it was my responsibility? Just because I'd taken it on my shoulders in the past, did that mean I had to do it forever?

When I got back home, the house was quiet. Singer had gone someplace where a eunuch might be welcome, maybe choir or choral practice. Bounce and Breakout were consoling each other in some bar with their bulked-up cronies, Damon was maybe at a playhouse, Robbie slept, Leroy held his own guilt to himself apart, even 'Fisto and Vigrid made no noise, although I was not so naive as to think that they were chastened. As to the babies, I was unsure. An unnatural quiet emanated up through the floorboards, but I couldn't bring myself to open that door.

I sat in the dining room, where I could watch Damon's light for some sign of counsel. The house was not the same, nor would it ever be. I'd raised them all from childhood, perhaps from the infinity out of which they were born, although I couldn't remember this. We'd all grown together with dreams of who we would become: Leroy, a great painter; Bounce and Breakout, pro athletes guarding bars to pay their way; Pleaser, an athlete of the sexual variety; Wendy, as I found now, a holy virgin mother to us all; Damon, a survivor, perhaps, with a little acting thrown in; Robbie, a found boy instead of a lost one; the babies, just to grow older, perhaps. And myself? What was my dream? A normal Only kind of life, working, married to Chloe, perhaps, with children in that little picket-fenced house. It seemed inane.

Where were those dreams now?

It occurred to me that the only solution, the only way to save us, was to get help. From a counselor? From the police? I'd thought of turning Vigrid and Mefisto in to the police before, but it had stayed just that, a thought.

If I did, what would become of us? I wouldn't confess to murders I had not committed. Perhaps I could just say that there would be others. But then they wouldn't believe me. And the thought of betraying all my people wracked my soul beyond sobs.

The light in Damon's living room was out. Leroy padded down the stairs at last and said it was a burnt-out bulb. I changed it. The next bulb flashed blindingly, and then burned out as well. Something about the wiring, I hoped. Not an ultimate loss of connection to all that had sustained me.

This must be what was meant by the "dark night of the soul."

43

BECCA PREFERRED TO WALK rather than drive the mile between her apartment and the hospital. She needed to stretch her muscles after the cramped tension of the clinic, and some days this was the only exercise she got.

Senior staff required students to fill in for them when they went off to dinner or meetings or the like, so it was dark by the time Becca started home. But Broadway, with the exception of a short three-block section of automobile and window repair shops, as well as hole-in-the-wall emporiums, was alive with cars and people. As long as she kept her wits about her, she didn't feel she was in much danger.

So it was, one mild night, that she was walking home deep in thought and with no wits about her at all, reviewing her day and toting a briefcase filled with clinic memos, copies of articles, and books. Her clinic work was both challenging and frustrating, her supervisory evaluations positive, perhaps because the hospital was so desperate for people to work with the mentally ill that they'd approve anyone whose screw-ups weren't too appalling. Cheap labor!

So engrossed was Becca in her thoughts that she noticed only peripherally the shadow ducking in and out among the cars of the parking lot she was passing. Alarms had only just begun to clang inside her head, when the figure emerged suddenly, a smallish presence, hands thrust deep into his pockets, which Becca recognized as a nonverbal sign of something hidden. A weapon?

Standing on the edge between the car lot and the sidewalk, he asked, "Are you Becca?"

Speedily assessing avenues of escape, Becca slowed. The street was deserted, shops shut for the night, but a gas station on the corner up ahead offered refuge. if she could get to it quickly.

"Yes, I'm Dr. Becca." Increasingly, patients bestowed the title on her, and she felt the need of its distance at this moment.

Her book bag could be a formidable weapon, if she had the strength to wield it. Why hadn't she taken those self-defense classes that McNalley recommended?

The man didn't appear threatening in his faded jeans and leather jacket that had seen better days, a face regular-featured but non-descript. If he attacked, he would not overpower her with strength, but he would be quick and agile. He paused, seemingly uncertain as to what to say next, as Becca moved on slowly, hoping at least to reach the streetlamp. Had he been the figure she'd glimpsed in the chapel? About the same size.

"Did you used to be Bec-Bec?"

Becca's heart lurched from her chest to her stomach.

"Some people have called me that," she said with trained evenness.

"Robbie called you that, didn't he?"

"What do you know about Robbie?" Her feet were transfixed to the pavement.

"He's asleep."

"Asleep where?" Asleep at the dinner hour? Or dead?

"Home. I'm Damon."

"How do you do, Damon. Have you seen Robbie lately?" As she spoke, she resumed her slow progress toward light and other people, without appearing to panic.

"Not lately. He stays up in his room in bed." He walked along the edge of the pavement, not crowding her, but keeping pace. "He was awfully upset that you didn't save him. He went through Hell, and it's your fault."

An odd take on the kidnapping!

"I tried to, but I didn't know where he was. Where is he sleeping?"

"In the attic."

"What attic? Which house? What's the address?"

"I'm not good with addresses. I can follow my nose, that's about it. Pleaser used to be, but 'Fisto and Vigrid cut him, and he's Singer now. I'm not sure if he still knows the way. We have to depend on Bounce and Breakout."

The names rattled her. They sounded like members of a group, but so odd! Was he mentally challenged, perhaps, reciting the nicknames of strangers without realizing that they meant nothing? Or could this be a patient, someone who'd seen her at the hospital and wanted to speak with her? Even if he were, he knew her childhood name as well as her brother's, and evidently knew her route home! It hadn't occurred to her a few minutes ago when he'd taken her by surprise, but alarmed now, she moved more quickly.

Becca managed to maneuver them under a streetlamp. Here in the light, she judged him to be about eighteen, brown hair betrayed by blond roots. Hair dye usually lightens rather than darkens, its purpose to appear more attractive. Darkening, on the other hand, is a disguise!

"How can I find Robbie?" Becca persisted cautiously.

"I don't know. Gregory might. I could ask him."

Becca wasn't sure she'd ever see this Damon again, so she didn't want to chance his disappearance after asking someone with a normal name!

"Where's Gregory?"

"Home, I guess."

"How do you get to his house?" Would it be too risky to go with him?

"The same way you go, except a little farther and then up the hill."

"How do you know where I live?" With steely self-control, she managed to keep the hysteria from her voice.

"Oh, that's easy. We've followed you." Then he added, "Watcher, mostly."

"Is Watcher a person?"

"He follows you for 'Fisto and Vigrid. Gregory says."

"Both of you?"

"Many times, in fact. That's how I knew where you'd be."

"But why?"

"I wanted to know you. You were our sister, once. Uh-oh, Gregory says I've said enough. I have to go."

"Gregory?" Becca looked around, but there was no one else nearby. Perhaps this Gregory had anticipated their conversation before Damon set out and warned him that he shouldn't say too much. "Wait! I need to know where Robbie is."

"Gregory says No," he called back. Without even benefit of a cell phone!

He seemed to fade up the street, and Becca, in spite of her better judgment, hurried after him as quickly as she could with her heavy briefcase. Then he was gone, although Becca knew very well he must still be there.

"You were our sister, once," the words echoed as she reached the busy section of Broadway. But how could that be? She'd only been sister to one. There was nothing familiar about this Damon. She'd never seen him before in her life, although he'd obviously seen her. Could he have been telling the truth about Robbie being asleep? Or was this the cruel prank of a sick mind? Robbie was long dead and gone, or a grown man by now, just five years younger than herself, about the age of Damon. If he spent all his time asleep, he was afflicted with major depression or possibly narcolepsy or even a coma, the result of an accident or illness.

No, this Damon was not to be believed. Too many absurdities in his words. The names he used for supposed people were bizarre. A patient, no doubt of it. Had he been experiencing auditory hallucinations when he said that someone named Gregory had said No to her request to see Robbie? He seemed otherwise rational, although not bright. But delusional patients can appear rational as long as you operate within their system. If Gregory were a real person, he might have cautioned Damon not to lead her to Robbie. If Robbie still existed, which as Becca reminded herself, she must not count on.

She'd keep her eyes out for Damon at the hospital.

When Becca got home, she dropped her briefcase on the sofa with relief and surveyed the place for signs of intrusion as she always did, even though there hadn't been any for a couple of months now, the third set of locks having apparently made entry too difficult. She was beginning to feel at ease here.

Two messages blinked on her machine, one from Annalyn who wanted to chat, and one from a friend. None from Craig, of course. He'd stopped leaving them when it grew apparent that she wasn't going to return them. At the hospital, they ignored each other when they passed in the halls or found themselves in the break room at the same time. If it was necessary for Craig to give Becca instructions, he did so professionally, and she received them in a similar manner. Otherwise, they steered clear of each other.

Sad, in a way. Very sad, in fact. She missed him, their late-night coffees, Thai dinners, and spirited exchanges on the state of the world. She missed the values and experiences that they had in common, and even the erotic fantasies that these fed.

He'd stopped asking about her intruder, of course. It was no longer his concern, and their new relationship afforded him no opportunity. This meant he'd also had to stop asking after her mental health — a relief and the major advantage of their break-up. She was behaving perfectly rationally, and she knew it. Not dissociating one bit. Less, in fact, if you counted erotic fantasy as one form. Without potential, it had faded from her life.

Becca's thoughts returned to Damon, as she reheated the "veggie mess" she'd prepared last night. What, if anything, should she do about him? Could he be her intruder, he and the man Becca thought he alluded to as "Watcher?" A voyeur, perhaps? Could these be her crank callers? They were a group, certainly. Should she tell the police? He'd done her no harm or even threatened her. Her contact with him was little more than the daily contact everyone had with the street people. Except that he knew personal details that ordinary street people did not know.

Becca took her vegetables and leftover chicken into the living room to eat. Her favorite comedy was in reruns, so it couldn't distract her from the events of the past hour. Certainly, if Damon were a patient, she was required to report any outside contact. The problem was, she couldn't be sure. He wasn't *her* patient. She'd never seen him before, either in her office or on the unit. Besides, if the whole experience got back to Craig, he might find a way to discount it as another manifestation of her dissociation! Now she was meeting strange people in the street! He could use it to discredit her. Would he? If there had been a gauge for measuring her paranoia similar to a blood pressure monitor, she'd have hit 200 over 99!

She could ask her supervisor if she should report meetings with people she thought *might* be patients. As soon as she worded this to herself, she heard how absurd it sounded. Perhaps she should hold off and not make a decision tonight. Meanwhile, she could take different routes home, alternating randomly among them, or she could even drive back and forth for a while. If she ran into him again, she could tell him that these meetings were inappropriate, that if he wanted to speak with her, he should make an appointment at the hospital. Of course, if he were an ordinary average guy, he might get insulted at even the suggestion of a mental health problem. But that might get rid of him.

Or it might arouse such ire that he would finally take his hands out of his pockets!

Early one morning, a few days later, Becca was passing the hospital chapel when she heard that beautiful voice again, singing a hymn in Latin. She paused to listen. "*Cantate Domine,*" sang the voice, and then what was almost a trill, "*Ca-a-a-a-a-nticum novum.*" She couldn't be sure that these were the exact Latin words, but this was what it sounded like. When she entered to ascertain who the singer was, she saw no one. The voice seemed disembodied, emanating from nowhere and everywhere. Could it be a recording?

Back in her closet office, a message from Officer McNalley awaited her. After several minutes of trying to get through, she finally reached him. When she identified herself, he immediately preempted her.

"I was just about to call you again. We can't be sure, but we think we may have your stalker."

"Smallish, needs a hair dye job, jeans and old leather jacket?"

"No, as a matter of fact, he's of medium height and well dressed. Why? Have you seen someone you suspected?"

Becca told him about running into someone named Damon on the street, someone who claimed to be following her with another person as well.

"Why didn't you tell us?" asked the officer testily. "You were going to keep us posted."

"I wasn't sure. I thought he might be a patient, although I hadn't seen him here at the hospital." And there was nothing threatening, which you people seem to require, if it's to hold your interest, Becca finished to herself.

"Well, we'll sure want a report from you. Especially if he's saying he's following you." She could hear the noise of papers shuffling in the background, because she was not important enough to require his undivided attention.

It wasn't going well.

"Who's this other person you suspect?" she asked.

"He turned himself in to us a couple of hours ago. Says he knows you. Name's Gregory Warhol. Ring any bells?"

"Damon, the guy who was following me, mentioned a Gregory. But it was all very odd. Seems Gregory's his boss or something."

"The Gregory we have here says you might be in some kind of danger."

"What kind?" Becca's breath had disappeared. I told you so, she wanted to say.

"Nonspecific. Seems he knows the possible perpetrators. They've done it before. We're checking his story and holding him for an interview with the police psychiatrist. Also —" He broke off, muffling the phone with his hand to speak to someone else while Becca twisted in an agony of suspense. "Where were we? Oh, yes, Mr. Warhol says another woman's in danger, too, a Samantha Hearst. Do you know her?"

"Never heard of her."

"Actress? Also goes by the name of Chloe Lippincott?"

"I have no idea. Did he say anything about Robbie?"

"Let's see, now. That would be the brother whose picture got straightened on your wall?"

"Exactly," said Becca, clenching her anger between her teeth.

"No. Is there anyone you can stay with for a few days until we've got a better handle on this?"

Craig, of course. It was Craig whom Becca thought of instantly. But, no, not Craig. "I'll think about it."

"Let me know where you end up." The call ended abruptly.

Not Craig's, of course, not the person who had become her best friend in Seattle, not him. She realized with a flash that she felt too insecure in her mental well-being to spend time with someone who so seriously doubted it. If she wasn't dissociative, then what other serious mental or emotional pathology did she exhibit? If there were one, he'd discover it. Then there was his anger towards her, probably feeling betrayed by her both personally and professionally. After all, she'd cast aspersions on his psychological judgment and on the impact of his dysfunctional family. Following this, she'd withdrawn from him. Finally, she'd had the nerve to prove him wrong every day that she appeared apparently whole, healthy, and competent at the clinic.

She could stay with her mom and the twins, inflicting inconvenience that her mother would be at pains to share. She could even take a leave of absence and fly down to be with Annalyn, Jim, and Nia. All alternatives might put loved ones in danger, if there was anything to the threat that this Gregory believed she was under.

She decided to remain right where she was and await Officer McNalley's report.

Which wasn't long in coming.

Officer McNalley called her again at work the next day.

"Our psychiatrist says there may be some pathology involved. He's referred Mr. Warhol over to Seattle General for an evaluation. You'll be seeing him there."

"Probably not. There are a number of psychiatric units and intake centers here. Besides, it wouldn't be appropriate if I'm personally involved."

"Keep an eye out. See if you recognize him."

When Dr. Craig Austin appeared at her door, he looked drawn, stray strands of hair escaping his ponytail, and even his white lab coat was limp.

"Becca, there's a new patient named Gregory Warhol. Says he knows you."

"The police told me. He doesn't."

"He insists. There are details about you, where you live —" Craig paused, probably not wanting to alarm her.

"That's odd." Becca told him about her meeting with Damon, as Craig slipped into the chair customarily reserved for patients.

"Why didn't you say something?" Now Craig looked anxious — positively unprofessional of him.

"I wasn't sure." She didn't want to raise the delicate matter of her possibly delicate sanity.

"Apparently he thinks there's some threat to your life. I asked Noel to do a special work-up on him. And make it fast." As if speed might offer some measure of protection.

"I can't be part of any of this process, of course."

"Of course not. But I thought you might come round to meet him. Noel has him in Intake B."

44

BECCA HAD NEVER SEEN him before in her life.

Perhaps he did resemble Damon, but only vaguely, of medium build, sporting a yellow shirt that partially concealed a thin gold chain, black pants, a black full-length coat, a diamond stud in one ear.

"I'm glad to meet you at long last," he said, rising from the table, his diction cultured. "I've heard a lot about you."

"Mr. Warhol turned himself in to the police, who referred him here," Noel informed her unnecessarily. "He agreed to come here, because he has some concerns about you."

"The police are looking into it from their end," Gregory said.

"Sgt. McNalley and I have both told her," Craig said.

"It was the only thing left to do," said Gregory, his features taut with torment. "There have been at least two torture-murders, a rape, and a mutilation before this, and, if we don't do something, there are going to be more."

Becca couldn't quite process the parade of violent images his words conjured up, and while she might have expected some connection with Robbie, this wasn't it. The old pain of loss surged again. She nodded to everyone and fled back to her office.

Shortly past four, Craig invited Becca to discuss preliminary impressions with him and Noel in Noel's office.

Arms and legs at all angles from each other, Dr. Noel McKay perched on the edge of her desk, tendrils of dark hair curling across her forehead and down to her lab-coated shoulders. Clutching his clipboard as if it might shield him — or Becca — Craig leaned against a file cabinet, while Becca stood uncertainly in the doorway, wondering again if Dr. Noel was Craig's girlfriend. In an odd quirk of fate, because she had been stalked by their most recent curiosity, Becca was newly admitted to this inner sanctum of consultation among the psych floor elite. Before today, she'd barely glimpsed Noel's office with its posters of Italy obscured by sticky notes.

The goal of their evaluation was either to confirm that Becca was safe or to get her to safety if she wasn't.

"I know you haven't finished interpreting these tests," Craig said, "but I think these killers exist in his imagination only, rather than being real."

"With such names," Noel agreed, "they couldn't possibly be real. I mean, Pleaser? Bounce? Breakout? What kind of names are those?"

"Nicknames, maybe?" Becca ventured.

"What kind of nicknames?" asked Craig.

"They do seem to be part of a complex delusional system," said Noel.

"Exactly. I vote for schizophrenia," said Craig.

Becca reflected that if laypersons ever overheard the "voting" procedure that went on in these rooms, they'd demand write-in ballots. Mystique was what psychologists and psychiatrists sought to project onto the unsuspecting public, not diagnostic elections.

"I'd love to agree with you, Craig," said Noel. "Certainly, there are indications. His fear of the killers might be paranoid, to say the least, and his belief that he is saving lives by reporting them may be a delusion of grandeur."

"There are quite a few paranoid features."

"Yes. His MMPI indicates auditory hallucinations."

"To say nothing of his Rorschach results. So why are you holding out?"

"I have just a suspicion that bipolar disorder may be involved. Only a preliminary take, of course" said Noel, ignoring the ringing phone.

"History of manic episodes?"

"No. But he's certainly depressed. He feels he's betrayed his family. Which doesn't seem to exist. He says he lives with them, but the police sent someone 'round and found only a bachelor pad. They're checking previous addresses."

"The delusions again. What's your take, Becca?"

"Me? My time with him was so brief. I was thinking border-line." She noticed they were listening, even weighing her words, so she pressed on. "As you say, he's depressed, his history indicates panic attacks, and his relationships seem hardly stable."

"Although he has a steady job as a computer analyst," said Craig.

"Well, and of course borderlines do get mixed up with every other diagnosis, sooner or later," Noel nodded at the reasonability of it. "The lamp in his apartment dips when the spirits predict bad things," she reported with a sigh, "and the light comes up when he's making a good decision or when things are going to turn out okay. He even interprets the dips scientifically, to make a kind of scale. Now the lamp's off permanently. Becca, I think it would be helpful if you interviewed him. You might be able to elicit more information. He might feel freer to tell you things since he's under the impression that he knows you. In the presence of one of us, of course."

Becca nodded, well aware that they were obliged to throw Gregory Warhol into a category, with a neat number from the *DSM IV-R* in order to receive insurance. Then there were other tests that Noel wanted to do and still others that Craig suggested.

Noel concluded the discussion with, "I've saved the best for last. Bernie wants me to do the DDIS and the SCID-D." The Dissociative Disorders Interview Schedule and the Structured Clinical Interview for DSM-IV Dissociative Disorders.

"Uh-oh, I guess we all know what that means," Craig joked, appearing relieved that they could find something humorous in the situation, while Becca attempted a grin.

"The diagnosis is set," Noel laughed. "Dr. Bernie sees dissociative identity disorder in every living, breathing thing, including his two dogs," she confided. as if she were telling Becca something she did not know, her friendlier tone implying that Becca wasn't going to undergo her ordeal with anything but support from Noel as well as Craig.

"We're all multiples," quoted Craig. "Different selves appear as needed."

"Sarbin and others call them roles, but Dr. Bernie doesn't like this terminology because it implies that we are all continuously acting, which he doesn't think is true."

They could argue diagnoses until Christmas. If the department chief wanted to see this newest patient, Gregory Warhol undoubtedly suffered from DID.

"It seems Mr. Warhol knows the potential attackers," Craig told her later, as she was charting. "They've done it before. Both in San Francisco and Seattle. Killed, even. Becca," Craig paused to look earnestly into her eyes, "I know we've had our differences. But if there's anything you need — Officer McNalley said you should stay elsewhere for a few days. You're welcome at my place, at least until we get all this sorted out."

Good old Craig! Ever the therapeutic friend!

"Really, Craig, I can go to a hotel." She wouldn't do anything of the sort, of course, preferring home in time of danger, and she was pretty sure Craig knew it.

Craig dismissed the thought with a wave of his hand. "We'll pick up a few things at your apartment, then go to my place, where we'll settle you into the guest bedroom."

Of course! Where else would Craig have her? Certainly not in his bed.

"If Dr. Bernie's right, these characters, Mefisto and Vigrid, may be all in Warhol's head —" Becca protested, as she knew she should.

"We don't know where they are yet."

"But if they're real, they might come after me and put anyone I'm with in danger."

"I can take care of myself. I'm not letting you stay in that apartment alone."

"Not letting me!" The arrogance of it! As if he had the right. And she loved him for asserting it. "The nerve," she smiled.

"Not letting you," he repeated, softening his tone to a less dictatorial level. "We'll go out for a nice dinner at Thai Hai, give you a chance to ventilate and unwind, then we'll make it an early night, or a TV orgy, if you prefer." He seemed to catch himself on the word "orgy," as if he thought it might be inappropriate, but now it was too late. A nurse passing in the hall paused in mid-step, then continued on smoothly, as if she hadn't heard. It'll be all over the hospital that Craig and I are into orgies, Becca reflected grimly, then had to laugh at the absurdity of it. Craig wasn't into orgies with anyone.

Craig's house was in the Green Lake district a few miles from her Mom's and a few blocks up from the main drag which surrounded a nearly three-mile lakefront, bordered by lawns and trees. Here, a sizeable proportion of the Seattle population walked, jogged, biked, in-line skated, wheeled baby carriages, boated, sunbathed, cruised, and held hands while planning their future on a sunny Sunday afternoon. Several paths around the lake accommodated the different styles of exercise.

A blue and white Craftsman bungalow surrounded by hillocks of tulips, daffodils, and hyacinths, Craig's house nestled among many others like it with a view of the lake. Rhododendrons were beginning to bloom their frilly pink and white blossoms among the evergreens. Becca accompanied Craig up the path, surprised at her anticipation. Inside, his dog barked.

The moment they entered, Minnie, Craig's black Labrador, jumped them, so glad to have guests that she "talked" and entertained by chasing her tail. Craig gave her a doggie bone and freshened her water, while Becca looked around. Here was the inside of Craig, the very marrow of his being, a huge room lined floor to ceiling with books, a reading addict's paradise. Squirreled among them, windows looked out on lawn, flowerbeds, and a tulip tree that spread over all.

In the center of the room was a maroon damask sofa, a nod to the more conventional usage of a living room. But it was the books where Craig had spent his life and furnished the inside of himself that intrigued Becca.

"Are they arranged by interest?" she asked in awe, not knowing what else to say.

"By discipline, yes. And then within that by subject area." Craig fairly glowed as he explained his system to her. "Here's Psychology, arranged by subject matter, of course. This is American History. I nearly went into that field instead, American Studies, actually. Mythology and religion, Anthropology, Biology, Sex, of course, on the bottom shelf where it usually is; English including literary novels, popular novels, poetry, and plays," he counted off, indicating the various sections as they passed, "Travel, Reference, Children's Literature including those stories from my childhood. I've mixed the first editions and rare books in with the others by subject matter. At first, I had them in a separate section, but I decided I cared more about their contents than their value." There was also a sizeable collection of videotapes and CDs, and the library spilled over into a room that might have been meant for a spare bedroom or den. But Becca gathered that space wouldn't last very long in Craig's house. "I have books in the garage, too," he nodded, indicating the small building at the back of his lot. "Anthropology, Geography, Geology, Biology — sort of ran out of space to park," he finished sheepishly.

"I notice you have as much American history as you have psychology."

"My secret vice. Just as poetry's yours. As a matter of fact, I'm working on a special project." He paused, appearing undecided as to whether to tell her. "Promise you won't think I'm crazy?"

"You're a shrink. How could I *not* think that? Unless I didn't think you were very good at what you do."

Craig laughed and ducked his head in a rare show of modesty.

"Truth is, I'm working on kind of a psychology of American history. Psychohistory, it's called. Do you know about psychohistory?"

"I've read several."

"Hatchet jobs, all. Pretending to interpret biography using psychological techniques. I'm interested in the psychology behind our wars, social movements, how we lead our lives, that sort of thing. A sort of social psychological personality analysis of American history."

"All of it?"

"All of it."

"Well, I'm glad you're including social movements," Becca said, trailing her fingers along some of the gilt and leather-bound volumes. "I've always resented history for being about wars and governments, all male-oriented."

"*White* male-oriented. This isn't."

"Pretty ambitious." Becca had discovered the missing dimension of Dr. Craig Austin. Nerd extraordinaire. Or "Renaissance man," if one preferred, which she did.

"Ambition has nothing to do with it. I run on passion, not ambition."

Passion, eh? Not that she'd noticed. "I meant the psychohistory. It must be huge. How many volumes?"

"Just one gigantic tome. I could break it into four, but then, if the first didn't sell well, they might not want to publish the others."

"Where do you work?"

"I have a computer nook upstairs. Didn't want to sully this room with machines. This is where I read and do research," and indeed, the easy chair with its floor lamp and view of the garden beckoned invitingly. "Books were my earliest passion. All my money goes into them. If I ever lose my job at Seattle General and get sick of private practice, I can open a bookstore. In fact, I've had several invitations from bookstore owners to do just that, go in with them. It's an addiction, really. Well, come on, this can't be very interesting. Let's get you upstairs."

"Oh, it is interesting," Becca protested honestly. "I'd love to have a library like this. I think I might just stay home and read and never go out."

"Well, there, you know my secret. I'm really a nerd. Nobody else knows. Don't tell." He only seemed half-joking. "Come on, let's get you settled."

Craig conducted Becca up to the guest room with its own bath, early American wood furniture, an old American quilt over the bed, and pewter utensils. Here he left her to make herself comfortable and retired chastely downstairs. No sign of Noel's stays, either in the closet or in the bureau drawers, all of which were empty. But perhaps she'd kept her things in Craig's room. On Becca's way back down, a quick peek in that direction revealed a sky-lighted ceiling and a big-leaf maple outside the window, through which Green Lake shimmered in the distance.

Over tortilla soup and tacos at a neighborhood restaurant, Craig met Becca's eyes levelly and said, "I'm sorry for doubting you, Becca, I really am."

"You couldn't have known," Becca replied. In her gratitude for his support now, forgiveness was easy.

"No, no, I jumped to conclusions. Unprofessional of me. But then, our friendship hasn't been just professional. I was worried. I hoped that maybe it was all in your head, so it didn't have to be real," he said, taking her hand. "It's more dangerous for you if it's real."

"Thanks, Craig. Thanks for all you're doing."

"Not nearly enough," he said. "But I've always wanted you to count on me, and I hope you always will."

"Always is such a big word."

When they got back to his house, Craig suggested, "Why don't we get comfortable? Then, if you don't feel like sleeping, we can watch TV."

Becca did exactly that, feeling a little self-conscious in her jammies and white terry robe, as she sat on the couch beside Craig, whose terry robe was blue. She wanted to believe that Craig was restraining his almost irresistible attraction to her so as to remain a gentleman and not take advantage of her precarious situation, that, in actuality, he was filled with nigh uncontrollable lust. But soon they were watching some drama on cable, and before she knew it, her head rested on Craig's shoulder.

Days later, the police told them that the gallery murder Gregory claimed in San Francisco had indeed taken place and was unsolved, as well as the brutal acid assault reported by someone who disappeared. What was more, Gregory knew details that he didn't even reveal to his therapeutic team. The "Razorman" murders were, of course, a matter of record, easy enough for anyone to claim. McNalley concluded that they might need to arrest Gregory as an accessory to murder at some point in the future.

45

AS A NEW PATIENT, Gregory had no roommate. He had been assigned one of the "dedicated" rooms with a brass door plaque indicating who had contributed to its cost. "In Memory of Linnea Applebaum" read the plaque. Becca felt saddened by the plaques, paid for by grieving relatives who thus extended the lives of those they loved. To Becca, the plaques said, "Look at me. I was a person once."

Of course, there was always the possibility that the room had been donated by parents who were grateful to the hospital for saving their daughter's life.

Accompanied by both Noel and Craig, Becca pushed Linnea aside and entered Gregory's room.

"Hello, Becca," said Gregory, standing up politely. He was wearing the black pants and a daffodil yellow shirt, a chain just showing over the collar. For her part, Becca wore the white lab coat that was supposed to distinguish between patient and staff — except when some patient with delusions of grandeur got hold of one and started ministering to his cohorts.

Becca decided to let the familiarity of Gregory's greeting slide. Indicating that they were merely present to observe, both Craig and Noel seated themselves in chairs along the wall. Becca sat across the table from Gregory, a bit nervous that Noel and Craig would, incidentally, be observing her interview technique. She had supervisors who did this regularly, of course, but none with the status of Craig and Noel. Besides, as her friends, they might be more liberal with their criticism.

"Are they treating you well here?" Becca began.

"As well as can be expected, I guess. Not much variety in the food."

"Maybe someone can bring you something."

"I sure would like some Brie cheese."

"That's one of my favorites, too." Harmless personal details helped the patient and therapist bond. "Have you had any visitors yet?"

"Not yet."

"It's a little soon, I guess." Some patients were defensive about the lack, which could be interpreted as meaning that they were unlovable.

"They're pissed at me for coming here."

"I see." His imaginary family was pissed at him. "Do you happen to know Damon?"

"Yes, Damon's my brother, sort of."

"I met him on my way home a week or so ago."

"I know." He seemed about to add something, but thought better of it.

"He told me you said he shouldn't let me know where Robbie was."

"It's kind of complicated."

"Is Robbie still alive?"

"Oh, yes. As Damon told you, he's asleep in the attic."

"Why? What's wrong with him?"

"Nothing's wrong."

"Why does he sleep all the time? I mean, doesn't he have a job? A girlfriend, maybe? Why does he just sleep?"

"He's only five. He still naps. Just a little more than he used to, that's all."

Becca stared at him dumbfounded.

"He should be eighteen now."

"No. He never grew. Not like some of the rest of us."

"Maybe we're not talking about the same Robbie."

"He used to talk about you all the time. He called you his Bec-Bec."

Truly shaken, Becca didn't know how to respond to this. But she had to say something, because Noel and Craig were watching her. And psychologists never merely watch. They evaluate. For a comparatively naive colleague, this could be brutal.

"Tell me about your own work," she suggested lamely.

He told her about his job as a computer programmer for a software company, his education and A.A. degree, and how he organized the family and kept it together.

"It's very time-consuming to run a family," said Gregory.

"I'm sure it is."

"Do you have a family?"

"Yes." Trained in not disclosing too much personal information, she went on, "And I agree, it's time-consuming. Do you and your family do things together?"

"Not recently. Everything's been too much of a mess. Mainly we're just trying to survive. But when things are going okay, we sit around the dining room table, and Wendy makes us blueberry milk shakes. But Wendy got hurt, and she doesn't feel like making them." His face was taut, and the lines at his mouth sagged.

"What happened to Wendy?"

"They hurt her. And they're going to hurt me for turning them in."

"I think you're pretty safe here. We have a lot of security."

"They don't give THIS for your security," said Gregory, snapping his fingers. "They can get in or out anywhere. Breakout learned the trade from Pleaser — I mean, Singer. They hurt Pleaser. Even Leroy can't keep them under control."

"Who are these people who hurt Pleaser and Wendy and want to hurt you?"

"Vigrid and Mefisto." He shuddered, and his head snapped to one side. "Ow! I guess I shouldn't have told you."

"What happened just now?" If Becca didn't know better, she'd swear she'd just seen a manifestation of switching, one of the major symptoms of DID.

"Onlys have a hard time understanding. I'm supposed to keep them in line," Gregory went on. "It's my responsibility."

"Can't they control themselves?"

"They don't want to."

"Are they part of your family?"

"Yes."

"I understand you live with your family."

"Yes."

"But, the police went to your apartment and found one room." Reality testing.

"That's Damon's."

"Oh, then you all live in one room?"

"No, we have our own places. It's kind of hard for Onlys to understand."

The second time he'd referred to her this way.

"Onlys?"

"People like yourself. You live alone, right?"

"Sometimes," Becca answered defensively. He caught her reticence immediately, and she realized she'd made an error. He took it for something else.

"I think I'm saying too much," he said nervously, glancing at Noel and Craig.

"That's okay, Gregory," said Noel. "Go ahead."

"See, we're not like other people. We're different."

"How different?"

"Just different."

"A lot of people feel they're different. Can you be more specific?"

But he seemed not to know what to say, so Becca decided to take another tack.

"Some of the members of your family have unusual names. Bounce, Breakout, Pleaser — as you said, Singer, now. Where did they get those names?"

"I'm not sure. They just took them, I guess."

"Took them from someone?"

"No. It's just whatever's appropriate."

"Are they nicknames?"

"No, they're real names. But when they go outside, they say they have ordinary names. Like Emmanuel Lacelaw or Humbert Pumpernickel or whatever."

"Why don't they use their ordinary names all the time?"

"'Cause they're not theirs." He shrugged and sighed impatiently, as if helpless to explain. "Can you control Vigrid and 'Fisto without hurting the rest of us?"

"We'll certainly try."

When Becca got up to leave, Gregory asked, "Will you come again?"

"I hope so," Becca replied with a glance to Noel. "Yes, I will."

"I know Robbie wants to see you, if I can wake him up."

"I never understood where he is exactly."

"I could go get him. I have to bring him to you."

"Maybe later, at some point. After you leave Seattle General."

"No, I don't have to leave here."

"You mean you can just phone him to come? Will someone bring him?"

"He can come by himself. He can take the spot if the others let him."

"The spot!"

Becca felt the shock surge through her and saw that Noel's leg had jumped and Craig was staring at Gregory. The spot! Classical DID language!

"The spot," Becca repeated.

"Sure, he never does, but he could."

46

DR. BERNIE DECIDED THAT Gregory Warhol was indeed afflicted with DID. Noel, Craig, and Becca met with him in his office, a massive windowed and leather affair as befit his status, with objects from his travels throughout Africa, Alaska, and China on his bookshelves. Not Europe. Everyone went to Europe. These art objects sat among the multiple editions of his own works, both domestic and foreign. Very different from Craig's library. But nobody kidded Dr. Bernie to his face about *his* multiplicity!

"Classic symptoms," he pronounced sonorously. "What he calls his family is just a bunch of identities living inside his head. He can remember his home and the rooms of his family members, but he remembers nothing of his past before the age of nineteen. However, and this may come as a shock to you, Becca, he seems to remember some of the details of what he claims is Robbie's past."

Becca felt the blood drain from her head at the elusive connection.

"Are you saying that he knows Robbie because he *is* Robbie?"

"Exactly so. Gregory says that Robbie remembers his Bec-Bec making him baloney and cheese sandwiches to take to the playground. Is that true?"

"I'm sure lots of sisters make sandwiches for picnics."

"Of course. He says you used to climb a pine tree in the backyard and watch him and your dad play baseball. Sound familiar?"

"The whole neighborhood must have seen that."

"You're thinking he might be a neighbor instead?"

"I don't know," Becca managed. "But if Gregory's Robbie, why does he keep insisting he's asleep in the attic?"

"Have you made contact with Robbie yet?" Noel asked Dr. Bernie, giving Becca a minute to recover.

"It's too early in the process, but we think Robbie had to change his name to Damon, and that's when he took refuge in another corner of his mind. We've just started diagramming him, finding out who's in there. We have to take a list of family members from each one, discover the role each plays, and get a history. But you're the reason he's here, Becca. He looked you up on the Internet, and when he was in too much danger of being tracked down as a murderer — or I should say, his other identities were — he moved here, partly to make contact with you, although some of the others were against it."

"It's hard for me to believe. He doesn't look anything like my brother would."

"A grown version of the little brother you knew at five? With blond hair and all that baby fat?"

"I think I'd know my own brother," Becca snapped, while she crumbled inside.

Dr. Bernie ignored it, perhaps because it was to be expected.

"What really clued me, Noel, were your test results — so different from mine."

"How different?" Noel was frowning.

"Your MMPI Lie Scale is moderately elevated, whereas mine is off the charts. In addition, I gave him two EEGs, and they were as different as Freud and Skinner. I even asked if Gregory had trouble with doctors finding contradictory medical problems. He asked how I knew."

Becca fought back tears again. Was it possible? Her dear brother a police case, and now a psychiatric one? Leaching his humanity in the process? It couldn't be.

Robbie! Robbie! she cried in her head, trying to assimilate the idea. Aloud, she asked, "But if Gregory really is Robbie —"

"Actually, another identity of Damon's, who was forced to split from Robbie."

"How did he get this way?" Becca asked, managing to keep the note of pleading from her voice.

"You could answer that on an exam, couldn't you?" Dr. Bernie said, not unkindly.

"Severe childhood trauma and abuse, often sexual," Becca replied. "Oh, my God!" She buried her face in her hands, as if to escape the images. On one side of her, Noel's hand rubbed her back, and on the other, Craig squeezed her shoulder.

"When your own brother's involved, it's got to be another story, doesn't it?" Dr. Bernie said gently. "Well, I've talked to three of them. So far, they give differing accounts of the abuse they suffered. One of them even says he doesn't remember any. They're not in good communication with each other, typical in the beginning, so they have different pasts and different experiences, and they say they fight about it all the time. They tell me Singer was castrated, long after he was Pleaser. Gregory has always been as he is. They say Bounce and Breakout were beaten up repeatedly until they grew big enough to defend themselves. But I'm inclined to believe the one who calls himself Leroy. He was horribly assaulted by one of his captors when Robbie was about six."

Becca felt dizzy and began to fall to one side. Craig caught her arm, his face peering into hers.

"Are you okay?"

"Yes."

"Becca, I think you should keep interviewing them," Dr. Bernie suggested. "As Noel says, he seems to trust you, because he thinks he knows you. Which it turns out is probably true. It might be good for you as well. There *is* some bad news, though."

Becca's emotions were so confused; the news that Gregory might be her brother hardly seemed good.

"According to Gregory, and I have to say he seems quite truthful, I'm persuaded there are two vicious psychopathic personalities, two that he knows of, the ones who committed the murders. When he turned himself in, he was trying to protect you and that actress he and Damon are so dippy over."

"So, if they're locked up in here, Becca isn't in danger any longer?" Craig pressed.

"As long as we have Gregory here, no. If he left, the vicious personalities might take over, as they've apparently done before. No, it's Gregory who might be in danger. Sometimes, one alter will hurt the body in order to get back at another alter."

If Becca believed that Gregory was her brother, a number of whose personalities had been stalking her, she could also believe she was now safe. She returned home from Craig's and toured her apartment. No one had been in here since she left. The intruders were sealed on a locked unit inside Gregory. She'd have no more unwelcome visits. So why did the hair on the nape of her neck stand on end?

And how could she even dream that she was in danger from her own brother? That her beloved brother's alters were bent on killing her?

Craig called at about nine that night to ascertain that she was all right. She assured him she was. He repeated his invitation to phone at any time, even for silly reasons. As she hung up, she realized that she missed him. Maybe, he missed her as well? They'd had one week of companionship, and even without sex, she'd deeply enjoyed it.

Becca couldn't sleep. She tried the old remedies of a hot bath, hot milk, and a mystery novel. Finally took a pill.

She'd just set off for dreamland like an ocean swimmer, arms and legs plowing the waters, when she heard it again. That click! The same one she'd heard in her terrifying nightmare.

In one fluid motion, she was sitting on the edge of her bed, heart thrumming in her chest. Nothing else. Just that click. No other sound, no smell, no change in light or shadows. She told herself it was another hallucination. Then she got up, flung her bathrobe around her shoulders in the night chill, flicked on every light in the place and began to search, pushing and pulling things around, everything that could possibly have made that sound.

Finally, she told herself that this was a normal reaction to all she'd been through in the last week — the last months. Still, just in case, she put a rolling pin beside her pillow. In the absurdly unlikely case that she was in danger, she didn't want to be defenseless.

Even though she was.

47

I CAN'T SPEAK FOR myself, because I don't feel like myself. I don't feel
like Gregory either. Gregory isn't me any longer, he's Gregory I and
I'm Gregory II, but as I watch him, I feel like I'm nobody. Which, in
a way, is a good thing, because I can feel sorry for Gregory without
feeling sorry for myself. Leroy says you're not supposed to feel sorry
for yourself. It's against the law.

Ever since Gregory got in here, here in the hospital — he's not
some crazy person doesn't know where he is, although they keep
asking him —'Fisto and Vigrid the Avenger have been threatening
him with death and mutilation. In no particular order. They've been
doing their best to carry out their threats, too. Leroy says it's only a
matter of time.

'Fisto grabbed the spot and bashed Gregory's head against the
bathroom door until he passed out. Hurt like Hell! A good thing I'm
not Gregory, or it'd be *my* head split open like a watermelon and *my*
neck in traction. Nurses came buzzing like flies over a corpse, lighting
on him here and there. Thought he'd done it to himself, of course.
Got him to the infirmary, where they bandaged the hollow in his
head and stitched the crescent in the middle of his forehead where the
door handle almost broke through, making him look quite the dash-

ing romantic figure, I thought. When they asked over and over, his answer, "I ran into a door," was fairly accurate. They shot him up with morphine, waking him every couple of hours for what they said was a concussion, but the real reason was that if he got a good night's sleep, he'd recover faster, and what other work would they have to occupy their time? How else would they earn their wages of sin?

Leroy tried to get Vigrid to stop 'Fisto before he killed Gregory — he's so virtuous, that Leroy is — but Gregory had it coming and a lot more. He brought it on himself, Leroy says. "No call to turn us in," he says. "We could have worked it out." "I'm not taking the pain for you." He says that to me, but he means Gregory.

There's always someone intruding on us unannounced. They don't knock even, just barge in. Gregory could be beating his meat for all they know. Pulling Peter to pay Paul. Makes no difference. Probably they hope they'll catch him at it. Gotta have some excitement in their lives to cream their little holes. Sometimes they even slam through the door, then turn right around and slam out again, as if they've forgotten something, but then they never return; somebody else does that. They're spies like the Watcher, hired by the great eye in the sky, Dr. Bernie Leonard, master of all he surveys and a good deal he doesn't. If you don't believe me, ask him.

Their excuse is that we're on suicide watch.

Dr. Bernie wanders in and strokes his pointy Machiavellian beard, as if he's thinking something important, and asks Gregory stupid questions like, "Do you know where you are?"

Of course, Gregory knows where we are! No other place could be so goddamn infantalizing — that's the word, "infantalizing" — although sometimes Gregory knows he's *not* in the hospital, but he also knows that's the answer he's supposed to give, so he gives it. Even as he's telling the doctor what he wants to hear, he dimly makes out the outline (like a ghost) of the home he and the rest of us share with Damon, the dining room where Wendy used to serve her milk shakes before she was hurt, and the stairs leading up to his room with the Victorian bedstead and the cupids up to their eternal mischief with each other on the ceiling, and Robbie's attic off to one side like a cock-eyed hat with the view of Alex's house and the trees in a season that's always autumn, and then up to Bounce and Breakout's primary-colored sports den that they're putting back together, and Leroy's studio that's building out across the alley and reeks of turpentine, and up the concrete castle steps to 'Fisto and Vigrid's lab, and the roof garden that Watcher tends with such exquisite care. Gregory doesn't tell them any of this, however.

Good thing about Dr. Bernie, he believes Gregory when he says we're family.

Sometimes Dr. Bernie asks him questions he can't hear with the basement kids making such a ruckus. So he lets one of the others talk, because they can cover their ears and block out the noise, whereas Gregory can't; they'd see his hands go to his head and take that as another sign of what they call "auditory hallucinations." If *they* had them, of course, that's what they'd be. After all, *they're* Onlys.

Then there are the questions Gregory doesn't have the answers to, so he gives any old one just to get them off his back. For example: "Does Leroy know where you are now?" How would Gregory know that! He replies, "The moon is moldy cheese," which it is if it's green. Dutifully, they take these down and assign their own meanings to them. They look these up in their *English to Psychology Dictionary*.

And always with us, the hospital "Staff" as they call themselves, as if that were their identity, something larger than Gregory because he's just one lone patient and they're an ant colony that can interrupt and demand to know what he's thinking, stealing crumbs of thought like they're nothing and marking them on their charts in ink that can't be erased, then scurrying away. Like their cousins, the roaches, they can get in anywhere through any nooks and crannies. Which is why they call us patients "cracked."

Talk about your denial! "Staff" is a whole bunch of people, too, calling themselves by one name. Why aren't *they* patients?

Some "Staff" want to talk about their nights with their boyfriends; both the men and the women want to do this; nobody has nights with girlfriends anymore. Oh, they start out by asking, "How are we feeling this morning?" because that's why they're supposed to be here, to decide how you're feeling. You couldn't possibly figure this out for yourself. They'll write it on your chart and pick up their payroll check and go spend it on fancy clothes for the dates they don't have. But what they really want to talk about is last night, which didn't really happen, but they want you to think it did, so you'll treat them as if.

One of them carries this bunch of keys around like it's a badge of honor. She'd be nobody without those keys, just another homeless madwoman across the street on her way to her next rape and already ranting about it to unseen witnesses. But keys make Staff important because she can get into things the rest of us can't. Like broom closets and patients' rooms and drugs that don't help the rest of us but boost or depress their spirits on an "as needed" basis, and community meeting places where all the patients except Gregory get together to fight over the TV. Anyhow, she drops this key ring like a lady's handkerchief in the fan and bustle days, and Vigrid picks it up all polite like he was a gentleman, what a laugh! And she simpers her "Thank you" with a flick of her hips, like he'd be interested in that except to cut on. Doesn't even notice that he's swiped a key with sharp edges and hidden it in his surgical hand.

Next thing Gregory knows, good old Vigrid's operating on his wrists while 'Fisto holds them bent back enough to break. Then they trot him off to the bathroom to soak in hot water and cut some more, real thorough like, so the blood spews up like twin geysers, but one of the spies barges in and sees him and does her "call the code" bit. Gregory's back in the medical wing with his wrists taped in bandages so bulky he can't do anything with his hands, and one of the sweet little pink volunteers, that Pleaser would have deflowered in a minute if he was still alive, has to spoon feed him with no idea how close she is to a long excruciating dissection.

The last thing Gregory did before turning himself in was to visit Chloe and tell her that he'd gone to the police to save her life, and now he was going to the hospital to pretend he was mad. No more danger for his sweet Chloe, he said, kissing her on her cheek, since her lips were Damon's. Not that she knew the difference.

"That's loverly of you," she said, practicing for her newest understudy role in *My Fair Lady*.

Now, here comes Chloe to visit Damon in the hospital, because that's what friends are supposed to do. She's wearing a bunch of new ear cuffs, purple and pink spangles and sequins twisted around tufts of yarn hair, and nipple rings that glisten through her black lace bra, and a skirt that snugs over her hips below her zircon belly button and stops short at the tops of her violet lace stockings.

"I had a time finding you," she announces in her latest accent, something between English and cockney. "They all think you're Gregory Warhol here. When I asked for Damon Hearst, they said there was no such person. 'How about Damon Warhol,' I ask, and they say they have a Gregory Warhol, like one person's the same as another so long as they're names are similar. You'd mentioned Gregory, so I figured, what's sauce for the goose —"

"I'm Gregory here."

"As long as you were going to change your first name, why not change your last to Hearst?"

"That's Damon's stage name, not mine."

Chloe huffs impatiently but decides to let it go. "So how's my snuggly huggababy?" she asks, nuzzling his neck and rubbing against his thighs like a cat in heat.

"How's Fyodor?" Gregory asks.

"Oh, he's history. What do you want to ask about him for? What kind of a greeting is that to your old lover, hmmm?" Her hand is bolder now, but he's limp.

Gregory's trying to get her off sex since he's feeling he can't. That's the difference between him and me.

"I thought you and Fyodor were an item."

Chloe's eyes widen. "*He cut my lines!*" she exclaims in a paroxysm of indignation. "Imagine that. I hardly had any, and he cut them. Dirty cheat. Better he slept with another woman than *cut my lines*. Let's not talk about Fyodor. You're my main man again," she adds, resuming her fiddling.

"Someone might come in."

"That's their problem. Come on, honey, I came to comfort you like I'm supposed."

"I can't."

"Can't?" She pulls back.

"It hurts. 'Fisto punched me in the progeny."

"The what?" Chloe is clearly uncertain about "progeny" but gets the drift. "Shall I kiss it and make it better?"

"No, don't."

She gives an exaggerated shrug and takes a turn around the room, as if there was something to admire in the cheap picture of a farm scene framed in fake wood and the linoleum floor flecked with pink and gray to hide the dirt the cleaning lady can't be bothered mopping and the stains of suffering on the walls, including the place on the bathroom threshold where 'Fisto banged Gregory senseless.

Chloe's outsized embroidered tote is poking out in all directions, first one, then another, as if there were something alive in there, and Chloe says, "What's the matter, Go-Go? Need a tour?" She removes the shaggy beast and lets him run senselessly around the room, feet splaying both east and west, as he tries to get everywhere at once. He's only partially successful, ending in a belly slide across the floor.

Chloe lights an invisible cigarette and blows an invisible ring of smoke. "Want a puff? No? I had a fella once."

"Another fella?"

"Not just any old fella. English, actually. Velly British. Impotent, ya' know? Couldn't get it standing for the life of him. And he tried. Oh, yes, he tried. Afraid of losing me. I helped. Mouth to mouth resuscitation and that.

"One night he's telling me about his mum who says it's a sin to masturbate 'cuz horrible things will happen. It'll turn his wingwang into this horrible diseased thing all scabs and sores, and then it'll decay and drop off like a pimple into Hell, where it'll fry forever. 'When you get the urge,' she says to him, 'Close your eyes and think of England.'" Chloe says this in her heavy cockney accent. Good practice.

"So I says to him, I'm asking 'cuz I can't believe it, 'Close your eyes and think of England?' and I think I'm using his mother's voice 'cuz he used it, see? Right away, I feel this twitch against my thigh, you know? And then a wriggle, and before you can say 'jack rabbit', he's saluting the flag and panting over me like a wet dog. From then on, all I had to do was say 'Close your eyes and think of England,' and then I shortened it to 'Close and think England' and finally 'Think,' and he was ready for me."

"He must've been grateful," says Gregory. "I know I would be."

"Oh, yes, the whole time we were together."

"How come he broke it off?"

"He didn't. I did."

"Why would you do that?" He hadn't cut any of her lines, had he? Actually, Damon was more anxious about this than Gregory.

"Too much thinking for my taste," says Chloe dismissively.

"Time's up," sings Staff, barging in.

"Gracious! People come and go so quickly here," says Chloe, doing her best Judy Garland in Oz imitation.

"Gregory needs a shower," says Staff.

"But we didn't do anything yet."

"Tomorrow," says Staff, like she'd remember. "Come on, Gregory," taking a firm hold of his arm.

"He's Damon."

"Damon's in mourning for Kenny. He died, you know," Gregory tells Chloe.

"So he doesn't shower?"

"Damon sees his ghost sometimes."

Chloe was losing the thread. "*Then* does he shower?"

"He does now," says Staff grimly. "Now, Gregory."

"Damon. Don't you even know your patient's names?"

Gregory wasn't getting anything to eat or drink. They'd stopped making him go to the dining hall with the really crazy coots — that's a technical term for lunatics — and were bringing him his tray to him. But the basement kids drank his coffee, which made them so hyper that they were up at all hours, and Wendy wasn't around to tell them it was bad for them. Gregory took to pouring his coffee down the sink before they got hold of it, so they snatched his water, and when he wasn't looking, they grabbed his food with their grubby little hands and stuffed it into their grubby little mouths. Wendy wasn't around to clean them, and Gregory had to do it or let them grow germs on their faces. Regular germ farms these babies were, their cheeks veritable petri dishes of bacteria colonies. Vigrid would have found them useful. At least, when they were fed, watered, and deprived of coffee, they subsided into something resembling peace and played off in the distance.

The medical police didn't remain in the dark for long. They weighed Gregory every day and talked about how his tray was always empty and he'd lost pounds.

"Healthy metabolism," Gregory explained.

"Where are you putting it?" they asked. "Are you pouring it down the toilet?"

"Gross!" said Gregory.

"It's a shortcut," Leroy reminded him.

When Becca heard that he was losing weight, she checked his chart to make sure he wasn't on some anti-depressant like MAO inhibitors, which he refused because this would mean he couldn't eat cheese, sausage or chocolate or, for that matter, drink wine or beer lest they prompt a hypertensive crisis. Then she brought him a box of crackers, a wedge of soft-ripened Brie, and even a spoon to spread it.

"Thanks," says he. "But I don't think the kids will let me eat it."

"The kids?" Becca asks quickly. "They eat your food, do they?"

Gregory pauses. He's said something he shouldn't, and he's trying to think how to recoup their privacy.

"I don't remember eating," he says finally.

"So you think the kids ate it?"

"What kids?" he asks. It's the only thing he can think to say. Then, in a flash of inspiration, he says, "Robbie wants to see you."

"He does? I'd like to see him, too."

"He's in the attic," Gregory says, as if that explains it. For a bright guy, sometimes Gregory can be obtuse.

"Can I talk to him now?"

"He's asleep. It's not a good idea to wake him. He gets cranky and rubs his eyes until they bleed."

"When does he usually wake up?"

"He doesn't wake up hardly ever these days."

"Maybe if you tell him Bec-Bec's here."

"I'll ask him."

This is truly a masterpiece of manipulation on Gregory's part, although I'm not sure he realizes it. He can keep the sister going for weeks, months even, promising that she'll see her brother. You'd think she'd be over him by now. Whenever she's on his case or he's slipped up, all he has to do is mention Robbie, and problems are forgotten. Of course, it would be a good idea if he produced, but with Robbie, who knows?

The doctor with the Christmas name comes in.

"Sorry I'm late," she says, and Gregory shuts the fuck up.

A few days later, an aide brings Gregory a glass of milk. It appears there's been a confab around the conference table with docs, nurses, social workers, and a dietician. The upshot of this one-hour, high-level meet (that must have cost the state several grand) is the decision to supplement Gregory's diet with an extra glass of milk per day.

But, the kids don't grab it. Now, this is peculiar, because these kids never leave him anything to eat or drink. Is there something wrong with it? Gregory sniffs. The hospital's added a few drops of almond flavoring, perhaps to tempt him to drink up and regain the weight he's lost. Gregory takes a sip. It tastes almondy, too. Not bad! But just to be on the safe side, Gregory puts the milk aside to see what happens.

At last, one of the toddlers, wearing only a dirty diaper around her ankles, crawls over to it. The others watch intently, but they don't say anything. Some instinct has prevented them from doing the same, although I can't imagine what that could be.

The baby pulls to a standing position, leans against the table, and tips the glass into her mouth. She glug-glug-a-glugs until she's finished half, then puts the glass down, giving us a triumphant look through the ring of foamy milk around her mouth. A few minutes later, she begins to whimper and then to howl. Clutching her stomach, she collapses, rolling in agony over the linoleum floor with the pink and gray flecks. I watch perplexed. Part of me feels I should call the nurse, but whenever I draw attention to one of the others — the "alters" as they like to call them here — they act like I'm crazy. Maybe half an hour later the little one's dead.

I have no idea who poisoned this milk or why. Maybe Vigrid got hold of it. Maybe the therapy is beginning to kill us off, one by one, as they warned us it would. Not in so many words. "Integration," they call it. But the poisoned milk episode has definitely put Gregory off his feed.

I tell Dr. Bernie I want an autopsy.

"Do you think someone's poisoning the food here?" Dr. Bernie manages to guess at their next session.

"That would be paranoid," says Gregory. This place has not made him altogether lame-brained.

"Even paranoids have enemies," quotes Dr. Bernie with Solomonic wisdom.

Gregory is screaming in the middle of the night. I have no idea what 'Fisto and Vigrid have done this time, but it's horrible. Gregory is particularly vulnerable when he's asleep, because then anybody can grab the spot. Looks like somebody did.

Staff shakes him awake and ask questions he can't hear because he woke the basement kids. Staff gives him a shot, although he squeals at them not to, that someone will take the spot, and he struggles to yank his arm from the burly orderly, who's having the best darned time. Without realizing it, he's gotten into a wrestling match with 'Fisto. The shot sends them both off to sleep.

The next morning, Dr. Noel, accompanied by Becca, asks him, "Was it a bad dream you had last night?"

"It wasn't a dream. It really happened. 'Fisto and Vigrid pushed me out the window. I tried to hang on, but I couldn't. I can't." He stops, unable to go on.

"Where are you now?" asks Dr. Noel.

"I've crash-landed on the pavement. I hear my bones crunch and break. A curtain of blood is coming down over my eyes."

"But you know you're really here in your room, don't you?"

"No. I'm really there. I'm dead, now."

Leroy says, "I told you so."

"You must be alive if you're talking to me about it," says Dr. Noel.

"How can you be sitting on your bed and dead on the pavement?" asks Becca.

"That's the conundrum, isn't it?"

"Can you tell me how you can be in two places at once?"

"I'm often in two places at once. Aren't you?"

Dr. Noel pauses. She's not going to tell him where she is.

"Show me which window they pushed you out of," she says. That's called "tacking." If you can't go forward one way, you turn into the wind. Kenny showed Damon this when they played with their boats in the bathtub.

They stand together in front of a double window that is solid with no cracks in it, wire netting between the two panes, and bars on the outside.

"See? It's not broken, is it?"

"They fixed it."

"It would take a window specialist to do that. I haven't seen any window specialists here this morning, have you?"

"I don't always see."

"What about the bars?"

"They're fake. Death is nothingness. The priest lied."

Staff takes him to music therapy, where they play a CD of soothing music, but Gregory can't hear it, because the kids are squalling. They won't eat or drink anything after the death of their sister, and they're hungry and thirsty and tired.

"You've got to feed the children," Gregory says to Dr. Bernie.

"I don't know how. How would I do that?"

"Bring Crunchy Bunchies," he suggests. "They love Crunchy Bunchies."

But they won't even eat Crunchy Bunchies.

Gregory falls into a deep depression. 'Fisto and Vigrid are calling him names, and Leroy is saying, "Serves you right."

For spite, Leroy wakes Robbie up and tells him they've found his sister.

"I want to see Bec-Bec," he says, wandering over to Gregory in his jammies and rubbing his eyes until they bleed.

"Vigrid and 'Fisto are getting out," Gregory warns Becca.

"Oh, I don't think so," says Becca.

"They're still mad as hell at you for getting them into this predicament."

"There's a lot of security here."

"Breakout can get them out any time he wants." He doesn't even try to hide their contempt. "Vigrid and 'Fisto are working on him."

48

WE'VE HAD A NUMBER of visits from the sister now. I don't think she really believes in Robbie. Maybe like the tooth fairy.

Usually, she's with Dr. Christmas or Dr. Bernie or both. Once, she brought Dr. Craig, who held her hand when they entered my room, as if she were about to get a shot. (Vigrid says, "No, a pelvic. Women hate those," he says. The more I get to know this Vigrid, the more I appreciate his humor. Grisly, but funny. Gregory One just doesn't get it.) Dr. Craig stood back and nodded at her every word, not so much at mine, even though I'm the star here. They're supposed to listen to me more than to each other.

That was the day she asked which one of us had been in her apartment.

What were we supposed to say to that?

We huddled together, trying to come up with the best answer. When we finally agreed, I replied for all of us,

"Watcher."

Watcher was the only one who wasn't here to defend himself, see?

"Watcher?"

"It's his job. He was supposed to watch you and report back." I thought it best not to tell her who he was reporting back to and why, although my suspicions had been confirmed in the interim.

"Why was he supposed to do that?"

I was stumped. Then in a flash of genius to which I must admit I'm prone, I said, "He's a gardener. He really likes your plants."

"She forgets to water them," says a bland voice, belonging to no one we can see.

"He says you forget to water them."

"Thank him for helping me out," says Becca.

"You can thank him yourself."

"Thank you, Watcher."

"He's gone." Giggles all around. What does *she* know about who's here and who's there?

Singer pipes up, "I visited you, too."

"Oh, you just don't want anyone else to take the credit," says Bounce.

"You've always been a credit hog, Singer, even when you were Pleaser," says Breakout. "That's why you pleased so many people."

Lately, I've noticed that the twins don't quite repeat what each says, rather they rephrase it or supplement it. Is this a new stage of evolution for them? They're supposed to be merging, not dividing — or engaging in mitosis, as Vigrid calls it. Should I report this to Dr. Bernie? Heck, let him find out for himself.

Disregarding us, Singer says to Becca, "You have a lot of great music, y'know? I don't have a piano yet, although I'm working on it."

"So you were the one who looked through my music?"

I was pretty sure she'd avoided saying "messed up." They're nothing if not tactful, these psychologists. Have to be to get what they want.

"Yes. I have a rather unusual specialty for a singer," said the eponymous alter. "I specialize in singing the instrumental parts rather than the vocals."

"I think I may have heard you in the chapel," Becca says.

"It's a challenge, you see. Your voice has to be very supple, agile even, like a gymnast or a ballerina. Your breathing has to be split-second, moving the notes up and down the vocal cords. Your —"

"Oh, cool it, Singer. She doesn't want to hear about your *castrati* vocal cords."

"I was there, too, I have to confess," I interrupt. "Robbie made me bring you the big troll doll."

"I bought it for him a long time ago," says Damon.

"Damon and I both bought it for him. It has yarn hair like Chloe's."

"When he heard you liked trolls, he wanted you to have it."

Becca's all professional now. See, there's the sister side of Becca and the psychologist side, and that's what she's becoming. Sort of sliding from sister to doctor. Leaving the sister behind the way she left her brother. But she's not split, oh, no!

Gregory One insisted that Damon have his stud removed. Says it's not him, and he's becoming the main man, with a little help from me, although he tries to forget this. Damon complains that the diamond is all he's got left of Kenny, at which we all bombard him with reminders of what Kenny did to him. He whines and sniffles and says we're being mean. Tough shit! Gregory the Main comforts him, wuss that he is!

Me, I'm Gregory's alter ego, wuss draining from him like pus. Wuss-pus. Vigrid, 'Fisto, and I mediate between him and the world — meaning Dr. Bernie. I'm Gregory II like the pope, but that doesn't make him Pope Gregory. Just plain Gregory is what he is. Kept the family together when they didn't know who they were. Credit him with that.

"He's got delusions of saviorism!" laughs Leroy. I never saw him laugh before. I didn't even know he had teeth. Admittedly, his laugh's kind of bitten off.

Dr. Bernie's been fairly honest with us, well, as honest as an Only can be without the checks and balances of a whole community. To be fairly honest, then — not scrupulously, just fairly — Dr. Bernie wants to make us an *Only* like the rest of the world, which in turn is trying to make all the *Onlys* into a community like we already have. Try making sense out of *that*, why don't you?

There are advantages of *Only*-ism, though. Or *Only*-ship. That is, if you believe Dr. Bernie. If you don't believe him, you're paranoid. He'll tell you so himself.

We've been making a list entitled, *The Advantages of Being an Only*. Each person contributes. Leroy contributes the most because he talks the most, not necessarily because he has the most ideas. Gregory doesn't, so I have to prompt him. Over and over. Bounce and Break-out have plenty to say, but it's the same idea in different clothes.

I list the advantages as follows, along with their contributors, so you know who to blame. Since you, the reader, are an Only, I presume, you tend to want to blame. In a community like ours, we don't dare, because there's a thing called "payback."

Okay. *The Advantages of Being an Only.*

Damon: No basement children screaming their bloody heads off when you're watching TV after a hard day's work.

"Doing nothing," adds Leroy.

"Nothing worth doing," says Damon.

"You mean, it's worth doing nothing," says Leroy.

"Anything worth doing is worth doing well. And Damon does nothing exceptionally well."

"People!" Dr. Bernie calls us back to the task at hand.

Gregory One: No more kids stealing your food until you're dead of starvation.

Gregory Two (that's me): You get credit for being an *Only* when everybody knows there's no such thing. *Only*-ness, like Dr. B. says, is next to godliness.

Leroy: Means it's clean.

Wendy: Multiples take just as many showers as *Onlys*.

Leroy (painting the air): No more chaos. True

Creativity flourishes in chaos like mushrooms in a dank forest, but edible and poisonous flourish equally, and you can't always tell the difference.

"Keep to the point, Leroy," I tell him. I'm sick to death of these meetings.

"So less chaos is a disadvantage of *Only*-ness," says Dr. Bernie, trying to keep up.

"The baby died of a poisonous mushroom, distilled to a fine puree. Vigrid says."

"Vigrid's a liar," says Gregory.

"Not necessarily," says Leroy. "He may be a lot of things —"

"Whaddya mean, MAY be," Bounce explodes.

"I don't think he's anything at all," Singer says, rather prissily, in my opinion.

"As I was saying about   creativity, without chaos you get to do your work in peace. But peace   that begat art, as the good Book of Genealogy says, becomes retro.

Now retro is good. It sells. So the critics slam it."

"Oh, stuff it, Leroy," says Breakout.

"I'm the one does the stuffing around here," says 'Fisto.

"No, you don't," says Bounce. "I been wanting to stuff you for a long time."

"You met your match, Weenie boy."

"You been in the lab too long," says Breakout. "You don't know what a match is."

"Could we stick to advantages, please?" says Gregory One. "Without fighting? Jeez, maybe I'd like it better being an Only after all. Write it down," he tells me. "It's an advantage of *Onlyism*. No more arguing with stupid ox-brains."

"Who are you calling —?"

"If it fits."

"Twat-mouth."

"We were listing advantages," says Dr. Bernie.

"AND disadvantages. You can't have it all your own way, Doc," I remind him.

"I'm sure there are disadvantages," Dr. Bernie nods sagely, tugging on his manipulative.

"Machiavellian," corrects Gregory One.

If we ever get out of here, I'm going to shave him clean.

Wendy: Okay, advantages. There's no one else you have to cook and clean for. Unless you're married. Maybe I'll be one of the ones to disappear when we merge. But where? Nobody knows where the alter goes.

"Sounds like a song in a musical," says Singer, humming a few bars of "Nobody's Knows the Trouble I Seen" and singing "Nobody Knows Where the Alter Goes."

Wendy: It's not polite to interrupt. As I said, nobody knows. Heaven or Hell? It's anybody's guess. Or Limbo in between. Like after death. It is like a death, isn't it?

"Would somebody shut that broad up before I do her again?"

"What was that?" asks Wendy, shrinking back.

"Just a nobody who thinks he's somebody," I assure her. Communication is still incomplete. We can't all hear each other or see each other. Wendy can hear Vigrid, but she can't see him yet. Couldn't even see him when he raped her. Just this invisible force. So we make it up as we go along, and we can tell we've done this, but Dr. Bernie can't.

The longer we keep the process going, the longer we live.

"I'm an *Only* already," Singer boasts.

"No you're not," says Gregory the Main.

"Would you all do me the courtesy of shutting the fuck up?" asks Damon. "Or I'll jump out that window. Right now. Mess you all up real good."

"Is that rhetorical?" asks Singer. Receiving no answer, he continues, "I'm an *Only* already. Only I can sing. Vigrid can't. He made me this way, but —"

"Like God," says Vigrid.

"But he can't sing."

"I wouldn't want to."

"Tee-hee," laughs 'Fisto. "Vigrid singing. Well, he does sing in the shower."

"How often is that?" asks Breakout.

"Saturday night," says Bounce.

"No, I don't," says Vigrid. "I don't sing in the shower or any place else, and I'll slit your throat if you say it again."

"Only if I let you. I'll mash your hand before you can slit."

"Blow it off, clit sucker. He did Wendy's."

"She liked it, too. Oooooh, she wriggles in pleasure. The Virgin's a slut."

"Gregory, you said I wasn't," Wendy cries out.

"You're not. 'Fisto, shut up."

"Or you'll —" 'Fisto waits for the threat.

Damon says, "Jump out that window."

"Through bars?"

"Shut the motherfucker up," yells Damon.

Gregory admonishes him, "Damon, that's a sensitive subject around here."

"I didn't mean it that way."

"How is Wendy to know that?"

Dr. Bernie interrupts. "You were listing the advantages and disadvantages of being *Onlys*."

Bounce: The advantage of *Onlyness* is, we can play on any teams and go National.

Breakout. Right now, we can only play with each other.

"I suspected as much," says Vigrid.

"Not enough of us to form teams," Breakout continues, disregarding him. "Not that that's bad. For teams, you have to get picked and go through contracts and that."

"We could split up," says Bounce.

"That's not exactly the point of this therapy," says Dr. Bernie.

We talk endlessly about who's dispensable, and who's not. Who can leave now, and who has to stay. We do this sensitively, because we don't want to hurt each other's feelings. Or get them so mad they'll stay on forever. The fact is, no one's indispensable except Gregory One. And me. Because I'm indispensable to him, or vice versa. And sometimes, I'm not even sure about me. But then we'd be left with no one, and the Devil would grab the spot. The chaplain would have to exorcise him.

We analyze the situation into atoms of argument. Take Singer, for instance. Singer only has one aspect to him now. He's a single-sided record, a classical one admittedly, but he hardly has the diversity of a Pleaser, who could fuck and get us police protection and stuff our cupboards with delicacies and spin stories. But he insists to Dr.

Bernie, "I never was this Pleaser. How disgusting! Don't you think I'd remember?"

The kids are growing at an alarming rate, and nobody seems to know why. Still, they haven't developed any talents they may have, and we got here first. They haven't become who they're meant to be yet, so it wouldn't hurt them to merge like a bunch of potatoes in a dank cellar all mashed together. Whereas, integration for the rest of us can become downright painful, suppressing bits and pieces of ourselves and letting the part that's needed grow.

Wendy's more rounded, but with the kids grown, she'll have nothing to do except be good, and the *Onlys* won't stand for that. They'll think she's mad as a hatter, although there are precious few of those around these days. If she couldn't keep safe as a Multiple, what hope is there for her as an *Only*?

Damon's been out in the world just enough to know he doesn't function well. Not as well as the Gregorys, if I may say immodestly. Bounce and Breakout keep to themselves. Together they're like one *Only*. Ditto Ball and Shayne. Leroy's only half a man without pain to take, but he functions well as an artist. Robbie, the Sleeper, wouldn't have a chance outside, even if Becca took him in. 'Fisto and Vigrid would wreak havoc. They've got to go.

We've forgotten about Watcher. We don't know him, so he's easy to forget. And Dr. Bernie says there are others, but I think he just wants to multiply us to enhance his reputation for his article. If there were others, at least one of us would know.

We decide that *Onlys* are a lot more dispensable. Take Staff.

Dr. Bernie asks, "Would you all be willing to become a sort of advisory council for Gregory? You could teach him how to defend with the quick jabs he needs in business in order to get ahead. And the poisonous words he needs to destroy his rivals. And the antivenin he needs to survive." This seemed specifically directed towards 'Fisto and Vigrid. I think it's in bad taste to pander to the threat they pose, just because Dr. Bernie finds them most perplexing.

"They'll be gone," I inform Dr. Bernie.

"What's in it for us?" demands 'Fisto.

"Lamebrain," says Leroy. "We don't have to kill each other off."

"As I was saying," Dr. Bernie raises his voice above the others, "Bounce and Breakout could teach Gregory enough about sports for him to survive as a man. Our culture defines masculinity as sportsmanship."

One of the things I've been noticing is that old allies are fighting, and old enemies are more cordial with one another.

"I'd rather like to teach pugilistics," says Vigrid, smacking his lips. "I'd start with old Gregory here."

"You'd have to deal with the two of us," I say, rushing to Gregory's defense.

"The four of us," say Bounce and Breakout.

"The five of us," says Leroy.

And Singer swivels his hips up to them and says, "Guess."

Wendy stands tall and straight, looking pleased.

"He who lives by the sword —"

"Dies by the 'Fisto."

"What use is Singer then?" asks one of the children. We look about, startled to find them joining the discussion. This could complicate matters.

"Yeah, what use?"

"Don't interrupt your elders," says Gregory.

"And betters," says Bounce.

"Art is the meaning of life," says Leroy. "Without music, art, and poetry to interpret our experiences, there's no reason to live."

"That's right," says Singer. "Anybody doesn't know that's an ignoramus."

"Sport is the meaning of life," says Breakout.

"We need us all," says Wendy. Then with a look in 'Fisto and Vigrid's direction, their outlines just becoming visible to her, she amends, "most of us."

"I don't see why we have to merge," says Leroy. "*Onlys* have different parts of themselves just as we do. And they don't merge much. At least, not for long."

You can see that Dr. Bernie's been searching for an opening.

Sometimes, the scientist part of him wants to study us in our cage. He jots down his observations for his article on *Dissociative Identity Disorder in a Case of Kidnap and Abuse of a Five-Year-Old Male: Rape, Mutilation, Murder, and Arrested Development in Early Childhood Learning*. When he's working on this, he leaves us alone. Other times, the clinician in him wants to help us integrate as he's promised. Then, there's that third part of him that isn't there at all. No one knows where he's at, but every once in a while something slips, completely out of character.

"Another advantage of being *multiples* is that we'll all be still alive," says Wendy. "None of us has to die completely."

"Until we do," snaps Leroy. "But the biggest disadvantage of becoming *Onlys* is that we can't remain as we are. Separate and distinct people."

"We're not."

"Oh, yes, we are. Try painting a mural, birdshit."

As for me, why would I endure becoming part of someone else? I have the brains to make it on the outside by myself. And the personality.

This was where we were, mired in the swamp of indecision.

As integration treatment began, many of us became confused and uncertain as we never had been before.

"I wish I'd been born an *Only*," Gregory One said one morning after a particularly painful session. "*Onlys* don't have to kill off parts of themselves in order to survive. They do, but they don't have to."

"It feels like killing?" asked Dr. Bernie.

"Parts of me are dying or going to sleep or moving away. Whatever you want to call it."

"That happens with *Onlys*, too. We grow out of wanting to be a rock star. We're fired from a job. We lose our loved ones."

"Even Becca?"

"Yes, even Becca. It's called 'growing up.'"

"It's not the same."

"Maybe not, but very like. Becca lost her brother, don't forget. Just as you're losing yours."

"Some of us think that was her fault."

"Many of us don't," said Dr. Noel.

"Tell us what you remember of your childhood," said Dr. Bernie.

"Why would I want to remember," Gregory replied, while I remained silent. Watcher had said the very same thing, but they didn't know this.

Dr. Bernie, Dr. Noel, and Dr. Becca, as we call her now, all tried to resuscitate Robbie. I helped by waking him up and bringing him to the sessions. Wendy gave him treats, and Singer sang him songs. But he said nothing to anyone except Gregory.

"I don't want to grow up," he told Gregory, rubbing his eyes until they bled. "I want to stay a boy, like Peter Pan." Gregory relayed Robbie's message to the rest of us.

49

BECCA'S STOMACH CRAMPED AT the prospect of her upcoming interview with a so-called identity who claimed to be Robbie. He had finally agreed to take the spot in order to be reunited with his beloved Bec-Bec. As for Becca, she vacillated between belief and doubt that Robbie occupied the innermost recesses of this man named Gregory, whom she now recognized as Damon, and who bore so little resemblance to the man her brother might have grown to be. She could be headed for a potent reenactment of the major tragedy of her life with no defense, and who knew what effect it would have on her? Probably a revival of her bereavement reaction.

Craig led the way down the hospital cafeteria line, selecting coffee, a yellow-centered sweet roll, and an almond Danish. Becca chose tea, telling herself it would calm her nerves. She didn't believe that either.

Once seated at a table reserved for medical personnel, Craig pushed the pastries toward her.

"Have some. Danes call this yellow one 'the sailor's poisoned eye.'"

"That's disgusting," Becca giggled.

"Perhaps you'd rather have the almond — 'grandmother's toenails.' The Danes have a wonderful sense of humor. So, you're finally getting to meet Robbie. How do you feel about that?" asked Craig, ever the psychologist.

"Confused, mainly. I'm not sure what to expect. I can't believe I'll be in contact with the real Robbie, the brother I knew and loved when he was only five."

"The goal is integration, of course, as you know."

"But this is just the initial phase."

"Right. They're telling the different alters about the diagnosis, that they've dissociated and how that came about. Leroy's been explaining how he's taken the pain for Damon, but Damon doesn't remember it or even the abuse that started it. A lot of work to do there."

"Dr. Bernie estimates at least two years."

"Gregory has to learn to live as an *Only,* as he calls it. That's a long adjustment."

Becca's role today was to interview Robbie, reuniting him with his long lost sister. But who was the patient here, and who the therapist?

It was as if the entire dissociation scenario were a play like Chloe's, destined to close at some point in the future, when all the members would relinquish their roles and props, leave the sets, and go out into the real world. Nevertheless, Becca was required to believe in the reality of it, to act "as if," because this was her profession — her religion, actually, with texts, credo, vestments, ministers, altar, and parishioners supplied. Not only that, but her superiors would judge her by the quality of her performance. The possibility of Robbie's presence inside this technology whiz ex-porn star seemed to be more imaginary than the computer projection created when children have been missing long years. In fact, the whole idea of it seemed bizarre. Yet, she dared not reveal her misgivings about DID as a psychological phenomenon to anyone except Craig, who shared her doubts but had to admit to the persuasiveness of the evidence.

So she went to the meeting, as if it were her yearly evaluation, fearful that she would betray her heathen doubts and be excommunicated. Dr. Bernie mustn't even suspect that he had a heretic in their midst. She must act her part to perfection.

And what if he really were her brother? She didn't think she could bear it.

Dr. Bernie sat on the edge of his desk — they did a lot of edge-sitting here, as if actually using chairs were for the masses or committed them to more time than they were prepared to take or might even appear as though they were — God forbid! — resting. Noel, balanced on the arm of a chair positioned to face Gregory when he came in. She divined Becca's nervousness immediately.

"Thanks so much for coming, Becca." As if she had a choice! "It can't be easy," she added.

Craig motioned Becca to the seat across from that destined for Gregory and sank down beside her.

"We were just saying . . ." Dr. Bernie began, continuing with something inconsequential that she didn't even hear.

Escorted by an attendant, Gregory looked more like Damon than previously, his two-tone hair growing out, the blond section longer, because Damon couldn't dye it here in the hospital.

He hung his head, twisted his face around in what Becca recognized as a switch, and then nodded to Becca.

"How're ya' doin'?"

"Damon?"

Small talk about the hospital and the Brie that Becca had brought previously when Gregory wasn't eating. Pleaser would liked some but Singer doesn't much care for it. They spoke of the therapy group he was in, his anxiousness to get out and get on with his acting "career," as he called it.

Then came the electric moment when Dr. Bernie asked to speak with Robbie.

"He's asleep," Damon said irritably. "Gregory told you that."

"Yes, and we decided that today he'd get to talk to his sister. It's something he wants to do."

"He's a pest."

"Robbie? Bec-Bec's here to talk to you."

Becca knew what signs to look for by now, the closed eyes perhaps, the facial changes that seemed like a muscular restructuring, eyelids fluttering, twitching at the corners of the mouth, as if there were a battle for control going on, which there well might be among the various identities trying to seize the spot.

Then his face seemed magically younger, baby fat restored, his chubby chipmunk cheeks working around some unseen food. And his voice?

"Bec-Bec?" Unmistakably Robbie.

Becca fought to control the tears that flooded through her. Oh, God, don't let her break down again, not in front of Dr. Bernie, Noel, Craig, even. But she couldn't trust her voice to respond.

"Becca's here," Dr. Bernie said, mercifully giving her time to swallow thirteen years of grief.

"Hello, Robbie," she managed.

He looked around, puzzled at the strangers in the room. "Where's Becca?" he asked.

"I'm Becca, Robbie."

"No, you're not. I want my Bec-Bec," he said, agitated. "They said my Bec-Bec would be here. Where is she?"

"I've changed, Robbie. I grew up while you were — asleep. But I'm still your same Bec-Bec." No she wasn't, not really. Too much loss and work, too many people moving in and out of her life, dying, being born. She wasn't even Becca any more.

"You sort of sound like her, sort of. But my Bec-Bec is small like me and climbs trees. She taught me how so I could get away from Carl." They'd heard about Carl from Leroy, Damon, and Gregory I, of course. "I climbed my tree all the way to the sky where Bec-Bec was, but then Carl chopped it down," he said, his voice rising to the edge of hysteria.

Becca's heart caught in her chest at the image of the sweet little boy assaulted to the point of disintegration.

"Carl's gone, Robbie," Dr. Bernie reassured him to keep him from recoiling back into his attic haven. "Carl can't hurt you ever again."

"Why? The other boy gonna come again? Do the nasty with him?"

"Carl's gone," Becca said.

"Where's Mom?" Robbie asked. "I want my mom and my dad, too. Where is everybody?"

How was she going to tell him that his dad was dead and that he had new teenaged brothers? She should have discussed it with Dr. Bernie beforehand.

"They're not here right now. What have you been doing, Robbie?"

"He sleeps," said Gregory irritably.

Robbie went on as if he hadn't heard. "I play games. I built a block tower all the way to the sky. Wendy doesn't get mad when I wet my pants sometimes. I go to school, when Carl lets Kenny take me, and I play with Alex, but I'm not s'posed to," he said, his voice dropping to a whisper. "I have to pertend I'm Damon. Carl's the Monsterman. Kenny was going to get us spistachio ice cream but Carl wouldn't let him. He tied me up." Robbie started to sniffle again, wiping his nose on his sleeve. "Why didn't you come and get me, Bec-Bec?"

"I tried to, Robbie. I tried so hard," Becca struggled to keep the desperation of those years from her voice, as Craig reached out his hand and covered hers. It was glaringly unprofessional, but Noel didn't seem to mind, and Dr. Bernie didn't seem to notice. "We looked for you everywhere. We put up pictures of you."

"On the milk carton?"

"No, but everywhere else."

"Is Mom at the hospital?"

"Yes, as a matter fact, she is." At least, she could be truthful about that. Just not about which hospital.

"Is Dad selling houses to buy food?" Clearly, he was trying to orient himself within the world he'd come from. "I want him to come out and play ball with me."

"I'm sure he'd love that," Becca said. Was there any point in bringing him up to a date he could never live in?

"I still can't believe you're Becca. You got too big."

"I know. You've been gone a long time, Robbie."

"I haven't been gone. You been gone." The old mischievous smile played around his lips. He hadn't forgotten their game.

"Tell me about where you live," Becca said.

Then her mind joined Robbie as he took her up to his attic room, and Becca looked around, so much familiar, so much that she was seeing for the first time. His bed was covered with a spread in his favorite color, red. The trucks and cars were lined up around it like a guard. His Peter Pan book lay open on his night table, but not the book she'd mended. Outside the window she could see the trees in their fall colors, although here it was only spring. There was Alex playing on his big wheels across the way, not a grown-up icky ichthyologist that she and Annalyn had run into, mowing the lawn. On the sill, a sweet potato vine grew in a glass of water, crawling up the window shade. Robbie's hand stole into hers.

"That's Kenny's," he told her. "He's sick of it." The Kenny for whom Damon was in mourning? "He said I could have it."

Colorful wooden blocks lay in a heap in the corner, red, blue, green, orange, and yellow, but there was something odd about them; they seemed to have sprouted twigs and branches, with the sap running down the sides like blood. And in another corner, there was a heap of bloody bandages, that he needed to throw away but somehow had not, and now they smelled of putrefaction, like suppurating wounds that had not been tended and continued to fester.

At a little table that Becca had never seen, child-sized chairs were ranged around a game of Candyland.

"Who plays with you, Robbie?"

"Gregory, sometimes. Wendy. Or Alex. Or somebody else, I'm not s'posed to tell. It's a secret," he whispered into her ear, but not the name of his secret playmate. Instead, "He sneaks up from the basement." Then aloud, "Will you play with me?"

"I'd love to, Robbie."

It would be her contribution to his therapy.

She became aware of musty smells she couldn't identify. Mold in the walls, perhaps?

"Does the rain come in?" she asked, pointing to the holes in the roof where the shingles had dropped off, and she could see the sky through the crisscrossed timbers.

"Sometimes. I catch it with my hands."

Here was where her little brother had lived for thirteen years since his disappearance.

Here was the place where he never grew. Gratitude to the invisible alters who'd cared for him, nonsensical as that might be, swelled inside her.

After the interview ended, Becca took refuge in her office, trying to control the conflicting love, anger, grief, agony, and sense of betrayal all fighting inside her. It was no use. She collapsed in her chair, letting her heart break all over again.

It was as if she herself had splintered, part of her carried back to that day so long ago, and part of her struggling to stay in the present.

She couldn't feel glad that Robbie was back, because he never grew.

The tragedy of it! He never grew, she said to herself over and over, banging her desk with her fist as the tears coursed down her cheeks. Hastily she wiped them away, but there they were again, an underground spring that wouldn't be shut off. And yet he's not quite dead. That tiny part of him is still alive.

She had lost him all over again. And she had to re-grieve.

What had she expected — a joyful reunion with her brother?

It might have been better if she had finally found his dead body decaying in the Cowell Redwoods of Santa Cruz. He was forever lost to her and even to himself.

The phone startled her, as if it had no business here.

"Ms. Merrow? Sgt. McNalley. Bad news, I'm afraid. As you know, an artist named Carmine was indeed murdered in San Francisco about five years ago. There's new evidence linking Gregory Warhol to the crime. I understand he turned out to be your brother after all?" He paused, waiting for her reaction.

"So, what happens now?"

"We're still investigating. We think we have enough evidence to indict him. Let me ask you something. Are you his legal guardian?"

It hadn't occurred to her. But, yes, she probably would be, or could get herself legally declared. She couldn't imagine Mom wanting to shoulder the responsibility.

Hearing her hesitate, McNally went on. "He'll need someone to help him hire a defense lawyer."

"But he wasn't himself," Becca argued, clinging to the DID paradigm now for her dear brother's sake. "It was one of his alters that did it."

"Yes, well, the law doesn't distinguish, you know. Unless, of course, he's legally insane."

Very difficult to prove. The law's idea of insanity was crazy in itself. And even if they could prove Robbie incompetent to assist in his own defense, they'd simply demand he be treated until he could. And then try the newly sane person for the acts he'd committed when insane. She'd read and heard about other cases of mental illness; Becca feared they'd condemn Robbie as if he'd had his new mental wholeness at the very moment he'd committed the crime.

"What will happen to him if he's convicted?" Becca asked.

"Probably he'll go to prison for a while. I doubt very much that they'll put him to death, given his illness and all."

Put him to death! What was the State of Washington's death penalty? She hadn't paid any attention. Hanging! That was it. Becca remembered how one prisoner had gotten his sentence delayed by gaining so much weight that he claimed hanging would be cruel and unusual punishment. The thought rattled around in her head. If it got desperate. . .

"But that's not fair," she argued. "It's not right. He couldn't help himself. It wasn't really Robbie who did it."

"They all say that, you know."

50

So preoccupied was Becca with her thoughts on Robbie that she failed, at first, to perceive the changing relationship between herself and Craig until he appeared at her door on Saturday night with a bouquet of stargazer lilies whose cinnamon scent perfumed the entry, the hall, and the kitchen on their way to a vase.

"What's the occasion?" she couldn't resist asking after expressing her pleasure.

She took note of the fact that he'd changed from his uniform hospital suit and tie to a casual blue cashmere sweater over gray trousers — smashing with his blue eyes.

"No occasion. Haven't I brought you flowers before?"

She searched his face for evidence of guile, but there was none.

"Not that I recall," she answered softly.

"Well, I should have," he said, stepping forward and kissing her cheek. "Where do you want to go for dinner?"

"I thought we were going to Thai Hai."

"We could. Or perhaps somewhere else? Where would you like?"

This was another startling development. He'd never asked before, just assumed.

"I think it's too late to get reservations anywhere else. On a Saturday night," she added, as she carried the lilies into the living room and deposited them on the coffee table.

"For the future then."

Back in the kitchen, she was pouring them each a glass of cabernet, thinking how nice it was to be asked. Other women probably took it for granted.

"You know that place in the market with the view of the Sound and the Olympics? Summer's coming, and the sunset will be gorgeous."

"Cutters Bayhouse? I'll make reservations there next time."

She felt as if he were courting her, and she enjoyed it.

Over spring rolls, Becca asked, "So how's your psychohistory coming?"

At last, Craig had someone he could talk to about it, and his enthusiasm for his project was infectious. Discussing the psychology of World War II, he reached over to the counter beside them to sneak little pots of hot mustard, chili, and red pepper, placing them between himself and Becca. At present, he was researching with voluminous notes, and Becca envied him the excitement of a long project.

"At least, they can't reject it until you're finished. It's perfect and undefiled. That's the great thing about a book. Me, I write a poem and it's turned down the next day."

"A book's cherry for a long time," he said, sipping his Thai Hai iced tea. "You should embark on a collection. That'll keep you busy and unrejected for years."

"But you have to publish poems in small magazines no one's ever heard of."

"That's a requirement? That no one's ever heard of them?"

"If people have heard of the magazine, the poems must be trite. At least, they can't be very good."

"But if they've appeared in unknown publications —"

"Preferably out of print—"

"Then an editor will give you a contract?"

"Exactly."

"From a publisher no one's ever heard of," Craig joined Becca's laughter.

"I could always self-publish a chapbook."

As Becca's green curry arrived with its eggplant and string beans *al dente,* they slid into a discussion of Gregory's treatment.

"I'm concerned that Gregory himself seems to have split," Becca said.

"Yes, that's one of the tricky aspects of working with DIDs. The whole system is based on defense against outside incursions, which Dr. Bernie and the rest of us are. Gregory himself split to defend against us, causing even more chaos."

"Chaos is a generally unrecognized defense mechanism, I think," said Becca.

"Good point! You should write a paper on it. Call it 'Displacement of Atoms.'"

Becca laughed. "You know that title's not nearly long enough for academia."

"How about *The Structure and Displacement of Atoms in Chaotic Defense Mechanisms?*"

"Better."

"Seriously, it's a lot harder to change someone's personality structure into something resembling order if it's chaotic. I can't help wondering if Robbie's personality may have had earthquake faults to begin with."

"Robbie was just the darlingest little boy. No cracks, not even hairline fractures, nothing."

"But he wasn't perfect," Craig said, more of a question than a statement.

Or was it a reminder? Take the scales from your eyes, Becca dear.

"He had an imagination, it's true. Very creative. He used to talk to the milk carton children. He'd sit them in the chair beside him and offer them tastes of his cereal."

"Just the normal, highly creative child. Subjected to who knows what kinds of stress, although we're getting a pretty darn good idea from some of the rest of the alters."

Becca's eyes slid to the gilt statues of Buddha around the room, their hands in various *mudras,* or positions, signifying enlightenment, compassion, and teaching. Serene. An ideal to be hoped for?

"Will there be more splits, do you think?"

"No way of telling. We're doing our best, of course."

"It sounds like a repeat of the Damon One-Damon Two dyad."

"Except that we're pretty sure Damon One was a real boy, the victim of a snuff film. The police are investigating. Want a taste of this barbecued pork?"

Becca reached her chopsticks over to Craig's plate and dropped most of her catch at various points along its way to her mouth, while Craig's snort of laughter quickly escalated to an eruption of full-blown mirth.

"I told you, you're crazy to use chopsticks," he said, handing her a solid forkful.

"Wood tastes better," she said.

"What do you mean, wood? They're plastic."

"Not metal."

"Would a plastic fork be okay? How about a plastic spoon?"

"You're merciless when you're on a roll. If you want some of my curry, you'd better spear it yourself."

"I wonder how we could do an objective scientific taste test comparing forks and chopsticks."

"Your pork would be delicious if it didn't have a slightly metallic flavor," she teased back.

"Your imagination. You don't eat American food with chopsticks, do you? Doesn't it taste metallic?"

"It would if it did," said Becca, resorting to the cryptic.

"What kind of an answer is that?" he laughed. He had her and knew it.

They were attracting less than benign looks from the other patrons, so they stifled their merriment and ate quietly for a couple of minutes until those around them had returned to the silences indicating they'd said everything to each other that needed saying.

"The alters are keeping a diary. Noel showed it to me. It's amazing to me to see all those different kinds of handwriting from one person."

"Isn't it, though? Large, rounded letters, pointy angular ones, some tall, thin and fine. Mefisto's letters are big and uneven, ill-formed. Vigrid stabs the paper so hard his 'i's' are dotted with holes."

"They do seem like indications of different characters. Some of them print, some write in cursive script, some thick and heavy, which graphologists say indicates a dominant personality."

"Mefisto and Vigrid, especially," Craig said. "And one thing we're finding is that there are a lot more different handwriting specimens than there are identified alters, so there are more of those than Gregory and the others know about."

"I thought their comments about what the others have written were fascinating. They sure disagree a lot."

"To the point of insult. Leroy says Gregory's got his head up his rear."

"Not precisely how he phrased it," Becca laughed. "One thing I still don't understand though. How can some alters be so much older? Gregory was a teen when Damon first met him at age five or six."

"That's one of the many reasons critics dismiss DID. As I understand it, the younger core personality observed the behavior of older ones and took sanctuary in it, identifying with it to protect himself. That's one explanation, anyway. Being older is safer. Same as when people identify with the aggressor or the torturer; some identify with the protector. Robbie's first discovery of an alter was in a mirror, a reflection of the world as he'd seen it."

"That makes it less mystical. I still don't understand how they have time for so many occupations though. How could Singer be off in a cathedral while Gregory's at work, and Damon's at the theater. I mean, the commute alone . . ."

They were polishing off their meal with a dish of lychee nuts between them.

"They're often absent from their activities," Craig explained. "Their consciousness takes up where they left off, maybe hours later. When someone asks them where they've been, they improvise excuses."

Becca and Craig grinned at each other over the last lychee nut, sitting unconsumed in a puddle of syrup.

When it came time to say goodnight, Craig asked to come up. Becca hesitated, not wanting to be rebuffed again, her lust having always been so much more powerful than his.

Craig leaned against the entry wall, his spicy breath wafting over her.

"You're not going to force me to make out here like a teenager in front of the whole neighborhood are you?" he asked with a hint of pathos.

"I'm not sure," she said.

"I promise not to make you do anything you don't want to."

Becca had to laugh at that. "Oh, that'll work!" Had he any idea?

Upstairs, they kissed for a few minutes, until Becca asked,

"Aren't you still worried that I love you like a brother?"

"If so, I hope the relationship's incestuous," he grinned. Then, seeing the hurt in her eyes, he added, "No, I was way off base. I don't think your feelings for me ever were linked to your feelings for Robbie. Perhaps there was some transference from Dr. Connie, but — I always seem to be apologizing."

"No need," she said, reaching for his hand. "You've been a good friend. Better than I had a right to expect."

She wanted no more mistakes, so she had taken a step backward from fevered desire. Now, she was just playing. He pressed for more, as so many men feel duty-bound to do in their defense against imagined slurs on their vaunted masculinity, but his attempts, while not half-hearted, were not inordinately insistent, either.

A few days later, Craig told her that he had tickets for the critically acclaimed Pioneer Square production of "My Fair Lady," starring Chloe Hearst.

Rarely did Becca wear anything dressy. There was hardly any occasion. The last time was Christmas with Craig's family. But a night at the theater was, after all, a dressy event. She couldn't even remember what she owned. Such clothes were stored away in her dining room closet behind the seduction fireplace.

Later, she remembered each little seemingly inconsequential act in slow motion. Nothing was important enough for her to notice immediately. When she approached the closet door, she did not notice that it was incompletely closed. Such a detail was trivial. The latch was only partly sprung back, resting on the door plate. Becca didn't even have to turn the knob to open it. She simply pulled. As she did so, she heard a click.

The click of her nightmare! The click of her return to her apartment after a week with Craig!

Someone had been there after all. But why would an intruder want to see what was in her closet? He'd had plenty of time and opportunity to do so before. Why now? And if Gregory's alters had been her visitors, as everyone assumed, now that he was locked up, who was it who got into her apartment in the early morning hours? Who was it who didn't take anything? Who didn't attack her? Who eluded her most thorough search, a thoroughness born of terror? Who, for all she knew, just looked into her closet. What was he doing here?

Or perhaps it wasn't an intruder, after all. Perhaps the door just naturally didn't close completely, and the slightest shake — perhaps a truck rumbling by — made it spring open in the night. That's what Sgt. McNalley and Craig and Annalyn would tell her.

She closed the door completely and then tried to pull it open without turning the handle. It was shut tight.

51

ROBBIE'S LITTLE BODY JERKING and twisting in the wind, head down, blond hair hanging in his eyes, words of reproach soundless — the image haunted Becca's dreams, both sleeping and waking.

That Gregory or Damon or Robbie or whoever he was might be compelled to undergo the ordeal of a trial for murder and be sentenced to death was more than she could endure. The fact was that the experience of encountering five-year-old Robbie in the body of a stranger — the way he spoke, the words he chose, the experiences between them, the affection — was growing inside her from strangeness into recognition. Although she tried to deny it, she couldn't resist the thrill of this recognition. That a multiple, or for that matter, anyone afflicted with a serious mental illness must suffer prison or death seemed incredibly cruel. The blatant exception, of course, was the psychopath or sociopath. Now Dr. Bernie was telling her there was little doubt in his mind that two of Robbie's personalities were psychopaths, and that it was they who had committed the torture-murders and other heinous crimes in San Francisco and Seattle.

Becca scanned a hundred articles and books concerning the law and the mentally ill, where she discovered to her horror that Gregory could be in even graver danger than she thought. Almost without exception, those dissociative patients with a criminal history who were tracked down and captured by the police, were indicted, appeared before a judge, and were then discovered to be mentally ill and found legally incompetent to stand trial. They were discharged to a mental institution where they were treated, and if they were lucky, they went through the process of integration. Assuming the personalities responsible for the crimes had fused, and for practical purposes, no longer existed, the patient might eventually be released back into the community.

But Gregory had turned himself in and was already undergoing treatment. Suppose that, by the time the police had enough evidence to indict him, he was integrated and declared competent? Could he then be convicted?

Seeking help, Becca waited in Dr. Bernie's office. Several of the books and articles she'd read referred to Dr. Bernard Leonard as an expert witness at these trials.   Dr. Bernie stomped into the office in a rage and tossed a reprint onto his desk.

"How dare they? How dare they? Stupid robot behaviorists — they have no idea. They attack my paradigm, which is acclaimed as brilliant by most experts, and what do they suggest in its stead? 'Dissociative Identity Disorder is therapist-created,'" he mouthed, oozing sarcasm. "Therapist-created! I ask you, Becca, I ask you right now — no, I order you — get out there and create a case of dissociative identity disorder. Right now. Pick a patient, any patient, and give me a case by the end of the day. I'll make it easy on you. By the end of the week. Can you do it?"

"I haven't a clue," Becca said honestly. "I suppose I'd have to arrange a horrible sexually abusive situation in their childhoods which, of course, I couldn't."

"Supposedly you'd do it by persuading your patient that his mother inflicted herself on him sexually when he was a child. Beat him into submissiveness. Perhaps you'd induce catharsis until finally he really had those memories, even though he didn't. Honestly, these psychoanalysts and cognitive behaviorists are worse than Freud."

("He's possessed," Becca later told Craig.)

"But that's not what you came to talk to me about." He finally settled down into his chair, crumpled the paper and threw it into the trash, retrieved it, and put it in his incoming box. "I'll show them. What did you want to ask me?"

"About the possibility that Gregory, Damon, and Robbie might be convicted and sentenced to death for what Vigrid and 'Fisto did. The rest of them are normal," she argued, forgetting her usual deference. "I mean, if you call dissociation normal. None of them is completely sane. But it's not fair to hang them for what the two sociopaths did."

"I don't think you need worry, Becca," Dr. Bernie assured her. First of all," Dr. Bernie continued in oratorical mode, "Integration takes several years —"

"To complete, but he might be far enough along —"

"The police are standing by to arrest him momentarily. They've got the evidence, but they're amenable to remanding him to the hospital until his trial."

Becca felt herself blanching. McNalley hadn't told her this.

"Gregory must be competent to stand trial," Dr. Bernie continued, "and multiples are often ruled incompetent. They don't have the memory for it, or rather, they have too many individual and conflicting memories. Gregory can't be sure that Vigrid and 'Fisto committed the murders. A trial would be too confusing for the alters."

"Like Billy Milligan," who had twenty-four personalities, several of whom had committed crimes, including three rapes. After years in Ohio mental institutions, he was considered no longer a threat to society and released.

"One of our more notorious trials, yes," Dr. Bernie was saying. "I see you've been educating yourself." Little had Becca known, when she borrowed that book from Dr. Connie so many years ago, that someday it would play such a significant role in her life. "The fact is that the stress of a trial makes the alters switch back and forth more rapidly like eye blinks, and then one of them doesn't remember what another one said or did the moment before. That's hardly helpful to their attorneys, which is one of the definitions of competence that the court insists on. The DID patient must be able to assist her attorney."

Dr. Bernie used female pronouns, even if they were inappropriate, to signal his emancipation from machismo.

Becca's thoughts tumbled over each other as she tried to convey to God the multiplicity, appropriately enough, of her anxieties. "They've got DNA on Gregory, and jurors think DNA is the ultimate proof, no matter how much defense attorneys try to discount it."

"They'll say it was left from one of Damon's previous visits."

"All over Carmine?" Vigrid had not taken precautions in those days. Besides, as he freely admitted with the transcendent expression of a saint in ecstasy, he loved the touch of flesh quivering in pain and finally expiring.

"They know Carmine fondled little boys," Dr. Bernie assured her. "It's to Gregory's credit that he turned himself in, remember. You see, Becca, juries are loath to condemn an innocent man like Gregory, but they also don't want to see a guilty one like Vigrid get off scot-free. It's a dilemma for them. In this case, two of eleven major identities are guilty, but the rest are innocent in varying degrees, from Damon, a porn actor, to Wendy, a virtual saint."

"A raped saint."

"The jury's out on whether or not one personality can commit a punishable crime against another. In any event, it's more likely that they'll find Gregory innocent by reason of insanity and then recommend treatment."

"But that's what I'm afraid of," Becca said, not even trying to conceal how upset she was. She saw Dr. Bernie blink at the unprofessionalism of her behavior, but she plunged on. "If he's ever sane again —"

"Which, of course, he will be with me treating him."

"That's right!" Becca had no doubt. "Then he'll be sane enough to stand trial. We've got this crazy system of treating the mentally ill until they're normal and then putting them on trial for things they did while they were insane. The newly sane shouldn't be held accountable for their actions when they were crazy."

"One manifestation of a dissociated society," Dr. Bernie nodded vigorously." "Whole society needs treatment for its multiplicity which they like to call 'diversity.'"

"To promote 'integration'," Becca agreed.

"Precisely. But it's not likely that Robbie will be tried after he's cured. Vigrid and 'Fisto won't even be there. Your brother will be a new person, a perfectly healthy young man out working in the real world and making love every Saturday night."

At Dr. Bernie's mention of his favorite topic, Becca started uncomfortably. But she had to know what Robbie's fate was likely to be and how she could help him.

"Will you recommend a lawyer for him?"

"I'll do better than that. A top attorney happens to be a good friend of mine. I'll contact her and ask that she take the case as a personal request."

Personal? And what *quid pro quo* would Dr. Bernie expect for such a "personal" effort?

"I've heard that different identities should maybe have different lawyers."

Dr. Bernie threw back his head and roared. "That sure would make an indelible impression on the jury, a long line of lawyers sitting at the defense table, each representing a different alter, while only one defendant sits among them. Acts out the multiplicity in a vivid way. But it's expensive. I'd leave that decision to my lawyer friend, of course. She might feel that it's better for them to have one attorney, but for each of them to plead differently. Similar impression but cheaper. That way, Damon, Robbie, Leroy, and the rest can plead innocent. Gregory not guilty by reason of insanity. But 'Fisto may want to brag. I doubt Vigrid will plead guilty. A lot of mitigating factors here, too. Leroy recalls Carl's horrible abuse, which caused the splitting. Juries are sympathetic to that."

Becca got up to leave. "I can't thank you enough, Dr. Bernie. I feel fortunate to have an expert in the field as my mentor."

"*The* expert," he corrected her, and she pretended she'd never heard of Colin Ross, Frank Putnam, Richard Kluft, and the rest. "I enjoy it. Being the expert in the field of dissociative identity disorder is a bit like being a detective. Who did what? And when? And why? You seem to be becoming quite a pro yourself."

"In self-defense."

"You might want to specialize."

"I'm not sure," she stammered. Of course, she didn't want to specialize in DID. She'd chosen sibling loss as her specialty; but she didn't want to offend His Honor by telling him.

"You won't feel completely relieved until it's over, of course. If there's anything else I can do for you . . ."

"There is one other thing. Gregory says 'Fisto and Vigrid are threatening to break out."

Dr. Bernie's look was reproving. "They can't break out. They're on lock-down."

"Yes, I know that, but they're experts at breaking in and out of places."

"In their own minds, I'm sure," he guffawed.

"They have a history."

"*Their* history."

"Of course." But the fact is, patients break out of mental hospitals just as prisoners break out of jail. Usually, it's a patient managing to get hold of a white coat and badge, and spouting word salad that sounds like arcane psychological jargon to anyone who challenges him.

"Meanwhile," Dr. Bernie was saying, "if you and Craig ever call it quits, be sure to let me know."

Becca couldn't conceal her shock. He knew? He'd been holding back because she was involved with one of his staff? He probably thought they were more involved than they were, but Becca wasn't of a mind to disabuse him of the notion. At her surprise, Dr. Bernie laughed uproariously and gave his chair a gleeful twist.

"Not much goes on around here that I don't know about. I've known about you and Craig for ages."

But they hadn't been involved for ages. Truth to tell, they hadn't been involved at all. Only recently had their friendship metamorphosed into courtship. "We're good friends," she should say, but that could open her up to his unwanted advances. Instead she thanked him for helping her improve her brother's prospects and made her escape.

That night, Becca lulled herself to sleep listening for clicks — her new soporific. She'd told Annalyn about them, but no one else. Not Dr. Bernie, who might suspect they were "in her own mind," nor Sgt. McNalley, who couldn't fingerprint them, nor Craig, who'd insist on smothering her in protection unless he reverted to the possibility that she was doing this to herself.

Weeks ago, a click meant someone else had been in her apartment. When she got home from the hospital, she hadn't conducted a thorough enough search, and when they figured she was asleep, they came out to explore. But that had changed. Now, she dropped her briefcase on the couch and immediately checked under and behind it, as well as the bed, the desk, and certainly the closets, especially the one she feared behind the false fireplace with the knight and lady in hammered metal across, courting each other. Why did the intruder wait until she was asleep? Maybe her return had interrupted him. Each time?

Restless, Becca switched on her bedside lamp again and padded out to the dining room. The door to the wall-length closet was closed. She'd shut it tight after checking it earlier tonight. She opened it slightly now, then pulled it, eliciting a satisfactory click. After surveying her clothes, her eyes focused on the square in the ceiling. Was it her imagination or did it seem slightly awry? A flashlight beam showed a crooked gray line along one edge where it had been moved after having been seated tightly for years. Whether this had been so before, she was unsure. She hadn't examined it before.

The square appeared too small for a normal human frame to squeeze through, but this must be an illusion. Why else was it there, if not for someone to gain access to the roof? The ceiling to her apartment had been lowered, and large tiles enclosed in aluminum frames had been substituted as being more decorous than the original high ceiling, although why she could not imagine. It was then she noticed that the closet ceiling was unlowered and at the original height, three feet at least higher than the one in the dining room. So, the square must lead to the attic, the same one that was accessed by the stairs on the back porch.

Could the click have indicated someone *entering* her apartment from inside her closet, rather than opening the door from the dining room? The stairs on the back porch led to a door with a padlock on it. She had seen this with her own eyes. So that entry was out. How else might someone gain access to her ceiling entry? Perhaps through the apartment across the way?

To be sure, Becca eased into her bathrobe, went out to the back porch, and looked up the short ladder to the door. Sure enough, the padlock was still attached to the handle and hasp. But to be absolutely certain, she climbed the stairs and pulled on the lock. It came loose in her hands. Nor could she lock it by simply pushing the shackle into the body. The cylinder must be broken. She'd call the manager tomorrow.

What was up there? Teetering at the top of the ladder, she removed the lock, dropped it to the porch floor, and managed to push the trap door up and open. A cold, dank wind rushed out at her, with smells of mildew, rotting wood, dead rat, and other unidentifiable stenches. As she suspected, another door in the attic ceiling about three feet above led to the roof. Becca herself was eye level with the floor and could just make out the pattern of something clearing away the dust in the direction of her apartment, reminding her of her plant movements months ago. She couldn't bring herself to explore any further. Letting the door fall, she reattached the padlock to give it the phony appearance of security.

Becca made herself a cup of cocoa as she puzzled over the intruder and who it might be. They'd always assumed Gregory or one of his aliases. Leroy himself had admitted that Singer and Watcher had been here. But they were all locked up, and Dr. Bernie didn't believe it was them. If it wasn't, then once again she was faced with the terrifying possibility that it was someone else entirely. Someone they did not suspect and were not remotely aware of.

Becca returned to bed with her cocoa, settled it on her nightstand, her rolling pin securely beside her pillow, and opened her mystery. Eventually, she fell asleep.

Click!

52

BECCA SHOT UP, FUMBLING in the dark for her rolling pin. It thudded to the floor, and the next instant, she was knocked sideways back onto her pillow, head pressed down, face smothered by a coarse rag saturated in the ether-like substance of her nightmare. She tried to twist from side to side, but the grip was too strong. She tried to hold her breath and avoid inhaling the fumes. But a brutal blow to her stomach forced all the air out of her.

She gasped and involuntarily spun into darkness.

As Becca began to regain consciousness, her first sensation was of pain all over— bruising pain in her legs and arms, throbbing in her head, sickening in her stomach where her attacker had punched her. She faded in and out, the ether still pungent in her nostrils. Attempting to move, she discovered that she couldn't. She lay immobilized, a blinding white light beyond her eyelids.

Then she realized that her wrists and ankles hurt because they were bound. Cautiously, she tested first one limb and then another, trying not to give away her efforts with too much movement in case someone was watching. But there was no slackness whatsoever. In fact, someone giggled. *Giggled?*

Squinting her eyes open, she saw herself naked and spread-eagled on the dining room table, her legs raised over chairs in an ingenious pelvic position, lashed by ropes extending over them and anchored below.

The light from the floor lamp burned into her retinas. Someone had replaced the three sixty-watt bulbs with one-hundred-and-fifties.

A figure stood over her in green surgical scrubs. He looked like Gregory, only he didn't. Damon, maybe, but not him either. Rapid conversation sparked between him and someone she could not see. The figure reached for something that scraped metallically. Raising her head, Becca was shocked to see a tray of surgical instruments beside her.

"What are you doing?" Becca gasped, terror rumbling through her bowels. She might lose control right there.

"Told you we should tape her pie hole."

"'Fisto, haven't I taught you anything? Agony's nothing if you can't hear it. To paraphrase a famous magician, it's all in the scream."

"Vigrid, you're such a card. Might wake the neighbors, though."

"I don't think so. Remember that first time? No one heard."

This was true. In her nightmare, Becca had screamed and screamed, but no one knocked at her door, front or back, to ask what the problem was. Her struggles gave the duo a lot of amusement.

"'Fisto's an expert at tying people up," Vigrid said to her. "But go ahead, knock yourself out."

She must have fainted again. The ceiling reeled dizzily above her.

"Now, Becca, you're a scientific type, aren't you?" the nursey-nurse voice inquired.

"Sure. Psychologists are scientists, aren't they?" asked 'Fisto gruffly.

"In their own minds, at least," said Vigrid.

It occurred to Becca that, when these two were speaking, their movements slowed or were even suspended. Talking and operating each required their total concentration. Desperately casting about for any topic that might halt the proceedings long enough for someone to come to her rescue (*who?*), she asked,

"So, how did you two meet, anyway?" Admittedly, the question was asinine. They'd never "met" in the normal sense of the word; they'd just both come into being.

"Oh, that's an interesting question," said Vigrid, gloved hands suspended over Becca's open thighs. "I needed an assistant, so I advertised."

"You did not. I offered."

"In the college paper. All kinds of weirdoes wriggled out of the woodwork with ideas for experiments."

"I wrote an application."

"You couldn't."

"I wrote my name."

"'Fisto, dear, you're a magnificent bulk of bulging brutality. That's what first attracted me to you. But you can't fill out forms."

"Nuh-uh. I filled out a form to get into college."

"You weren't in college. You were wandering the halls, looking for a score. I filled it out for you, after you came to work for me. It was easy. Colleges these days take anyone who's warm and breathing. And fills out their forms."

"I signed it."

While their attention was distracted by this little tiff, Becca struggled to loosen her ropes to no avail. She kicked at one of the chairs in an attempt to knock it off the table. Maybe someone would hear it downstairs. But it sat solidly entrenched in its position. Her wrists were becoming raw.

"The muscles you need for writing are small and delicate," Vigrid was explaining patiently. "That's just not you."

"I remember now. We met in the campus beer joint. You helped me fill it out over a few pitchers."

"Doesn't sound like me," said Vigrid. "Then again, maybe. Now I think of it, weren't we reminiscing about our childhood in the cafeteria?"

"In Mexico?"

"Big Bend, Texas. Now I remember. I found 'Fisto beating on a professor. He knew instinctively where to hit to cause the most pain. I admired that in him. But, here we are, wasting our Becca's valuable time. I apologize, Becca." Vigrid resumed palpating and exploring. "Those are her ovaries."

"I'd like to hear about your childhoods. Your mothers?"

"Our mothers!" exclaimed 'Fisto. "Bor-ing!"

"We didn't have mothers. We were originals. We're going to perform a little experiment."

"A bunch of them, actually," 'Fisto giggled.

"To be accurate, yes."

The instrument clattered to the tray, and Vigrid had to pick it up again.

Later, when Craig demanded an explanation of the Central Nursing Station, they told him that the night nurse was charting when Staff said Room 810 was missing.

"What do you mean, missing?" asked the nurse.

"Not in his room."

"Say that, then. Don't say he's missing. That's serious. Have you searched all the other rooms, the TV room, the kitchen, the offices?"

"They're locked," Staff said, pursing her mouth sullenly.

"Under the beds, in the cabinets, the closets, the stairs, the elevator, the other floors? Have you hunted for him in any of those places?"

"No, I'm too busy."

"Not the dispensary, but maybe?"

"No. I have to —"

"Then he's not missing. He's just not in his room. He's somewhere else. Whenever someone isn't in one place, he's in another," said Nurse didactically. "It's a principle of physics. Search thoroughly. Leave no bedpan unturned. Then, if you don't find him, *then* he's missing."

Staff didn't look for Room 810 because the FBI was cursing out Room 822, calling him nasty names from the TV tower across the rooftops, and Room 817 was wandering the halls, and Room 838 was in Room 841 with Room 805 doing God knows what. In other words, Staff had other fish to fry. Not the way she put it to Dr. Craig. To him, she gave the eternal inarguable excuse. "We're short-handed," she said.

When Room 810 didn't show up, Night Nurse pulled his chart and learned that he had a name. Gregory Warhol. If he escaped, she was supposed to inform a Sgt. McNalley at the East Precinct station. Did she want the police on her case? Not hardly. Not with all those unpaid parking tickets. She waited for Staff to come back with her search report. Which she didn't.

An hour later, Nurse saw Staff padding down the hall with Room 5 in tow.

"Any luck with Room 810?"

"Not yet."

Nurse gave it another hour, and when Staff still remained mystified, Nurse reluctantly phoned the East Precinct and asked for Sgt. McNalley.

"Ma'am, I can't exactly contact him," said the buttery southern voice.

"He's not on duty?"

"Not exactly, ma'am."

"We've had a patient wander off, and I'm supposed to call him. Where is he?"

"Ma'am, he's in crisis?" he said, ending his sentence with an odd questioning inflection.

"In crisis? What's wrong with him?"

"Ma'am, I don't mean personally. The sergeant's never in crisis personally. It's unprofessional. He's at — an event."

"Can you reach him?"

"Depends."

"Would you give him a message then?"

"Ma'am, I go off duty in five minutes? But sure, I'll leave it on his desk?"

"Will he be coming back to his office?"

"Ma'am, I doubt it."

"This is Seattle General." The hospital didn't have unpaid parking tickets. At least, she didn't think so. "Tell him Gregory Warhol's whereabouts are not known."

"Gregory Warhol missing," the officer repeated what he thought he'd heard.

"We're not sure he's missing exactly." That could set off a frantic protocol, including media coverage.

"Well, if he's not missing . . ."

"He may be."

"Ma'am, I'll inform Sgt. McNalley. If he gets back from the riot."

Nurse also noted that Becca Merrow was to be called. She dialed the number, but an automated operator came on the line and told her the phone was temporarily out of service. As for Dr. Bernie, he was away at a conference in Atlanta.

"Now this will be just a little uncomfortable," said Vigrid.

"For you. Not for us," said 'Fisto.

Vigrid inserted an instrument, and Becca screamed.

"It's only a speculum, for God's sake!" said Vigrid. "You've had them inside you a hundred times at your age."

"Usually they warm them first," 'Fisto reminded him. "So we've heard."

"Like we care. She never cared if our Robbie was warm, did she?"

Becca was listening frantically for the help that didn't come, the knock on the door, the voices on the stairs as she replied, "I was a good sister to Robbie."

"Not what we heard."

"I did everything for him. I was his mother, practically."

"Until you got sick of him and traded him for a mall certificate."

"I didn't! I did everything I could to find him." Tearfully, Becca listed the Search and Rescue team, the police station, the private detective that she tried to hire. As she spoke, once again they were more intent on what she said and stopped probing inside her. "I even made flyers and posted them all over town. The grocery, the record store, the library, the post office . . ." Becca could go on forever if it made them pause.

"Didn't do much good, did it?" Vigrid summed up acidly, resuming his activity.

"It's not my fault. They took him."

"Have you any idea what they did to him? Leroy knows. He had to take the pain."

"Damn straight," came a gravelly voice she hadn't heard before. "Hard work, taking pain. Couldn't do my art."

"Leroy, get out of here. We've got the spot now."

"I was only agreeing."

"All right, you agreed, now git!"

"You guys don't know what it's like. You make the pain instead of taking it."

"What pain was that, Leroy?" Becca asked, the glimmer of an idea rattling around in her head like a pinball.

"Carl raped me in the bum, over and over. I bled in the bed, on the carpet, in the bathroom, and Dr. Phillip had to sew me up. Lots of times."

"Yes, it was awful," said Vigrid. "Now, let us get on with our work."

"Thank you so much, Leroy, for taking the pain for Robbie. You must be a wonderful brother to him."

Becca felt a sudden poke deep inside her and screamed again.

"Shut the fuck up," said Vigrid.

"I've got a right to talk about it," said Leroy.

"Want me to tape her, huh?"

"No, I want to hear her scream when I cut the labial nerve and transect the *glans clitoris*."

"Will that hurt?" 'Fisto asked with gusto.

"Beyond her wildest imaginings."

"Ooooo! And then what will you do?"

"Dissect her little box. Slowly. Very slowly. We want her to appreciate it, don't we, 'Fisto? And then, and then, we head for the uterus and the endometrium. Myself, I can't wait to twist these wires into her Fallopian tubes."

"Like snaking a drain?"

"Very like."

Vigrid had donned a mask. With only his eyes showing, he was scarier than ever. She must have been out only a few minutes, because they hadn't made progress.

"We were waiting for you," said 'Fisto, as if reading her mind. "We don't want you to miss any of the gory details. Right, Vigrid?"

"When have you been wrong, my dear 'Fisto? Tell us one single instance. We're opening you up, Becca, to see what's inside," he explained, twisting the instrument inexpertly, as Becca flinched. "Now, let's have a look, shall we?"

Frantically, Becca tried to think of another question to ask them. But fear blanked her mind.

Vigrid and 'Fisto took turns peering into Becca, although only a single figure was bending over, looking inside, straightening up, and bending from a different angle.

"Not very impressive," 'Fisto opined. "You take a cock and balls. That's a sight to see. They've got mass, you know what I mean? Even Pleaser's, you gotta admit."

"Even Pleaser's," Vigrid agreed.

"This here's just a little box like you said, pink and spongy. You could put jewelry in it."

"She's got a collection of earrings," Vigrid reminded him. "You can stuff her later."

Becca was cramping uncontrollably and trying not to pass out again. She had to keep her wits about her if she had any chance of survival.

"You and Leroy seem close," she said through a groan of pain.

"What do you mean by that?" 'Fisto demanded.

"You do him a lot of favors."

"What favors? What's she talking about, Vigrid?"

"I mean, you've been very kind to him."

"Kind!" 'Fisto exploded so violently that Becca jumped, resulting in excruciating pain all over her body.

"When we take his side, she thinks it's kindness," Vigrid explained, having paused long enough in his dissection of Becca for her to catch her breath. "She didn't mean it as an insult. She's bleeding again. Sop that blood up for me, will you, 'Fisto?"

"I forgot the gauze pads."

"Grab the roll of paper towels we used for the turkey. You see, Becca, we don't like bullies. Not one bit. Carl was a bully, so we helped Leroy turn him in and get the place shut down. Took care of

Mickey for aiding and abetting Carl, didn't we, 'Fisto?"

"Took care of him good and proper, I'd say. Bleeding's stopped. For now."

"Leroy's the only one in the pack with guts. Not Gregory."

"God, not Gregory."

"Gregory's a wimp. Robbie's a crier. Damon's a whiner."

"What about Breakout and Bounce?"

"Okay for sports freaks. Not really contributing to the world, like we are. But you gotta respect Leroy. He's the one taught me about pain. I looked up to him. Still do. That's how I became a great surgeon. Like the Bible says, I do unto others what they'd done to Leroy. Leroy would have been my assistant, but he already had a job. Besides, he was pretty focused on his painting. Still, he does medical pictures for me."

"Very colorful," said 'Fisto.

"Photos, too. Doesn't like to. Cameras are mere machines, he says. Not art. But he does them. As a favor to me."

When Becca came to again, the last pain still stabbed through her to the place she thought of as her 'baby room'. 'Fisto seemed not to have realized she'd lost consciousness.

"We had another woman," he said as he checked her ropes almost absently, tightening one that he imagined to be slightly loose.

"Dessa. Her name was Dessa. Leroy's girlfriend, only she wasn't."

"Bad girl! Hurt our Leroy no end."

"See, the way it works," said Vigrid, holding a shiny steel instrument in each hand, "anybody hurts our brother, we avenge him."

"Not our sister, though."

"I've told you not to mention that."

Wendy? The one he raped?

"We opened this Dessa up, but we didn't get very far. Didn't even make it through the cervix. Fainted dead away."

"As in dead," 'Fisto giggled.

"Have you ever tried to operate on a dead person?"

"Bet she hasn't." Giggle giggle.

"Blood stops, coagulates in the veins, no more circulation. And that's just for starters. I mean, you can do an autopsy. I've done plenty of those." As he probed inside, he pinched her. "Ooops. Sorry. Unintentional."

"It really was," said 'Fisto. "The intentions come later."

"Along with the autopsy."

Becca was trying to swallow her panic. This must be what it's like to have a baby, the grinding cramps in depths farther inside her than she'd known she had.

"What do you two do for fun?"

"You mean, besides this?"

Vigrid and 'Fisto broke into guffaws that had them reeling around the dining room and high-fiving each other.

"This is what we do for fun? What else is there?"

"Playing games, maybe?"

"You mean, like checkers? Sure we do that sometimes."

"Yeah," said 'Fisto. "We use those blue buttons you attach to wires for a cardiogram."

"Discs," Vigrid corrected.

"And you glue them to the poor schmuck's chest for an EKG. Except we jolt 'em."

"Toenails or fingernails will do."

"After we've jolted 'em."

"Sure. They don't need them anymore."

As Vigrid and 'Fisto bent once again to their work, Becca took a wild stab at putting these two back in touch with reality.

"Do you two know that you're aspects of Robbie? Alter identities?"

"You got it wrong, Sis. We're the primaries. He's just an alter. A weak, puny alter. And he's on his way out. We got no more use for him."

There was just one hope, an outside chance. Probably, it wouldn't work and might earn her another episode of grinding pain. But she had to risk it. She waited until Vigrid had withdrawn the instrument to exchange it for another. Metal clattered into the tray, and another instrument scraped.

"Robbie," she called out suddenly. "Robbie, it's your Bec-Bec. Can you take the spot?" During the few minutes that Leroy had been on the spot, the others had not hurt her. 'Fisto clamped his dirty hand that stank of alcohol and her own blood over Becca's mouth, before his face suddenly softened, as if it were made of butter.

"Bec-Bec? You don't got no clothes on."

"Get back to your room, kid."

"You're not my Bec-Bec."

"Or we'll hurt you real bad."

"I'm sorry, Robbie." Damn! She'd called on the wrong one. "They're right. Get back to your attic, where you're safe."

"Nice try," said 'Fisto, slapping one cheek so hard it snapped her head to one side, and then the other. "But we're in control here."

"Gregory," Becca shrieked. "Gregory, help me!"

"Get out of here. You're not supposed to take the spot," said Vigrid.

"You said so yourself," 'Fisto added.

"It's one of your rules."

"I'm breaking my rules," came the cultured voice, more suitable for literature or the opera than for dealing with thugs.

"Not now." Petulance edged Vigrid's response.

"We're busy, now."

"You're not supposed to be doing any more surgery. Dr. Bernie's orders."

"None of your business. Get away."

"Back to your labs," Gregory ordered. "Becca, how awful for you. Here, let me untie you."

"We'll kill you if you interfere."

"Bounce! Breakout!" Gregory shouted suddenly. "Hold them down."

To Becca it looked as though the figure was having a seizure, arms, legs, torso and body twisting every which way, as the identities battled it out.

She felt her ropes loosen and drop to the floor. Her legs still wobbly from being bound for so long, she limped quickly to her room for the rolling pin, the excruciating pain throbbing deep inside her. Damage? She'd think about it later.

"I've got Breakout," came 'Fisto's unmistakable voice.

"And I've got Bounce."

Did she have time to phone the police? It was all happening too fast. Vigrid and 'Fisto seemed to be taking the spot again. She swung the rolling pin at them with all her might, over and over.

The next minute, Robbie was crying to her, "Ow, Bec-Bec, stop, that hurts." Blood spurted from her beloved brother's forehead and streamed from his eyes.

Horrified, Becca paused. She couldn't defend herself without hurting her sweet brother. Then, she was even more horrified to see Robbie's face rearrange itself into the hardened features of Vigrid once again. He grinned triumphantly.

Like a ventriloquist, 'Fisto called "Robbie, Robbie, it's your Bec-Bec."

"Now for your punishment," said Vigrid in a rage.

"Sure, we've been easy on you."

"Even trusted you."

Becca glanced around her frantically for any weapon, any idea, 'Fisto's hands already on her wrists. Feeling as though her insides were dropping out of her, she stomped his instep, and he yelled, "Ow!" Holding her stomach, she ran to the kitchen back door but couldn't get it unlocked fast enough. Managing to duck under 'Fisto's ham-handed grasp, she dashed to the front door, but 'Fisto just giggled.

"Why didn't you run around the dining table? That would have been more fun."

She thought of throwing herself out a window. They were open but screened.

"I'm on lockdown," she said to herself stupidly, out of breath with terror.

"Come on, Becca. Make it fun. I'll let you get to the table, and we can chase each other around that."

"Stop the nonsense," said Vigrid.

"Aw, we're just having fun."

Trailing blood, and sure she couldn't make it another step, Becca tried to think. 'Fisto giggled madly as he chased her, first one way, then the other. Pain made her slow and clumsy.

"'Atta girl. Ooh, you're too fast for me."

She had to save both Robbie and herself, even if it meant hurting him. They'd said they had no more use for him. Becca was the only chance he had.

"Gregory," she yelled, "You've got to get the others. All of them. All together."

Then Gregory was calling, "Bounce, Breakout, Damon, Singer, and Leroy, you too. We need everyone we can get. Wendy, let the kids out. Leroy, please, you have to help us. All together now."

The fighting erupted again. Becca grabbed her rolling pin, unsure of who was who and therefore unsure of when to hit. To her astonishment, even though there was a single writhing figure before her, a crowd of shadows struggled and fought with each other on the walls. She must be hallucinating.

"Ow, Singer, cut it out, or we'll cut you again."

"My pleasure," said Singer. "This'll teach you not to cut on your brothers."

"Tear up our room, will you?" said Bounce or Breakout.

"You really went too far with Wendy," said Damon.

"Leroy, after all we've done for you."

"You didn't do it for me. You did it for you."

"Robbie, get out of here. It's too dangerous for you."

"Watcher," called Vigrid at last. "Watcher?"

A moment of suspended animation. Then the violence erupted again.

Vigrid sank to the floor, attacked by a pack of invisible demons, his arms pinned behind him.

Becca ran to the phone, found it off the hook and jostled it to get the dial tone.

"Want my duck phone, Bec-Bec?" Robbie's voice asked as clearly as he had thirteen years ago. "It always works."

At last, she was able to dial 911.

53

"DID I TELL YOU that Dr. Bernie thinks we're involved?" Becca chortled a few weeks after her terrifying encounter with Vigrid and 'Fisto. They were in Craig's kitchen, and she was feeling happier than she had in a long while. Her only reminders of the attack were sudden stabs of pain from bruises she forgot she had, and she suffered these gladly — the alternative so much worse. A gynecological exam showed no permanent damage. Dr. Bernie assured her that the two psychopaths couldn't get at her again; for one thing, hospital security had been tightened, and for another, the other alters wouldn't allow it, if only for Robbie's sake.

"Dr. Bernie thinks everyone's involved," Craig informed her gaily. "He sexualizes everything and everyone. It's a fetish with him."

Craig was leaning against the counter, his long legs gracefully bent in his blue pants like swans necks, she thought. He turned to season fresh Copper River salmon with what he claimed was his own secret recipe — mayonnaise, nonfat yogurt, shallots, cilantro, fresh basil, and a secret ingredient, all blended and generously spread over the fillet. Around him, the rest of dinner was in various stages of preparation, the asparagus *al dente* (he promised) and the herbed pilaf. Salad in the fridge.

"Histrionic personality disorder," Becca diagnosed Dr. Bernie with relish.

"Oh, now he's got a womb, has he? He'll love that! What did you tell him?"

"I didn't want to say we weren't involved, for obvious reasons. So, like it or not, in Dr. Bernie's eyes, we are."

"Let's not lie," he said, letting the spoon clatter to the counter and putting his arms around her waist. His kiss was delicious.

"You've made an honest woman of me," she giggled. "Very thoughtful."

"I'm a gentleman," he reminded her, then turned to pour the gefiltemilch. As he handed her a glass, he drew her to him and kissed her again. They both sipped before he turned back to the range. Was this a game? Kiss, wine, kiss, food, kiss, kiss? She smiled to herself. Couldn't wait to find out. She prepared a cracker of ripe, runny Brie and raised it to his mouth. As he took it, his lips grazed her fingertips, and she shuddered with unexpected pleasure. When he'd finished it, he kissed her again.

"This is getting to be a habit," she smiled. Part of his new courtship, she decided, the purpose of which is usually to get a woman into bed. Did he imagine he was seducing her? Of course, he didn't need to. Becca would have let him mount her with no courtship whatsoever. But she'd decided not to share this with him. If he wanted to think of her as an old-fashioned girl, a virgin, even, let him. When they finally got to bed, she'd surprise him. "Surprise me," he said in her fantasies.

They carried the dishes into the dining room and set them on the trestle table, where Minnie anticipated them, seated on her haunches like a proper show dog, waiting patiently for any crumbs that might be forthcoming.

"She's well-behaved," Becca commented.

"Not as well-behaved as she should be. My fault. I can't resist those pleading doggie eyes. It's no good making an occasional exception, as you know from Psych 101. Occasional reward is a stronger incentive than steady. How's your salmon?"

Orgasmic, she almost said. "Absolutely delicious," she really said. "Everything is. I'm letting you do all the cooking from now on. The heck with Thai Hai."

"These are the only dishes I know."

"I can live with that."

Too late, she realized the *double entendre* and felt herself flush. Craig caught it and grinned at her discomfort, kissing her ear. His kisses were always slow and deliberate. He'd lean into her, as if warning her of what he was about to do, then kiss her gently, increasing the pressure at the end.

"Compliments are handsomely rewarded in this household."

"In that case, I can go on about the food indefinitely."

"You can?" He met her eyes intensely, until she felt she'd said more than she'd intended.

"Well," she amended, feeling off-balance and looking away, "almost indefinitely."

"Don't break the connection," he admonished. A favorite phrase of his. As they connected more and more, he wanted it held, not piddled away.

But she'd already broken it. If it was real, it would reestablish itself.

When they'd finished dinner, Craig announced ice cream topped with frozen fruit for dessert, but both of them were sated. They scraped together a few scraps for Minnie's dish, although she wasn't supposed to have anything but dog food. Do dogs actually taste differences, or are they just pleased to have something from the table?

Craig rewarded Becca's help with periodic kisses. Carry a dish into the kitchen, kiss. Return the mayonnaise to the fridge, kiss. Rinse the tableware for the dishwasher, kiss. She returned his kisses in equal measure, but there didn't seem to be any progression in intensity. At least, not at first.

"You should have a kiss for each chore you do, too," she told him.

"Then you owe me one for the salmon, one for the asparagus — I figure about eight in all."

"I figure about twelve."

"I defer to your superior judgment," he laughed.

"First time," she countered.

"That you showed superior judgment or that I deferred?"

"Oh, the latter, of course."

"Come, now." He poured them each a liqueur glass of Cointreau, saying, "Let's take these into the living room." If she hadn't known better, she'd have sworn this was leading to a seduction.

They sank into the couch amid the bookcases that stood like those sentries guarding a religious site — their own Stonehenge. Appropriate in that Craig's psychohistory project was a religion all his own.

"So," he asked, "have you told your mother that you found Robbie?"

"I haven't known what to do. She wouldn't recognize him to look at him. She might not believe that he was Robbie, in which case it might seem like a cruel prank. Even if we managed to get him on the spot again, and even if she believed Robbie was still alive inside this man she's never seen before, it might cause her so much grief that it would be like losing him all over again."

"As it's been for you."

"Exactly. I'm not sure whether to put her through that."

"Maybe that's a decision she should make."

"I could tell her and give her the choice of meeting him. But then she'd have to know his history, what Damon did all those years, that there are killers inside. I'm just not sure."

"I think you have to tell her at some point."

Craig put his liqueur glass on the table, took hers and put it beside his, drew her into his arms, and kissed her the way she'd always dreamed he would, her breath catching with surprise at the intensity of their desire. After a few minutes, their passion seemed beyond control.

"Let's go upstairs," Craig said hoarsely.

"Why now?" she asked.

"I can't put it off any longer," he said simply.

"That's a good reason," she replied. "You're sure it's not for therapy?"

"I never do sex for therapy, Becca dear," he said, pulling her to her feet and pressing her full body tightly to him. "But I don't want to take advantage of you. I know you've been grieving for Robbie all over again. Is this too soon?"

"You're always worrying about taking advantage of me."

"I guess I am. You seem so vulnerable."

"Listen to me carefully, Craig. I want you to take advantage of me."

"Put it that way," he laughed, snugging his face into her neck and then her breast as he pushed her up the stairs.

Their night of lovemaking was not stodgy or uncreative in the least, spiced as it was with suggestions of every fetish they could think of, which they jokingly promised to explore in more depth in the future. She was taken by surprise at how well he seemed to know her body, how he anticipated her needs and fulfilled them lovingly.

As the dimpled morning brightened through the big leaf maple outside their window, she asked him, "What would you think of doing it in a cave? That's a test question," she warned, recalling how Hugh had flunked.

"We'd have to bring sleeping bags. Those rocky floors get pretty sharp and lumpy."

"Oh, you've done it?"

"Anything you can think of, I've probably done, Becca dear. Next question, which cave?"

They fell into a discussion of developed caves versus dirty, how to get past the locks on the famous ones like Mammoth in Kentucky, or the secret entrances to remoter sections of Carlsbad, planning future orgies and adventures until their desire rose again.

54

I WASN'T THERE FOR our arraignment. Neither was Damon. Said he was sick of being dumped on for every little thing. Leroy told him that the San Francisco murders and the attempted murder of his sister weren't exactly "little things," but Damon said he didn't do it so why should he take the fall? Again?

Dr. Bernie didn't want Vigrid the Avenger and Mefisto on the spot. Thought they'd make an "unfavorable impression on the court." Talk about your masterpiece of understatement! Like they'd scare the judge into putting us away forever.

As for me, I didn't know as much as Leroy. So Leroy gave an interminably terminal sigh and sacrificed another hour away from his art — where would we be without him? When I pointed out to him that he was the one who got Vigrid and 'Fisto steamed in the first place — the instigator of the mess we were in, so to speak — he shrugged and said, "Oh, well, being in court will give me new scenes of craziness to paint." After it was over, he was promptly signed for a gallery show by an art dealer who happened to be in court as an observer and spotted him sketching.

Pope Gregory Two helped Leroy out with the little snippets of advice that are all he's good for, but I guess Leroy took them. Two told me he did. Not that he was bragging! Insufferable! Bounce and Breakout held the spot for brief periods to "set the record straight." Being sports addicts, they're fanatical about records. Occasional brief outbursts from Vigrid and 'Fisto, in spite of Dr. Bernie's orders ("he's not the boss of us") almost got us canned. The judge kept trying to guess which one was on the spot now. And guessing wrong. He got so confused that he didn't know who he might be penalizing. Occasionally, a kid piped up, although most of them were older by this time and, at Dr. Bernie's suggestion, leaving home to seek their fortunes in the world.

All this activity was enough to demonstrate our "switching" to the uninitiated or the unconvinced.

I hear Singer sang the Hallelujah chorus for the court. Just before the judge rendered his decision. He's laid out his papers, and we're standing beside my brilliant attorney, who is Dr. Bernie's paramour. Drs. Bernie, Noel, Craig, and Becca with a big yellow bruise on her cheek are seated solemnly behind us and praying to St. Dymphna, as Dr. Becca told us later. The judge opens his mouth to speak, and suddenly this gorgeous soprano voice fills the courtroom with "Hallelujah!" Just that! One bar of music.

The judge frowns at Singer, but since nothing else seems forthcoming, he begins to speak, only to be interrupted by another "Hallelujah!"

"Interesting that the bar is both the legal profession and a scrap of music," observes Gregory Two. That man is getting on my nerves. "Another case of one word meaning two opposites." And then he adds, "Baseness and transfiguration." As if I didn't get it. Let's all pretend we're brilliant, shall we?

Our attorney nudges and shushes us as the judge intones, "In the matter of Gregory Warhol, aka Damon Hearst, aka Robbie Merrow," and then Singer launches into full aria. The bailiff moves to escort him back to his cell, he struggles, and the judge says, "Let him stay a moment longer. Really, a remarkable voice! I'm in a barbershop quartet myself. The effects of the surgery? Young man —" but the rest of his words are lost in full throat, as it were. With the judge's permission, Dr. Bernie approaches the defense table and orders Singer to stop.

"You're not the boss of me."

"I certainly won't be if you end up in jail."

Singer pipes down, and the judge pronounces us "Not Guilty by Reason of Insanity" (more like inanity, I think).

"Who's insane," Vigrid yells, leaping to his feet. "Who's insane, you pompous old bag, you twit, you swillbelly, you pusillanimous pus-pot, you poor excuse for a bugger! I'll razor your *vagus* into skin-thin slices like cucumber and serve them up on crackers, I'll puree your balls and make you swallow them with prune juice, I'll —" This time the bailiff does restrain him and hauls him off kicking and yelling imprecations to a cell, until Dr. Bernie can arrange for some muscular attendants with a straitjacket to transfer him back to the unit.

Singer's "Hallelujah!" plays big in the media, where he gets to sing several bars to TV cameras set up in his room in order to illustrate the story. He's dubbed "the singing madman." Certainly, performing a religious piece in a court of law is indisputable evidence of madness.

The story of how his voice got to be soprano is a topic of much speculation from knowledgeable professionals, who compare him to the eunuchs or *castrati* of ancient Egypt and China, employed to guard the harems of the emperors. Dr. Bernie points out that, actually, we all have our balls, and so, of course, does Singer, except that he can't feel them. When he goes to poke around himself, they're gone, in spite of Dr. Bernie's attempts at a reality check.

The tabloids do their usual painstaking research and discover that Singer's a two-thousand-year-old alien born of the Virgin Mary, which would make him Jesus' brother.

Dr. Becca brings around an old lady wearing a nurse's uniform and a tan cardigan. She calls herself our mother. None of us wants to meet with her; in fact, we don't want a mother. We can't see any use for one. Mothers are supposed to protect you, but she failed miserably in that department, and now we're grown up and can fend for ourselves. Besides, Wendy has been our mother for as long as we can remember, and we aren't about to kick her out of the dining room, if we ever get back to it.

Finally, I make a deal with Singer. If he will take the spot the next time Dr. Bernie performs his odious psychic surgery on us, (Singer being the most experienced as a surgery patient), I agree to talk to "Mom."

So, when Dr. Becca ushers her in, I take the spot and call her "Mom" and say Robbie's asleep, she doesn't want to wake him up, does she? She cries the whole time she's with us. Is she glad to be with us or what? We finally give in and sic Robbie on her, who rubs his eyes, having been awakened from a deep and dreamless sleep. But he doesn't remember her, which makes her cry harder.

"Don't you remember the milk carton children?" Mom pleads, thinking to lead him into recollection by association.

"I remember the milk carton children."

"But you don't remember me?"

"No." Robbie's sincerely trying.

"Don't you remember Crunchy Bunchies?"

"I remember Crunchy Bunchies. I still eat them. Wendy makes them."

"And the time I bought you your red bedspread?"

"I remember the red bedspread. Maybe I remember you," Robbie says, in what's clearly an effort to shut this crying woman the fuck up.

The next time she comes, she brings a couple of teen-aged guys, who she says are our half brothers, Ike and Mike. Are we supposed to act as if they're long-lost buddies, or something? They slouch around the door like they don't want to be here. The feeling's mutual. It's flat out embarrassing to try to talk to them. They aren't our brothers at all. We don't know them. Ike's in his first year at college, majoring in football. Mike's in his third year, majoring in the physiology of chemical reactions, or maybe it's the chemistry of physiological reactions. He and Vigrid have a nice chat about nerves, Vigrid clearly the senior chatterer.

When the visit's over, Mike and Ike heave a sigh of relief and slouch out the door, and "Mom" says she'll be back. But she never is. Once in a while, we catch her peeking around the corner from the hall. Then she disappears.

Chloe comes by to see us a number of times, not that she's that crazy about Damon, but she seems to be growing attached to the place. She makes friends with the nurses and cozies up to Dr. Bernie, who takes her to lunch and who knows what else? Before we know it, she's doing some of the work around here, carrying charts back and forth, eating the food the patients refuse, and flirting with them to make them feel better. The hospital is like another stage set to her, and she's getting good at it.

"I'm thinking of becoming a sex therapist in my spare time," she informs Damon. "I've had all this experience. Oh, don't take it so seriously, Damon. It's not like I'm being unfaithful. I don't even get off on it. But you have to give back, you know? This is my contribution to the world."

"I do porn," he answers sarcastically.

"And wash dishes," Leroy prompts.

My Fair Lady has closed, and Chloe is in the next production of *Jesus Christ, Superstar*, "a small part but very important," as small parts are if they're yours.

When the time comes for us to move out of the hospital on a trial basis only and with a strict outpatient clinic schedule, Chloe takes us in — "in" being her new theater basement. But she won't allow Damon to sleep with her. After all, it isn't even winter. Finally, she starts introducing Damon as her fiancé. "Sounds more respectable than live-in boyfriend." Damon kind of likes the sound of it. It's fun pretending you're normal. You get treated with respect. Another acting role for which he's getting good reviews from the hospital staff, the doctors, the director, and the acting troupe.

When Chloe shows up with a ring for group therapy (just our group) and asks Damon to give it to her in front of witnesses, he does so.

"That makes it official. I knew a fella once —" she began.

"Chloe, please. No more fellas!"

"Why, Damon Hearst, I do believe you're jealous."

"Jealous of a door-to-door bra salesman? A garlic king who tastes like his produce? A fella who could only get it up if he thought of England? I don't think so."

"This one was different."

"They all are," said Damon.

In celebration of their engagement, Chloe decides to let Damon sleep with her. Afterwards, she lies beside him, stroking his head, murmuring, "you have such soft bumps. They remind me of spring buds on a tree. I knew a fella' once —"

"Not another fella!"

"You think I had too many?"

"I don't know. You haven't told me about all of them, have you?"

"You want me to?"

"Tell me about your fella."

"He was bald. Not a lick of hair on his head. Even his scalp was thin. In fact, it was so thin you could see his brains."

"The brain's covered with a skull, silly. Gregory says."

"His skull was thin, too. You could really see his brains, all jelly and beating like a heart. He wore a bicycle helmet to protect it. He got awfully sick of the same helmet, though, so he bought different ones, and people gave them to him for his birthdays, Christmas, tips. Finally, he ended up with this huge collection of just thousands. So guess what he did. He sold them for a million dollars on the Internet and got a skull transplant."

At long last, I had my dream wish. As we began to merge, Dr. Bernie decided that it was time for me to take my place as the main man. This carries a lot of responsibilities, like always being on the spot — well most of the time — and taking the blame when things go wrong, and listening to the others, but then making the decisions. It isn't easy, but as Dr. Bernie points out, it's the situation *Onlys* find themselves in regularly.

"I wish I'd been born an *Only*," I told Dr. Bernie. "*Onlys* don't have to kill off parts of themselves in order to survive."

"Is that what it feels like? Killing?"

"Yeah!" said Vigrid enthusiastically.

"Cool it!" said Leroy. "This is serious."

"We'll cool you!" said 'Fisto.

"Guys, guys, come on now," said Dr. Bernie.

I said, "Parts of me are dying or going to sleep or moving away. Whatever you want to call it."

"That happens with *Onlys*, too," Dr. Bernie reminded us. "It's called growing up."

"Some of the kids don't want to grow up. 'I want to stay a boy like Peter Pan' they say."

"That's what happened to Robbie, don't forget," said Dr. Bernie.

It didn't look so hot from that perspective.

The only perk of this whole *Only* gig is that Chloe has become my fiancée as well as Damon's. Dr. Bernie talked Damon into sharing her with me. Since Damon's been feeling sort of faint a lot of the time, he agreed I should look after her.

Robbie was the first to die. At first, we thought he was just asleep. I went up to his attic room to try to wake him. Nearly broke my neck on his trucks scattered on the floor, where he'd left them with his Lincoln Logs. I accidentally stepped on his Peter Pan book, but the spine was long broken anyway. In the corner, he'd built a splendid block tower, reaching to the ceiling, the wood not dead, after all, miraculously sprouting branches that massed into vines at the top. He should have been an architect.

"Come on, Robbie, time for your Crunchy Bunchies," I told him. "You can't sleep all the time."

He was turned on his side, snuggled under his red quilt, too still. Any minute, he'd fling off his covers and sit up grinning, "Fooled ya', didn't I?"

I noticed that everything had vanished outside his window. There was nothing there, no trees brilliant with autumn leaves, no house where Alex played. It was just a window like one of those stage ones that are actually a piece of plastic with a light bulb behind, only this was gray. Not even a light.

"Robbie!" I called, shaking him. "Robbie, come on, wake up."

"What's going on?" Leroy asked with alarm.

"I can't wake him."

"Let me see," said Vigrid, elbowing past us and putting a nursing finger on the pulse at Robbie's neck.

"He's dead," he pronounced without much feeling at all, sort of clinical, a preview of how he'd feel about the rest of us if we didn't get him first. "I'll call it as 6:32 a.m."

"Pacific Standard or Daylight Savings?"

"We're still on Pacific Standard."

"We turned our clocks ahead last night."

"I didn't."

"We were supposed to."

"Nuh-uh, we were supposed to turn them back, dummy. Spring forward, Fall backward."

"Spring backward, like you just met a snake. Fall forward flat on your face."

They wrangled on until Two cut through.

"Poor little fella!" said Two. "Like Becca says, he never grew."

"Maybe he climbed his tree tower through the ceiling up to the sky," said Leroy. "He used to try to do that before Carl chopped it down. He didn't remember, of course. But I do."

"Romantic claptrap," said Vigrid.

"I'd like to think he did," I said to Leroy, feeling a lot closer to him.

"Did he have to die?" I asked Dr. Bernie. "He's my brother."

"They all are," said Dr. Bernie.

We buried him in our graveyard that only we know. It lies in the depths of our soul. Dr. Becca cried when I told her. She came to the funeral, too. We all stood around the little white coffin, scattering rose petals — red for passion, white for innocence, yellow for ascension, as Wendy told us. Singer lifted his voice in a hymn of faith, with a stunning instrumental between the words, and we lit candles. Then we filed into our chapel to pray, as best we knew how.

It's a small structure with a statue of St. Dymphna behind the altar. She grows more beautiful by the day, forest tendrils of hair trailing down her pink and white porcelain face and a blue dress flowing over her hips to her sandaled toes that peek out from under the hem. At her feet, she holds the devil by a chain attached to a collar. His resemblance to Vigrid shocks me.

I go there often now to pray for the dead. Robbie was only the first. I leave flowers and light candles. It helps. She nods to me sometimes and smiles, but on the day Robbie died, I glimpsed a tear glistening at the corner of her eye — just one. Robbie had been her child, too.

The others cleaned out Robbie's attic room, as his and Becca's mom had done so long ago. I couldn't bear to. They tell me it's shrinking like a dead thing, browning at the rim, curling into itself like a leaf. Now we understand what Becca went through. Like Becca, I too must lose my brothers and sisters. It's like a family curse, written somewhere in our universe. And we have no idea how it came about.

Everybody's been fighting about who should leave and who should stay. Naturally, each of us feels he's more important than the rest, and it's getting kind of nasty. Nasty politics. Such a great talent as Leroy's shouldn't be consigned to the dust heap, he claims, and believe it or not, he defends Singer, too. Says Singer has a right to exist. "We artists stick together. We have to save the world by giving meaning to life. Bounce and Breakout aren't important. They're just athletes. What good did an athlete ever do for anyone except make money?"

"Not like artists," Bounce gibes.

"Art's of no use whatsoever," says Breakout. "Ask any sports fan."

"I'll go," Wendy offers. "I've never amounted to much anyway. Just a shadow of my possible self. A tainted one at that."

"You're not going anywhere," says Leroy gallantly. "We need you."

"What for, exactly?"

"All sorts of stuff."

"Name one thing."

"Blueberry banana milk shakes."

"I'll leave you the recipe."

"We need the feminine touch. A little more androgyny in our lives. I think Gregory Two should be next," I say. "Nothing personal," I add to the little aper.

"You bet it's personal," retorts the great Two. "I wouldn't stick by you if my life depended on it."

At which Vigrid and 'Fisto snigger.

"Hey, whatever happened to Watcher!" I flash. "Vigrid? 'Fisto?"

Their shrugs are too elaborate to be believed.

"Haven't seen hide nor hair of him," Vigrid claims.

"Me, neither," says 'Fisto. "Hair nor, what? I sure haven't seen his hair."

"Leroy?"

"Swear to St. Dymphna, Gregory. I haven't even heard from him."

"He must be somewhere," I say.

"You heard Vigrid. He's hiding," says Leroy.

"A figment of Gregory's imagination," Vigrid suggests.

"How's Gregory's advisory council coming?" Dr. Bernie asks us.

"Damon's superfluous," says Vigrid.

"Supernumerary," Two adds, as if in explanation.

"You are!" Damon flares.

"Are what?"

"What you said."

"Vigrid, are you teaching Gregory how to stick up for himself?" asks Dr. Bernie.

"I'd advise him to stick his finger up his nose," says Damon, at which Leroy actually claps him on the back.

"Put 'em up, Gregory," says 'Fisto. "Let's see what you got."

"Bounce and Breakout, are you teaching him sports like we agreed?" asks Dr. Bernie.

"We're teaching him to talk the talk. Walking the walk's another matter."

"We only need one of them," says Leroy.

"True! They're practically merged already," says Dr. Bernie, as the twins shrug into each other.

There are more tombstones now. The babies are all gone, either grown away or passed. We have graves for everyone, no matter how they died; in fact, for some of them we have several, different alters not satisfied with only one. We can fight about everything, even about grave markers, and we do.

The carnage continues. We cried when Wendy passed. Nothing

dramatic. She just faded to nothing as she'd always threatened to do. "Farewell," she told us at the end. "I can't live in such a horrible world. The Virgin is assuming me," she added faintly.

We built a beautiful monument to her, a statue of the Virgin welcoming her to Heaven with cherubs flitting about and a garland of flowers for her hair. St. Dymphna smiled down on us the day we laid our Wendy to rest. She left us her milk shake recipe, and Dr. Bernie says we can make them in the unit kitchen, but we haven't had the heart.

We're back on the DID Unit temporarily. Not that we've failed or anything. Dr. Bernie assures us that we haven't. Just that Chloe went to Holy-wood to star in a tampon commercial and hasn't come back yet. Ours is now a long-distance engagement, and there's no one else for us to stay with.

'Fisto and Vigrid taught Gregory what they could about defending himself, then took off for Washington, D.C., after doing a lot of Internet research on other places to live. Before they left, they told Leroy that they wanted to find a community of like-minded people where they could "torture and murder in peace."

To our dismay, Leroy said that Singer had merged with a choir in order to become something bigger than himself. Evidently, he didn't think Gregory was it.

Leroy says he agrees with Singer, and he's damned if he's going to merge with "that wuss," but he sticks around. Ever since he had his "Courtroom Show" at a major gallery (a gallery is major if it's showing your work), which got rave reviews as being the essence of deconstructed neo-retro, his work is in demand, and he says he doesn't have time to think about someplace else. He's too busy painting the same pictures over and over and selling them for outrageous prices. His work has earned him the highest recognition in the art world, similar to the Pulitzer in journalism; that is, a moving company stole a dozen of his paintings that they were transporting from Seattle to New York for a showing at the Metropolitan. The driver has been apprehended and will stand trial for sacrilege.

Like *Onlys*, I visit the graves of my brothers and sisters less and less.

55

THE AROMA OF COFFEE wafted up the stairs. Becca snuggled into one of Craig's terry cloth robes, still damp from their multiple showers the night before, preliminary to doing outrageous things with each other. They sure had needed a lot of showers.

She descended to the kitchen and discovered a pot on the coffeemaker and Craig at the dining table, reading the Sunday *New York Times*. He kissed her good morning, wrapped his body around her, then broke it off, saying,

"We'd better not get started again. We'll die of starvation. Your tummy's been rumbling for hours."

"In my sleep?"

"In your sleep. You snore, too."

"You toss and turn as if you were in a wrestling match."

"Sounds like fun. Let's add it to the list."

"If my snoring keeps you awake, I can always move into the guest room for the rest of the night."

"Not a chance. I want to take you while you're sleeping."

"Did you?"

In mock hurt, he asked, "Don't you remember?"

"I was sleeping."

"Let me get you a dry robe."

He returned a minute later with a yellow one.

"Do you have a different color for every occasion?"

"Now you know what to get me for my birthday."

"What color?"

"Red looks great on you."

With her coffee, Becca seated herself at the table. Craig removed "The Book Review" from the *New York Times*, gave Becca the rest, and went to the kitchen to whip up scrambled eggs. Becca slid Craig's section of the paper over to her place and began reading it.

"Hey, I give you the whole paper, and you snitch my few pages?"

"I figured that, since you took it, it must be more interesting."

"I've been thinking," Craig said, as he sat down beside her with a couple of plates of eggs and toast that smelled heavenly. "I know it's premature, but if you move in with me — *when* you move in with me — " then, to her look of surprise, he reminded her, "You did mention being able to live with my limited cooking repertoire."

"So I did. Months ago."

"It was your idea, not mine."

"I didn't think of that at the time," she said.

"Women are so inconsistent."

"Consistency is the hobgoblin of little minds. And, as you're so fond of observing, I have a big one."

"Only a foolish consistency. Anyway, as I was saying, your poetry collection can go right into that bookcase between the windows there."

"My Poetry? What about my Psychology?"

"Oh, those can go in with mine. I figure we'll have a lot of duplicates."

"You figure I'll be reading that much poetry?"

"Absolutely. Writing it, too."

"Instead of Psychology? This wouldn't be a little dragon of competitiveness rearing its ugly head, would it?"

"Not at all. So don't go looking for it. Poetry is something you can do in your spare time. A poem here, one there. They add up."

So Craig had not only recognized and acknowledged her main

passion; he was already providing for it. But the great poets Becca knew wrote fulltime. Perhaps in later years?

"If you have a whole bookcase, there'll be plenty of room for your collection to grow," he added, spreading orange marmalade on the rest of his toast. "I'll shift Science Fiction and Cultural Anthropology to the garage."

"Not Cultural Anthropology."

"Something else, then."

"Business and Finance."

"Oh-ho. I can see we're going to be poor."

"You hook up with a poet, you've got to expect it."

As to the prematurity of Craig's assumptions, Becca knew she should demur. But the fact was that she didn't want to. She wanted to be with him forever, and his suggestion seemed eminently practical.

They would be two dreamers following their bliss.

Epilogue

He never found me,
    Although he knew I must be here in the
    Interstices between one thought and another.
        His dirt fingers probe
        Into crevices where moldy memories creep
Amid living lichen.

Others told him,
    Warned him, even,
        How the cloud of all-knowing sees through
him
        — He didn't believe that.

I am a mere reflection on the lake,
    Giving back mountains, loons, leaping fish, and wil-
lows
        that drag their hair in the water.
    Lacking substance of my own I am,
But how can they exist without me?

Like Nostradamus, with less catastrophe,
    I see.
I see Robbie in his tomb, showered with starlight,
    As in her womb, Becca's black-haired baby
        sucks her thumb,
While Craig mines history for meaning —
        Never mind that it's pyrite.
And she pens poems of long dreaming, for the small jour-
nals
    That weigh her art in a thimble
        and find it full.

Triumphant, they come in glory, they.
    The poet, the artist and the singer,
    Holy triumvirate, they.
        Their mission,
That art will not be analyzed into extinction.

As for the rest,
    They are not gone while I am
still here to reflect them.

The cloud of all-knowing, I am,
    St. Dymphna's newly appointed angel,
        (The devil of madness chained at my feet),
    Healing in memory.
I watch to save them.
Why would I not?

ACKNOWLEDGMENTS

WHERE DOES ONE BEGIN to thank all those who have contributed to creating the book you hold in your hands? Does one start with the graphic artist who designed the entire work — text and cover? But that couldn't have been done without the careful professional copy-editing of the text itself. Perhaps, first, one should really thank the phalanx of friends and relatives who encouraged, even insisted on, *Mindstalker's* emergence into the light of day. But without the savvy business advice of the volunteer council, Rubythroat Press would not even exist.

Where does one begin? There is no solid answer.

Mayapriya Long of Bookwrights designed *Mindstalker* with an eye to frightening you out of your wits. She is an artist of exceptional creativity, and I am fortunate to know her. This is the third book she has designed for Rubythroat Press. Many more, Mayapriya! She did so with the copy-edited text of Karen Olson. It astounded me that Karen discovered so many errors in the flawless manuscript that I submitted to her, and her middle name should be "Tactful."

Melissa Overdorf is my talented business manager, a godsend in the changing world of publishing where small independent presses are offering a variety of options for publishing a broader range of work than traditional publishing, including digital print-on-demand in addition to offset. Print-on-demand avoids the printing of huge quantities, the necessity to store and ship them, and the probable returns when they don't all sell. Melissa has a natural god-given business talent as well as wide experience.

I am also indebted to our widely knowledgeable and reassuring attorney, Michael Graham, as well as The Authors Guild and the Independent Book Publishers Association with its affiliate, Book Publishers Northwest, for their invaluable advice.

As for our sales phalanx, Pamela Marott buys multiple copies and gives them to her friends, some of them in book clubs, urging me to overcome my reticence and fly down to Los Angeles to speak. Valerie Marott sends out press releases to everyone she knows — and she knows everyone, probably including God — although I have no solid evidence of that. Both persuade readers to write on-line reviews. Anne Gray writes them as well, and Anonymous wrote three! Thanks, Anonymous, whoever you are!

This book is the product of many years of research, writing, revision, deletion, and more revision. Many people who helped me with it have probably long forgotten the assistance they rendered when I came to them for help. They include Officer Sean O'Donnell of the Seattle Homicide Division's Media Relations who gave me a short course in what every writer should know, for which I am profusely thankful. You will find your information scattered in bits and pieces throughout this book. Detective Steve Kirkland's file review was immensely helpful. And finally I want to take notice of Officer Kim Bogucki, who, as a professor, I had a chance to teach some years ago, and of whom I am immensely proud.

I first met Mr. Douglas G. Dahl in a line for something in 2003. We got to talking, and he was kind enough to send me his own copy of the Prayer to St. Dymphna, which he will discover in this book. It has stood me in good stead personally as well!

Last, but you know he isn't least by the very fact that I put him in this enviable final position, is my webmaster who, believe it or not, possesses the name of John Webster, President of Abacus Graphics. With Francesca Droll's partnership, his beautiful websites urge everyone to visit and stay awhile. And a word in the ears of those of you who are writers or publishers — he's a dream to work with!

PATRICIA WEENOLSEN
Seattle, 2010

MINDSTALKER BOOK GROUP QUESTIONS

1. It is 1985. Why do you think Robbie is so intensely interested in the "milk carton children"? Could it be normal childhood curiosity or because he's already met Toyman who's told Robbie that he will be a milk carton child? Or is it just intuition?

2. Does Becca do everything she can for Robbie, both before and after he is kidnapped? Is she a good sister to him? Does she fall short?

3. Are Robbie and Becca's mother and father "good parents" in your opinion?

4. Does Doctor Connie help Becca through her grief over losing Robbie? What methods does she use? How do the trolls help?

5. Why is Becca having false memories of Robbie?

6. How is Becca's garage significant in the Merrows' lives? How is it a setting for both dealing with the present and moving on into the future?

7. How does Kenny's life with his brother, Timmy, lead to his kidnapping Robbie? What parts do the boats play in the episode?

8. Why does Damon show different results on different biological tests?

9. Why does Damon have so much trouble remembering both dates and events?

10. How do the various boys who work in the films, such as Dicky-bird, Flip, and Mickey, manifest the damage done to them?

11. What do you think is the significance of the tower/tree that Damon builds on his bunk bed?

12. Do you think that Trent and Barry's son, Adam, was always abnormal, or have his experiences of being kidnapped and of living with Trent and Barry made him that way?

13. Is Mickey a good friend to Damon? Why does he betray him?

14. Does Kenny really love Damon? What evidence can you give for and against? On the one hand, what does he do to protect Damon from Carl? On the other, what does he do to harm Damon?

15. Robbie has a good personality (Gregory), two bad personalities (Vigrid and Mefisto), at least two artistic personalities (Leroy and Singer, formerly Pleaser), and two athletic personalities (Bounce and Breakout). Where do you think they came from? If they were created to protect Robbie/Damon, how do they do this? How do they help him deal with his traumatic ordeal of life with Carl and Kenny?

16. Damon is really just one person. How do you think he is able to do the following:
   a) As Pleaser, associate with the police?
   b) Assume the identity of both Vigrid and Mefisto, and nail Carmine to the wall?
   c) Escape from the hospital?

17. Is Chloe a real person or one of Robbie's personalities? How do you know?

18. Do Gregory's "haunted lamp" signals help him? In what way? What causes them? Is Gregory afflicted with mental illness, do you think, or is he just imaginative?

19. How do you see Robbie's favorite book, *Peter Pan and Wendy*, manifesting itself in various ways during his experiences?

20. It is 1998. Becca is working as a psychology grad student intern at the hospital and dating Craig. What signs of intrusion into her home does she endure?

21. Do the relatives of the mentally ill suffer? In what ways? How does Becca hope that St. Dymphna might help them?

22. When Damon is treated for Dissociative Identity Disorder (DID) and becomes one person, he may be put on trial for the crimes committed by his other personalities. Do you agree with this legal situation?

23. On the other hand, should a person who has committed murder get away with it?

24. How has Robbie's kidnapping changed Becca's life? For the worse? For the better?

25. Does Watcher survive?

BONUS QUESTION: Do you believe that this book, *Mindstalker*, deserved to be written? Give your reasons, pro and con.